ASHLEY BEEGAN

The Advocate

Three Book Collection

Copyright © 2022 by Ashley Beegan

All rights reserved. No part of this publication may be reproduced, stored or transmitted in any form or by any means, electronic, mechanical, photocopying, recording, scanning, or otherwise without written permission from the publisher. It is illegal to copy this book, post it to a website, or distribute it by any other means without permission.

This novel is entirely a work of fiction. The names, characters and incidents portrayed in it are the work of the author's imagination. Any resemblance to actual persons, living or dead, events or localities is entirely coincidental.

Ashley Beegan asserts the moral right to be identified as the author of this work.

First edition

ISBN: 9798439215201

This book was professionally typeset on Reedsy.
Find out more at reedsy.com

Contents

I   Lucy's Coming For You

Summer	3
Summer	13
Summer	17
One. Two…	28
Summer	30
Summer	32
Lucy's Coming	38
Summer	40
Aaron	44
Summer	46
Summer	49
Summer	55
Summer	58
For You…	61
Summer	63
Summer	67
Aaron	70
Summer	72
Summer	78
Summer	80
Summer	84
Summer	88
Summer	92

Summer	96
Summer	101
Swanson	104
Summer	108
Swanson	114
Summer	118
Summer	123
Three. Four. I'm knocking…	126
Summer	128
Summer	131
Swanson	136
Summer	139
Summer	143
Summer	147
Summer	152
At Your Door	156
Summer	158
Summer	162
Summer	167
Summer	173
Summer	180
Summer	183
Summer	186
Swanson	190
Summer	193
Summer	196
II Mother… Liar… Murderer?	
Prologue	205
Astrid	209
Summer	212
Astrid	219

Sophie - May 2007	222
Astrid	227
Swanson	232
Astrid	237
Sophie - June 2007	240
Astrid	243
Summer	246
Astrid	249
Sophie - September 2007	259
Astrid	261
Swanson	266
Astrid	269
Swanson	275
Sophie - January 2008	280
Astrid	283
Swanson	286
Astrid	293
Swanson	297
Sophie - September 2008	303
Astrid	306
Swanson	312
Sophie - August 2009	317
Astrid	321
Summer	326
Sophie - October 2009	332
Astrid	334
Sophie - June 2010	338
Astrid	342
Summer	345
Swanson	348
Summer	350
Swanson - June 2010	352
Summer	355

Swanson	357
Astrid	366
Summer	369
Swanson	375
Astrid	378
Summer	382
Astrid	386
Summer	389

III   The Hospital

The Servant	395
Swanson	400
Summer	406
The Servant	413
Swanson	415
Summer	418
Swanson	422
Summer	424
The Servant	432
Swanson	435
The Servant	441
Swanson	442
The Servant	446
Swanson	449
Swanson	460
Swanson	467
The Servant	472
Swanson	474
Swanson	480
Swanson	484
Swanson	490
The Servant	496

Swanson	497
Swanson	503
Summer	507
Swanson	512
Swanson	518
Swanson	523
Swanson	526
The Servant	530
Swanson	533
The Servant	536
Swanson	538
Summer	542
The Servant	545
Swanson	547
Summer	551
The Servant	553
Swanson	556
Swanson	559
Swanson	562
The Servant	566
Swanson	572
Swanson	576
Swanson	580
Summer	582
Also by Ashley Beegan	585

I

Lucy's Coming For You

Summer Thomas questions her own sanity when violent patient, Lucy Clark, disappears from a locked hospital ward.

Because no one else will admit that Lucy exists.

As Summer digs deeper into the disappearance, it becomes apparent that Lucy is looking for her too, but Summer should have stayed away. Now, Lucy is coming for her...

And there's no escaping someone who doesn't exist.

Summer

For a moment, I thought about trying to escape. Her cold eyes stared straight into mine. They were like two emeralds. Bright, serene, and angry. We stood in a showdown position reminiscent of the wild west fights from old cowboy movies. Not that I would ever watch a cowboy movie.

The sound of the cheap clock infiltrated my muddled thoughts. It was to my right on the white-washed wall behind me, above my head. *Tick. Tock. Tick. Tock.* The clock was far too low in such a dangerous place. Didn't they ever learn? Unless absolutely necessary, nothing should be within reach here. Anything, without exception, could be used as a weapon.

Annoyance plagued my mind, briefly overshadowing the anxiety instigated by the owner of the green eyes. She was in her forties and still staring at me with intense focus. Despite this and the rising nausea which sat heavily within my stomach, I kept my head straight. My face was expressionless, not unusual for me, and my eyes were wide and unblinking. I needed to show confidence as my training informed me. I was on guard. I allowed a small smile to line my lips, disguising any evidence of unease.

As beautiful as the emerald eyes were, they were surrounded by a mass of angry, red welts. The wounds encroached upon her features, from her forehead to her chest. Each raised mark was surrounded by a patch of white, where there used to be smooth skin. They looked like small lava pools across her face. Both eye sockets drooped towards her cheeks. Her lips were nothing more than slits. It was as if someone had pulled the skin off her face in one fell swoop, like a child removing a Halloween mask. Except she had removed her human disguise, revealing the monster.

She was not my friend on this particular day. Some days, she would be my friend, and we would laugh and joke like two high school girls. She would show me her jewelry and her adult colouring books. She always wanted to brush my long brown hair, though I couldn't allow physical contact. I was ten years her junior and, in her mind, we were two *normal* young women. But not on this day. On this day, I was her enemy.

I knew it. I could feel it. She revealed her distaste for me through her unfriendly stare. Her anger. Her need to lash out and to hurt me. She didn't move but stayed as still as the painted human statues on the nearby cobbled streets of Derby city centre. My body stiffened as I attempted to move my legs forward towards the young woman with the cold eyes and angry red face. The narrow hospital corridor did not assist with the claustrophobia that grabbed at me from every angle.

The corridor opened out into the ward, but this was not your usual hospital ward. Everyone has been inside a normal hospital at some point, even if just visiting a loved one. No. This was the kind of hospital most people are lucky enough never to see. The red brick building wasn't impressive to look at from the outside but was modern and purpose-built to keep people inside at all costs. It lay on the banks of the River Derwent and was a short walk from my home city, the quaint east midlands city of Derby.

The key to the air-locked doors behind me was attached to my elastic belt. Many items were hanging from my belt, mostly keys and fobs for the maze of doors within the hospital, but there was also an alarm to be used in emergencies in case I was assaulted, or if I were to see someone else being assaulted. However, I could not go through these doors. If I'd made it to the other side, I would have been safe, but to turn my back would be dangerous. I shouldn't have been in that position, a lone patient between me and the ward, but rules weren't always followed, so there I was.

I knew I was being absurd. I spoke to patients like Lucy every day, but most were unlikely to attack me. It was as if an unknown horror was waiting for me if I proceeded further. My legs were laden with fear, as though all my blood had sunk to my feet, adding to their weight. I took small steps towards her. Beads of sweat made my palms sticky, whilst my lips felt dry. It was as if the natural moisture in my body had gravitated to the wrong places. I forced my lips to curve into a larger smile. It was my signature move when nervous, though not always helpful. I hoped it wouldn't irritate her further.

Whatever happened, I knew I must absolutely not let my fear show. That would have been dangerous. I needed to get past her with no issues. There was no going back through the locked doors, so I needed to take the other route to safety on the other side of the corridor. I needed to walk past her with as much confidence as I could muster. The weak did not last long in such a hospital.

"Hi, Lucy," I said, trying to keep my voice warm, and friendly, although I felt the opposite.

Lucy said nothing as I expected, remaining statue-like and cold. She continued to glare at me, making her anger clear. Her muted features made it impossible to read her emotions.

Her black hair was tied back, so tight and slick with grease it appeared to be stuck to her head. There were bald patches visible on her scalp, old scars where the skin had been badly burned. She still wore her nightie despite it being 2 PM, an oversized t-shirt stating *Mother knows best.* My mind wandered to her child. Lucy certainly did not know best as a mother, but I forced those thoughts out of my mind. My face needed to appear friendly, not disgusted, and never angry.

To get to the other patients who did wish to speak to me, I needed to walk past Lucy. I was their confidante, their voice, and their advocate. Like I used to be hers. I forced myself to walk quicker and with more confidence. I wanted to show her I was not a threat, but nor was I an easy target. She needed to know that I had taken her hint. I wouldn't talk to her again that day unless she changed her mind, which she often did.

Lucy's head did not turn as I got closer. Her unwashed stench stung my nostrils as I walked past her without getting too close. The nauseating scent of dirt, grease, and body odour hung about her in an invisible cloud. She continued to stare at the space I had occupied rather than allow her eyes to follow my movements. My heartbeat slowed as I walked by Lucy without being attacked. The nausea subsided, and I realised it relieved me that Lucy was not my friend that day. A pang of guilt overtook the anxiety. Not for the first time, I considered that I needed a new job. I was there to help after all, and I *wanted* to support most of my patients. I knew for the most part they were far more likely to be victims of crime than to be violent to me. However, I also knew what Lucy was capable of, and she would happily do the same to me if in the right mood. Lucy worried me, and for good reasons.

But as I made my way by her, Lucy's cold, lank fingers wrapped themselves tightly around my wrist. I jumped round so fast my vision blurred, and bile burnt the back of my throat as nausea threatened to overcome me. Lucy's grip tightened, her sharp, icy nails digging deep into my wrist. I should have known not to turn my back on her. I reached for the alarm strapped to my belt. Lucy was strong. Strong enough to be hurting my wrist, but she released me as soon as she saw the panic in my eyes. She smiled, revealing yellow teeth.

"Don't grab me, please, Lucy," I said sternly. She laughed a high-pitched, girly giggle and turned to the door behind her. She skipped into her bedroom, slamming the door shut. Despite attempting to show no fear, my hands tremoured. I swallowed the bile in my throat. The warm air of the hospital was pungent as it filled my lungs. The scents of medicine, sweat mixed with cheap deodorant, and food didn't help to ease my nausea.

I cleared my throat, trying to regain some sort of grip on my emotions. My hands were still shaking, and I needed a glass of water. I turned around again and continued up the white corridor. It felt shorter now that Lucy had gone. I supposed the corridor was brighter than the average hospital ward. There were hand-painted pictures of happy hillside and beach scenes with inspirational quotes stuck to the walls. They reminded me of the drawings I had on my own walls created by my son, Joshua. Though these images were not a child's artwork but the result of the patient's art therapy sessions. The room still felt clinical, though. There was nothing homey about Bluebell Ward, despite these feigned attempts. It certainly didn't live up to its bright and flowery name.

The corridor opened up to a communal living space with lime green walls. There were several couches and armchairs arranged in a U shape in front of a medium-sized TV. A dozen patients had spread themselves out on the furniture, all of them female. Multiple members of staff sat amongst them. Some were nurses, and some were support workers. Support workers cared for the patients in much the same way as the nurses, except they could not touch medication. Or at least they *shouldn't* touch medication. Two staff members sat on hard kitchen chairs across from the youngest patient, 17-year-old Aaliyah.

Aaliyah's every move was watched. Two members of staff were with her at all times, and one would even watch her as she slept. Aaliyah suffered from anorexia nervosa, depression, and severe self-harm tendencies. She was tiny and skeletal but lethal, at least to herself. She wouldn't hurt anyone else unless they were trying to restrain her from hurting herself. Self-imposed cuts and bruises covered her body. I saw a fresh, deep cut in the middle of her forehead near the hairline. It was about two inches long, angry, red, and looked in need of stitches. She clearly had not had a good day. I decided I wouldn't talk to her today for fear of distressing her further. She would approach me if she wanted to chat.

Before I had the chance to sit and say hello to anyone, another young patient approached me. Louise walked right up to me with zero concept of personal space. It was a problem I found common among the patients and one I had always struggled with due to my need for wide personal space at all times.

Again, my hand sat near my alarm. I hadn't had to use it in my eight months of being an advocate, but I needed to be careful. I was constantly surrounded by instability, terror, and people who thought the unthinkable.

Louise's dark-skinned face was red and blotchy, more so than usual. She took loud, deep breaths, as if she were having a panic attack. Her skin wasn't burnt like Lucy's, but she had pink scars from deep cuts. Line after line of scar tissue from her forehead to her chin. There must have been fifty lines on each side of her beautiful face. At 21-years-old, her face was destroyed forever. She would never leave the house without people staring at her and instantly knowing she was severely damaged.

"Hi, Louise," I said, my voice soothing and warm. I was well aware of how important being calm was when talking to someone in distress, particularly if they suffered from disordered cognitive processes. Speaking in a calm tone was an attempt to convince a distressed patient into subconsciously following my placid body language. "Everything okay?"

"They're in there, look!" She pointed to the nurses' station next to us. The nurses' station was a long, soundproof room with an end-to-end window that overlooked the living area. Unlike its name suggested, it was not an area specifically for nurses since it was not where the medication was stored. Instead, it was a meeting area for all staff. Private discussions could be had, such as meeting arrangements, handovers, and quick updates if a particular patient became *poorly*, which is staff code for violent. Right now, though, the ward manager was sitting in there, smiling and talking with two women I'd never seen before.

"They're talking about me! They've been in there for ages. Can you ask them to come and speak to me, please? I can feel myself getting wound up, Summer. It's so rude of them to sit there talking about me, and all I can do is sit here and panic! You wouldn't like it, would you? They wouldn't like it!" Louise spat the words at me, her voice getting louder with each one. She was verging on hysteria. I struggled to take in what she was saying.

A nurse approached us, her steps brisk. "Louise, sit down! The manager and the ladies will come and speak to you when they are ready," she barked. From her tone, I could tell that Louise had already tried to talk to them numerous times. The nurse must have felt fully justified in speaking to Louise like that in front of me.

I'd seen this particular nurse a few times. Her name was Emma. She was blonde with always perfect hair. It was hard to tell how old she was because of the amount of makeup she wore. Some of which had dried into her skin, giving it a patchy look. I guessed she was around forty. She came roughly to the same height as me, so about 5'4. I'd noted on a few occasions that she appeared firm but fair. Though it was hard to tell. As an outsider with the power to report to authorities, most staff were on their best behaviour around me.

Louise threw me a desperate look, although she did as she was told and sat down. I noted a fresh cut on her cheek. I smiled at her, hoping she trusted me enough to leave it with me and stay calm.

I stepped closer to Emma and asked, "Who are they?"

Emma glanced at Louise and lowered her voice. "They're from Louise's previous care provider. They're checking in and looking to arrange the next steps for her. They've been in there for about two hours. I'm not sure exactly what they're discussing, to be honest." She didn't sound like she cared too much about the subject or their conversation.

Although she was next to me, she didn't look at me once. Her eyes constantly moved as she surveyed the ward. Emma was distracted, her mind elsewhere. She was likely overworked and tired. She smelled like she hadn't made it home for a shower in between shifts. I took a step back as anger rippled inside me. Not directed at Emma, but Sue and the two women with her. Sometimes the staff seemed to forget they were working with actual people. Damaged people. People who were tormented enough as it was. Women who did not deserve to sit there and watch three clinicians discuss their lives with no involvement.

Yes, private conversations needed to be had. Patients cannot be present during discussions that may negatively affect their mental health. However, conversing for two hours behind a giant window right in front of Louise was not fair and not good care. It must have been extra torturous for Louise, with her severe anxiety building every minute. This was her freedom they were discussing. They could have had a conversation in an office downstairs where Louise was not forced to watch them. I knocked on the door of the nurses' station before using my key to gain entry, and smiled politely at the manager, Sue. She was another petite, milky-skinned blonde. However, Sue was pushing sixty with soft wrinkles lining her face and was much meeker than the defiant Emma. She reminded me more of a loving, smartly dressed grandmother than a stern ward manager.

"Hi, Sue." I smiled brightly, knowing she would not like me coming in here and undermining her. But she deserved it. If she had made a better decision on where to discuss Louise's care, I wouldn't have needed to undermine her. "I wondered if you could speak to Louise soon, please? She is getting very anxious as she can see you guys talking about her. Or maybe you could go into a private office so she can't see you, at least?"

My smile grew bigger again. I had no genuine power in this situation, other than the staff wanting to appear competent and willing in front of an outsider who knew how to report them, if necessary. An outsider who would be taken seriously if a complaint was made and who could make their lives difficult. Confrontation was never easy for me, though, and if Sue was to refuse my polite request, I wasn't sure what my next step would be.

To my immense relief, Sue smiled back. "Of course, yes! Poor thing. Tell her we will be with her in two minutes." She appeared genuinely concerned. I thanked her gratefully and returned to inform Louise. The tension in Louise's shoulders visibly eased. I smiled as she thanked me, feeling a bit more confident again after remembering why I was there. This was why I enjoyed my job...most of the time.

I spent some time chatting with a few of the other women about menial subjects, building rapport. Some patients started putting on their coats and shoes before standing near the exit door. They were being treated to a cinema trip to The Quad in the city. It was a creative center of Derby's historic cathedral quarter. It boasted a nice cafe and an art gallery as well as an indie cinema on the top floor.

I knew The Quad building well. Three years ago, fresh out of university, I presented life skills classes for adults with autism in one of their upstairs rooms. I analysed the patients who had been allowed such a treat. It was the quieter patients, the ones who were not as ill as the others still vegetating on the couch.

The patients often saw it as a punishment if they were not allowed to attend such outings. As if they were a child who wasn't being allowed on the school trip because of naughty behaviour. I got a lot of complaints about this type of event. It might not feel fair, but sometimes a patient was too much of a risk to the public and could not be allowed to leave the hospital grounds. Hence why they were in a secure hospital in the first place.

I noticed Lucy was not among the crowd. I wondered if that was why she was not my friend today. Maybe she blamed me for her missing out on the trip. The trust between us was well and truly shot. Thanks, psychosis.

I looked through the nurses' station window again. Sue and the other two women had left, and it had been around two hours since I'd spoken to Sue. It was time for me to move on to the next ward. Aaron Walker, one of two male nurses in the hospital, was in the nurses' station alone. I decided to go and speak to him about Lucy. I recognised him as a friend of a friend from my university days studying Psychology. I didn't know if he remembered me too, and I had never found an appropriate moment to discuss our university nightlife on the ward. I let myself back into the nurses' station.

"Hey, Aaron," I said to his back. Even though he wasn't yet looking at me, I smiled again and hoped he didn't now dislike me because I was an advocate. I wanted him to see me smiling to show I was still friendly. Plus, it was harder to say no to someone who was always nice and friendly. It was human instinct to be nice in return.

"Hey, Summer." He turned to look at me and grinned back, showing uneven white teeth through his dark stubble. He was tall, about 6'1, and his thick, black hair flopped over his forehead, partially obscuring his left eye. Aaron's paler than usual complexion made me wonder if he was sick. He still wore black guyliner around his eyes which had always accentuated his light skin, but there was a sweaty sheen to his cheeks.

"Still going to Rednote?" he asked me.

"Oh god, no! Well, sometimes when I'm drunk enough!" I replied with a laugh. So he remembered me from our favourite student nightclub. "But I don't drink much these days with a child around. What about you?"

"Every weekend!" He winked. "How is the little one? Not so little?"

"He's six. So no, not so little! Makes me feel old!"

"You're not even thirty, shut up!" He pulled a mock confused face before retrieving his grin. "Anything I can do to help ya?"

"Yeah, actually, I wondered why Lucy Clarke hasn't gone to the show? She was acting a bit off with me earlier, and I wondered if it was me or if she's been ill again recently?" I knew he would understand what I was asking. *Has she been violent lately?* However, he looked confused for a moment. Then his dark eyes darted away as if he was looking around for an answer. I watched as his confusion turned to panic.

I wondered if Lucy had done something more serious and braced myself. If something serious had happened, I should have been told before entering the ward so I could protect myself from a particularly violent patient. However, his answer was not one I could have ever anticipated.

"Lucy Clarke? There is no Lucy Clarke on this ward."

Summer

I laughed at him at first. "I spoke to her like two hours ago."

Aaron looked uncomfortable, but I couldn't fathom why. It was a simple enough question. Surely he knew who I meant. There were 15 patients on the ward. As a nurse, he needed to know them all well enough to deliver medication.

"Lucy," I repeated. "Lucy Clark?"

He pursed his lips and looked deep in thought for a moment. Then, finally, he shook his head. "Nope," he said. "There's definitely no Lucy."

"Stop playing games, Aaron." I laughed again, convinced he was playing a trick on me.

"I'm serious, Summer. There's no Lucy." His face was sombre, and I began to doubt myself.

"You can't miss Lucy. She has burn scars covering her face," I said.

He looked deep in thought again. The word *overacting* sprang to mind.

"We don't have any patients with facial burns. There's Izzi, but only her hands are scarred noticeably. There are no scars on her face."

I crossed my arms over my chest and glared at him. A joke was fine, but I genuinely wanted to know how Lucy was doing.

"Her room is number 15," I said.

"Number 15 is empty," he replied without missing a beat.

"Show me then." I knew without a doubt that Lucy was in there. She hadn't left since our earlier interaction. I would have seen her on the ward.

"Come on, then," he replied.

I tried not to let my surprise show. I'd half expected him to decline. Yet, he walked straight out of the nurses' station and beckoned for me to follow. I willed my legs to move, but they refused. I had a bad feeling about what was going to happen next. Something was nagging at my brain, warning me not to go looking for trouble. I told myself I was being ridiculous. Of course, Lucy would be in the bedroom. I followed him, shaking off my doubts.

As we walked through the main lounge, Louise ran up to me again. "Summer!" she shouted in my face, making me jump back.

"Hi, Louise." I smiled at her, trying to recover from the scare she gave me. "Is everything okay?"

"Yes, they came to speak to me." She beamed now, all her earlier anxiety calmed. "They wanted to see how I was doing. Sue told them I was doing well!"

She reminded me of Joshua whenever he did well in school and came home with a good behaviour certificate. "That's great!" I told her.

"You are doing well, Lou," Aaron said. "I'm going to show Summer something. We'll catch up later." He continued through the lounge and I followed, despite my nagging reservations. *Stop being ridiculous,* I repeated to myself.

The lounge was practically empty by that point, with half the patients having left to visit The Quad. That left about half a dozen patients milling around the ward in various rooms. I wished I was going on the visit with the others. I got to accompany the patients on trips sometimes. It was my favourite part of the job, getting to see them happy and doing normal things. Activities that other people take for granted every day, such as shopping or going for a walk. I couldn't imagine having every aspect of my life be in the hands of others because I was ill. I would hate having someone else making my decisions for me because of something out of my control. It seemed so unfair, but then what else can the doctors do? The patients needed to be looked after somehow. They needed to be protected. And sometimes, the public needed to be protected from them.

I looked around for some sort of distraction as we walked silently to

Lucy's room. Anything to stop the feeling of impending doom, which was getting stronger and stronger within my gut. The stench of some sort of burnt meat filled the lounge. The kitchen was right off the back of the room, partly open so the staff could watch patients as they used it. There was a sink, a microwave, and drawers full of paper cups and plastic knives. The cupboards were filled with food the patients had bought themselves. Sticky labels covered everything. To the back of the kitchen was another door leading to where the oven and proper cooking utensils could be found. If they had been behaving well, some patients were allowed to cook with supervision. Others were rarely allowed because of their history. Although, for those particularly ill patients, they didn't need an oven to cause harm to themselves. A patient once took me into a private room and simply lifted her sleeve. My eyes met with the most horrific sight. A single pen jammed right into a vein on her arm. That was three months ago, and I was still not over it.

But there was nothing to distract us, and we reached the corridor a few seconds later. When we reached her room, Aaron tried to open it. It was locked, and I knew right then he was right. The rooms couldn't be locked from inside, and staff wouldn't lock anyone inside their bedrooms. There was a safe room for patients who needed to be locked away. It was a padded cell with a shatter-proof window to the ward and an opening in the metal door to pass food through. It was straight out of a horror movie. People probably thought rooms like it no longer existed. Yet, it was still used as an alternative to overmedicating patients and, therefore, seen as the more humane option. Straitjackets were no longer a common item in the UK, at least, but the padded cell was still used.

Aaron jangled the keyring on his belt, looking for the key to Lucy's room. He had many more keys than I did. At least when he opened the door, we would see Lucy's things, and I would be proven right. Less than a minute later, he unlocked and threw open the door. The smell of bleach stung my nostrils. An unmade bed sat in the far right corner, and the chest of drawers next to it was open and empty. The closet by the opposite wall was also open, with just hangers inside. Clearly, this was not Lucy's room.

"I don't understand…" I fell quiet as words escaped me.

Aaron glanced at me. "You're probably thinking of a Lucy from another hospital?"

Cold fear grabbed hold of my stomach and twisted around it, like Lucy's icy fingers around my wrist. I shivered at the thought of our interaction as one terrifying thought took over.

Is Aaron lying to me, or am I going insane?

Summer

I spent an hour visiting the male ward of Derby Hospital before I could finally leave for the day. I tried to put Lucy out of my mind, but the feeling of her stiff fingers snaking around my wrist was stamped into my brain. I looked down at my wrist. There were no marks.

It was real. It was real.

Fridays were usually a good day of the week for people. The last day of work for lots of office workers and contractors. The beginning of the weekend, time with family and friends. For me, Fridays were the worst day of the week. I never got to spend time with Joshua on Fridays because he was always at his dad's house. I was so happy he still got to spend time with his dad, but for me, Fridays sucked.

So did the Friday afternoon traffic. I weaved my blue BMW one series in and out of traffic along the dual carriageway, desperate to get home. I needed to be alone to sit, to think, and just *be* for a while. Ten minutes after leaving the hospital, I arrived at a car park in front of an immense building. The car park was enough for ten cars, five on either side. It was for flats one to eight, with two visitor spaces for guests. I noticed a FIAT Punto in the guest space. I would usually try to figure out which neighbour it belonged to, but not that day.

The front wheels hit the kerb with a thud, jolting me forward, but I barely noticed. For once, I didn't bother to check if the wheels were okay. I levered my short self out of the bucket seat and slammed the door behind me, clicking the key fob's *lock* button three or four times as I walked away. Cold evening air stung my face, and a damp smell hung in the air. It hadn't stopped raining for three days. That wasn't unusual October weather for Derby, which averaged at less than ten degrees celsius. It was my biggest gripe about living here. I hated being cold.

I leaped over the sludgy grass to reach the pathway leading to the colossal Jacobean building that soared in front of me. Gravel crunched under my thick-heeled boots as I rushed to the steps. Over a year had passed since I made this walk for the first time, with Joshua's tiny hand holding mine, his other holding Richard's. Our lives had fallen apart one month later. The flat Joshua and I lived in was small, but the 170-year-old building it was a part of was stunning. In a funny twist, famous architect Joseph Danbury originally built the building as an asylum. It stood within a ten-acre site and included the original chapel further down the road.

I hurried up the thirteen curved steps to the entrance. An unlucky number for some. I wasn't superstitious, but I had always been glad for the additional three steps that led to the great double doors. Engraved above those grand entrance doors were the words *ANNO DOMINI MDCCCLI*. The shallow part of me loved it, finding it poignant and elegant. I'd lived nowhere even remotely classy before. I grew up on a typical council estate with my mum and two brothers, one older and one younger. A hundred feet above the engraved words was the striking bell tower with a red brick column on either side. The building continued at a right angle past each column, albeit at a much lower height. Blue Staffordshire brick and stone detailed the red brick in a sectional pattern.

At the end of the gravel pathway, I fumbled with my key before finally fitting it into the external door of the old asylum. Once inside and out of the freezing wind, I took a moment to embrace the welcome warmth of the central heating system. My shoes tapped loudly off the antique flooring as I hurried towards the marble staircase that ran to the left of the vast entrance hall. The hall was stunning. The dark floor contrasted with duck egg blue walls. One solid dark oak door was on each side of the hall, leading to flats one, two, and three. The doors were not that old, but they were made to look antique. The hall always smelled earthy, although I'd never been sure why. An ormolu and cut crystal Victorian chandelier took centre stage of the pristine white ceiling. The icicle drops and rosette crown scowled down at me as I climbed each marble step, criticizing me. I was an imposter living amongst such opulence.

At the top of the staircase was a double door which conflicted with the grand hall. It was made from light oak and modern, and a sign of the rest of the building's decor. Externally, many original features had been saved, but the hall was one of few original interior features. Through the modern doors, the narrow corridor floor was covered with deep red carpet tiles and surrounded by plain, white walls. It reminded me of a budget hotel. I had been tempted to redecorate it myself and then feign surprise along with my wondering neighbours. Lack of money stopped me, and I wasn't sure if I actually had the balls.

I reached the third door along on the first floor, flat number six, and again fumbled with my keys for several seconds. My fingers felt much thicker than usual. They trembled, although I was unsure why. Probably anxiety. Maybe fear. I cursed before the key finally slid into the lock and turned. I walked straight through the door on my left to head into the living room. Relief hit me as my own belongings enveloped me like a comfort blanket. The beautiful antique blue paint on the walls, the pine table in the corner, the black leather sofa complete with cracked arms. None of it matched, but it was mine. It was home.

I threw my old handbag onto the floor, kicked off my boots and ripped off my socks, not caring where they landed. My bare toes squeezed into the soft, grey carpet underfoot. It had been a gift from my successful younger brother, Dylan, named after Bob Dylan. I grabbed my old laptop from the table and plugged it in to charge. It always needed charging. I left it and exchanged my black suit trousers for comfortable joggers and my white blouse for a soft, warm jumper. As it often did when I was preoccupied with work-related matters, my mind wandered to my eldest brother, Eddie. His actual name was River, but nobody could call him that. I was eleven years his junior, and I'm not sure when he changed it, but I'd always called him Eddie. I was also 11 years old the last time I saw him, so I was hardly a reliable source of information regarding his name.

I'd tried to look for Eddie many times once I was old enough to do so, but I'd gotten nowhere. I even tried looking for his girlfriend, Marinda Tanda, but I didn't know where to look for her. I stopped looking once I found out I was pregnant. I didn't want him near my son. *Hypocrite.*

Guilt ate at me whenever I thought about Eddie. I was supposed to be an advocate for people like him, but that was work. I knew I was safe when I left the hospital at the end of any working day. I knew Joshua was safe. Work eased my guilt. If I helped enough people like Eddie, wasn't it the same as helping him? Better even, since I helped lots of people rather than one. Though Lucy had been playing on my mind since early afternoon, and I didn't leave the hospital until 5:30 PM. It was now 6 PM.

Maybe it was a good thing that I didn't have Joshua. I would be distracted by Lucy, anyway. At least I could be alone with my thoughts, but I yearned for a cuddle, as I always did. I didn't know what I would do when he got too big to cuddle me. I tried to convince myself I was glad for the peace, requiring it to untangle my mind from the web of Lucy-related thoughts. With a sigh, I flopped onto the couch and opened the ancient laptop. I only used it for job-related record keeping. My phone was much newer and worked far quicker for anything else. The laptop screen welcomed me with an image of bright, colourful flowers as it struggled to open the login screen. Whilst I tried to keep my patience with the slow machine, I sent Richard a quick text to ask if Joshua was okay.

As I waited, I considered what I knew about Lucy. She used to open up to me because she believed we were friends. Until a couple of weeks ago, when she had accused me of betrayal. She had screamed at me in the middle of the ward, to the point where staff had to restrain her. I had never had a patient be so angry with me. Usually, they got upset with others and asked me for my support. That was my role in, after all. I was to have no opinion of my own and provide factual information and support only. Lucy thought I had spoken to her nurses and instructed them to ignore her. It was untrue and unfounded, but unfortunately, psychosis knew no truth. It was not uncommon to lose rapport with a patient through no fault of your own or theirs.

My knee bounced up and down in frustration as I stared at the laptop, willing the login screen to appear. I needed my work files and reports. Every conversation I'd had with Lucy was recorded, despite what Aaron had told me. He was nearly believable, but I knew I saw panic and fear in his eyes. Thanks to working with pathological liars in several jobs after studying psychology for five years, I was a fantastic lie detector. I read facial expressions intently. I saw minute movements of the forehead that most others missed. I watched which way the eyes gazed as lies were told and in which direction oblivious hands pointed and waved. I noticed jittery legs, which bounced like my own did when I was nervous or anxious, an annoying habit I picked up from my dad before a car crash had taken his life.

Aaron knew who I was talking about. He knew Lucy. I could tell that much. But where she could be and why was he lying, that I could not fathom. I needed to ring my mentor, Natalie. She was my immediate supervisor, a thirty-five-year-old who lived in Birmingham. My supposed guide through being an advocate. The thought of calling her made me bristle with annoyance. I was forced to check in with her weekly, much to my dismay. Not only did I prefer to be left alone, but she had also made it acutely clear that I was her first supervisee. As a result, she was overzealous in monitoring me. I got it. She was trying to impress our big boss Alexia. I still disliked it.

I was more highly qualified and had far more experience at working with people who suffered from mental health problems. She had no psychology degree and certainly no master's. She had been an advocate for barely a few weeks longer than me and, previous to becoming an advocate, only had around a year's worth of experience in mental health. On multiple occasions, she would tell me I was wrong about something where I knew I was right. She once told me to ignore it when I informed her a male patient was being mistreated. She said I was probably wrong, so monitor for now. I ignored her and reported the hospital to the CQC, the Care Quality Commission. Though I was still waiting on their response three months later.

Regardless of my feelings, she was officially my first port of call for any issues. But I couldn't call her yet. I would sound delirious. Plus, she would likely tell me to ignore it again. *Monitor for now.* I scoffed at the memory. I required some sort of concrete evidence first, so she had to listen and get Alexia involved. I'd only been an advocate for eight months, and I didn't want Alexia to think I was losing my mind either. So, evidence was a must. I would prefer to die than end up in a *secure* hospital as a patient. After witnessing the experiences of my patients and brother, I knew I was not as strong as them. I could never cope with the torture that their minds put them through on a never-ending basis. Too many of them never got better, trapped in nightmares decade after decade. There was no way I could ever do it.

I gave a long sigh of relief as the login screen finally appeared. Once logged in, I frantically clicked on a folder titled *DERBYC*, hoping the laptop would recognise my urgent need for information and suddenly decide to work quicker. I desperately needed a new one, but my employer, Rowan's Advocacy, refused to supply them. And they were far too expensive for me to buy one on my wage. The folder eventually opened three times, thanks to my incessant clicking. I clicked on the separate files within the folder. I always entitled each with a date and nothing more.

Time dragged by as I waited impatiently for the files to open. After a minute or so, which felt like at least ten minutes, a multitude of excel documents opened all at once. I pressed *Ctrl* and *F* simultaneously on the largest file, a daily report named *Fri7:09* — Friday, the seventh of September. I visited Derby Hospital twice a week, on Mondays and Fridays. This report would have been created around three weeks ago. I entered the initials *LC* into the pop-up search bar. We were not allowed to write names in our reports for data protection purposes, meaning any notes on Lucy would be under her initials. When *LC* popped up on the report, a wave of relief washed over me. I was not crazy. I read the first entry to see what I had written.

Spoke to LC briefly today, but she is very ill at the moment. Mood was down, paranoid, anxious. She thinks I have betrayed her somehow - psychosis seems to be taking over. Did not want to communicate about her care and did not want assistance. Verging on abusive. Will try again next week if no longer confrontational.

So I hadn't woken up in a parallel universe. Lucy existed. She was not a figment of my imagination. I had spoken to her. I wouldn't have written it down otherwise. At least that's what I told myself. I clicked on the next excel file, which had since opened up. This one was named *Fri31:08,* one week before the other file. I searched for her initials again, looking for anything that might help me understand what had happened.

Friday, 31st August

Spoke to LC today. She was chatty and smiley. We are building good rapport- would like me to attend the ward round on Monday, which I've confirmed is fine if it is between 9 and 11 AM.

My heart skipped a beat. If I had attended a ward round meeting with Lucy, there must have been other people present. Other people who could confirm she was a patient and tell me where she was. I didn't recall Lucy speaking to other patients or even staff whilst I was there. This hadn't struck me as unusual, as I was on the ward for an hour or two twice a week. It would be easy for me to miss such interactions. So this meeting could be my only evidence to show Natalie. I opened another file to check.

Monday, 3rd September

Tried to speak to LC today. She did not want to talk or attend the ward round at all, with or without me.

Damn. We didn't go to the meeting together. My note seemed short and did not consider why Lucy missed the ward round. I assumed I couldn't get anything out of her during the visit. Plus, missing the meeting itself was not unusual. Ward rounds were formal meetings between the patient and their multi-disciplinary team, or *MDT,* to discuss how they're doing and the next steps of their care. Patients could request things such as new medication or section 17 leave from the hospital grounds. The regularity of ward rounds depended upon the hospital. It may be weekly, fortnightly, or monthly, which had always struck me as unfair. It was a chance for the patients to be involved in their care plan and what happened to them. Why should some patients only have the chance to request this from their RC once a month? I imagined four weeks was a hell of a long time to be detained in such a noisy and often violent environment, unable to even request leave.

Sometimes the patients liked to *threaten* the MDT with my presence at ward rounds. Some patients viewed them as the bad guys. They were in control of everything the patient did, from where they slept to whether they were allowed outside. Patients often thought that having me at their side ensured the MDT acted appropriately, for I was an outsider. I was not mentally ill. Therefore, I was to be respected. When the time came for ward rounds, a patient would often change their minds about me being there. If they had an enjoyable week, they might decide they no longer needed me to speak for them after all. Or if they had experienced a dreadful week, they may not want to go to the meeting. Any meetings Lucy attended would be in her patient file. This was the file completed by her MDT and kept in the nurses' station on Bluebell Ward. I needed to get my hands on that file.

Frustration hit me as I realised I was not back at the hospital until Monday. I didn't work on weekends, but I wasn't sure how I could wait. I was usually good about not bringing work home, but the whole situation with Lucy was so strange. Maybe I could visit the next day regardless and tell the staff I'd forgotten something. I could then go to the nurses' station to look for it. I was allowed access to a patient file if that particular patient provided their consent, and Lucy had never given me consent. But I didn't think she would care. Despite our fallout, I was trying to help her. Wherever she was, I had a bad feeling about it.

I looked at my watch. It was 7 PM, and far too late for me to visit the ward. I needed to put Lucy out of my mind. Otherwise, I would be no good to her. If I allowed myself to become too preoccupied, I knew I would not be able to sleep properly. And I did not function well on too little sleep. I would happily sleep for ten hours a night if my schedule allowed for it. As it was, I probably managed six-ish hours a night on average and found myself exhausted most days. Often it was a struggle to concentrate.

I picked up my phone from the sofa and waved it in front of my face until it recognised my facial features. It took a second or two before the screen unlocked. I scrolled down the list of contacts and tapped the name *Kelly*. Kelly was a couple of years older than I but had been my best friend for over a decade now. A mutual friend had introduced us. The ringing went on for quite a while. I was ready to give up when she answered the call.

"Hello," Kelly answered in a gruff voice as if she were half asleep.

"Sorry, did I wake you?" I asked, although I was unsure why I bothered. She wouldn't care if I'd woken her. It was only 7 PM.

"Nah, just having a few drinks at home. What's up?" I heard her inhale deeply. She was smoking. My cigarette craving grabbed at my chest, and I took a puff of my electronic cigarette to shake it off. Clouds of sweet-smelling smoke filled the air around me.

"Nothing, I'm a bit bored." I wasn't sure how to broach the subject of what was wrong without sounding psychotic myself.

"Oh," she replied. "How was work?"

Fuck it, I thought. I needed to speak to someone about it before my brain exploded. And Kelly was my most trusted friend.

"Well, something kinda strange happened today."

"Go on." Kelly sounded a lot more interested. Most people were fascinated by my job, mainly because I didn't work in the average mental health ward. I worked with people who had been identified as *criminally insane* by the courts.

"So I was speaking to a patient, we'll call her patient Z, and then I went off to speak to some other patients. It must have been like, two hours later, bearing in mind this patient Z touched me and everything. Like she grabbed my wrist and hurt me!" I paused for dramatic effect. There was another deep inhale. "Anyway, two hours later, I went to speak to the nurse about her. He told me she doesn't exist! He said there's no Lu... I mean patient Zs, in the whole hospital."

"Dickhead," she stated simply. "He's obviously not good at his job if he doesn't know his own patients!"

I laughed loudly. I knew I could trust Kelly to make me think straight. Her blunt nature was always a help, and she saw life as far more black and white than I did. For me, the world was a mixture of colours. Yes, some things were black and white, others were shades of greys, blues, and whites, or even shocking pink. I needed to know why things happened, what made people do what they did, and I couldn't rest until I had the answer. Kelly didn't overthink any situation. I would be more like Kelly if I could control my intrinsic need for information. I would likely be a lot less exhausted and probably much happier. Maybe it was that simple. Maybe Aaron was simply wrong. Maybe he was not good at his job.

"But he showed me her room, Kelly. The room I thought was her bedroom, and it was empty." A chill ran down my spine at the memory.

"Maybe you're not good at *your* job!" She laughed, as did I. "Honestly, mate, it sounds like nothing. I wouldn't worry about it. He's an idiot, and you got your bedrooms mixed up. Or this patient Z lied to you, told you the wrong name or wrong bedroom or something."

"Maybe," I mused. I was unconvinced, but her straight-talking made me feel better.

After a few more minutes of general chitchat, I hung up. Whilst talking to her, a wave of calmness had passed through me, forcing away the anxiety that had been squeezing my insides all evening. Kelly was probably right, and if she wasn't, I'd find out on Monday. No big deal. I ate some leftover chicken pasta from the fridge, and then grabbed a hot shower to wash away the residual stress. The bathroom was my least favourite room in the flat. It was so cramped that we couldn't fit in a bath, which made Joshua sad. I'd promised him we would have a bath next time we moved house. That led to him constantly asking for a new house.

I let the hot water trickle over my body for some time, not wanting to get back out into the chilly flat. I didn't put the heating on too much when Joshua was away, not wanting to spend the money unless it was to keep him warm. Eventually, I left the warm shower and selected some fluffy blue pyjamas to sleep in. They were super warm, despite my hair still being soaking wet. I threw on some old soft slippers to match. I felt much calmer, but needed something extra. I sloped into the kitchen and grabbed a tumbler glass from the high cupboard above the oven. The kitchen was more stylish than I could have ever made it myself. The glitzy charcoal countertops with brilliant white cupboard doors were here when we moved in. I loved it. It wasn't big, but looked stunning.

I poured some Jameson's whiskey into the tumbler and then poured some more for good measure. I added some coke and brought it back into the master bedroom so I could sip it in bed, as I browsed Netflix for something easy to watch. My brain couldn't take much more deep thought. *Plus, the quicker I fall to sleep, the quicker I get Joshua back*, I told myself.

I ended up knocking back the large tumbler quicker than usual. My mind clouded over as I lay in bed, a silly comedy playing in the background. I got super hot as the alcohol filtered through my veins and stripped off my fluffy pyjamas, abandoning them on the floor next to my bed. A few minutes later, I was asleep. But not for long. She was coming for me.

One. Two...

I watched Summer stride around the ward as if she owned the place. She shimmied her hips as she walked like she thought she was God's gift. Her shiny brown hair reached her waist. She always wore it the same way. Long, straight, and unstyled. Sometimes it was all hocked up in a boring ponytail, even though her nose was too big for the style to be attractive. But mostly she left it down, as if she couldn't be bothered to do anything nice with it. Not like I would if I had such long hair. Mine wouldn't grow, but that was okay. I had my own new shiny hair by then. She didn't deserve her hair. Someone should chop it off. Maybe I'd chop it off.

The first time I saw her on the ward, she was shorter and fatter than I thought she would be. She had lost weight now, though, and was too skinny. She looked bony. Like she would be uncomfortable to touch. I bet she was single. Nobody would want to have sex with that. It would be like fucking a skeleton. And I hadn't even seen her wear makeup once since she started visiting the ward. She constantly smiled, attempting to appear genuine and nice. She wanted people to see her that way, but I knew the truth. No one else knew, but I could see it. The words were green when spoken, like a green mist escaping the truth teller's lips. The mist was purple when people lied.

Summer stopped smiling when she thought no one was looking at her. She was a destroyer of lives. She was fake and evil. It shone around her like an aura, deep red and so dark it was almost black. It was the aura of the devil. She didn't even *recognise* me. You'd think she would after all the time we spent together, but that's typical of her. All Summer thinks about is Summer. I was happy that she didn't recognise me. I'd hoped for it. I could take my time and mess with her head.

I'd told the ward all about her, so they knew not to trust her. I told the nurses and their assistants that she spreads lies and to tell her nothing. I told the patients that she tells the MDT everything they say.

Frustratingly, it didn't seem to bother her. *Typical.* She carried on coming. Every Monday. Every Friday. Like clockwork. I stayed well back when I could. I enjoyed staring at her, watching until the facade dropped. Her fear was obvious whenever a patient was agitated. Laughable that with her history, she feared the patients.

It wasn't obvious, at least not to people who did not have my gift. She always looked calm, but I knew the truth. I could smell fear. It had the metallic scent of blood, and she reeked of it. No one else could smell it. It was a gift of mine, one of many powers I'd possessed since my vision, like the power to see truth and deception. I couldn't wait until she saw what I had in store for her. She would be scared then. The dread in her would grow and grow until everybody could smell it. I was going to ruin her like she ruined me.

She would be so ugly she wouldn't want to go out in public ever again. I used to be ugly, but I changed that. I was clean, re-birthed, and free of my ugly skin. She would not have the same luck.

She spoke to an agitated Louise next. She looked concerned, as if she cared about Louise's stupid, insignificant problems. But I knew she didn't care. People like her didn't care about others. She was there for selfish reasons. Being near these pathetic souls, pretending to help them, pretending to care, it was all to make her feel better about herself. Deep down, she knew how disgusting she was. Summer could help her brother instead of these idiots, but chose not to. Which was all the evidence I needed to know that she was fake. A smile lingered on my lips as I wondered how she would feel if she were aware of how much I knew about her. If she knew I was there, watching her, always watching her.

Summer

Spidery wisps of moonlight reached through the blinds as I lay in bed. They danced and lingered on different objects, and my sleepy eyes followed them slowly across the room. The wisps spun around, a shadow in the doorway—a human shadow. Lucy.

She stared at me with her cold green eyes. She had pulled the hood of her black jumper tightly over her head, but I could still see those eyes lit by the moonlight. There was no life in them. The fire had disappeared. She was not friendly today. I could feel it, smell it, and taste it. Every fibre in my body told me to run.

I jolted up into a sitting position, desperate to create some space between us, and banged my head off the wall. *Shit, that hurt.* I wrapped the duvet tightly around my naked body as if for safety, but I didn't feel any more secure. Goosebumps covered my naked skin, and I cursed myself for taking off my pyjamas.

I watched Lucy for a moment and waited for her to say something. She was silent. I was unsure whether I should say something or wait for her to talk. All I could hear was my heart. *Thump. Thump. Thump.*

It was so loud I wondered if she could hear it. My breathing was ragged, and there was no pretending to be calm. It was my bedroom, not the hospital. She had invaded my space. The hair on the back of my neck had risen like tiny pinpricks, and my teeth felt cold against my tongue. I shivered hard. Why did the room feel as if it was below freezing? Yet sweat beads tickled my forehead as they slowly dropped into my eyes.

My dry lips moved as I attempted to say her name, but no sound came out. I tried to move again, but my body refused to obey. The room spun, and I blinked a few times, trying to clear my head. My face was sticky with sweat. I wanted to close my eyes and pretend it wasn't happening and that she was not here, but I couldn't look away.

A giggle escaped her deformed lips, the high-pitched laughter of a child, and I didn't feel bad for her anymore. I no longer wanted to find her. I wanted her gone. The laugh got louder. The air was so thick with evil and her greasy stench I struggled to breathe. I raised my hands, pressing them tightly over my ears as the laughter slammed my eardrums. Louder and louder until it penetrated my brain, and I couldn't take it anymore.

I squeezed my eyes shut and heard myself whisper, *no, no, no* repeatedly. A rustling sound broke through the noise, and I forced my eyes back open. Lucy was moving, and yet her legs did not move. Instead, she glided rapidly towards me. *What the fuck was going on?* Bile rose in my throat as she came within inches of my bed. I could not move. I sat and watched with my hands clasped over my ears, elbows pointed out as a hopeless defence. My bedroom was not a large room, and she was across the grey carpet and on the opposite side of my bed in seconds. She was still laughing as her grossly burnt hands reached for me. I closed my eyes and prepared myself for pain, a gurgled scream piercing the air between us. And the laughter finally stopped.

Summer

I raised my hand to rub the thumping ache at the back of my head and willed it to disappear. There was no lump, and Lucy was gone. One minute she was inches from my face. The next, I opened my eyes, and she had disappeared.

I *had* heard a thud, and I *had* banged my head. The pain shooting through my brain was proof. The soft bed sheets and duvet still protected my shivering, naked body, pulled up tight around my chest. I looked at the bedroom door where she'd first stood.

It was closed as it always was when I went to bed. I couldn't sleep with the door open. So Lucy was never there. She couldn't have been. Yet the stench of her greasy, unwashed hair still hung heavy in the air. I had to make sure she was gone.

I flicked on the bedside lamp, the warm glow and familiar objects calming me. My second-hand TV sat on top of the pine drawers adjacent to the bed. The cute elephant teddy Joshua had bought me last Mother's Day sat next to me on my *Paris* bed sheets. The framed picture of Joshua and I watching dolphins in Lanzarote was on the bedside table.

My anxiety eased as the familiarity of my surroundings soothed me. I snuck my hand down to the side of my bed to grab my pyjamas and hurried to put them on whilst still under the duvet.

"Hello?" I called out, feeling silly, and yet terrified that I might hear a response. Deathly silence greeted me. No laughing, or breathing, or footsteps. Thank God.

I needed to get a grip. I'd never had a nightmare so real. My ears still rang from the evil laughter that had penetrated my brain. But what if it wasn't a dream?

My patients told me about their hallucinations all the time. I had one sixteen-year-old patient who saw a blood-covered witch whenever she felt stressed out. The witch told her to hurt herself, and the girl did so to make the witch go away because she was so terrifyingly real. Another patient spoke to God like he was sitting on the empty chair right next to him. And then there was my brother and his devil.

These hallucinations were completely real to the person experiencing them. I'd never had a hallucination before, despite my fear of becoming ill like my brother, but I guessed it would feel like what had just happened.

I grabbed my phone from the bedside table. It was two o'clock in the morning. I couldn't call Kelly this late. She wouldn't be impressed if I called her in the middle of the night over a nightmare, for God's sake. *Fuck this.* I needed to get out of the flat. I needed to be around people.

I gingerly got out of bed as if Lucy were still hiding somewhere. Every time I made a noise, I froze, and listened for a second. I removed my pyjamas and quickly threw on some clean underwear, a pair of old jeans, and a thick black jumper before grabbing my car keys. I didn't know where I was going, but I needed some fresh air.

I ran from my flat to the car park, still on edge from the dream or vision or whatever it was. There was nobody around, yet I felt as though I was being watched. I shivered and cursed myself for forgetting my coat. It was freezing outside. Once safely in my car. I locked the doors and drove off at speed.

I drove nowhere in particular initially, but eventually went to the twenty-four-hour supermarket. It was a ten-minute drive away, and I knew it would have bright lights and other people. Not lots of people, but still better than being alone. Better than my flat with no Joshua. I needed to get the food shopping done whilst he was away, anyway. There's nothing worse than having a bored kid around whilst you're trying to shop or an over-excited one throwing everything they see into the trolley.

I parked right at the front of the store in the parent and baby spot. It wasn't something I would normally do without Joshua, but I was still pretty freaked out from my dream, and the car park was dark. Besides, few parents would be shopping with kids at 2 AM. With my conscience eased, I left my car and jogged over to the trolleys, keen to get inside and wander around in the familiar, safe environment.

In my younger days, I probably would have gone to a bar. Now, at almost thirty, my priorities had shifted. The loud noise of a night out and the following three-day hangover did not appeal to me. However, that night was an exception. If I'd known anyone who would be up for a night out at 2 AM, I would have called them.

There were one or two other shoppers in the supermarket. As I entered the first aisle, I attempted to remember what food I needed for the week rather than think about what happened earlier. Or *the dream,* which I was pretty sure it was. *No, it definitely was.*

I eyeballed the ridiculous amount of different vegetables that lined the aisle, trying to remember which ones I needed. I was in a world of my own and didn't hear any footsteps behind me or feel the presence of another body. Not until icy fingers gripped my shoulder. *Lucy.* My breath caught in my throat as I spun on my heel to face her again.

"No!" I squealed. I tried to sound stern but could not keep my voice steady.

"Whoa! It's me. I'm sorry. Are you okay?" Instead of Lucy's sharp eyes, I gazed into the dark eyes of Aaron Walker.

"Oh shit, sorry, Aaron. Shit. I was in a world of my own then!" I could not stop cursing as I tried to calm my heartbeat. A rush of heat spread across my face, and I looked at the floor. *Please swallow me up.*

"It's okay. Are you okay?" He looked concerned. My face flushed further, and I wished he would laugh at me or make a joke like he usually did.

"Yeah, I'm fine! Well, actually, I had a horrible dream, so I went shopping to take my mind off it." I giggled at how daft I sounded and flashed him a smile in some vain hope of convincing him I wasn't crazy, despite my actions earlier.

"Ah, that sucks! I've just finished work. I had to stay late." He rolled his eyes. The hospital was always understaffed, and people often had to take extra shifts or stay until a bank nurse arrived. "Why don't we go for a drink? I can take your mind off it more than shopping!"

I laughed at his offer. I couldn't remember the last time I had an impromptu drink offer in the middle of the night. It's not like the stereotype of single mothers getting drunk every weekend is true. I never had the time. Most of my child-free time was spent sitting around missing Joshua and looking at the chores I should do whilst he was gone.

I looked down at my old jeans, suddenly self-conscious in his presence. "I'm not dressed for a drink!"

"We can go to my mate's bar. No one in there will be dressed up. You'll fit right in." He winked at me.

I supposed it couldn't be that bad, and I could see what he had to say about Lucy after a few drinks.

"Okay, sure, why not!" I said with a grin, pushing down the nagging feeling in my stomach. I walked away from the few items I had managed to get in the trolley.

We talked about some memories of nights out as students as we drove back to my place to park my car. Neither of us mentioned the time we had kissed outside a nightclub as students. He came inside the flat with me to grab my coat. I still didn't want to be alone in there.

The ten-minute walk back to town was quiet at first. It was just Aaron and I strolling through the frosty night air. But as we got closer, more and more people milled around. Most were falling around in a drunken stupor, getting kebabs and taxis home.

I'd forgotten how much Aaron could make me laugh. He was quirky at times. Some mutual university friends thought of him as strange, but I didn't mind strange. People thought I was strange, as an advocate for murderers, rapists and stalkers. His jeans were super tight and paired with a long Nirvana t-shirt. He wore black eyeliner and a large silver earring in his left ear, which stretched the piercing hole to the size of a penny piece.

As we walked by the pubs we used to frequent, I remembered him dressing up as Captain Jack Sparrow once on a night out. It wasn't fancy dress anywhere. He then wore the same costume for about a month's worth of nights out, purely to make people laugh. Well, I'm pretty sure it was a conversation starter, and he was able to pull lots of women. His movements when he spoke were sometimes like Jack Sparrow, not as theatrical but somewhat similar.

It was around 3 AM by the time we reached his friend's bar. I looked up at the bright letters lit in neon orange above the door, spelling out *Charlie's*. I'd been there before with my own friends. It was a tiny place, usually frequented by lovers of indie rock and nowhere near clean. But the music and atmosphere were always great.

"Don't worry. He'll stay open until about 6 for me!" Aaron winked at me again.

I smiled at how he was showing off for me. I asked for a double vodka with soda water, a splash of lime, and a shot of tequila. He looked surprised.

"Have you forgotten how I can drink?" I laughed. "Well, until I got pregnant!"

I might not get the chance to go out drinking often, but I certainly made the most of it when I did. Plus, I hated being sober and surrounded by drunk people. We sat in the corner chatting about mutual friends and drinking. The front door of the bar was locked by then, but there were around ten other people still inside. Everyone was laughing and joking, having a good time. A couple swayed together on the tiny dance floor, holding each other up and giggling.

The drinks tasted metallic and flat, but I didn't care. I felt tipsy within an hour and couldn't remember the last time I'd laughed so much. Aaron made me feel so comfortable. I ordered more vodka and shots for us both. Our legs rubbed against each other as we sat drinking and laughing together. He caressed my thigh, and I didn't push him off. At 5 AM, I allowed him to walk me home.

I didn't stop him from following me into the flat. I didn't stop his lips from reaching for mine, either. Or his icy hands from slipping up my top and closing firmly around my breasts. Instead, my nipples tightened, wanting his attention. I was on a high, drunk and happy with a funny man who was easy on the eyes. Fuck it. Real life could wait until tomorrow. I'd forgotten all about Lucy.

Lucy's Coming

Summer didn't see me as I watched her wander slowly around the shop. It was fun to catch her outside of the ward. I had to stay well back, as there weren't many people around to hide behind. Even still, I was pretty sure she wouldn't notice me. She appeared to be in a world of her own, and I looked different now, anyway. I'd taken off the mask to hide. I knew she wouldn't recognise me without it.

She looked tired. Her face was white, and black bags marked her eyes. She wore fading jeans with a scraggy old jumper. I wondered why she was here in the middle of the night rather than in bed. She stood in front of the vegetable aisle, but didn't appear to know what she wanted. As usual, she was indecisive. Weak. I wondered if she ever thought about me. I reckoned she'd forgotten all about me and the hours we'd spent talking. The times we'd shared.

A figure caught my eye, and I turned to see a man. I couldn't see his face, just his profile. He stood at the other end of the vegetable aisle, watching her too. So I watched him for a moment instead. He was a tall man with black hair, dark jeans that were much too tight, and a baggy black hoodie. I couldn't place him from this angle, but he looked familiar. He must have felt my stare because he turned and looked straight at me.

Shit! Aaron. What was he doing here?

He must not be allowed to mess up my plan. I rapidly changed my shocked expression and smiled at him instead. But then I remembered I wasn't wearing my mask so he wouldn't recognise me, anyway. Yet despite my missing disguise, his face turned pale against his dark stubble.

He cracked open his mouth as if to say something. Did he recognise me? I risked it. I raised one hand and waved, enjoying how much I was freaking him out.

He turned back to look at her. Shit, was he going to tell her? No. He wouldn't be that stupid. Still, I turned and ran down the aisle where he could no longer see me. I slowed to a brisk walk and calmly strolled out of the supermarket. I didn't want the burly security guard to think I was a thief.

My body shook with adrenaline, but I laughed once outside. I probably sounded hysterical, but so what? The look on Aaron's face was priceless! I ran around the corner of the supermarket car park and down an alley to where my old Punto was parked. I had to get out of there, sharpish. I could always wait for Summer at her flat.

Summer

The morning light seeped through the blinds. It danced on my eyelids, and I groaned as I struggled to open them fully. The pain in my head did not help matters. I glanced over at Aaron. He lay in the bed next to me, snoring softly. I couldn't help but smile despite my head feeling like a tiny person was drilling into my brain. A small pang of guilt pulled at my stomach, but I pushed it away. I refused to bother with any regret. We'd had fun as two consenting adults, a lot of fun.

My throat felt like sandpaper. I reached out to grab the glass of water next to my bed and gulped it down. It soothed my dry mouth and made the drilling in my head a bit more bearable. The one thing I regretted was not asking Aaron about Lucy. I had enjoyed myself too much, and Lucy had gone completely out of my mind. Aaron being drunk had been the perfect opportunity. I needed to know if he'd somehow forgotten who she was or if she was safe on the ward. Safe for her, but safe for me, too.

Do I really need to know? Can't I forget what happened? Forget about Lucy?

I pushed the thoughts aside. I needed to know I wasn't crazy. If Lucy existed, then I wanted to help her and make sure she was okay. If she didn't, then I had to figure out what that meant for me. And, if I was hallucinating, what that meant for Joshua. That settled it. It was vital that I knew what had happened to Lucy to protect Joshua. I looked back over at Aaron and watched his chest move up and down rhythmically. I tried to figure out how to bring Lucy up again. He stirred and half flicked his eyes open before closing them again.

"Come here," he whispered. His muscular arm snaked around my stomach as he prised his eyes open again. "Good morning." He smiled sleepily. "I've been waiting years for this."

His smile widened into a grin as he reached up to kiss my cheek. I laughed and lay with him for a moment, enjoying the feeling of his powerful arms around me. I slid down, so my face rested against his warm chest. The small hairs tickled my cheek, but I ignored them. I couldn't ask about Lucy right now. It had been a long time since I cuddled an adult, and I didn't want to ruin the moment.

We lay there for half an hour, alternating between talking and just being. But that was about as long as I could manage before getting up and taking a hot shower. As nice as it was, I couldn't lie in bed for long. Even with an adult to cuddle, I got bored. It was a side effect of becoming a mother. I ignored his pleas to stay in bed but promised to buy him breakfast at a cafe down the road from my flat. *Barbara's Baps* was a greasy spoon that made the best cheese toasties I'd ever tasted. Perfect for a hangover.

The winter sun was warm on my face as we walked down the street. We dodged the puddles from the night-time rainfall and joked about the previous evening's antics. He reminded me about my terrible dancing as I tried not to blush. *Barbara's Baps* was one street away, so it didn't take us long to reach the cafe's blue and white front door.

Aaron gripped my hand and led me inside. I enjoyed the gesture, though it was not something I would normally allow to happen. It wasn't normal for me, but I liked the human contact. The one person I would usually allow to touch me was Joshua. I lived for his little arms to be wrapped around me, but I rarely hugged anyone else. Not even my own mother, for instance, and never would I hug either of my brothers. I saw Dylan at Christmas, and would likely never see Eddie again.

The cafe was a small building. It was previously a mid-terrace home and, as a result, did not have much space downstairs. There were six plastic tables dotted around in three uneven rows of two. Cheap waterproof checked cloths were draped over the tables, matching the blue and white colour scheme.

The counter was at the back of the room, and two women stood behind it, chatting. Both looked to be in their early fifties. They were rotund with greying hair, thick Derbyshire accents, and wore the same blue and white plastic aprons. They looked like sisters.

Four builders wearing yellow hard hats and matching high-vis jackets sat at the table to the left of the entrance. They joked and laughed loudly at each other's expense. Aaron led me to the right to take a seat on the bench furthest away from the door. I decided against a cheese toastie today and ordered a full English with an extra sausage and toast. Aaron ordered the same. I was supposed to be dieting to squeeze back into my skinny jeans, but I needed to soak up the alcohol. I had to pick up Joshua at lunchtime, and it was already eleven.

Our food arrived promptly and, halfway through our breakfasts, I still hadn't asked Aaron about Lucy. I needed to know before I picked up Joshua. I wanted to put it out of my mind. It was then or never.

"So," I smiled at him slyly, not sure how to word my question, "are you going to tell me the truth about Lucy yet? Because you're a terrible liar."

Worry lined his face for a split second before he forced his smile to return. But it was long enough for me to notice.

"There's nothing to tell. If we had a Lucy, I would know." He shoveled more sausage into his mouth.

"Aaron, I've checked my notes, and I record *every* conversation with *every* patient. I have had many conversations with *LC*," I said, attempting to sound jokey rather than confrontational. I smiled at him as I watched his face. Part of the reason I'd studied psychology may have been that I was naturally good at reading people, but I was not so good at confrontation.

"We do have some LCs. Izzy's proper name is Laura Coughlan." He dismissed my evidence with a mouth full of egg and bacon. "Why are you so bothered about one patient, anyway?"

"The dream I had last night that made me go shopping in the middle of the night? It was about Lucy." I looked away, not wanting to see his face when he got to thinking I was pathetic. Or even worse, that I'd lost my marbles.

"You....you saw her?" Aaron's voice was unsteady, and I looked back up at him. There was no smile now. His face had turned an even paler shade of white, the black stubble on his jaw was more pronounced than usual.

"Well, I dreamt I did. I think it was a dream, anyway. It was so real. She was in my room, and she sort of floated towards my bed..." I trailed off as I realised he was gawking at me with his mouth wide open. I had expected him to laugh and tell me I needed to chill out. Instead, he jumped to his feet, pulled some notes out of his pocket, and dropped them onto the table. I looked up at him, my face still and calm. I was used to keeping a straight face when shocked. It came with working in mental health.

"Sorry," he stammered, "I...er...I've just remembered that I have a shift at lunchtime. I have to go."

"I can give you a lift?" I offered, but he was already halfway out of the cafe. The noisy builders went quiet and looked at Aaron, and then at me sitting alone. I faced my head down towards the table so they couldn't see the red sheen I could feel appearing on my warm cheeks.

What the hell was that about? I had hoped for reassurance or an answer that would stop my mind constantly whirring about Lucy. But I'd ended up even more mystified. Something had happened to Lucy, and Aaron knew what. I needed to get my hands on that file.

Aaron

Aaron reached his flat at 11:45 AM, thoughts of Lucy racing through his brain. His breath heaved in and out of his chest. He wasn't used to running so quickly. *Fucking Lucy.*

It took a lot of effort to push open the heavy door to the building. He was glad they'd ended up at Summer's flat. It was much nicer than this dingy hell hole. He ran up two flights of grey stairs and finally slowed to a walk when he reached his corridor. His chest couldn't take any more running. The hallway had its usual aroma of damp and dirt. It made his stomach churn after eating most of that massive fry up. His flat opened straight into the living room with no entrance hall to speak of. He sat down on his battered couch, his head in his hands.

Stupid. Stupid. Stupid.

He tried to catch his breath before his lungs gave up altogether. He needed to calm down and try to think. Lucy must be following him. He was sure now. It wasn't a coincidence at the supermarket last night.

Lucy had also been at the cafe.

He had spotted her through the restaurant's window, watching them from across the road. She had been watching them, just as Summer was talking about her. It was as if Lucy had known Summer was asking questions about where she was. But why him, and what did she want? He kicked himself for going back to Summer's the previous night. What if Lucy had followed them there and he had put Summer in danger? No, wait, didn't Summer say Lucy had been in her bedroom before the supermarket, was Lucy following Summer? Confusion impaired his mind as he struggled to think straight.

He jumped up off the couch and raced to the window, which showed a view of the busy front street below. His flat was right off the centre of town, and he could see Derby Cathedral looming close by. He scanned the street, but Lucy wasn't anywhere to be seen. So where was she if she hadn't followed him home? A jolt of panic ran through him as he realised she may still be watching Summer. *Shit.* He had to warn Summer. But he couldn't tell her the truth. She would call the police. Maybe he didn't have to say it was Lucy. A crazy ex might do. She probably wouldn't believe him, but at least she would know to be more wary. He was especially concerned about Joshua after what Lucy had done to her own child.

He took his phone out of his pocket, having to stretch his leg to do so because of the tightness of his jeans, and searched for Summer's number. He thanked God he'd saved it last night as he typed out the text.

Summer

I struggled to concentrate as I waited for another driver to allow me to turn right into Richard's street. It might have been the alcohol from last night or Aaron's response to my questions about Lucy's whereabouts. I had no idea why he would have reacted in that way, and I didn't have time to think about it. I needed to concentrate on Joshua, but the questions refused to leave my mind.

A friendly driver finally allowed me to turn, and I pulled right up on the kerb outside Richard's semi-detached house. I took over most of the pavement, trying to ensure other cars could get by on the tight side street, then I grabbed my phone to call Richard. We got on better than when we first split, but I still refused to enter his house. He answered his phone as though he was surprised at my call.

"Hey, I'm outside," I said in my usual neutral tone.

"Oh, okay." Again with the surprised tone despite pickup being the same time every weekend. I bristled with irritation, but shook it off. One thing I'd learnt was to pick my battles with Richard. He was a good dad, after all. Though he kept me waiting for another five minutes before the door finally opened. Joshua ran outside, and my heart soared. All was well with the world again. He could barely move in his padded red coat and skinny jeans. I hated skinny jeans on young kids. They were so uncomfortable. I'd rather he was in comfortable joggers, but Richard preferred he looked stylish. I rolled down my car window as he ran up to it.

"Hi, baby!" Simply looking at him made me much happier. "How are you? You okay?"

He nodded and planted a wet kiss on my forehead before pulling open the rear door to jump into his booster seat. Richard followed him out. He wore his slippers and his dressing gown as a coat, which made him look much bigger than his actual slight frame. He was tall but skinny with it. His thick black hair was abundant with gel.

"Tell Mummy what you ate," Richard encouraged Joshua.

"I ate pasta!" Joshua shouted in triumph.

"Wow! Well done!" I exclaimed, my enthusiasm a tad over the top. "With what sauce?"

"Urgh! No sauce!" He stuck his tongue out and looked at me like I was mad for suggesting pasta should be eaten with sauce. "I had cheese with it." He gave me a big grin. He was so proud, but I fought the urge to roll my eyes.

"Oh, right. Okay, well done, baby." I flashed him another smile.

Richard attempted to help him with his seatbelt, but Joshua batted him away impatiently, insisting he could do it himself because he was six. Six going on sixteen. He said goodbye and gave Joshua a tight hug before closing the rear door.

"Bye, Daddy." We waved to Richard as we drove away.

Joshua chattered about his day for the whole twenty-minute drive home and repeatedly told me he loved me. The immense comfort I felt at being with him again was unbelievable. I hated being away from him. I hated sharing every weekend and only getting two full days with him a month, thanks to work. I hated not having every one of his birthdays with him and sharing Christmas. I hated seeing our ex-babysitter in his second home, pregnant with his younger sister. It should have been me with a swelling stomach, not her.

When we reached home I allowed Joshua to choose a film to watch. We settled down for a cuddle and to watch Lego Batman for the 127th time. I decided to enjoy the rest of my day with him. I could think about Aaron and Lucy later. Joshua and I didn't get much time together, so I always made the most of it. As soon as we got comfortable, I noticed a new text message notification on my phone from Aaron.

Aaron: *Sorry, I had to run off. I completely forgot I had a shift! Can we meet later? Need to tell you something. And no, I'm not married! Don't panic :)*

I threw the phone away from me and tried to concentrate on the film, even though I could likely have recited most of the scenes from memory. But I considered my options as Joshua lay next to me, his sweet head on my lap. He giggled every so often at the film and looked up at me to make sure I laughed too. I tried to figure out if I wanted to see Aaron. I wanted to know what he had to say, but felt as if I was digging into an open wound. How deep could I go before it became infected?

I hugged Joshua tighter. Maybe I could stay in this little bubble of Joshua and me. I didn't need to get involved further. I could believe Aaron and move on. That wouldn't give me closure, though.

We ate plain pizza after the film, followed by bath, book, and bed. He squished himself into me as we lay in his bed together.

"Don't go, Mummy," he said as he did every night. "Stay with me."

I stayed with him and wrapped my arms around him tightly. I didn't ever want to let go. The familiar scent of strawberry shampoo and natural sweetness calmed me completely. If I could have chosen a moment to get lost in forever, it would have been that one.

"Mummy, I have an important question." His serious blue eyes looked up at me.

"Go on then," I said.

"How many miles away is Africa? Because Daddy said that's where lions live, and I don't want to be eaten by a lion." He looked up at me solemnly as I tried not to laugh.

"It's thousands of miles away," I kissed his forehead. "Now go to sleep."

He settled back into my arms. Within minutes his breathing had slowed, quiet snores escaping now and then. I stayed with him, not wanting to let go, and knew right then that I had to learn more about Lucy. I couldn't get lost in the moment and forget. If I were hallucinating, I needed to know. I needed to make sure I wasn't turning into Eddie.

Summer

I sat at the same table where Aaron had walked out on me the previous day. I faced the window this time, wanting to see him coming. The hangover had stuck with me for a second day. Not as bad, but the greasy aroma of the cafe did not do me any favours. There were no builders. Two men sat on the opposite side of the cafe. They spoke in whispers, for which my delicate head was grateful. I felt out of sorts. Like I was not actually in the cafe, but was watching from somewhere else.

I'd dressed in tight jeans and a yellow top which showed off my cleavage a bit. I'd even worn some light makeup. A part of me wanted Aaron to think I looked good. But mainly, I wanted to feel confident and in control. The makeup was like a mask of confidence. I wanted to be prepared to demand the truth. Anxiety still sat like a heavy knot in my stomach at the thought of what Aaron had to say. It must be about what happened to Lucy. Or that there was no Lucy, and I needed professional help.

I had dropped Joshua off at my mum's house an hour before. Despite us not having a close relationship, she loved having him, and he loved being there. They adored each other. Mum was different these days, and she was great with him. She was a stereotypical grandma, or *Mamma*, as Joshua called her. He could do whatever he wanted when she was around and eat all the treats in her cupboard. Joshua got on better with her than I did, but then he didn't know what she was like after my dad died. He didn't know about the drinking. Nor would he, as long as she stayed off it. So there was no rush for me to get back to him, but I was not going to admit that to Aaron. Kids are a great excuse to get out of any situation, and one which I often used to its full advantage. After all, there had to be some perks to being a single mum.

I saw Aaron before he entered the cafe, as I'd hoped. His head was lowered, his shoulders pulled upwards to his ears, and his hands in the pockets of his black parka. I guessed he was attempting to keep the weak, but freezing, wind at bay. My heart surprised me with an involuntary flip that I immediately ignored. There was no way I was getting close to anyone after my last shit show of a *relationship* with Richard. The last couple of days didn't fill me with confidence in Aaron being a reliable and trustworthy partner either.

The bell above the front door jingled as he pushed it open and took one enormous step inside with his long legs. He closed the door behind him immediately. I liked that gesture. Most people would think nothing of closing the door quickly. But to me, it showed empathy for those around him. Of course, it may also be that he was cold. But then, my habit of overthinking human behaviour was likely another reason I enjoyed studying psychology so much.

Once over the threshold, he lifted his head and searched the cafe, his expression serious. It didn't take long for his eyes to land on me. As soon as they did, he smiled anxiously. I returned his smile with a confident one, hoping to make him feel more comfortable. I needed to ensure he didn't back out of whatever he wanted to tell me. I wanted the truth about Lucy, and then I could move on. I could be with Joshua and carry on, making sure he was happy and safe. He was my priority. Everything else was background noise.

We greeted each other as he took the chair opposite to me, sprawling his elbows and arms out on the table once seated. He almost reached for me, but wasn't brave enough. I didn't bother making this any easier for him.

"Are you okay?" I asked, still smiling but with a lift of my eyebrows.

A part of me didn't care. The same part of me that wanted to run away and forget all about Lucy. It's anxiety, I told myself. I felt like my and Joshua's lives were on pause until I found out the truth about Lucy.

"Yes." He sounded surprised, as though he had no reason not to be okay. I raised my eyebrows even further, and he stopped smiling. "Well… I wanted to talk to you about something."

I waited, but he didn't continue. His mouth was half-open, but the words wouldn't come out.

"Go on," I encouraged him.

He smiled again and cleared his throat, but still he said nothing.

"I assume it's about Lucy?" I tried again.

"You're obsessed!" he retorted, snorting with laughter.

I threw him an annoyed look, and his expression sobered. "No, it's not about Lucy. It is about a girl, though."

"Oh God, you have a girlfriend?" I asked probably too loudly, but the suspicion angered me. I knew all too well the damage cheating could cause.

"No! Jeez, shhhhhh!" He spat the words at me and looked around. The couple at the other table glanced over but went back to their conversation when Aaron caught them looking.

"It's my ex-girlfriend. I'm having issues with her."

"Oh." I relaxed and considered him for a moment. I was unsure why he was offloading this on to me. I didn't care. Well, not enough to meet in person to discuss that, anyway. I said nothing further, and glared at him until he continued.

"Erm…I'm not sure how to say this, but she has issues. She's a bit of a nutter, to be honest. I didn't meet her at work, mind you!" He laughed at his grim joke. My glare intensified. His use of the word *nutter* had not helped my irritation towards him. "Erm…I think she's following me."

At first, I still didn't see why he'd brought me here. Then it dawned on me.

"Oh shit, the other night? She saw you come to mine?" I asked.

"Well, I don't know." He looked apologetic.

I didn't feel sympathy for him. Why the hell had he come back to mine if he had a potentially dangerous stalker?

"I saw her earlier on in the night, but that was before I saw you. I'm pretty sure I had lost her by then."

"Jesus, Aaron, what do you mean by nutter? Dangerous? Violent? Still in love with you?" My voice was still way too loud, but I didn't care. Let the others look if they wanted.

"Well, she has attacked people before, but I don't think she knows about you. She did *not* follow me here today. I made sure."

His revelation took me by surprise. Of all the things I had imagined he might tell me, this was not one of them. I disliked being on the spot with no conversation prepared.

"Attacked who? Have you called the police?" I asked, not knowing what else to say.

"No, no. No need for that. She hasn't hurt anyone recently. Not since we split. She won't leave me alone. I'm sure she will give up soon. It's only been a couple of weeks."

I studied his face carefully. He looked agitated, troubled. That didn't mean he was lying, I supposed. I would probably look the same if I had a *nutter* for a stalker. But something felt off to me. Maybe this was his way of making sure I didn't want to see him anymore, but then that seemed extreme. Why not ghost me if that was what he wanted?

"If she doesn't know about me, then I'm not sure why you're telling me this," I said. I kept watching his expression for evidence of lying.

"Well, it was just in case, really. In case I'm wrong, and she *did* see us. I wanted you to be aware, I guess, what with having Joshua and all."

I stewed over his words for a moment. The nagging feeling that had bothered me since Friday intensified. One of my greatest fears was someone breaking into my home and me being unable to defend Joshua. And now there's a chance it might happen, thanks to Aaron. I didn't want to go home, and I certainly did not want Joshua there right now. I made a mental note to call my mum once I was finished with Aaron. I needed an excuse for Joshua to stay at hers for a night or two until I could make sure we were safe. Maybe I could say I found a rat.

"You could have told me this on the phone." My usually calm voice had a clearly annoyed undertone that I struggled to hide.

"Well, I wanted to make sure she wasn't near you. Can I come back to yours? I can make sure you're safe. As I said, it's just in case. I don't think she knows, and she definitely did not follow me here. I'd swear on my own life. Can I please hang around with you, to make sure she isn't about? I don't want anything to happen to you."

"Maybe you should have thought about that before." I couldn't help but retort.

I tried to think about whether I wanted Aaron with me. I didn't. But I supposed I'd be safer with him around if someone were to follow or attack me. I had been in a fight-or-flight situation before, and I'd done neither. I froze. My legs turned to jelly and wouldn't work. Like in the dream with Lucy, I couldn't move, never mind run or fight back. If it were Joshua in danger, I knew I would fight like hell. I had no doubt I would kill for him in an instant. But if it was me in trouble, well, I already knew I was useless. If Aaron's ex wanted him, it was surely safer not to be around him.

"Please, Summer." His eyes stared deep into mine.

"Look, I get you want to make sure I'm okay. But I'll be fine. I think you need to stay away."

"Well, can I at least call you later?" He looked like a kicked puppy.

"Okay." I agreed. "I need to get Joshua, anyway."

"Okay, I'll walk you out."

We left the cafe together. I tried not to look at the men who had clearly heard snippets of our conversation. Aaron followed behind me, wary of my prickly vibe. He was good at reading people, too.

The cold air nipped at my bare face as the cafe door closed behind us. The glare of sunlight bouncing off the roofs of nearby cars momentarily blinded me, but didn't do much to warm the air. I stood still for a moment and took in the fresh air. My nauseous stomach was much happier away from the greasy stench of the cafe. A strange feeling washed over me, though. I shifted uncomfortably, feeling as if someone was watching me. I glanced at Aaron, but he was looking at the ground again, still standing behind me. It was nothing. I was feeling paranoid after Aaron's revelation about his ex.

    I chanced a scan across the road, and fear hit me in the stomach like a freight train. A dark figure stared at me from across the road, a figure with bright green eyes.

Summer

I turned to Aaron. I couldn't speak, but he felt my stare and looked up. My horror must have been obvious, judging from the worry on his face. No words came to me. I looked back towards Lucy, but she was gone. The street was empty. Some parked cars and a lamppost lined the street, but Lucy was nowhere to be seen. *Had she run away? Was she hiding somewhere?*

Aaron followed my gaze and looked across the road. I turned again to look at him, not sure what to say or do. His skin turned pale. He gulped. He knew what I had seen. It was written all over his face.

"Lucy was there!" I finally gasped, pointing over to where I had seen her.

He didn't look surprised, or like he thought I was crazy. He looked scared. I didn't know what he was about to say, but I could tell he believed me.

"Lucy?" He gathered himself back together and attempted another snort of laughter. He relented when he saw my serious face staring at him.

"Come on, let's get you home." He said with more sincerity.

"No, Aaron, she was there!" I had lost my calm exterior yet again.

"Okay," he said simply, taking my hand. It shivered, and he held it tighter.

I allowed him to lead me home. I kept checking behind us, across the road, down side streets, looking for Lucy, but she was nowhere. I still couldn't think straight when we reached my building a few minutes later.

My mind was a fog of swirling thoughts as I tried to unlock the main door. Aaron took my keys from me and led me upstairs. We hadn't spoken a word to each other the entire way home. He led me inside the flat and straight to my couch.

"Let me make you some tea," he said.

I said nothing, and he disappeared into the kitchen. I could hear cupboard doors open and close again and again as he tried to find his way around. I didn't actually drink tea, but I did have tea bags hidden somewhere for the rare occasion we had a guest. It occurred to me I should help him, but I didn't move.

I took the steaming mug from him upon his return. The warmth of the cup felt good against my chilled fingers, if nothing else. Aaron sat beside me and put his hand on my leg. I didn't push it away.

"Did you see her?" I asked him.

He shook his head. "Babe...what exactly did you see?" he asked.

"It was her!" I pulled my leg away from his hand and scowled at him.

"Did you see her face?" he asked.

He appeared genuinely curious as to what I had seen rather than disbelieving. At least he didn't accuse me of seeing things. Which, to me, was more evidence that he knew Lucy was real. I thought about how to answer his question.

"Well, yes...I think so." I frowned and thought about it some more. I knew I'd seen a female figure with dark hair, a large coat, and dark trousers. But no. I hadn't seen her face clearly. Not at all, honestly.

But I knew it was her. Like when you see a friend in a random place and you *know* it's them without seeing their face. Except Lucy wasn't a friend.

"I'm not sure," I admitted. Tiredness overtook me and I hid my head in my hands.

He placed his large hand back on my leg and squeezed. I put my hand on his and looked into his eyes, searching for signs of dishonesty as he spoke.

"I believe you." He looked so sincere I wondered if he was about to admit to something. "I believe you think you saw Lucy, but I also believe I freaked you out with all my bullshit about my ex. Think about it. I tell you some girl might be following me, then we walk outside and you see a girl looking at us? Obviously, you still have Lucy on your mind, so you're going to assume it is her, but babe, *think*. Have you seen Lucy at any other time, other than that horrible dream?"

I shook my head. I supposed he was right. I hadn't seen Lucy at all since my nightmare. The timing was suspect too. Maybe I was jumpy, and my mind was seeing things. Or maybe it was some random person.

"And if she was there, if it was Lucy, why would she be following you? And where did she go?" He pressed further.

I shrugged my shoulders. I had no answers, still only questions, but Aaron knew about Lucy. If she was following me, then Joshua and I weren't safe. I knew what I had to do.

"I'm going to ask my mum to keep Joshua for the night," I told Aaron. I looked up at him. "Will you stay with me tonight?"

"Of course," he nodded, "whatever you need. Go to your mum's and see Joshua. I'll go to the shop for some drinks and come back here when you're ready." He winked at me, and I managed a smile. "Then you and I are going to chill out and watch a movie together."

I ached for Joshua to come home, not Aaron. But I had to make sure we were safe. I had to get the truth out of Aaron.

Summer

I allowed Aaron to guide me outside to my car, and dropped him off at the supermarket on the way to my mum's. She lived twenty minutes away in the old mining town of Ilkeston, near Richard. I arrived at her two-bed semi feeling better, though still not myself. I pulled up on the street outside, ignoring her empty driveway. I liked to have a quick escape from the awkwardness of our stilted relationship. I checked the mirror, my pale face looking back at me despite the smattering of makeup I'd applied earlier that day. I tried to neaten my windswept hair by running my fingers through it but gave up and closed the mirror.

I pulled my coat tighter and made my way up the tarmac driveway. I knocked on Mum's door and waited for her to open it as a stranger would. We were close too when I was Joshua's age, but it all went wrong after my dad's death. At ten years old, I'd been devastated and in desperate need of her guidance. Mum was devastated and turned to alcohol for her guidance. It terrified me that Joshua and I might someday grow apart. I couldn't imagine it. I would do anything in my power to ensure we didn't end up little more than strangers. It didn't take long for Mum to come to the door. She smiled but held her head down rather than look me in the eye. I gave her a tight smile back. I could hear Joshua's shouts the second I entered the tiny grey entrance hall.

"Mummy!" he yelled. I dodged Mum's tired-looking shoe cabinet and coat stand, entering the living room through the open door.

I don't think I'd ever squeezed Joshua so hard. He moaned at me for hurting his sides, but I wanted so badly never to let go and bring him home with me. He fit so perfectly in my arms, he always had done no matter how much he grew. I reminded myself repeatedly that I was leaving him there for a good reason.

"Are you okay, Mummy?" He looked at me quizzically. He knew me better than anyone, despite his young age, and could always tell when something was wrong. No matter how hard I tried to hide it. He worried about me far too much. It was as if he thought he needed to take care of me rather than the other way around.

"Yes! Just sad that you can't come home, baby." I kissed him again. He seemed to believe me and gave me another tight squeeze.

"It makes me sad too." His bottom lip stuck out as he looked up at me with big eyes.

My stomach flip-flopped as guilt tore at me. I should never have gotten involved with Lucy's disappearance. I should have believed Aaron and moved on with my life.

We played games for a bit on his tablet before I put Joshua to bed in my mum's spare room. I bought him a new audiobook on my phone, and we listened to it for a while. We giggled together at the silly story of a naughty boy who liked to cheat. I lay with him until I heard quiet snores. I stayed a little longer in case he woke, and then snuck out. Downstairs my mum was sitting on her red recliner watching the news, her glasses perched on the end of her nose. The decade of alcohol abuse was visible in her aged skin and lack of teeth. She had lost a lot of weight since she stopped drinking and looked far more fragile. Another pang of guilt grabbed at me. She had been through more than most people.

"Hi, Mum." My words were always stilted around her. I wished they weren't, but I couldn't help it. There were too many unspoken words between us.

She smiled up at me. "Is he asleep?" she asked. Wisps of her shoulder-length grey hair fell around her hollow cheeks. I nodded. "I would have been happy to lie with him, you know. He's such a Mummy's boy."

I tried not to let my irritation show. What does it matter if he's a Mummy's boy?

"Well, yeah, we're close," I stated simply. "I'm going to go to the shop to see if I can get anything to sort out the rat."

"You'll need a proper store, not the supermarket. Why don't you stay here too? For one night."

If someone had told me last week that I would consider sleeping at my mum's house, I would've laughed in their face. But as I looked at the fragile old lady, watching the telly alone, I felt a need to sit with her. I realised I felt safer here than in my flat. I considered my options. If I was to stay here, then we'd both be safe. For tonight at least. It would be short term, though. To make sure we were safe forever, I needed to speak to Aaron. I needed to find out what he wasn't telling me.

So instead, I said a rushed goodbye to my mum. We were closer than we used to be, thanks to Joshua. But I still didn't hug and kiss her or tell her I loved her. We weren't there yet, so instead, I threw a graceless wave her way before I walked away.

Back in the car, I felt stronger now that I had some semblance of a plan and finally felt a sense of calm. Seeing Joshua's sad face had given me new strength, and no matter what was happening with Lucy, I needed to stop it. I needed to make sure Joshua was safe. I needed to find her before she found me again.

For You…

I had a good view of them both through the window. Though I had to be careful that she didn't spot me. It didn't matter if Aaron saw me, he wouldn't tell. But it wasn't time for her to see me yet. She had her tits on show for him, which didn't surprise me. She even wore makeup. Not that it made her look any better, she may as well not have bothered. She won't be able to wear it when I'm done with her, anyway.

I was pleased to see that she didn't look too happy. Her brow furrowed as she looked at him, but I couldn't tell from this distance if it was anger or disappointment. I wondered what they were discussing to make her feel that way. It better not be me. *No.* I laughed the thought away. Aaron wouldn't be that stupid.

I was still reeling from my earlier discovery. Summer had a child, a young boy. He was the image of her with the same brown hair and light eyes. He had darker skin, though. Despite looking like her, the boy was beautiful. I had heard her shout his name when he ran too far ahead to the car. *Joshua.* I knew the second I saw him that I was going to have him. He would be mine, and I would love him and cherish him far more than *her*. I'd share him with no one, and she would have no one. Loneliness could be her punishment. It was far better than simply making her ugly. She'd made me lonely, she'd taken my home, so I would make her lonely and take her home. I would take her boy.

I would still make her ugly as well, though. I needed to have some fun. Plus, that way, she wouldn't be able to look after anyone when I was done with her. She would be ugly, and everyone would stare, but not because they wanted her. No one would want her. Joshua wouldn't want her. Aaron wouldn't want her.

She would be completely alone. They won't even notice when she doesn't return home. No one would want her.

Summer

I picked Aaron up from his flat on my way back and apologised for taking so long. He didn't seem to mind. He was much perkier than when I had left him in the supermarket, and I was feeling much better myself, thanks to my plan. He had two bottles of white wine in his bag, along with some vodka and a bottle of lemonade. I was certainly not planning on drinking that much, but I wondered how much alcohol it would take to get him to open up about Lucy. I was feeling confident I was going to get the truth. When we arrived back at my flat, I poured each of us a large glass of wine.

"How about we watch a film?" Aaron asked.

I agreed. I'd get him talking eventually, and a film was the perfect opportunity for him to get some alcohol down. I let him choose the movie, and he picked a comedy with Eddie Murphy. I took small sips of my wine and went to the toilet shortly after to pour the rest of the glass down the sink.

"I'm going for a top-up," I told Aaron. "Do you want one?"

"Sure," Aaron replied. I felt guilty as he smiled at me, but then I thought of Joshua, and the feeling dissipated.

By the time the film finished, both bottles of wine were gone. Aaron was smiley and chatty. His hand had made its way to my leg, and he was feeling braver. I moved closer to him, and he turned to face me. I smiled at him, inviting him to come closer. He moved forward, and his rough stubble gently grazed my face as we kissed. His touch was light at first but quickly deepened as our hunger for each other grew.

I felt his fingers graze my hip as he slowly manoeuvred his hand beneath my top. His cold fingertips tickled my stomach as he reached for my breasts.

I pulled my mouth away. "Wait. We need to talk, Aaron."

He carried on kissing my neck, his stubble digging into my skin. I couldn't help the moan that escaped my lips as he moved his hand back down over my stomach. I had to be cautious not to scare him off. I needed him to know he could open up to me and tell me the truth. But as his hand slipped into my trousers, I didn't want him to stop. He inserted a finger deep inside me, and my moans became louder.

Lucy's face flashed in mind, invading the space between us. I pushed him up so I could wiggle away.

"Aaron, I know you're not telling me something," I blurted out. *Shit*.

He sat back with a disappointed look on his face. "I thought you were enjoying it," he said.

"I was." I smiled at him, and he leaned towards me.

"Then let me carry on," he said with a smirk.

"I want to know about Lucy first. I need to get her out of my head. I can't relax."

He sighed and sat back. "Okay, but you're going to think I'm crazy," he replied.

A tremendous sense of relief washed over me. He was finally going to tell me the truth.

I laughed. "I won't!" I said. "I need to know that I'm not crazy."

"Okay, look, there *was* a Lucy Clarke who stayed on Bluebell Ward, but… she doesn't stay there anymore." Aaron looked pointedly at me.

"Okay. So she's moved on? Why lie about it?" I asked.

"No, I haven't told you everything yet." He sighed and looked down at his knees.

"Aaron, tell me, please."

"She died, Summer."

I heard his words, but I didn't understand. "I spoke to her a couple of hours before I spoke to you and asked if she was poorly. I'm pretty sure I would have noticed if a patient died whilst I was on the ward! And again, why would you lie about it?"

He was quiet for a moment before finally replying. "No, I mean, she died a long time ago. Before I was even working on the ward, it must have been about ten years ago."

Shock vibrated through me like an electrical current. Of all the things I thought Aaron might tell me, Lucy being a ghost, was not one of them.

"So I've been seeing a ghost?" I laughed quietly at first, but within a few seconds, I was verging hysterical. I couldn't help it. I thought about her cold lank fingers on my arm and the way she had drifted towards me whilst I lay in bed. My laughter stopped, and Aaron stared at me, full of concern.

"I don't know what you've seen," he said and shrugged his shoulders.

"It can't have been a ghost! She talked to me in front of others. She must have!"

"I don't know what to say." He looked at me, more dismal than I'd ever seen him.

I examined what he'd told me. *Lucy* and *Clarke* are both common names. It's possible another Lucy Clarke had been on the ward years ago.

"What happened to the Lucy Clarke you're talking about?" I asked him.

"Well, apparently she had paranoid schizophrenia, and she was in on a section 37/41. She had voices in her head, they told her to be violent."

"A section 37/41? What crime did she commit then?" I asked. Patients convicted of a crime could be detained under Section 37 by criminal courts. The additional Section 41 was included if the Crown Court thought the patient was a serious risk to the public.

"Something about stalking that got out of hand." He shrugged his shoulders, and looked away again. There was a wistful look in his eyes. He probably wanted to be anywhere else but with me. "I know some patients talk about her, so I asked Emma, and that's what she said. The patients think they see her too. I've thought I've seen her once or twice, Summer." He looked back at me. "Once on the ward, and outside once, too. Hence why I freak out whenever you think you see her."

"Well, what happened to her in the end? Did she leave the ward?" I asked.

"She died in a fire."

My stomach flipped upside down and I closed my eyes, trying to steady myself. I knew there had been a fire at Bluebell Ward because of a plaque that was stuck to the wall in the corridor. It listed the names of patients who had died in that fire. Was the name Lucy Clarke on it? I couldn't remember, but I'd never read the names in any great detail. I opened my eyes.

"I think you should go. It's late," I told Aaron.

"Really?" He looked disappointed. "I was hoping I could stay and make you feel safe."

"I'm fine. I do feel safe," I lied. I'd feel safer without him.

"Okay, if you're sure." He placed his empty glass down on the coffee table and stood up to leave. "Bye." He stood awkwardly with his hands in his pockets.

"Bye." I got up to walk him out. I smiled at him but stayed a few steps back. I didn't want him to touch me, and I wanted to make that clear.

He looked solemn as he left, but as harsh as it sounded, I didn't care. He'd lied to me again. I needed a new plan.

Summer

I sat in my living room after Aaron had left. His story made no sense to me. I refused to believe I was speaking to a ghost the whole time on the ward. I would have known. Other people would have seen her, or I would have looked like I was talking to myself.

Lucy had touched me. She'd grabbed my arm on more than one occasion, brushed her fingers through my hair. I shivered remembering how cold her hands were. I didn't understand why Aaron had fed me such a ridiculous story. There was fear in his voice as he spoke about her that made me wonder if he believed it. Maybe someone had told him. He'd said Emma had said it, but she didn't strike me as the kind to believe in patient ghost stories.

I wasn't even sure if *I* believed in ghosts. My nana had a ghost in her bungalow, according to my mum. I couldn't remember my nana as she died when I was six. She and Mum were not close. But when I was small, Mum would tell me tales of a ghost who watched her and her three siblings in the bedroom. Things would move on their own, and in the dead of night, they could hear heavy breathing. I'd thought she was making it up. I'd never seen a ghost before or heard of any concrete evidence.

I thought of my older brother Eddie, and tried to remember the last time I saw him. It was a few months after Dad died. He was twenty then. It was eighteen years ago, yet I remembered the violence as though it were yesterday. How he had threatened Mum as I hid. How Marinda had tried to stop him. His hallucinations were no longer auditory. The devil was following him everywhere he went, and he had to do what the devil said.

I am not my brother. I am not my brother. I am not ill.

My laptop sat on the dining table, so I meandered over to review my diary entries once again. I tried to remember every time Lucy and I had spoken as the old laptop kicked into gear. I couldn't remember seeing her speak to any other patients. That wasn't unusual for the people living on the wards I visited, because they mainly consisted of severe personality disorder patients. It was a wide spectrum of possible illnesses. It was common for people to keep to themselves, and I didn't blame them. People who suffer from poor mental health are more likely to be victims than perpetrators of a violent attack. But every ward I visited had some particularly violent patients living there. It was a high-stress environment, and the patients were already burdened by mental health. These were not people I would want to live with whilst trying to work through my own problems. I often wondered how forcing ill people together helped them to overcome their issues. I could guarantee that being forced to live in such a place would drive me completely over the edge.

But there must have been at least one time Lucy spoke to someone else. I remembered her threatening aura, the stench of cigarettes, and the shiny grease that coated her hair. She was solid. I shook my head. Ghosts weren't like that. *Were they?* Then there's Aaron, but I clearly wasn't getting the truth out of him. Whatever the truth might be, he was hiding it from me. I opened up the files on my laptop and started scrolling through notes again. One, in particular, jumped out at me, and I realised what I'd been missing. *How could I have forgotten?*

I'd had my evidence that Aaron knew Lucy all along. I grabbed my phone and brought up Aaron's number. He answered on the second ring.

"Hey, Summer. Good timing. I just reached my flat. Are you okay?"

"No, Aaron, I'm not okay. You're lying to me, and I know it now." I listened for his reaction. My words were met with silence, so I continued. "Lucy fell out with me a few weeks ago. She went mad and thought I'd been telling lies to the staff about her. She thought I was responsible for her ward round being cancelled. You and Emma had to restrain her." I left my revelation hanging in the air. I could hear him breathing, but nothing else.

"I don't remember," Aaron replied. His voice was hesitant.

"You're lying to me." I couldn't be bothered to argue with him. "And I'm going to find out why."

Aaron

Aaron's phone made a thud as it fell from his hand. His legs gave way, and he dropped to the floor with his head in his hands. He felt panic rise as he tried to figure out what to do next. Giving up was what he *wanted* to do. Maybe he should tell the truth. His crazy ex-girlfriend lie hadn't worked, but he had hoped the story about Lucy's death would scare Summer off. Clearly not. He needed to get her off the scent somehow before she got hurt. But now she didn't trust him, and he was running out of options.

He lowered his hands and raised his head. Hot tears ran down his cheeks, wet circles appearing on his jeans as his tears dropped. He needed help, but he couldn't go to the police. There was one person he knew that might be able to help him, but calling them would be dangerous. He wasn't even sure if he had kept their phone number.

Aaron ignored the ache in his legs as he pushed himself up off the ground. He stalked over to the open kitchen and frantically searched the drawers, looking for the tiny scrap of paper that had recently been pushed through his letterbox. But it was nowhere in sight. He moved into his bedroom and rummaged through the bedside cabinet. Again, he found nothing. He racked his brain, trying to remember where he had put the note as he walked back into the kitchen. His eyes fell on the bin. He remembered scrunching up the paper and throwing it away. He hadn't wanted it then. The risk was too great.

Now, it was the one thing that could help him, Summer, and Joshua. He had seen a picture of Joshua on Summer's bedside table. The boy had the same light brown hair, beautiful big blue eyes, and freckle-spattered nose as Summer. He had even fantasised about meeting Joshua despite Summer and him only recently sleeping together for the first time. Aaron couldn't believe his luck when she'd walked onto the ward a few months ago. She was way out of his league, though. He'd always been too shy to say anything to her. But now he could have his own ready-made family and maybe even add another child. His mother would love Summer. She had far more class than any other girl he had brought home.

Holding his breath, he opened the bin and carefully took out the top layer of rubbish and threw it on the floor beside him. Eventually, he saw the note beneath a piece of tin foil. It was stained orange with what looked like bean juice. He gingerly took it out and wiped it down with a kitchen towel. He could have kissed it if it weren't covered in God knows how many germs. The note in front of him had a name and a phone number written in a sprawling, child-like handwriting. The name was Lucy.

Summer

I'd spent the entire night on the sofa, drifting in and out of sleep. Lucy visited my dreams, but it wasn't as realistic as the previous nightmare. It was Monday and I was due back on Bluebell Ward that morning. I forced myself to get off the sofa and take a shower. My hair was getting so long that it was a pain to blow dry, but I took the time to wash and dry it, anyway. It desperately needed a good trim, but I hated going to the hairdressers. All the physical contact and small talk meant I'd sit in the chair, itching to leave.

I threw on some black suit trousers and a pretty cream blouse. I chose a black cardigan which was smart but not lawyer-like. It was important to be smart but approachable. I couldn't look intimidating like a lawyer.

A part of me didn't want to go back to Bluebell Ward. I wasn't sure why, as Lucy obviously wasn't there. But I knew I needed to get her file. Aaron had told me during the previous night's film that he was not on shift today. I hadn't heard from him since I hung up the phone. I'd meant every word about finding the truth, and knew what I had to do. I rang Joshua before I left. We spoke for a few minutes, and I told him to be good for his mamma and get ready for school. I felt calmer after our chat, but my head began to pound when I started driving. A heavy cloud of dread surrounded me as I pulled into the hospital car park, making my headache feel even worse.

I forced a few deep breaths in through the nose and out through the mouth before pushing myself out of the deep front seat of the BMW. Despite my forced breathing, the cloud of dread grew heavier as I walked through the doors of the reception area. I needed to sign in with the receptionist and get my ward keys.

Though they made me feel like a jailer from an old prison movie walking around with twenty-odd keys swinging off his pockets. Once I had them and had placed my coat, handbag, and laptop into the reception room locker, I entered the first of many corridors to get to Bluebell Ward.

Every secure hospital I visited was a maze of locked corridors. It took time to learn the correct way around the building with each one. Staff left me to it. They were worried that if they helped me, they might say something that would get them in trouble with the advocate. Not wanting to appear panicked, and be mistaken for one of the ward's patients, I tried my quiet, deep breathing all the way, but it didn't help. The anxiety wouldn't leave me. I kept expecting Lucy to jump out of a wall or something equally ridiculous. I walked through the winding, tiled corridors, unlocking what felt like a million doors as I went. By the time I'd reached the Bluebell ward entrance, my apprehension was suffocating me.

I stopped still, unable to raise the keys. Instead, I stood in front of the doors, looking through the glass panel to the corridor on the other side. The same corridor where I last saw Lucy. *I didn't have to go in there. I could quit my job, move house, move Joshua's school...*

I realised that was ridiculous. I didn't have the savings needed to move house. Although, if I did, I'm pretty sure I would have chosen the simple way out to protect us. Again, I half expected to see Lucy as my eyes searched the corridor through the panel, but Louise stood there alone, leaning back with one foot against the wall, her head down. She must have been able to feel my gaze because she raised her head and looked straight at me. Her eyes widened. She didn't smile, but she was clearly eager to see me. *Shit.* I had to go in.

With my rising anxiety attempting to suffocate me, I forced my hand to open the door. I had to be quick and alert around patients for fear they would try to escape. None had ever managed it in this manner to my knowledge, at least not recently, but it was drilled into all staff to know that it could happen.

I wasn't moving fast. My legs felt like jelly and were difficult to move. I looked at Louise as I entered and forced a smile before slowly turning my back on her to lock the door. Another thing I shouldn't do ideally, but Louise wasn't much of a risk to me. Like most patients, she was more of a risk to herself than anyone else.

"Can we talk?" Louise asked without saying hello. She clearly had no time for manners, but that was okay. The women on this ward usually had far bigger things to worry about than good manners. Plus, it took much more than that to offend me. Like multiple lies from someone I'd slept with.

"Sure, see you in the room in two minutes?" I asked. I needed to let the ward staff know I was there and would be alone with Louise in the room.

The room I referred to was a private space on the ward where patients or staff could have meetings without leaving the secure area. This was only allowed with certain patients who did not have a history of violence towards staff, like Louise. It was a room I was familiar with, a claustrophobic space with no window. All four walls were whitewashed, turning grey with age. A round wooden table sat in the corner with some chairs gathered around, and a white bench lined the far wall. It wasn't an easy room to be in if you were already struggling to breathe.

I walked over to the nurses' station and let them know I was on the ward and going to the private room with Louise. They were friendly enough and confirmed it was safe to go into the room alone with Louise. They warned me about a couple of patients who had shown aggression already and let me on my way. I looked around the ward. It was quiet that morning. A lot of patients were on medications that made them docile, so it was not unusual for them to sleep in. It was barely 10 AM after all, and they had nowhere to be. There were two patients in the communal living area, and both were draped over the sofas with their eyes closed. The TV quietly showed an episode of some daytime talk show. The smell of porridge hung thick in the air.

I entered the meeting room, still a bit unstable on my legs but moving easier than before. Being on the ward was not as bad as I'd thought, everything seemed so *normal*. Louise was waiting for me. She seemed okay, if maybe nervous. She jumped right in, speaking about her ward round meeting. She was going to be first today. The meeting was at 10:30, and she wanted section 17 leave. I didn't blame her. The hospital gave all patients the same deal when they first arrived. They could not leave the ward until their behaviour and mood had been assessed by staff. Eventually, with good behaviour, the patient would be allowed to go out by themselves. If anything untoward happened, or they did not return by a certain time, one hour a week at first, then two hours, then three, etc., their privilege would be revoked, and they would have to go back to the beginning to build it up again.

Louise was allowed out with a staff member for two hours every alternate day. She wanted her leave to be alone now and needed me to attend the ward round in case she got too nervous to ask. I forced my own feelings aside and agreed to help. We moved back into the communal area and talked until one of the support workers smiled at Louise and shouted her name. The support staff could get super friendly with the patients, although they had to be careful not to let their guard down. I'd seen violent attacks happen to staff and had been threatened myself on a couple of occasions. Most recently was the Lucy incident. The one that Aaron *did not remember*.

I walked next to Louise as we left the ward with the support worker. We made our way down one of the winding corridors, through three air-locked doors, and into a conference room. It was a stark contrast from the patients' tiny meeting room on the ward. It was sunny and cheerful, with a large, oval table taking up the middle of the room. A crisp breeze came in through the open window, making the room cool.

There were already a few people sitting around the table, all looking at Louise, smiling, and saying hello. Some smiled at me, too. Some ignored me, unsure how to act around me. These people made up the multidisciplinary team, or the MDT, at the hospital. The team consisted of the lead nurse from the ward, Emma Fahy, the consultant psychologist, the art therapist, social worker, occupational therapist, and key support worker. It was no wonder patients felt intimidated in such meetings with all of these authorities around them. I knew I would be daunted if they were discussing me, and that was without being mentally fragile.

I took a seat next to Louise and looked around at the people in front of me. A moment of clarity ran through me as if someone had turned on a light in my fog-addled brain. I realised who could help me.

Everyone sitting here should know about Lucy. *But who would tell me?* I had to be careful. I was there to support patients, but the hospital was my employer's customer. The hospital paid for our advocacy service. Therefore, although most staff didn't realise it and patients certainly did not know, I could not annoy or upset the staff. If they complained about me, my employer could replace me, or the hospital might cancel their contract. It was a dynamic I'd always hated. Not all advocacy services worked this way, but the private ones did.

As Louise and I took our seats, the lead psychiatrist, Dr Rears, entered the room. His colossal frame took up most of the doorway, despite being stooped from age. I wondered if he was past retirement age. He must have been at least pushing it. The quicker he retired, the better. He smiled at us all from under his fluffy white moustache. Dr Rears would tell you he does not drink alcohol, but his skin suggested otherwise. Like my mum's skin.

I had disliked Dr Rears since our first encounter, when he was training all staff on how to *deal* with the patients. There had been lots of *us* and *them* mentioned. I had secretly diagnosed him with Narcissistic Personality Disorder. I had voiced my concerns to Natalie once, but she dismissed them as usual.

His sly eyes lingered on Emma as he took his seat next to Louise. She didn't seem to notice. Her head was pointed down as she read the patient file in front of her. Her blonde hair fell in front of her face. Such behaviour was typical of Dr Rears and made my stomach churn, but my detest came from somewhere deeper. Ever the professional, I smiled and greeted Dr Rears as usual. He did not appear pleased to see me. The psychiatrists never were. Advocates got in their way. I imagined having an advocate in the ward round was like the dynamic of having a new boss watch you while you work. It would be dangerous to do anything too stupid in front of me.

The meeting began with Dr Rears asking Louise how she was, what she had been up to. Had she been feeling positive and sleeping well? Louise responded optimistically, trying hard to remain calm and give off a confident aura. Dr Rears then spoke to each staff member in turn, asking for an update whilst Louise looked on. I could never imagine how difficult it must be to have these professionals in charge of your life. Everything being scrutinised under their watch and right in front of you. Luckily for Louise, all were positive for the day. Dr Rears asked her if she had anything further to say, and she looked at me. Her large brown eyes were full of anxiety and fear of rejection. I heeded her sign.

"Louise feels she has been making significant progress, and she would like to request unsupervised leave, please." I smiled at Louise and turned my attention back to Dr Rears, who answered Louise directly, as he should.

After considering the feedback, he confirmed that she could have two hours a week unsupervised. If it went well, she could look to increase it in thirty days. Louise beamed from ear to ear, clearly delighted.

Once the meeting was finished, I asked Dr Rears if I could have a word with him. He confirmed he would find me once ward rounds were completed for the day. I thanked him and left the room with Louise. She skipped back to the ward. I was smiling too, but my happiness was more to do with being one step closer to finding Lucy.

Dr Rears might disgust me, but he must have been Lucy's psychiatrist and, therefore, her responsible clinician. He must have known where she was. He couldn't lie about that.

Summer

Dr Rears did not come and find me after the final ward round had finished. So an hour after the last meeting, I went looking for him. I checked all the wards, the smoking area, and his office but eventually found him in the staff room drinking a cup of tea. He looked up as I entered, and his eyes widened when he saw me standing at the doorway.

"Oh, hi!" he exclaimed, throwing his hands up in an exaggerated expression of relief and standing up. "I'm glad you found me!"

He spoke as though he had been looking for me rather than hiding from me.

"Hi." I smiled and stepped closer to him despite my mind screaming at me to stay away from him. "You got a sec now?"

"Sure." He beamed from ear to ear and walked around to my side of the table so we were face to face. I resisted an urge to punch him in the mouth. "Which patient is it regarding, by the way?"

"It's a strange one. I'm looking for Lucy…" I trailed off to watch his expression. His face showed no reaction at first, but then his forehead wrinkled and his lips pursed.

"Lucy? Hm. I don't think she's one of mine? I don't have a Lucy. Which ward is she on?" He was a good liar. It clearly came easy to him.

"Bluebell. Lucy Clarke. In her twenties, lots of scar tissue on her face from burns. Section 37/41," I replied.

"Nope, I don't know of any Lucy Clarke, sorry." He shrugged his shoulders and stood up. "She must be in one of your other hospitals."

He left his tea on the table and dashed out of the kitchen before I could respond to his suggestion that I was confused. Him undermining my professionalism hadn't bothered me. It took much more than that to insult me. But he had intrigued me further. He was also lying. I had no desire to follow him out of the kitchen. Now both Dr Rears and Aaron were lying, I thought about who else I could turn to. I didn't want to speak to the patients for fear of scaring them. Most were paranoid enough without me making it worse.

I headed back to Bluebell ward and visited the nurses' station where the patient files were stored on the computer. Each patient had their own personal case file. It contained their background, childhood traumas, diagnoses, and notes of all of their care-related activity whilst in the hospital. The files fascinated me, though some were heartbreaking.

I didn't automatically read a patients' file, I only read them where necessary. I was legally allowed access to any file as long as the patient gave me permission, but the ward staff never double-checked with the patient. They never even asked *me* if I had permission.

But then I was a professional. Why would I lie? Plus, too many staff didn't care about such rules. They liked the *nice* patients, the daytime outings and the money. Even the staff who cared about the patients didn't fully understand my role. To be fair to them, I usually would never lie about something so serious. However, I needed to check for Lucy's file, and if there was no chance of being caught, there wasn't any real risk.

As I entered the ward again, the plaque on the wall caught my eye. I knew Aaron was lying about the fact he thought I'd been talking to a ghost, but I scanned my eyes over the plaque anyway, searching for Lucy's name. I was saddened to see that it was a long list. Each name had an age next to it. *Anna Bishop, aged 53. Rose McDonald, aged 42. Amber Vish, aged 19.* Annoyingly it was not in alphabetical order, and it wasn't until I reached the end of the list that I saw a name which made goosebumps rise over every inch of my skin. *Lucie Clarke, aged 25.*

Summer

I told myself it couldn't be her. Lucy Clarke was a common name. Plus, they'd spelled it differently. I was sure she spelled it *Lucy Clark* and not *Lucie Clarke*. And Lucie had been twenty-five. The Lucy I knew was older than me, at least in her forties. I racked my brain, trying to think where I'd seen her name written down other than how I imagined it to be spelled. Then I remembered the patient files. There must be answers in there if Lucy was real. Which she was. I knew she must be. I couldn't even consider the alternative. *I am not like my brother.*

I continued through the ward and let myself into the empty nurses' station. The staff were out on the ward by then. Most were watching TV with a few of the patients. My anxiety dissipated once I'd rationalised that it *must* be a different Lucy. I was invigorated with a newfound confidence. I didn't know what was going on, but I knew I was not crazy. Although I was acutely aware that anyone suffering from hallucinations would say the same.

I sat down at the desk and opened the password-protected folder on the computer. I scanned through the list of names. As with most patient documents, they were all saved under initials for security. Most of which I recognised. Not all patients wanted to use an advocate. Some had great family support or enough confidence of their own. Some did not trust us. A lot of patients with such debilitating mental health had traumatic experiences with authority figures that resulted in them not trusting anyone, so it was no surprise. It wasn't my job to help them with such issues. That was what therapy and medication were for.

I soon lost hope as I flicked through the initials. There was one file named *LC*, but on closer inspection of the documents inside, I found it was for Isabelle, as Aaron had mentioned to me previously. As I was about to give up and log off, an unusual file caught my eye. It was at the bottom of the list of files and entitled *ZZ_AG_Duplicate*. I double-clicked into the file and, at first glance, it appeared to be another dead end. AG stood for Alison Gile. I'd spoken to her once or twice but didn't know her well. All the files inside the folder were entitled *AG:Therapy1* or *AG:Ward_round_week37*. It seemed like a duplicate of the original AG file. But nobody else had a duplicate file, so why did AG? I opened the file entitled *AG_Background*.

What I saw made me feel a way I had never experienced before, as if my heart had risen and sank simultaneously. I was nauseous yet so completely triumphant that I wanted to grab the nearest person and scream *I fucking told you so* in their face. There it was in glorious colour, a picture of Lucy. I couldn't believe it at first, but I zoomed in on the tiny photo, and there was no mistaking her scarred features and shocking green eyes. I began to read.

LC, aged 29, was committed to Bluebell Ward following a transfer from Havensfield Hospital in South London. LC was in Havensfield for 2 years and has been in different institutions since the age of 19, following the death of her infant son. It is believed LC caused the death of her son by drowning him in the kitchen sink when she was 19.

A shiver chilled my bones. I knew Lucy had somehow hurt her child. She had mentioned causing her child pain in previous conversations. However, I did not realise she had *murdered* her own baby. My stomach turned as I ordered myself to keep reading.

LC was removed from the care of her parents at the age of 10 following a report from a neighbour that she was being neglected. Following a visit from social services, LC was found to be living in squalid conditions and covered in suspicious looking injuries. These included severe bruising to the breast and thigh area and marks that looked like cigarette burns on her arms and legs. LC will not discuss this part of her childhood. She was sent to a foster home at age

10, where she stayed for 18 months before moving to another foster home due to violent outbursts. Her initial foster family reported her as being defiant, staying out all night, smashing ornaments in the house, and uncontrollable. She stayed at the second foster home from age 12 to 14, when she reportedly ran away and was never found. LC has informed us she was homeless and lived on the streets until the age of 16 when she moved in with a man. She will only refer to this man as 'Bainsy' and will not reveal his full name. She has said she had sex with his friends for money. She did not see this money, but in her words, Bainsy took care of her and bought her anything she needed. She got pregnant aged 18 and gave birth aged 19. She was still living with Bainsy but stated that she did not know who the father was. She will not discuss the death of the child, but police reports show that Bainsy found the dead child in the sink, and he started to beat Lucy. He tied LC to a chair and set the flat on fire, taking the infant with him. A neighbour called the fire brigade. Bainsy told the police it was LC who murdered the child. They saved LC from the fire but she suffered severe burns. LC did not speak a word to police and ended up being charged for the filicide but committed under a section 37/41.

Tears for Lucy and her baby stung my eyes as I read. She was clearly extremely vulnerable but also dangerous. There was no way I was letting her near Joshua no matter how much sympathy I had for her childhood. The sound of voices alerted me to a nurse walking towards the station. I pulled myself out of the black hole I had fallen into whilst reading Lucy's file. A curse escaped me as I realised I had no way of copying it for evidence or for further information. I snapped open the therapy contacts file, grabbed my phone and stole a picture of the names to check later. I shoved my phone back in my pocket and closed the file, smiling at the nurse as she entered the office. She smiled back.

"What are you up to?" she asked innocently enough, but concern heaved up from my stomach.

"Oh, looking into something for Louise," I replied, grinning like an idiot. "What about you?"

"Grabbing some phones." She picked up the mobile phones she was referring to and took a seat to record what she was doing. Some patients were allowed supervised phone access at certain times of the day. As I watched her, an idea came to me of who else might be able to help me.

"Is Emma around?" Surely Emma would know where Lucy was.

"She's off sick." The girl replied without looking up.

"Oh, I saw her this morning in Louise's ward round. She seemed fine."

"Yeah, she went off sick after ward rounds, not sure what's wrong with her."

I gave in and left the office to finish off on the ward. I made a plan to look at the contacts for Lucy later. I promised myself I was going to find her. I was going to catch her. And then, I was going to help her.

Summer

After hastily visiting the other wards to say hello to the patients, I sat in my car outside the hospital. A light rain drizzled down my windscreen. I was leaving ninety minutes earlier than usual but hoped no one would notice. I pondered the situation with Lucy for what felt like the billionth time. Patients had escaped from the facility on plenty of occasions. They spent months, or even years, building up the trust of the staff to get unsupervised leave. Then the temptation became too much, and they went AWOL. I'd seen it happen at many hospitals, sometimes with devastating consequences. Patients with personality disorders commonly lacked insight into their condition and actions. Empathy was often missing. Any human being who lacked empathy was dangerous in my book. Although I knew of a few people devoid of empathy who were not locked up in a secure hospital.

Runaways sometimes happened even with escorted leave. The patient was not handcuffed to the support worker and the hospital always advised staff not to put their own safety at risk to stop someone from running off. So, although most patients didn't realise it, they could actually run away at any time during leave if they were so inclined. However, with the patient being so ill, they were often not in any fit state of mind to remain hidden. They were far more likely to get drunk, take drugs or cause trouble somewhere, so the police soon found them and brought them back. Actions such as this were partly why it took so long to earn unescorted leave. It was a tremendous security risk and one which always needed to be investigated fully.

What I had never come across was a hospital lying about a missing patient. There simply wasn't any need. Yes, an investigation would be required but, unless it was a regular occurrence, or there were clear signs suggesting leave should not have been granted in the first place, there wasn't any genuine risk to the hospital. A good hospital would not get shut down over one patient escaping, or even two or three. It happened. It was understood that mental illness is an ongoing battle that is difficult or even impossible to *cure*. It wasn't like physical health where it was easy to run a few tests to get confirmation of a disease. A disease which you could cure with drugs and then confirm it had worked by repeating the same tests. You couldn't do a blood test or brain scan and hear the doctor say *yes, you have bi-polar*, or do a brain scan and hear the words *all clear*.

As a responsible clinician, you couldn't use a lie detector test to check if someone is telling you the truth when they promise they're feeling better and won't run away if you give them leave. But there would likely be dismissals, hospital closures, and even possible prison if a patient escaped and the clinician covered it up. That would be a major issue and one which would not go away following a quiet investigation. The risk wasn't worth the severity of the consequences.

I kicked the car into gear and began the drive home. I tried to figure out what *was* worth the risk. What had happened that was so terrible that Dr Rears and even Aaron would cover it up? *Did she sneak out somehow? Was she dead? Had someone murdered her?*

I arrived home twenty minutes later to an empty flat, and slumped onto the sofa, not bothering to remove my shoes or jacket. My mum had picked up Joshua from school and was giving him dinner for me. I'd promised Joshua I would visit him at 6 PM. That gave me two hours. I opened up my phone to look at the names listed in the picture I took of Lucy's file. I didn't know a lot of the staff by name and didn't recognise many. There were lots of staff who couldn't handle it and quickly left, and lots were bank staff rather than permanent fixtures. However, there were two names that caught my eye. One was Dr Rears. He was noted as Lucy's psychiatrist and RC. A strange mixture of relief and anger ran through me. I knew he had been lying to me. The question I needed to answer was *why*. Why would he risk his prominent career over one escaped patient when he was so close to retirement? I knew the answer to that part. He wouldn't risk his career or notoriety for *any* patient. He was selfish and egotistical. *So why risk it all over Lucy?*

The other name I recognised on the list was Aaron. It listed him as Lucy's lead nurse. Another liar. Another narcissist? I struggled to believe it. Aaron had always seemed so genuine in the days of getting drunk together as students. Back then, he appeared to be honest, caring, easygoing. I had never seen him show a nasty bone in his body. That didn't mean he didn't have one, of course. But it was unthinkable to me that he was somehow in league with Dr Rears, especially after I had shared my body with him. Something was making him lie though. Or someone.

I looked again at the list, moving my eyes down past staff names, and noticed a section underneath labeled *family contacts*. I expected that section to be empty. However, there was one name, Hannah Bridgeford. According to this document, Hannah was Lucy's sister. The part of her file I had managed to read earlier did not mention a sister or any other siblings. It may be a foster sister, I supposed. They did have different surnames. Both Hannah's phone number and address were listed. 12 Coppice Court, Edwinstowe. About an hour away from my own home. I felt my excitement growing. I was getting close to the truth. This sister could be the answer to my problems.

I wondered if Hannah still spoke to Lucy, or were they like Eddie and me? So close when we were young, but oceans apart since psychosis took him over. I thought about Eddie often, probably once a day. Sometimes I envisioned our reunion. He would tell me how sorry he was for the attack and that he'd forgiven me for calling the police. He would tell me he is all better now, so there was no need to worry about him being around Joshua. Dylan and Mum would be with us. One big, happy family.

A bang at my door shook me out of my fantasy. What the hell was that? It sounded like one big knock. My heart thumped as I tentatively walked out of the living room to look at the front door.

"Hello?" I called out loudly and instantly regretted it. Now they would know I was inside. As I stood in my hallway frozen with fear, nothing happened. There was no answer, no banging, no footsteps. Was I hearing things now as well? *I am not crazy. I am not seeing things. I am not hearing things.*

I turned my attention back to the phone in my hand. Hannah Bridgeford. What would she think of Lucy's disappearance? She must at least admit Lucy existed and confirm I wasn't having hallucinations. I punched in Hannah's number before I had a chance to think about what to say. I was still scrutinising the front door, as if it was going to explode at any minute. I racked my brain as I waited for the phone to connect, maybe I should say I'm calling to speak about Lucy to see what Hannah's reaction was. But to my dismay, a dial tone greeted me, and a female voice told me that the phone number was no longer in use. There was one other thing I could think to do. I needed to pay Hannah Bridgeford a visit.

Summer

Later that evening, I was back at my mum's house. Joshua was happy to sleep at hers again as long as I tucked him in. I stayed with him this time. The bang on the door to my flat had made me even more nervous. We shared the double bed in the spare room, though I pushed the bed right up to the wall. That meant no one could get to Joshua without getting past me. He was out of reach. I slept far better, knowing he was safe next to me.

The next morning I had no visits booked until 2 PM. I was due at another hospital called Antwelle Health Services in Radcliffe-On-Trent for two ward visits, one female and one male personality disorder ward.

Usually, I would have used the lack of morning visits to complete mundane admin tasks, such as writing up my notes and sending them to Natalie for review. I briefly wondered what she would think if she knew I planned on visiting Hannah Bridgeford. It was likely that I'd be formally disciplined, if not sacked. I needed to play it safe. I could not lose my job. The last thing I wanted was to end up as a single mother on benefits. I'd been there when Richard first walked out on me. I wondered again if I should contact Natalie about Lucy, but discarded the idea. She wouldn't help me the last time a patient was in trouble, so I saw no point in telling her now. I pushed her out of my mind.

I jumped into the car to drive home, shower, and change whilst Mum took Joshua to school. I even put some makeup on, a little foundation, blusher, and mascara, with a smattering of lipstick. It was a small amount, but it made me feel confident. Like I used to feel as a young student ready to take on the world, rather than the meeker version of myself I appeared to have become. I didn't like looking in the mirror these days, all I saw were eye bags and tired skin, but a bit of makeup helped. Once I felt more confident, I began the drive to Edwinstowe, merging on to the M1. It was fresh outside, and the cold air pinched my face. It was getting closer to winter weather as November fast approached. I hated being cold. I was much happier feeling warm rays of sunshine on my skin. But I loved this time of year. I loved Halloween and bonfire night. I adored Christmas and New Year. The family time with Joshua and Dylan, the food, the presents, and the fireworks. But mainly, it was the joy. I loved seeing Joshua so happy.

As I trundled along in the left lane, I gave Kelly a quick call. I felt I needed to tell someone what I was doing, just in case. In case of what, I was unsure, but I knew I would feel happier if someone else was aware of where I was going. Kelly didn't answer, though, so I used the in-car system to send her a voice text.

"Hey, Kelly, I'm on the way to Edwinstowe. What you up to? I'll tell you about Edwinstowe later, but I'm visiting a house on Coppice Court. Speak later."

I hoped my text didn't worry her too much. I tried to keep it casual, but the message did still sound strange. Plus, she seemed to have an instinctive knowledge of whenever something was upsetting me.

I approached an old car doing well below the speed limit in the left lane of the motorway, so put on my indicator and moved over to the second lane to overtake, as did the FIAT Punto behind me. When I returned to the left lane, so too did the vehicle behind me. This in itself didn't deter me, but there was something about the car I disliked. I felt as if I'd seen it before. It gave me an uneasy feeling, and I slowed down to see if the car overtook me as well. As I carefully reduced my speed, the car swerved out into the second lane and overtook me. Thank God. I really was paranoid.

I arrived in Edwinstowe an hour later, as the sat nav had informed me I would. I turned on to Coppice Court and drove slower to read the numbers. It wasn't a long street. All the houses mirrored each other in their style of build. All were semi-detached with one-car driveways. I disliked streets where all the houses matched. I much prefer a mismatched street, full of character and intrigue.

Coppice Court was a tired-looking street. I assumed the houses were from the sixties with their style of build. They were all built from a dirty shade of red brick with ancient roofs barely clinging on.

I approached number 12 about halfway down the street. It was a property that had not seen much love recently. Tall weeds rose through the cracks in the paving. The UPVC front door was supposed to be white, but dirt made it appear much darker, and it was unevenly hinged. Grey nets in the dirty windows blocked the view to the inside of the house. It was not an inviting home. Everything about it screamed at me to leave it well alone.

I drove to the end of the street and around the corner, parking well away from number twelve. I walked back to the house with my large parka hood pulled right over my head, trying to ignore the light drizzle that had started. I dawdled as I attempted to make a plan. I did not want to tell Hannah who I actually was as I didn't want to get sacked. At first, I wanted to watch the property to see who lived there. I wanted to check Hannah out before I started asking her questions. I stood across the street, half-hidden behind a tree, pretending to be typing on my phone so I would look less conspicuous.

There were few cars on the road, so I assumed most of Hannah's neighbours were at work. Though when I glanced up at number 12, I froze in fear. The car from the motorway was now parked directly outside of number twelve. There was an enormous figure in the passenger's seat. A man, although I couldn't see his face well. A smaller figure was in the driver's seat, wearing a dark hoodie. I couldn't see them clearly, but they could see me. They were staring right at me.

I pulled my hood further up in a futile attempt to hide and turned around to rush back to the car. Alarm bells rang in every part of my body. Wishing I hadn't parked so far away, I began to run back to the car. I was so close to the end of the road when I heard an engine revving up. I looked behind me. The car was moving straight towards me.

Terror grabbed me, but for once, I didn't freeze from fear. I realised I wasn't going to make it to the car so scanned the street, searching for somewhere to hide. The pavement was wide and open, they could easily drive onto it to hit me. I ducked down behind a large van and hurried to a nearby garden. I hid right behind the car parked in the stranger's driveway, praying the owner of the property would not come out and give me away.

I couldn't see anything from my hiding position, but I did hear the car screech to a stop and its door open and slam shut. The thud of slow footsteps on the pavement made my heartbeat quicken as I thought about Joshua. I was stupid to have come here and put myself in danger when I needed to be around for him. I felt tears coming and desperately pushed them back.

It felt like hours had passed, but it was probably seconds before the car door opened and shut again. I heard the car drive away, but stayed glued to the spot. I couldn't move. What if they were tricking me and one of them was still out there? I willed myself to breathe again, staying as quiet as possible. My legs were rooted to the spot, and blood pounded in my ears, making it difficult to hear anything. As the street stayed silent, I realised I had to risk looking out past the car I was hiding behind if I wanted to get away.

Daylight seared my eyes as I slowly cracked them open. I blinked, trying to get used to the light, and turned to my left to snake my head around the car. Two green eyes stared straight back at me.

Summer

My vision had blurred from clamping my eyes shut so hard. Lucy's eyes glared brightly and, for a moment, they were all I could see. As my vision adjusted, I noticed the plump features of her face, her wrinkled, soft skin, and a normal nose that did not resemble a burnt stump. Her fine, grey hair was curled from a perm. The green eyes were worried and warm rather than cold. It dawned on me that this was not Lucy. It was likely the lady who lived in the house behind me. I attempted to apologise, but all that escaped my lips was a stutter.

"Are you okay, dear?" The lady's voice was soft, full of concern. It had a slight whine to it, like elderly people's often did.

"Yes, yes, I'm so sorry. I was…er…I'll go now." I forced myself to stand, but winced as I did so. Pain jumped up both legs like tiny bee stings after being bent uncomfortably for so long.

"No." Her face was lined with worry. "No, no. Don't run off. Come and have a cup of tea."

She put a withered hand on my arm to guide me. I smiled gratefully and allowed her to lead me inside the house. It looked like number 12 from the outside, but the door was a dark purple. The windowsills were still white and much cleaner than number 12. There were no weeds in the driveway, and a neat patch of grass lay to the left, surrounded by colourful flowers. I followed the lady through the front door and into a narrow corridor. I couldn't help but smile at the décor. The carpet was a deep red with a repeating pattern of huge purple flowers. The walls were a faded cream, and photos lined the corridor. There were many different shapes and sizes of photos, and mainly of one particular boy. He actually looked vaguely familiar to me, though I was in no state to figure out why. We entered an open doorway before the stairs and walked into a lounge. The carpet was the same, but the walls were a dull peach colour. They were lined with more photos of the same boy and different styles of clocks. None of the furniture in the room matched.

"Now, you take a seat here while I get you some sweet tea," she said sternly, pushing me towards the sofa.

"Water is fine." I managed. My stomach churned at the thought of forcing down sweet tea. I smiled at her to show I was not being rude.

"Okay, water it is then." She smiled back at me and gestured again for me to sit. I obeyed and perched on the sofa. My breathing was beginning to slow again, although I still felt a little weak. The walls of the old lady's house were a barricade between me and whoever the hell had chased me. Surely that wasn't Lucy. How would she have gotten a car, and what reason would she have to drive it at me? I cursed myself for not getting the registration number. The old lady returned within a couple of minutes with my glass of water, which I accepted gratefully.

"Is there someone I can call for you?" She looked at me warily as she spoke, like she was trying to figure out if I was going to panic again.

"Er, no…I'm fine now, honestly. My car is around the corner. I'll go back to it in a sec and get out of your way," I replied. I hoped I sounded better than I felt.

"What happened? Has someone hurt you?" she asked.

"Oh, no!" I smiled again. "It was nothing…really..I..er…had a panic attack. I suffer from anxiety. I needed a space to calm down again but didn't quite make it to my car."

The old lady gave me an understanding nod. "Do you have far to drive home?"

"Oh no, to the other side of town. I was here to see an old friend, but she doesn't appear to be at home." The lady seemed sweet, but I lied all the same.

"Oh?" The lady posed this as a question. "Who is your friend? I know most of the street. Lived here for 56 years now!"

I examined the elderly woman for a moment. "Hannah," I answered.

"Hannah?" Her forehead wrinkled.

"Yes. Hannah Bainbridge. I think she lives at number 12?"

"Number 12? Oh, dear honey, I think you must have the wrong street. There's no Hannah at number 12." She looked at me again with concern in her eyes.

"Do you know who lives there?" I ventured tentatively. I wasn't sure if I wanted to know.

"Why yes, an older man, although I forget his name. He's a doctor, I think."

For a moment, it didn't register. But slowly, it dawned on me who the large man in that car must have been.

"Dr Rears?" My voice was a whisper.

"Yes! That's it! Rears. Is Hannah a relative of his? I do see some young women visiting from time to time."

"You do? What do they look like?" The words rushed out, and the lady looked at me in surprise.

"Well…they are a bit strange." She started slowly, seeming to struggle for an appropriate description. "I can't see that far these days, but there is one lady who visits on a Sunday. She is quite petite with black hair and doesn't dress too good, if I'm honest. I keep my distance. I'm not one to judge people, but sometimes you know, don't you?" She looked at me for approval for her judgmental attitude.

"Know what?" I prompted again.

She looked hard at me for a moment before deciding to trust me with her opinions. "She isn't all there," she whispered, as though someone else might hear. Raising her voice back to normal levels, she added, "I think she must have had a terrible accident a few weeks ago. Strange marks all over her face." She looked at me sadly.

"Marks?" I prompted her.

"Yes. It looked like scarring from this far away. Like maybe she had been burnt. Awful stuff."

My stomach did a somersault. Lucy must have been at number 12 with Dr Rears, but her face had been burnt a long time ago. So the previous lady could not have been Lucy.

"What did she look like before the burns?" I asked.

"Well, she had lighter hair then. More brown than black. Still dressed the same, in old clothes every week she was." She tutted as if not dressing well was a crime to be ashamed of. "Could have been such a pretty girl if she had taken better care of herself. Now I suppose her accident means she will care even less."

I had no idea who the other woman might be, but it was clear that the lady was talking about two different women, even if she didn't realise it herself. The previous one had no scars on her face, and the one more recently with a scarred face. And Dr Rears had brought them to his home. A stormy wave of fury flowed through me at the thought. There was so much more to this than Lucy. I needed to get home. I needed to speak to someone. Someone I should have spoken to when all of this first started.

Summer

Two hours later, I was home alone. I had called in sick to Antwelle Health Services. Unless I had a stomach bug, I rarely called into work sick. Hospital rules stated we could not return until we had been well for a minimum of forty-eight hours following a sick bug, as the last thing they needed was it flying through all the patients and staff. So this was the excuse I used. It gave me a minimum of three days off work and was never questioned. I had slight paranoia that the law of karma meant I would end up actually being ill soon, but I pushed the concern away. Sometimes you have to tell lies to get to the truth.

Joshua was still at school. Mum was going to pick him up. She normally did when I was at work, anyway. I should be more grateful, and maybe take her out for dinner once this was over. Though the thought that she might decline put me off. Until I knew what had happened and Lucy was back at the hospital, I wanted Joshua to remain safely away from the house. I couldn't be sure if it was her that had nearly run me over, but it certainly looked like her. The car had disappeared when I left the old lady's house, who I'd found out was named Mrs Timpson.

I now sat back at my kitchen table with my phone, ready to make the call. I groaned inwardly at the thought, but I knew I had to do it. I had to call Natalie.

"Hey, Summer," Natalie answered after the first ring, eager as ever.

"Hey," I said, less enthusiastically. "You got a sec to talk?"

"Sure."

"Great. It's…it's a bit strange." I wasn't sure how to tell her, so I jumped right in. "There's a patient at Derby Hospital by the name of Lucy Clarke. Yet, she isn't there anymore. And when I asked her nurse and psychiatrist where she was, they said they'd never heard of her."

"What?" Natalie's voice was full of confusion. She was quiet for a moment. "Maybe she's from a different hospital?"

I rolled my eyes. Of course she fucking wasn't. "No, she was definitely in Derby. It's a bit weird, isn't it? I don't get why they'd lie?"

"I doubt they're lying, Summer." She scoffed. I put my head in my hands to keep the bubbling anger in check. I knew she'd be no help.

"Well, I've found her patient file on their computer. They have changed it to a different name." I delivered my evidence, expecting this to make her see that they *were* lying.

"Oh. Well, ask some other staff. I'm sure someone knows where she went. Probably a transfer."

I couldn't tell Natalie about my visit to Edwinstowe, so I wasn't sure how to get her to see the seriousness of what was happening.

"Yes, I will," I said instead. "But to be honest, Natalie, I think something strange is going on."

"Okay. Well, let me speak to Alexia, see if she has any ideas."

I rolled my eyes for the third time before letting her know about my sick bug and saying goodbye. I didn't know what I'd expected her to say, but I'd hoped for some agreement that it was a strange situation at least. I prepared my phone for the next call, another one I didn't want to make.

"Hello, Derby Police," a female voice answered.

"Hi, my name is Summer Thomas. I need to speak to somebody about a missing patient."

"Hello again, Ms Thomas."

"Er, again? No, I haven't called you before," I said with a voice full of indignation. *What was she talking about?*

"Okay, Ms Thomas, I'll see if I can put you through to DI Swanson again," she sighed loudly.

Music blared in my ear before I could respond. I lowered the phone and checked at the screen. I'd dialed the right number, but I had never called it before in my life. Less than a minute later, a deep male voice came on the line.

"DI Swanson," he said.

"Er, yes, hi, my name is Summer Thomas."

"Yes, Ms Thomas, I remember," he replied in a snappy tone.

"No, you don't." I snapped back. "We've never spoken." I heard him mutter something under his breath.

"Did you curse?" I asked him.

"Let me guess, a patient named Lucy Clarke is missing, and no one will admit it," he replied, still in the same curt tone. It stunned me into silence. I had no idea how to respond. "Well?" he insisted.

"Wh…I…yes," I said, stumbling over my words.

"Hmm, well, how did I know that if we've never spoken before?"

"I…I don't know. How did you know? Are you trying to tell me I told you this? When?" I demanded.

"Every day since Friday, Ms Thomas."

"I have never called you!"

"Well, you do sound different. Kudos for putting on a voice, but we both know the truth, don't we?"

"I'm telling you, I have never spoken to you!" I said, my voice getting louder.

"Look, Ms Thomas, I've told you before that I will look into Lucy Clarke's whereabouts. If you don't remember, then please contact your doctor." And with those words, Swanson hung up the phone and left me sitting open-mouthed at my kitchen table.

I thought about the likelihood that someone had been calling the police since Friday pretending to be me. Statistically, I knew it was more likely I was losing my mind, but I refused to believe it. Someone was messing with me. Aaron's voice was too deep to pretend to be me, the same for Dr Rears, that left Lucy herself.

I didn't know what to do next. If I called Kelly, would she think I was crazy too and tell me to see a doctor? What would Natalie think? She was no use at the best of times. Or my mum, who was already terrified that Dylan or I might get ill like Eddie? There was no one I could turn to.

Hot tears ran down my cheeks, and I was drawn back to my phone. Aaron had called me three times, but I hadn't answered any of them. I wanted to speak to him to tell him I had found Lucy's file photo and had proof of her existence. Now a surge of loneliness was ripping through me and I ached to be with him, even if he was lying. I was stuck in a nightmare, and no one could wake me up.

One person who always made me feel better, though, was Joshua. I forced myself to stand on wobbly legs and walked to the sink to splash my face. I needed to think straight. I considered what to say or ask Aaron when I called him. I wanted to prepare for either more lies or the truth. I had a feeling that the truth was not going to be happy news, but it was vital for me to be able to defend Joshua. My phone buzzed to indicate I had received a text message. I unlocked it to take a look.

Aaron: *Please pick up. Just want to make sure you're okay. xx*

I found that strange. Why wouldn't I be okay if Lucy was dead, as he claimed? I replied to tell him I was fine, but busy, and would call him soon. Despite our last argument, he was still my closest link to the truth. He replied again.

Aaron: *Ring me now please–it's urgent xxx*

I rolled my eyes. I didn't have the energy to deal with him lying yet again. But then it might be something to do with Lucy. I selected the call button next to his text message and held the phone to my ear. It barely rang before I heard his voice.

"Summer? Hey." He fell silent, seemingly unsure what to say now that he had my attention.

"Hey." There was still silence from his end. "What's so urgent?"

"Err," he paused, "can you meet me somewhere? Somewhere quiet, where we won't be followed. Just in case…ya know…my ex…" He added hastily. "The car park at the supermarket? The underground part."

"I don't know, Aaron. I'm exhausted." I yawned loudly, evidencing my point.

"Please. It's about Lucy."

He'd piqued my interest. Should I tell him about Dr Rears? I decided not to, wanting to see what he had to say first.

"Why can't you tell me over the phone?" I asked. I didn't want to go out again, despite wanting to be close to him a few minutes earlier.

"Please, come see me now. Trust me?"

He had a nerve asking for trust after lying to me, but I caved and agreed to meet him. My loneliness was too much. I was unsettled by the whole thing, though I couldn't put my finger on exactly what was bothering me. I still did not believe Aaron was a danger to me. Still, as a precaution I called Kelly. The phone rang and rang. I was about to hang up when she finally answered. I explained everything that had happened in the last forty-eight hours as briefly as I could. Though, I didn't tell her about the car trying to run me off the pavement, or about the police saying I'd called them. I didn't want her to panic.

"I'm going to meet Aaron at the supermarket car park," I said.

"I'm coming with you. Give me twenty mins to pull a sickie from work. I'll meet you there."

I agreed, but I didn't want to drag Kelly into it any deeper, so I set off straight away instead. Now that someone knew where I was going, I was a bit more at ease. I could meet Aaron and then talk it over with Kelly when she arrived. I'd tell her in full then. It was Aaron after all, and Aaron would not hurt me.

Summer

Ten minutes later, I drove into the underground car park, watching for any sign of Lucy whilst also looking out for Aaron. The supermarket had arranged the car park as one giant level underground, rather than having many floors. It was dank, and the thick smell of oil burnt my nostrils. There was a vast outdoor car park, so the underground one seldom got used. There were less than a dozen cars parked in spaces far away from each other, most of them likely belonging to the staff. It took my eyes a minute to adjust, and the weak wall lights didn't help that much. It was another long minute before I saw Aaron lurking in the far right corner.

I considered driving off for a moment as a pang of fear clutched me, but I knew that was silly. It was Aaron, for god's sake. I had known him for years. I knew he was a good guy. Whatever reason he had for not confiding in me, he wouldn't hurt me. I eased my car closer to Aaron. I hated underground car parks. The spaces were always far too narrow. All my previous cars had been worth less than a grand, and I'd bumped every one of them in similar car parks, or at least whilst parking. So I was wary of scratching the BMW and chose a spot about five spaces away from Aaron.

As I turned off the ignition, I realised how much I did not want to be there. It didn't feel safe. I was tempted to drive away from the situation then and there. But thoughts of getting to the truth to ensure Joshua's safety made me stay. I contemplated waiting for Kelly, but didn't want to drag her into a potentially dangerous situation, either. I sighed. I knew I had to speak to Aaron alone. Slowly, I opened the door and looked up at Aaron. I wasn't in a rush to see him. My earlier loneliness had vanished, and I suddenly craved being alone.

"Hey." He smiled at me meekly. He seemed wary too. He moved from one foot to the other, and his eyes darted around the car park. His usual easy manner was nowhere to be seen.

"Hey, weirdo." I tried to break the awkwardness with a smile. "What have you called me here for then?" My tone was light-hearted. Or at least that's what I aimed for.

He smiled back weakly for a second. "There's something else I need to tell you about Lucy."

"Yes, you said on the phone." I dropped my smile. I couldn't be bothered to pretend anymore. "But I want no more lies, Aaron."

"No. No more lies. Pinkie promise." He stuck out his little finger.

I rolled my eyes. "So you admit you lied to me about Lucy, then? You know she isn't a ghost."

"I didn't lie. Have you seen the plaque?"

I nodded my head in response.

"So you know there was a Lucie Clarke who died in the fire?" Aaron asked.

"Yes. A different Lucy, clearly. Their names aren't even spelt the same."

"Yes. A different Lucy," he admitted, finally.

"So... Why lie to me?"

"I didn't want to lie, Summer. I was trying to protect you."

"From who? From Lucy?"

"No, not Lucy!"

"Then who, Aaron? Who were you trying to protect me from?"

"I need to ask you something first. Why are you so bothered?" Aaron surveyed me with serious eyes.

"What kind of question is that?" I was getting more and more frustrated with his strange behaviour. " "Tell me what happened to Lucy!"

"Not until you answer my question. Why do you care what happened to her? Didn't you fall out with her and tell everyone not to allow her into the ward round?"

"She's my patient! Of course, I care about what happens to her. I'm her advocate. I'm here to speak for her when she can't speak for herself. And no, I didn't tell them anything. I would never suggest not doing a ward round for a patient. It's their right, and they're entitled to one, in my opinion!"

When I finished, Aaron was silent, as if trying to figure me out. I wondered if he actually had the balls to accuse me of being the dishonest one after all of his lies to me.

"To be honest, you're freaking me out, Aaron. Tell me the truth now, or I'm leaving."

"I know Lucy," he blurted out. I stared at him, willing him to continue. "I know Lucy," he repeated, slower and calmer. "And I know what happened to her."

"Yes, Aaron, I've figured that bit out. Now please tell me."

"What will you do when you know?" he asked.

"How do I know? I don't know what happened yet!" My voice was raised and bristled with frustration.

"Will you go to the authorities?" he asked.

"Well, yes, if I need to!" Days of confusion and fear were getting to me at this point. I was fast losing the grip on my usual cool exterior. And because it was Aaron I was talking to, I forgot to say the right things as I would when trying to get a patient to open up to me.

I was off my guard and didn't hear the footsteps creeping up behind me. By the time I noticed the shadow on my right side, it was too late. I saw a flash of green eyes before everything went black.

Swanson

DI Alex Swanson sat in his cramped and jumbled office outside the City Centre. The paperwork crowding the office belied the fact that Swanson was usually exceptionally organised when it came to his work in the Special Operations Unit: Major Crime. At that moment, however, he sat contemplating his phone and trying to figure out what the hell had taken place about twenty minutes before.

It was the fourth call this week from Summer Thomas. She sounded different. Her voice was much smoother, but that wasn't what was bothering him. Anyone could change their voice. There was an odd note to her voice that hadn't been there before. That note had settled uncomfortably in his mind, like a seed that he was not willing to grow. Swanson was far too busy to be looking for ghostly patients, but he couldn't throw the thought that maybe someone was fucking with both him and this Summer Thomas. He couldn't tell if she was lying over the phone. He considered meeting up with her, but what would they gain? More confusion and lies? He wasn't sure there was any point.

He had already had a discussion with Derby Hospital the previous day, and had spoken to the lead psychiatrist from the ward, Dr Rears. The doctor had confirmed there was not a Lucy Clark on Bluebell Ward or their other female ward. Although, there had been a Lucie Clarke who died in a fire a few years before. Dr Rears had also told him about the patients getting worked up over ghosts sometimes. It had seriously creeped Swanson out. Murderers, kidnappers, thieves he could deal with. They were an actual threat. You could see them, talk to them, hurt them, and best of all, catch them. But scary burnt ghosts who you couldn't touch or see? *Fuck that.* Swanson didn't even watch ghost films.

The last thing he wanted to do was visit that creepy hospital again. He had visited the hospital a few times. Violence, theft accusations, and absconded patients all brought him there a couple of times a year. It was a hub of constant crime, and full to the rafters of murderers, paedophiles, rapists and stalkers. Maybe googling Summer's employer would help, they might have a picture of her or a staff profile. He cursed as he realised he didn't know the name, and he had to use the hospital website to find out which advocacy company they used. Once he'd found it, he located the company website—Rowan's Advocacy. It looked appropriate enough, with lots of information on mental health. He noticed a page titled *Meet our Advocates* and clicked upon it. He scrolled down through the list. It started with a serious-looking older woman named Alexia. The boss by the sound of it. He kept scrolling and flicking through the other people. *David Geraghty. Natalie Brown.* Eventually, near the bottom, he found *Summer Thomas.* His eyes were drawn to her picture first. Light brown hair fell loose around her breasts. Her blue eyes were shy, as was her smile. She looked sweet, calm, and younger than he had thought she was, maybe in her mid to late twenties. He read her profile.

Summer Thomas holds a first class honours degree in Psychology from Derby University, where she also won Volunteer of The Year, Student Union Person of The Year, and published her undergraduate research to worldwide acclaim. Summer went on to achieve a Masters in Forensic Psychology from the University of Nottingham, where she completed her research and also won yet another award for creating and delivering innovative life skills classes for adults with autism. Summer covers the East Midlands area and dedicates herself to helping adults with mental health issues and learning disabilities.

Jesus fucking Christ. Looks, brains, and spending her life helping others. Why would this seemingly perfect overachiever be calling him constantly about a missing patient who didn't exist? Then again, the good ones always turned out to be nuts. He sat back at his desk and checked the time. It was five past three. The door to his office opened noisily, causing his neck to snap up from his laptop. His usual partner, DI Rebecca Hart, stood in the doorway.

"What are you doing?" she asked him sharply. Her head was tilted to one side, and her short, dark hair bobbed around her chin.

"Remember that nutcase Summer Thomas who keeps refusing to speak to anyone but me?" he asked.

She rolled her eyes and nodded.

"Well, she called again. She sounded different, though. So I checked her out. Come look at this."

Hart strode towards his desk. She never walked. One would think she was meek because of her small and skinny frame, especially when she stood next to Swanson, but she was the opposite. Loud, purposeful, and striding everywhere she went. She bent over his desk to look at the screen. Her strong, flowery perfume stung his nostrils. She spent a minute reading the text about Summer. Her small nose wrinkled with disgust.

"She sounds awful, doesn't she?" She didn't look at him as she spoke.

"Awful?" Swanson looked at her with raised eyebrows.

"Full of herself. All those awards and qualifications. Who cares?" She shrugged her shoulders and walked back towards the office door. "I'm going for lunch. I forgot to eat earlier. Want to come?"

"Okay." Swanson wasn't hungry, but he wanted to convince her that there was something off about the calls from Summer Thomas. He stood and grabbed his coat to leave with her. As he started to walk away, the shrill noise of his desk phone rang out.

"Leave it." Hart rolled her eyes again. "Come on. I'm hungry."

He ignored her and answered his phone.

"Hi…Er…DI Swanson." It was the same receptionist from earlier. "I've heard about something I thought you'd be interested in. It's about Summer Thomas."

His interest piqued, he turned his back to Hart so he could ignore her mouthing at him to hurry up.

"Go on," he said, pen poised above his desk notepad.

"Well, her friend has reported her missing."
"Missing? She called me less than an hour ago."
"Yes..she's missing under suspicious circumstances."

Summer

A sharp pain shot through the back of my head as I tried to open my eyes. I managed a split second before they involuntarily closed. A mass of dark shapes attacked my vision each time I opened them. It wasn't until I tried to raise my hands to rub my throbbing eyes that I realised I couldn't move. Something prevented my hands from moving any further than the small of my back. Fear stifled my throat, and a damp smell filled my nostrils. It felt like water surrounded me, yet despite the darkness, I knew I was surrounded by air. Thoughts of Joshua filled my head, causing panic to pull at my stomach. *How could I be stupid enough to let myself end up in this position? What would happen to him if I died cold and alone?*

In order to get back to him I needed to stay calm. I stopped trying to raise my arms and lay still instead. I listened. The silence pummelled my eardrums more than any noise I could ever remember. I used my body to test out my surroundings whilst my eyes adjusted to the dark. I was lying on my side. My face was against something cold and hard. I thought it was concrete at first, but it was too rough against my hands and face. It felt more like a stone floor.

I tried to piece together what had happened and figure out where I was. I reached out to the last fuzzy image in my mind of Aaron's face. He was talking about Lucy. I knew he hadn't told me where she was. We hadn't gotten that far. I had heard a noise and turned around. I remembered a flash of green eyes, pain in my head. And then I had awoken in the dark hell hole, unable to move my hands. Panic grabbed at my chest again. I closed my eyes and told myself sternly I would not die. I was going to get Joshua, find a new home, and forget all about this fucking mess. First things first, though. I had to figure out where I was and who had hit me. I knew it wasn't Aaron. He had been a few feet in front of me. The flash of green I had seen may have been Lucy, but I couldn't be sure.

There was no way Aaron had stood there as Lucy attacked me. It didn't make sense, so I concentrated instead on my surroundings. I could figure out the who later. My eyes were beginning to adjust to the gloom, and the edges of some shapes were becoming less blurry. I blinked again and finally noticed the thin shadow standing before me. I shrank back as much as I could in my awkward position on the floor. As my eyes adjusted further, I realised it was a person with slicked-back hair. They were wearing dark trousers and some sort of hoodie. I couldn't make out the face, but the eyes gave her away.

Lucy bent down and leaned towards me, her eyes glaring into my own. Her face was so close to mine that I could feel her stale breath. Her stench filled my nostrils. It was so bad I thought I would never be able to smell anything else for the rest of my life. That was probably true, as my life was possibly about to be cut short.

Her scarred face was clear by then, even in the dark. I wriggled back again as she leaned closer, trying to move my hands or stand or at least sit, but my feet were also tied. I was trapped. It made no sense that skinny Lucy could have tied me this tightly. That's when I remembered Aaron. I looked around the room, searching for Aaron. I didn't know if he was in on this attack or if he was hurt, too. He was my one chance, and I prayed he was nearby and would help me. I spotted Aaron sitting on the floor about twenty feet behind Lucy. He'd brought his knees up to his face, and his arms were resting on them, one elbow on each knee. He didn't look tied up. His head was bent towards the ground, and I couldn't see if his eyes were opened or closed.

"Aaron?" My voice sounded strange, like it was faraway. There was a slight echo reminiscent of being in a cave. Aaron didn't move.

"Summer!" Lucy exclaimed in an excited tone. Her face moved closer, her nose almost touching mine. She had blocked my view of Aaron. "It's me. Lucy?" She cocked her head to one side like a confused puppy.

I looked back at her, not sure what to say.

"Hi, Lucy," I ventured. It was all I could manage to force out of my dry throat.

"Hi!" she replied, as though we were long-lost friends. "I'm so glad you're finally here, Summer. I need you. Thanks for coming!" She nodded her head enthusiastically. Lucy was a different woman than when I had last seen her on the ward. She was my friend again.

"It's okay, Summer," Aaron mumbled from behind Lucy. Lucy shifted to look at him, and Aaron came back into my view. He had looked up, but he was rubbing his head as though it ached. "Lucy, untie Summer now."

"You need me?" I said blankly to Lucy. Confusion distorted my thoughts, and I couldn't decide who to focus on. Lucy turned back towards me as Aaron attempted to stand.

"Well, yes. You are still my advocate, aren't you? Your job is to speak for me?"

I didn't know what to say to her. "Well, I was, but then you went missing."

She laughed, the high-pitched, girly sound echoing in the strange room. "Yes, I ran off, thanks to *them!*" She spat the last word. Someone had clearly upset her. Multiple people by the sound of it.

"Them?" It seemed I was still incapable of forming a complete sentence.

"Yesss, them!" She pronounced each word slowly as if I were a child or an idiot.

I tried to sit up and Lucy jumped forward. Her cold hands twisted around the tops of my arms, her nails digging deep. I flinched and tried to shift back. To my surprise, she hauled me up and helped me lean against the damp wall behind me. I eyed her suspiciously as she moved back to sit on her knees again. There was now a gap of about three feet between us. Blood rushed to my head, and I closed my eyes and waited for the dizziness to pass. When I opened them again, Lucy was still eyeing me, and Aaron was back on the floor. Apparently, standing hadn't gone too well.

"Why am I tied up, Lucy?" I asked in a gentle voice. I didn't want to make her angry. She was not mad at me yet, and I didn't appear to be included in *them*.

"Oh, ya know, so you don't run off," she said as if it was the most obvious thing in the world.

"I won't run off, Lucy," I replied cautiously, "but my hands are really hurting."

"Okay, soon," she said. She sounded sincere, and hope started to replace my panic.

I threw another look over at Aaron. He was attempting to stand again, but Lucy paid him no attention.

"Is Aaron okay?" I asked Lucy, since she seemed more chatty than usual.

"No, not really," she replied. I waited for her to elaborate, but she didn't. Instead, she stood and walked towards Aaron.

I took the opportunity to force my wrists out of what felt like a zip tie, but it was no use. It was too tight, and pulling made it dig in more. I gave up and tried to bring her attention back to me so Aaron could do what he needed to get us out of here.

"Untie me and tell me what you need," I said, still keeping my voice light and friendly.

She turned back around and looked at me, her eyes suddenly full of suspicion.

"I will tell you first, *then* untie you. I need to make sure I can trust you like Aaron said we could," she explained. I threw Aaron a wide-eyed look, suddenly unsure if he would be my saviour. He didn't look up at me.

I turned back to Lucy and found her studying me. Her eyes were wide with fear. I had no idea why *she* was scared, seeing as I was the one trussed up and at the mercy of a violent person with disordered thoughts. A warm trickle of blood ran down my neck as I dutifully nodded my understanding, despite the searing pain in my head.

"I knew complaining to the hospital wouldn't help. That's why I've brought you here." She hesitated. "I am sorry about your head. It was the only way." Her eyes pleaded with me.

"Oh, okay." I tried to look thoughtful. "I understand."

She nodded back, pleased with my answer. She paced the room, her steps quick. Aaron had managed to stand by then and kept his eyes on her, one hand still resting against the back of his head.

"Don't be mad at Aaron. I needed him to check we could trust you," Lucy said.

I remembered the strange questions Aaron had asked me. *Why did I want to know what happened to Lucy? Would I tell the authorities?*

"You see, that…that…that," Lucy tried to find words that escaped her, "pathetic excuse of a man, is no doctor! He is an abuser." She said this fast, as though the words were poison on her lips. She stopped pacing and looked right at me, gauging my response.

I wasn't sure what to make of her words at first. Lucy was severely ill, and I knew her well enough to know she did lie a lot. All the time, to be frank. Sometimes she suffered psychotic periods where she wasn't lying, but her hallucinations made her believe certain things were happening. Other times she lied because she thought it was funny to do so. But Dr Rears also disgusted me to my core, and I was never sure why. There was something off about him. An unspoken warning I couldn't put my finger on.

"You see, Aaron knows all about this piece of shit. He's seen him, haven't you, Aaron?" She glanced over at him, but did not wait for a response before continuing. Aaron stood leaning against the opposite wall, still watching her. "He knows all about it."

"You need to untie Summer, Lucy," Aaron said again. He could have overpowered her. He was much taller and stronger, but he knew the best way out of the situation was to talk her down. He must have known I would understand what he was trying to do.

"But I don't know, Lucy," I reminded her. "Tell me. Please, let me help."

Lucy sat down to my left, leaning her back against the wall. She was inches away and staring straight at me. I looked into the green eyes that had haunted me since Friday. They weren't cold. At least not at that moment. They were sorrowful and childlike. I realised how ridiculous I'd been. I felt my fear dissolve. Lucy was a lost soul. Like my brother and most of my patients.

"I will tell you, but then you need to tell everybody else." Her eyes implored me. I could see that she was looking for signs of me lying. She was still trying to figure out if she could trust me.

I got it then. She knew they would believe me. She knew they wouldn't believe her, like I'd doubted her. Even though I despised Dr Rears, even though I'd seen his gaze linger on younger patients, and even though I was supposed to be her advocate, I hadn't instantly believed her. Why would the MDT at the hospital or the police? They wouldn't. I wasn't even sure then that I believed her, but that was not my role as an advocate.

"Yes. Okay, Lucy, I will. Now, untie me and tell me what you need people to know."

Swanson

Swanson sat in the claustrophobic briefing room with Hart and four police officers initially assigned to Summer's supposed disappearance. His hand absentmindedly stroked his beard. Summer Thomas had absolutely fucked his week up.

"She's probably faking it," Hart said. "She's a nut job."

"So, how many times did she call today?" asked a skinny officer named PC Townsend.

"I dunno. Loads, probably." Hart looked pointedly at Swanson.

Swanson shrugged. "I don't know if she's mentally ill or not," he said. "Talk me through who reported her missing."

"So there was an emergency call from the woman's mum," Townsend began.

"Summer's mum?" Swanson interrupted.

Townsend threw an annoyed look his way. "Yes, Summer's mum. She rang and said a friend of Summer's had told her Summer had been attacked and taken by someone. She didn't know who. So the mum rang emergency services and reported it."

"But how did this friend know, and why didn't they call the police?" Hart asked.

"She did, ten minutes later. She said she had planned to meet Summer and someone else at the car park. When she got there, Summer's car door was wide open, her handbag was on the passenger seat, and there were drops of blood on the floor next to the driver's door," Townsend said.

"What's the friend's name?" asked Swanson.

"Err...Kelly something. I'll need to check."

"Useful." Hart rolled her eyes.

"So the friend saw that, went to the mum's *house* rather than call, and *then* rang the police?" Swanson muttered to himself. The rest of the officers looked at him.

"There's something weird about all this." Hart liked to state the obvious. "Come on, let's go to the car park then."

"I'm not sure there's any reason for major crime to be involved yet," PC Blake, scoffed.

"Well, we are, so deal with it," Hart said before walking away. She looked at Swanson expectedly until he stood and followed.

They made their way together through winding grey corridors to Swanson's black Audi, parked at the back of the station. Hart quickened her pace to keep up with Swanson's long strides. The supermarket's car park Summer had allegedly been taken from was one both of them knew well. They often grabbed lunch or petrol from there whilst working as it wasn't too far from the station. It would take less than ten minutes to drive there.

"So, what do you think happened then?" Hart asked him once they were in the car.

"Fuck knows." Swanson's tone was grim as he reversed out of the car park space, an inch away from hitting a bollard in his rush.

"I reckon she's staged the whole thing. Rang her mate to meet her, left blood and everything there so we'd come look. She's been trying to get your attention all week with her bullshit story. It would make more sense than any other explanation."

Swanson said nothing. He knew Hart was right. It was the most logical explanation. But there was something about Summer's tone earlier on the phone that made him wonder if perhaps she was telling the truth. They drove through the midday traffic easily. Derby wasn't a big city and only got truly busy at rush hour, football matches, or during road works. He parked neatly in the outdoor car park, near the entrance to the underground space. Cold air whipped around them as they walked towards the pedestrian entrance, where Summer was supposedly taken. Hart pulled the collar of her coat up higher. Swanson hadn't bothered to wear one. Once underground, the pair inspected their surroundings. Few cars occupied any spaces. Despite dim lights on the walls, the atmosphere was gloomy. There was a blue BMW on the far side of the car park that matched the description they had been given. The pair glanced at each other.

"Why would Summer meet her mate here?" asked Hart, filling the silence again.

Swanson ignored her and instead headed towards the car. He surveyed the car park as he walked. Hart followed behind at a slower pace, taking her time. Swanson reached Summer's vehicle and bent down to look inside. Someone had closed the car door, but he noted the handbag on the front seat as Townsend had described. He didn't touch the door or try its handle. Instead, he knelt on the floor to study some dark spots of liquid, which did look like blood as the friend had described. He wondered why Summer might go to this much trouble to reach him.

"Stop," he instructed Hart. She had reached the vehicle and was about to open the door.

"Why? You don't actually think this is real, do you?"

"I don't know. Just don't fuck anything up."

Hart took out a package from her handbag and waved it at Swanson. Gloves. She threw them on and opened the car door. Voices echoed from the pedestrian entrance and the four officers from the briefing room appeared. Hart carried on and picked up the handbag to open it. She rummaged around in the bag and pulled out a purse.

"Yep, it's Summer Thomas," she announced after searching the purse and finding Summer's ID. She replaced the purse and bag in the vehicle as the officers arrived behind her. "You took your time." She raised a perfectly waxed eyebrow.

"Found anything?" PC Blake asked.

Hart proceeded to inform Blake about the handbag and the closed door as Swanson silently wandered off. He walked into the middle of the car park, his dark eyes surveying every nook and cranny of the surroundings. The place was dreary and smelled musty and damp. No one other than the officers had entered since he and Hart arrived. It wouldn't be too hard to have a fight with someone in here and have it go unnoticed. But how would you get an adult out of here against their will? You would need them to be quiet, knocked out cold perhaps. You'd have to be strong or know where to hit someone to knock them out. He flicked his eyes up to the ceiling. He smiled. Cameras. Now they were getting somewhere.

Summer

Lucy looked determined. "Okay, I'll untie you." She bent to reach for something on the floor.

There was a slight glint as the weak lights on the wall caught the item within their rays. Scissors. I noticed the wall lights were the same dim lights as in the underground car park. Lucy came closer and used the scissors to cut the zip ties from my wrists and ankles. I winced as she released each one. It was worse than the pain of them cutting against my skin.

"Sorry, Summer," Aaron mumbled. "It was the only way." He still stood over by the far wall.

He watched Lucy the entire time, never taking his eyes off her. I don't know why he bothered. If she'd been messing with us and actually went to stab me, he would have been much too far away to stop her. I shot him an angry look as I rubbed each wrist and ankle in turn, trying to rub away the pain. How could this possibly have been the only way? I concentrated on Lucy since she still had the scissors in her hand and was close enough to reach out and stab me. I cursed as I realised my phone was sitting on the passenger seat of my car.

"What's wrong? Is that not better?" Lucy smiled sweetly. That was the first time I'd seen her smile so widely. With her scarred face, it wasn't a pretty sight, but she seemed to feel guilty for hurting me.

"Yes, thanks, Lucy." I felt some claustrophobia lift when I could move more freely and my eyes had fully adjusted.

I scanned the room again, and noted there was a heavy metal door behind Aaron which looked like a fire door. I'd need to stand to have a chance at reaching the door, but Lucy was in my way. I had to stay calm and think my way out. She was too unpredictable. To the left of me were stacks of boxes. Dozens and dozens of them with black writing, though I couldn't keep my head turned away for long enough to read them. I wanted to ensure I didn't lose my bond with her. She may have been a lost soul, but she was also mentally ill with violent tendencies, severely stressed about something, and holding scissors. Lucy sat down across from me, with her legs spread out before her like a young girl. Aaron finally came over and knelt to the left of us. He smiled at me, and I flashed him another angry look before turning my attention to Lucy.

"I'll tell you what you need to tell others," Lucy said. "But you need evidence first, Summer. No one will believe it otherwise."

"Evidence? You want me to get evidence?" I asked. "Evidence of what?"

"Of what Dr Rears has done, silly!" Lucy laughed her high-pitched giggle again.

"What has he done, though, Lucy? You haven't told me yet," I said.

It was the wrong thing to say. Her face darkened. She changed right in front of me, back to the colder version of Lucy. The one from my dream. "Don't you know?" she growled at me.

Aaron noticed the change, and I saw his body tense. He looked ready to pounce if he needed to. Now that he was closer to me, I could see a trickle of blood rolling down the side of his face.

"Lucy," he said in a gentle voice, "of course, Summer knows. She wants to make sure she isn't missing anything."

I buried an urge to shout and scream and ask them what the fuck were they talking about. Thank God I was so used to strange situations. I pulled the face I always pulled when a patient was making no sense to me and at risk of becoming violent. I kept my expression blank, bar a small, encouraging smile.

"Oh!" Lucy giggled again and put her hand to her cheek. She had shifted back to the young girl routine again. "Of course! Silly me. Now, to get the evidence, you need to go to Dr Rears—"

Lucy didn't get to finish her sentence. The heavy metal door in the far right of the room burst open.

"She's in here!" A male voice boomed, shining his torch right at us.

We all winced at the light and covered our faces. The man stormed over, and two more men ran in after him. I could see their uniforms now. Aaron stood and immediately held both of his hands up in the air. The first police officer grabbed him and pushed him up against the wall, twisting his hands behind his back. He had obviously wrongly assumed that the male was the most dangerous person in the room, not the small woman opposite me still holding the scissors. Lucy jumped up and ran to the far corner, waving the scissors in front of her.

"Whoa," the second officer said. "It's okay, miss. No need to wave scissors around. We're here to check you're okay."

A third officer approached me, walking sideways so he could keep his eye on Lucy.

"Are you okay, miss? Can you stand?" He offered a hand to pull me up, and I took it gratefully.

"Yes, I think so. My head hurts," I replied.

Two more people came striding into the room. One was a female this time, the other male. They wore suits rather than police uniforms but had what I assumed to be some sort of police ID hanging around their necks. I guessed they were detectives, judging purely from movies I'd seen. The officer who had spoken to Lucy held his arm out to his side, motioning for the two suits to stop and stand still.

"Easy now," he said to them. "We have a lady here who is scared." He gestured towards Lucy.

I assumed *scared* was like the hospital version of *poorly*.

"Okay," the petite woman in the suit barked in an authoritative voice, belying her small stature. She didn't take her eyes off Lucy. "We'll take it from here. Get the others out."

The uniformed officer moved back a few paces as the suits slowly moved forward. The officer next to me held my arm, and we began to ease towards the door. Aaron was being walked out by the first officer.

"There's nowhere to go," the female suit said in the same bossy tone to Lucy. "Put the scissors down and come with us. We want to talk."

Lucy sobbed. She opened the scissors and held a sharp blade to her own throat. "Summer! Tell them." I couldn't help but turn around. Lucy looked at me, her eyes pleading.

"Tell us what?" the lady commanded without taking her eyes off Lucy. The male suit hadn't said a word but glanced over at me. He dwarfed the woman. He even dwarfed Aaron.

"Er…I'm not sure…" I stammered, looking at the man.

Lucy's sobs became anguished now. "You promised, you promised, you promised." She repeated over and over, getting louder and louder. The blade pushed into her neck, and a small trickle of blood ran down to Lucy's chest.

The suit lady tried again. "Hey, lady, scissors down, please."

I rolled my eyes. Jeez, she was going to get nowhere with that attitude.

"Lucy," I said in my own much calmer, authoritative voice, "I promised."

Lucy stopped bawling enough to look at me and listen. She still took deep breaths, as though it was difficult not to let the tears flow. She reminded me of times when Joshua had hurt himself but wanted to show he was a brave big boy.

"So I'm going to go with these nice police officers and tell them everything you've told me." I tried to reassure her.

"Tell them now!" she screamed at me. The scissors dug deeper, more blood trickled.

"But then it wouldn't be recorded!" I said in mock exasperation.

Lucy stared at me for a moment in silence. Her loud breaths had stopped and she cocked her head, before a wide grin spread across her face. Her child-like giggle escaped again. I knew I'd be hearing that laugh in my sleep.

"Oh! Goodie! Thanks, Summer!" she said through her laughter. The suits looked utterly flustered now.

"That's okay. I'm your advocate, aren't I? Now put the scissors down."

Lucy's face changed again. She looked at the suits. She could see by their baffled faces the effect she was having on them. Her lips curled into a smile. But not the young girl routine. An evil smile. It reminded me of when I saw her in the corridor, before she went missing.

"Lucy, I won't tell them if you don't put the scissors down right now," I said more sternly than I usually would have. Even I had my limits. She looked at me, smiled sweetly, and lowered the scissors to the floor as slowly as possible. The two uniformed officers who had been standing behind the suits ran at her with lightning speed. They pushed her up against the wall, dragging her arms behind her back as they had done with Aaron. Lucy howled out in pain. As awful as her screams were, I rushed out of the room as quickly as I could, with tears running down my face. I'm almost ashamed to say they weren't for Lucy. They were tears of relief. I was free. They had caught Lucy. I was safe. Joshua was safe. It was all going to be okay.

Summer

The bright lights of the hospital bored into my skull as I surveyed my surroundings. I sat in the emergency room of Derby City Hospital in a row of uncomfortable plastic chairs, with my back firmly against the wall. I knew Lucy wasn't there, but it would be a while before I turned my back on anyone again. One of the uniformed officers sat next to me. I'd since found out his name was PC Townsend. He didn't look like a cop. He was too skinny and not much taller than me. He was far too friendly, and had barely stopped talking on the way to the hospital. Thank God it was a five-minute drive. Though he was finally quiet, reading a fishing magazine he had picked up from the table in front of us.

I had since learned that Lucy held me captive in a rarely used storage room off the car park. She had been staying there since Friday. I'd noticed a sleeping bag and some other paraphernalia dotted around on my way out. I struggled to believe it had been three nights since she had gone missing. It felt more like months had passed. I'd also learned from PC Townsend that Kelly was responsible for saving me. In all the drama, I had forgotten all about calling her to meet me. I was so grateful I had. Thanks to the storage room not being too far away, it took around an hour for the police to find me.

I was thankful that the emergency room wasn't too busy patient-wise. There were five other people in the waiting room. I normally loved to watch people, but not today. Nurses, doctors, and porters ran around me, pushing in and out of noisy doors. I hadn't spoken to Aaron so I was still unsure how much of Lucy's plan he was in on. His head had been bleeding, too. Surely he hadn't realised that Lucy was going to attack me. I couldn't understand why he would let me get hurt. *But then why not talk to me on the phone? Why did he lead me to the car park? Did he not see her sneaking up behind me?*

Yet, he knew Lucy was there. He obviously wanted me to see her. And he'd allowed her to hit me and tie me up, no matter what way I looked at it. I yearned for Joshua. My mum was still looking after him for me. It was the first thing I'd asked once Lucy was arrested. She and Joshua were both fine, other than my mum worrying about me. PC Townsend had said this as if it was obvious she would be concerned. I doubted she was that bothered.

I was so deep in thought it took a few seconds to register a woman calling my name. I looked up to see a young nurse smiling in our direction. PC Townsend told me he'd wait for me in the chair. He would give me a lift to the station once I was sorted. The nurse walked me into a small private room with two chairs on either side of a desk. She sat facing the huge old-style computer screen whilst I sat down in the opposite chair. I explained to her what had happened. Not the full story, but that I got hit in the back of the head with a blunt object by a mentally ill woman. She made the usual sympathetic noises without asking too many questions. She didn't seem too surprised. I guessed being an emergency room nurse she had heard stranger tales and likely dealt with many mentally ill patients. I'd had to call the emergency services a few times for patients in my previous role as support worker.

She took me through the standard head injury questions and tests. She shone a torch in my eyes, made me follow her finger, and took my temperature. Luckily, it didn't take long for her to decide I was okay. She wrapped up my wound and declared I could leave as long as I called my doctor or the emergency services if any of my symptoms changed. I promised I would and thanked her, grateful it was over so quickly.

It was when I was leaving that something strange happened. I made my way back down the corridor to the waiting room. As I reached PC

Townsend, a figure outside the entrance to the emergency room caught my eye. Something about the person made my head snap around to get a better look. They wore dark trousers, a dark jumper, and had slicked black hair. I couldn't distinguish the facial features from where I stood, but I knew on some deep level that it was the same person who had been outside the cafe. Yet this time, I knew it couldn't be Lucy. *So who was it?*

Three. Four. I'm knocking...

Summer's silhouette was blurred as I watched her through the glass panelled entrance doors. She was sitting next to some skinny police officer. Though I couldn't enter because she would see me, and that couldn't happen yet. My plan wasn't quite ready, but it would have to do as it was, thanks to Aaron. I couldn't believe he had betrayed me. What an idiot. He was a spineless, diseased waste of space. He obviously didn't care about people as much as I thought he did. Unless maybe he didn't believe me. Maybe he didn't think I'd go through with it. Never mind, I had a plan to scare him. I knew how to show him I meant business. Aaron wouldn't tell the police about me, anyway. I was sure of it. He would have done it already if he had the balls.

Lucy probably would tell the police, but no one would believe that hot mess. She was a disgusting child killer. No one cared about child killers. No one cared about most of the patients. But an advocate? Aaron might tell *her*. And she might tell the police. I smiled as I watched her sit and stare at nothing. She looked pale and exhausted. Lucy had inadvertently helped me to start wearing her down. I squinted my eyes to get a good look at her injury. I couldn't see the wound, but I could make out blood around her head. My stomach fluttered as I thought about hurting her myself. I'd waited twenty years for revenge and I was now so close I could smell it. Her hair was dark and matted above her ear, and dry blood lined the neck of her ugly white top. Well done, Lucy, you psycho bitch. You made yourself even less believable.

She disappeared off down a corridor, following a nurse. I waited, enjoying that she looked so pathetic. I'd wait for thirty minutes. If she wasn't back by then, I'd go to her flat. Twenty minutes later, she returned. As she reached the cop again, she looked over at me. For once, I didn't move. I couldn't. The pull to see the same fear I'd witnessed outside the cafe was exhilarating, and I needed more of it.

She looked straight at me, but I couldn't tell if she recognised me. Her facial expression gave nothing away. In all the time I'd known her, it never had. But I knew her better than she knew herself. I had my gift, and I could see fear all over her face. I wanted to grab her, smell her fear, and tell her everything I knew about her. But then the plan would be even more screwed up. I needed to tear myself away. She turned away as the cop spoke to her, drawing her attention. I took my chance to sneak away. It wouldn't be goodbye for long, though. I would see Summer soon, and then she would disappear and Joshua would be mine.

Summer

I inwardly cursed PC Townsend for pulling my attention away from the staring figure. He'd only asked if I was okay, yet when I looked back a second later, they had disappeared.

"Sorry? Yes, I'm fine," I said.

PC Townsend hadn't moved from his seat and he looked up at me with concerned eyes. It was clear I hadn't convinced him I was fine. I smiled at him, and his expression relaxed.

"If you're feeling okay, are you happy to come over to the station with me? I'll drop you off at your car if you like, and you can follow me down. Or I can drive you there if you're not up for driving yet…" He trailed off as he stood up.

"Sure. I feel fine. Do you not need my car for forensics?" I instantly blushed when I saw him trying to hide a smirk.

"Not in this case. We could see from the camera that she didn't touch the car and we have all the photos we need. We've found you, got the suspect, and caught the whole thing on camera. There aren't any other forensics to obtain at this point."

I nodded. I wasn't sure if I should be driving, but I was too desperate for some time alone with my own thoughts to care. I needed to think about what I was going to tell the police. The truth, obviously, but I didn't want to be carted off to the hospital with Lucy. And I needed to figure out who the hell had been watching me. I was *not* going to raise that with the police.

I still hadn't moved, so PC Townsend took the lead and headed towards the hospital exit. The same doors that the figure had been standing behind. I convinced myself that nothing would happen while I was with a police officer and forced my feet forward to follow him. As we exited the hospital I pulled my coat up further around my shoulders to block out the harsh air. Winter was approaching, and leaves crunched under our feet as we walked. My gaze roamed the hospital grounds, but the mysterious figure had disappeared yet again, like a damn ghost. I stood still, trying to figure out where they could have gone. A separate department building flanked the emergency room on either side. Cars, trees, and other hospital buildings surrounded me in every direction. She could have disappeared into any one of them.

"Who are you looking for?" PC Townsend called out. He was about fifteen feet in front of me, standing by his police car. He was more perceptive than he looked.

"No one," I said. He raised an eyebrow. "Well, I wondered what happened to Aaron? Did he come to the hospital?"

"Oh!" He was livelier then, his arms moving everywhere as he spoke. "No, he refused hospital treatment. I reckon he's still at the station. He'll at least be answering questions, I assume."

"Will you charge him with anything?"

"Did he do anything illegal?" he asked. I'd forgotten PC Townsend didn't actually know what had happened at this point. He knew less than I did.

"Erm, I'm not really sure." I told a partial truth. I wished I could have spoken to Aaron before I had to give my statement to the police, but I knew that wouldn't happen.

I crunched through more noisy leaves as I joined PC Townsend at his squad car. He opened the door for me so I could climb into the back seat, and set off on the short drive back to my car in the supermarket car park. He smiled at me once he was in the front seat, but didn't say another word. I'd been in the back of a police car on one other occasion. The drive reminded me of that day and the last incident with my elder brother. The police had given me a lift home, and Eddie's girlfriend, Marinda, had sat next to me. She'd been my appropriate adult when they questioned me. She'd told me not to say anything to get my brother in trouble but I told them everything I knew. I hadn't seen Marinda since. My mum had been in no fit state to tell them anything. He'd nearly killed her. The memory of what my brother had done made me feel nauseous. The panic I'd felt, and all the blood. I'd seen the nightmare unfold as I hid under the rickety table in the kitchen corner, whispering down the phone to the emergency services lady. Eddie had thought I'd been to school, but I'd been off sick. For a moment, I wished I had an appropriate adult in the car with me. Kelly, or maybe even my mum, would do. I was fed up with being alone and always the appropriate adult. I was constantly scared of being unable to protect Joshua. It was exhausting.

Anxiety pulled at my stomach as the car slowed and we entered the dark space. I closed my eyes until we rolled to a stop. When I opened them, PC Townsend was already getting out of the car. He came to my side to open the door for me and held out his hand to help me out. I had an urge to bat it away, but managed to control myself and take his hand. My car was only a few feet away, but he walked by my side as we made our way over. I assumed he could sense my apprehension and my cheeks coloured at the thought.

"Don't worry. I'll be fine getting in." I smiled at him.

"Okay." He smiled back and walked back to his car. I jumped into the driver's seat before he disappeared from view. I didn't actually want to be alone there.

As I sat in my car, the anxiety dissipated. Being in my own surroundings and in control of the vehicle made me feel stronger. I shook away the ridiculous feeling of wanting company. Joshua and I were better off alone. Only the police to talk to, and then I could be with him again. I just hoped that the figure from the hospital stayed away.

Summer

The grey walls of the police station interview room were the opposite of the bright white walls of Derby Hospital. The two suits from the storage room of the underground car park were seated in front of me. I'd found out that the broad man was DI Alex Swanson. The bossy woman was DI Rebecca Hart. The name did not suit her personality from what I had seen of her.

Swanson hadn't spoken much, but he focused his deep brown eyes directly on me. I shifted uncomfortably in the hard chair. Not because he stared, but because he looked as though he was trying to figure me out, and there was something about him that made me believe he would succeed. Though his thick beard made it somewhat difficult to tell what he was thinking.

"So, Summer. Are you feeling well enough to talk to us?" she asked. Her short brown bob moved in line with her chin as she looked up. She gave off an air of being in control.

I struggled to tear my eyes away from him as Hart spoke. His suit defied his lumberjack structure, like he'd be more comfortable in a gym. I decided not to look at him again and focussed on Hart's perfectly symmetrical face instead.

"Yes. Yes, I do," I replied.

My eyes flicked straight back to Swanson. He had more hair on his face than on his head, which wasn't difficult to accomplish. I forced myself to turn away again, but I could still feel his intense stare.

"Let's start with how you know Lucy Clarke." She glanced up at me and smiled briefly before looking back down at her notepad. She looked at Swanson, then at the floor, then back at me. I couldn't tell if she was impatient or distracted.

"I'm her advocate," I replied. Hart looked blankly at me, so I explained further. "I work for Rowan Advocacy as an Independent Mental Health Advocate. Lucy resides on Bluebell Ward in Derby Hospital. I visit the ward twice a week as an independent person for patients to speak to."

"So you speak to all the patients on Bluebell Ward?" Hart asked. "I thought advocates were like lawyers? Available by appointment?"

"No, I visit twice a week and sit on the ward for an hour or so. Patients choose whether they want to speak to me. They don't have to, but they do all legally need to have access to someone like me. The advocates by appointment tend to be council advocates not employed privately like me."

Hart nodded. "Did you know Lucy was no longer on Bluebell Ward?"

"Yes. I didn't know where she was…" I trailed off, unsure what to say next. "When I asked the staff, they weren't sure who I meant."

"They didn't know who you meant?" Hart looked at me incredulously. I knew how she felt. "How do they not know their own patients?"

"I'm not sure. I've been trying to find out but have not had much luck. I'd spoken to Dr Rears and Aaron, who you met earlier. Then Aaron rang me today and said he had something to tell me about Lucy and asked me to meet him at the car park. But then Lucy hit me…I think." I trailed off and looked back at Swanson. He was still intently focused on me, and I felt my cheeks blush. I was babbling.

"So she was with you and Aaron? Why did she hit you?" Hart asked.

"Well, I don't know to be honest. She wasn't there at first. It was Aaron and me talking. Then I heard a noise, and someone hit me. I woke up in that room, and I was tied up with zip wire. That's why she had scissors. She had cut me free. She wanted to tell me something about Dr Rears. She seemed to want to check if she could trust me before she told me."

"By knocking you out and tying you up?"

"Well, she isn't very well." I shrugged my shoulders. I'd seen stranger things happen. I'm sure these two had, too.

"Hmm. That's one way, I suppose. So what did she tell you?" Hart responded.

"She kept talking about Dr Rears, the consultant psychiatrist from the hospital. She said he is bad and I need to tell people. But she didn't say exactly what he's done."

"Patients from there tell the police all sorts." Hart rolled her eyes. "We'll see what she tells us."

"What will happen to her? To Lucy, I mean?"

"Well, she'll go back to the hospital. She's under their care."

"No!" The word came out far louder than I had meant to say it. I rubbed my face in my hands and took a deep breath to regain my calm. "I mean, she can't go back to a place where she is being abused."

"We don't know that she is being abused. We get calls from the hospital all the time. The patients tell us they're being held against their will, physically beaten etc, etc. It's never true. It's their illness." Hart shrugged again.

"It doesn't matter if it's true." I sounded snotty, but I couldn't help it. "She believes it. Can't you imagine how scary that is for her?"

"Yes, but helping her with that isn't our job. That's her doctor's job." Hart crossed her arms and glared at me. I should have stayed calm.

"The same person she believes is abusing her?" I tried to sound less snotty, but I was pretty sure it hadn't worked.

"Yes, but even if she changes hospitals and doctors, she'll say the same thing, won't she? She is ill."

"As long as I've known her, Lucy has never accused anyone of abuse."

"How long have you known her?"

"Six months."

Hart made a snorting noise through her nose. "That's not that long." She reminded me of Joshua when he tried to win an argument. I decided that I'd had enough of the woman.

"What do you think?" I directed my question to Swanson. At least then, I could legitimately look at him without it seeming weird.

He shrugged his large shoulders and cast a glance over to Hart. They shared a look, and I briefly wondered if they'd ever had sex. Jealousy pinged at my chest. I knew it was ridiculous. I didn't know the guy at all.

"Like DI Hart says, we aren't mental health experts," he finally said.

I'd heard enough. I put my hand to my head then, feigning pain. "I need to go home. I need to—"

"We do have more questions for you." Hart interrupted.

"I need to get my son." I stood as if she hadn't spoken. I knew my rights and wasn't going to be bullied by this unempathetic nightmare.

"Oh, okay. Please give us your contact details. We will be in touch soon then," she mumbled.

I gave them my contact details and rushed out of the room. Swanson followed me to unlock the outside corridor door. As we walked along, side by side, I forced myself to look straight ahead. But we stopped before the locked door and he looked down at me, keys in his hand.

"Miss Thomas, have you called me this week?"

Oh shit. I realised then that this was the guy who that receptionist had put me through to earlier in the day. He believed I was some sort of lunatic who had been calling nonstop about Lucy.

"I called the station once today, and that was it," I said more sternly than I had expected too.

He studied me for a moment before asking, "Who do you think called me pretending to be you then?"

I paused before answering, unsure how to respond. "Well, maybe it was Lucy. Maybe she wanted to be found," I replied eventually. He nodded and unlocked the door to allow me to leave.

The autumn sun cut into my eyes as it set for the evening. It must have been around 6 PM. I raised my hand across my forehead to block it out as I rushed to the car. I didn't want to be out in the dark.

A shadow moved in the far corner of the car park. *Was that a person? A small animal? Was I being watched again?* I froze in the middle of the car park and peered in the shadow's direction. A painfully cold breeze hit my face, but I stayed as still as a statue. There was nothing there. *Was I actually losing my mind?*

I raced forward again towards my car and heard footsteps approaching behind me. I whipped around and stepped back, hands up to defend myself this time. She would not get me again. My breath whooshed out of me as I saw Swanson striding towards me.

"Sorry…didn't mean to scare you…" He trailed off as he reached me, eyeing at me in the same intense way he had done inside the interview room. I suddenly realised why he was so familiar to me. He observed me in the same way I observe others. He was calm and unreadable, too. We were the same, maybe we were connected. I wondered if he felt the same. I had a sudden impulse to let go of my emotions. To unleash my misery upon this man I barely knew. To hug him tight and beg him to protect Joshua and me.

"You didn't scare me." I lied instead. It was such a foolish lie. He had clearly scared me half to death.

"I wanted to make sure you're okay. You've had a rough day." His expression changed, and he almost smiled.

"I'm fine." I lied again. I didn't smile back.

"Okay. Well, if you need anything, here's my card." He handed me a small card with his name, division, and work number on it. I could have hugged him. Maybe he saw me, too.

"Thanks, but I doubt I will need it." I instantly regretted being so unpleasant.

"That's fine." He shrugged off my arrogance and smiled properly.

Every bone in my body wanted to stay close to him, but I turned and walked to my car. He watched me as I went, and I had to fight the compulsion to turn back to him. Sometimes, I really should listen to my intuition.

Swanson

Once Summer had driven off, Swanson made his way back to the station to collect Hart. They needed to get to the custody suite on the other side of town to speak to Lucy. Hopefully, she was calm enough. They had already spoken to Aaron while Summer was in the hospital. Swanson didn't know what to make of him. He was some sort of modern hippy man. He wore jeans that were ridiculously tight and looked stupid. There was a hole in his ear the size of a two pence coin and dark makeup smudged around his eyes. To each their own, but Swanson wouldn't be caught dead looking like that.

It was obvious that Aaron hadn't told them everything he knew. His story was that Lucy had somehow escaped, found out where he lived and followed him to the car park. Swanson had seen the camera footage from the car park before finding Summer. It was grainy and flickered, but it showed Aaron and Summer talking. It was like watching an old horror movie with no sound. He'd watched a flickering, grey Lucy crawling around a nearby car before creeping up to Summer with an object in her hand. She'd stood just behind Summer and whacked her so hard she fell like a sack of spuds.

Aaron had run over and knelt by Summer, but as there was no sound, they couldn't hear what was being said. After a minute or so of Aaron and Lucy speaking and waving their arms around at each other, Lucy began pointing in the direction of the storeroom. Aaron and Lucy then picked Summer up and walked off-camera. No cameras were pointing at the storage room, but it hadn't been too hard to find once they'd watched the footage. Aaron told them Lucy was living in the storage room and she said she had a first aid kit there. In his panic he hadn't thought that firstly, this was a lie because why would Lucy have a first aid kit? And secondly, it would be infinitely easier to bring the first aid kit to Summer rather than carry her dead weight all the way there. However, once they were there, as he laid Summer down, Lucy had taken the opportunity to knock him out as well. In his defence, he had clearly been whacked on the head with something pretty hard, though he'd refused hospital treatment. Neither Swanson nor Hart believed Aaron's reason for dragging Summer to the storage room. But they'd let him go home for now with a warning to stay away from both Summer and Lucy.

Swanson reached the station doors and noted that Hart was waiting for him on the other side. She caught his eye and raised an eyebrow. He nodded in return, signalling for her to come outside. He walked towards his car and jumped into the driver's side to start it up whilst he waited for her, and flicked on the heating to warm his icy hands. Hart joined him a minute later and he pulled out of the car park, headed for the custody suite.

"So, what do you think of her, then?" Hart asked, peering out the front passenger window. Rain began to drizzle down the glass, giving a distorted view of objects and people as they drove through town.

"I don't know. The whole situation is fucked up. It's pissing me off." Swanson's forehead was wrinkled in frustration. He'd had this feeling many times before, but this case was stranger than most. "I don't think it was her that called earlier this week. I think *she* called today, which is what she told me when I walked her out,"

"Then who has been calling? Lucy herself, maybe?"

"That's my bet. She wanted to communicate but maybe wasn't sure how."

"What gets me is the hospital not reporting her missing," Hart said.

"It's not that they didn't report it. They didn't admit it. I spoke to them myself. That doctor said he didn't *have* any patients called Lucy. Now that's weird."

Hart nodded her head in agreement, but they both fell silent, lost in their thoughts. They pulled up at the custody suite soon after and hurried inside to get out of the now pouring rain. A few minutes later, they were sitting outside the interview room waiting for an officer to bring Lucy to them and introduce them. With Lucy being ill, they had to tread carefully. The door banged shut as another officer walked through and approached them.

"Hi, guys. You're not speaking to Lucy tonight, I'm afraid. We're still trying to contact her doctor to get the medication she needs, and she has no legal support yet or an appropriate adult."

"Can we not get someone in as an emergency?" Swanson asked.

The officer shrugged. "It won't make a difference until we can get her meds."

Hart gave the officer a foul look as if it were his fault. The officer stared steadily back at her.

"Fine," Swanson muttered as he turned to leave.

"Where next?" Hart asked as they walked out of the custody suite. "The doctor?"

Swanson thought for a moment as he stood at the top of the steps where the rain couldn't reach them thanks to a roof overhang. Then he remembered the other event that didn't add up.

"The friend," he said.

Hart cocked her head for a moment before realising what he meant. "The friend who drove to the mum's house before calling the police?" She smiled.

Swanson nodded. "Yep, that friend. Let's see what she has to say about not calling the police straight away."

Summer

I sat in my mum's kitchen with my stiff fingers gripping a hot cup of sweet tea. It was disgusting, but it was helping with the shaking. The heat seared through my hands, and I was starting to feel them again. For the first time since Dad had died, I was comforted by being in my mum's environment. I felt safe with the scribbled drawings on the fridge, the rickety chair I was sitting in, and even the pictures of my brothers and me dotting the walls. Joshua would be back soon, and I couldn't wait. Mum had taken him to the park, but they were due to return at any minute. Lucy was locked away. Whether she was in the police station or the hospital, I didn't know, but I knew someone had incarcerated her somewhere, and she couldn't get to us. *So who'd been watching me at the hospital?*

I texted Kelly to confirm I was fine and would call her soon. I'd had thirty-three missed calls from her in her panic to find me. Lucy's marred face still played in my mind. She had been so desperate for me to help her, and I *wanted* to help her. I hated the thought of her going back to Dr Rears. If I was honest, it wasn't Lucy's desperate plea that convinced me she wasn't lying. I hated to admit it, but Hart was right when she said unfounded accusations happened all the time. It was Dr Rears himself. It was the way he drew his eyes over the younger female patients. The way he taught staff to have an *us* and *them* attitude. The simple way he had lied about Lucy not even existing. He was a liar and a pervert, so it wasn't a huge jump to believe Lucy when she called him an abuser. I made a promise to Lucy to help her, and I meant it. I also needed to know who was following me if it wasn't Lucy. To figure that out, I had to concentrate on helping Lucy. If I could get that part of the puzzle, then the rest would fit together. I hoped, anyway. It was all I could think to do and certainly beat doing nothing.

I'd borrowed a plain beige jumper from my mum's clean washing pile on the couch. I hadn't wanted Joshua to see the blood on my top. It was barely a few spots, but it was enough to be noticeable. I'd carefully washed my neck first, but there was nothing I could do about the padded bandage above my right ear. As long as he could see I was okay, he shouldn't be too startled by it. I'd tell him I'd simply fallen. Five minutes later, I heard the jangle of keys as Mum opened the front door. I stood, ready to show Joshua I was definitely okay despite the bandage. I heard his footsteps running into the entrance hall. He must have shoved past my mum as he came running through the door like a freight train. He wrapped his tiny arms around my waist as tight as he could. I held him as close as possible without cutting off his oxygen supply and kissed his head. I felt whole again with him in my arms. I was so focused on Joshua that I didn't notice my mum. To my shock, she was hot on his heels to embrace me. She didn't wait for a response but wrapped her arms around both of us. She sniffled, and I felt her tears on my cheek. I swallowed and bit back my own tears. I couldn't remember the last time I'd hugged her. If she had tried last week, I might have run away. But now I didn't want her to let go.

Joshua laughed. "Group hug!" he shouted, making both Mum and I laugh along with him. Tears still threatened to escape, so I stood up straight to release their grip and gather myself.

"I guess you both missed me then!" I looked at my mum. Tears were flowing down her cheeks. She smiled at me before walking out into the corridor. I assumed to collect herself so Joshua wouldn't see her tears. I felt an urge to follow her but turned my attention back to Joshua instead. He needed me more.

"Yes! I missed you a million gazillion times!" he shouted up at me with his skinny arms still locked around my waist. "I missed you more than you missed me!"

Everything was a competition with this kid. I laughed again. I'd missed him trying to outdo me.

"Not possible," I told him and squeezed my arms around him again. When I let go, he finally released me. I sat back down, and he kept a hand on my leg. I wasn't going anywhere if he could help it.

"How was the park?" I asked.

"Great! Mamma went down the slide and got stuck!" He laughed, showing his gappy smile, where his front tooth had fallen out a few days ago.

"Oh, I'd better check on her!" I said, squeezing his hand as I stood again. "Go into the lounge and put some TV on."

He eyed me carefully. "Okay. I'll be right there." He pointed at the couch. "Don't go anywhere?"

I smiled and reassured him I wasn't going anywhere. It seemed to help as he skipped away to put on his current favourite show about dinosaurs. I wandered tentatively into the hallway in search of Mum. She was leaving the downstairs toilet as I entered the corridor. Her face looked fresh now, and I wondered if maybe I'd imagined the tears. I hadn't imagined the hug, though. I smiled at her.

"Are you okay, Mum?" I asked, not sure what else to say. She grimaced and looked as though she might break down again.

"Oh, Summer. I'm so glad you're okay. I was so scared when that lady came round to say you were missing."

"It's okay, Mum. It was an escaped patient from work. She wasn't actually trying to hurt me. She wanted my help."

"You need to stop working with these people. You need to work somewhere safer. Mandy said there's a job going at the old folks' home. You could look after them instead. It's basically the same thing."

"I'm fine, Mum." I tried again, but she continued.

"You don't have to do it, though, Summer. You don't owe Eddie anything." She let her words hang in the air. Her face fell as though she was scared she'd said the wrong thing and made me angry.

"I know," it was all I could manage to say. We hadn't spoken about Eddie since I had failed to find him or Marinda over a decade ago. Mum had wanted me to stay away, so that conversation hadn't ended well. I did not want to argue with her right now. It was the closest we'd been in a long time and, after today, I felt a desire to protect her.

"Who told you I was missing?" I changed the subject instead. "DI Hart? That was quick. They found me within an hour, and Hart was with the police officers."

"Er, no. Your friend came round," she said. She looked away now, busying herself with organising the windowsill full of random knick knacks, including a nodding dog, an old silver clock, and some random papers.

"Do you mean Kelly?" I tried again.

"No, Kelly rang me later though through Facebook. It was your friend with black hair, tied up in a ponytail. She was about your height, a bit older than you, though."

Fear shot through me like I'd never felt before. There were two women I could think of with black hair. One was incarcerated. The other was following me, and now she knew where Joshua was.

Summer

There's a certain mode I always go into when Joshua is in danger. Like the time he fell from a ten-foot climbing frame in a park. Or when he got lost for less than a minute on the beach in Spain. I referred to it as *Mum Mode*. I never was any good at naming feelings despite my background. I didn't know if it was something that happened to all parents or not. There was no panic or fretting involved, as you'd probably expect from a distressed parent. It was a fear-driven sense of urgency, and business-like. I knew if I panicked, I wouldn't make good decisions, so I stayed terrifyingly calm. Every possible scenario and resolution flew through my mind in seconds. And I knew in less than a minute what I had to do.

For the first time since we had broken up, I called Richard and told him I needed his support. I explained what had happened with Lucy and asked him to have Joshua. I was unsure if Lucy was in custody and thought Joshua would be best off staying with him for the night while I sorted the situation. To my relief, he agreed instantly. Mum went to stay with my aunt, which she did at least once a fortnight, anyway. Again I didn't tell her the full story, and instead told her I thought that the girl who had visited claiming to be my friend was the patient's friend. She'd argued that I should go with her but eventually agreed to let me sort it. I barely listened to her as I helped her pack and waited for my aunt to arrive.

Joshua was even less impressed he couldn't go home with me but was excited to spend an extra night with his dad. I told him I needed to rest my head and would be back for him tomorrow, which he seemed to accept. I knelt at my mum's living room window, resting my knees on the frayed carpet. I peered through the glass, searching for any signs of the stranger with black hair. Mum had already gone and left me a spare key to lock up her front door.

It would be hard for anyone to hide on the quiet street outside. It was a narrow road with many semi-detached red-brick houses, and each had a short driveway, so there were few cars parked on the road. I had even parked my own car on Mum's drive today, wanting to be as close to the front door as possible. It was early evening so the sun had set, and the dull light of the street lamps was all I had to pick out a figure creeping in the darkness. I waited and watched for a few minutes, but I didn't see anyone. Joshua still sat on the sofa watching telly and ignoring my strange behaviour.

I casually walked outside under the pretence of vaping and wandered out past the drive to the tarmac pathway to look around. I had a hammer up the sleeve of the winter coat I'd borrowed from Mum. Luckily, she was a size bigger than me, so there was plenty of room to fit the weapon in without it looking obvious. The street was still quiet, the brisk autumn winds keeping most people in the warmth of their homes. It was then or never. I had to risk it. I hurried back inside and told Joshua it was time to go. We walked back to the car together, holding hands. He chuntered excitedly as he clambered into the car.

"Mummy, did you know twelve times twelve is one hundred and forty-four? And that plants give out oxygen? They breathe in carbon dioxide and breathe out oxygen!" He dramatically breathed in and out as he spoke to show me what plants did. Then he grinned into the rear-view mirror, awaiting my appreciation of his newfound intelligence.

"Wow! That's amazing, baby. You're so clever." I smiled into the mirror as I made sure our doors were locked.

"I'm at Daddy's for *one* night though, right, Mummy? Then your head will be better?" His voice was full of concern.

"I think so, baby, yes." I didn't want to promise, but if all went to plan, it would all be over tomorrow.

Once he had clipped himself in, I took another look up and down the dark street. I still couldn't see anyone lurking, so I kicked the engine into gear and set off on the short drive to Richard's house. I kept expecting someone to jump out from behind a lamp post or driveway. Richard's house was five minutes from my mum's, but I kept my eye out for any cars that seemed to be going in the same direction. To my relief, the roads were quiet. A red car sat behind me for a couple of turns, but it pulled off not long before Richard's turn. There were no cars behind me when I turned into his street. I pulled up to the house and decided to get out and walk Joshua to the door instead of phoning Richard. I wanted to make sure no one was lurking around and watching us. Richard looked surprised to see me at the door with Joshua. I didn't blame him, seeing as I normally stayed in the car.

"Hey, you okay?" His voice was strained, as though he felt more awkward than usual.

"I'm fine." I was getting sick of saying that.

"Hi, Daddy. Bye, Mummy. Love you more." Joshua gave me a big squeeze before he ran past his dad and into the house.

"He's had chicken nuggets for tea and been to the park, so should be fairly tired," I told Richard. "I'll get him tomorrow at dinner time if you're okay to pick him up from school, please?"

"Yeah, that's fine. See you tomorrow."

"Bye." I gave an awkward half-smile and turned to walk back to my car.

"Summer?" Richard called after me. I turned back around. He stared at me, seemingly forgetting what he was going to say. "If you need anything, call me." He finally blurted out.

I didn't bother pointing out that I had already called him for help. I got what he was saying. As much as I appreciated the gesture, I couldn't help a gremlin of annoyance flaring up within me. I didn't want Richard to think I needed him. I didn't need him. Joshua did. There was a difference.

"Will do," I said as I continued to walk away.

Back in the car, I wondered where to go. *Did I go home? Was it safe?* I thought about calling Kelly, but I didn't want to drag her into the situation any further. If I was not safe, then surely anyone around me wasn't safe, either. I took out my phone and looked online. There was a hotel down the road from me at forty quid for the night. I booked it immediately and drove right there, stopping off at the supermarket on the way for clean underwear and a cheap outfit. It would all be over tomorrow. As long as I followed the plan.

Summer

I awoke to a deep nagging pain above my right ear the next morning, courtesy of the previous day's attack. I grimaced as I carefully opened my eyes. Unfamiliar, white-washed walls enveloped me. They looked exactly like the walls on the Bluebell Ward. Panic grabbed at me as I sat up in bed and threw off the covers. *Had they carted me off to the ward?*

But as the rest of my surroundings gradually registered—the desk phone on the bedside table, the flatscreen TV on the wall, the bright purple armchair in the room's corner—the memory of checking into the hotel came back to me. I had spent so little time in the room before falling into a deep sleep. I wasn't sure if it was from exhaustion or the bang to the head, but it was the best night's sleep I'd had since last week.

An uneasy feeling overcame me as I remembered what I had to do that day. I grabbed my phone from under my pillow to text Richard, wanting to make sure Joshua was okay before anything else. I held my fingerprint on the lock screen to wake it up and saw I had three missed calls from Aaron. I glared at the phone and tutted, as if Aaron could see my reaction. I ignored his calls and sent the text to Richard. I had things to do and needed to get to work. I needed to shower and get ready to pretend everything was normal.

I had managed to wash the blood out of my hair last night before collapsing on the bed. So I tied it into a tight bun to shower, I pulled on the new khaki trousers and light grey blouse I'd purchased the night before, and slipped on my thick-heeled black ankle boots, grateful I'd had them with me. They were easy to run in and would be great for kicking someone should I need to. Again I added some makeup, just a bit of what I kept in my handbag. Foundation, blusher, mascara, and lip gloss before finishing with a spritz of perfume. I didn't remember ever putting perfume in my bag but was glad it was there.

I grabbed my laptop bag and keys before striding out of the hotel room and down the three flights of stairs. I ignored the elevator. They were horrible, claustrophobic things. It was barely 8 AM, yet the hotel was busy. Mostly with people in business-type suits waiting for breakfast or their taxis. Nobody paid much attention to me as I dropped my hotel room key into the check-out box and made my way through the exit. Icy air slapped my face as I strode confidently to the car. I'd parked as close to the entrance doors as I could get. I picked up my pace with each step, eager for the day to be over. Today was the day I would get evidence for Lucy and make sure Joshua was safe.

I slid into the front seat of the car, slamming and locking the door behind me. Anxiety had begun to manifest as a dense pit of nausea at the bottom of my stomach. I breathed in deeply until I could inhale no more and held my breath for ten seconds before releasing. My patients found it useful when they were stressed, and I could see why. I will do this for Lucy and for Joshua, I told myself as I repeated the breathing exercise. I clicked the seatbelt and put the car in gear, manoeuvring out of the car park and down the dual carriageway to the hospital. Once on the road, my anxiety was replaced by determination.

The characterless brickwork of the hospital came into sight not long after I took the exit from the dual carriageway. I swung into the car park and reversed into a spot in the far corner. I snuck into the back seat of my car. From there, the large entrance was in my eye line, but it was difficult for anyone to see me. My anxiety rose further with each passing minute as I sat, unmoving, for about half an hour. I forced it back down, using the same technique I'd used earlier. Doubt made me reconsider what I was doing. *Should I walk away? Should I call Swanson?*

A loud ringing startled me out of my thoughts. I looked at my phone

SUMMER

to see that Aaron was calling. I was wondering whether to answer when a noise made my head snap up. The familiar sound of Dr Rears's rambunctious laugh was close by. He had appeared by the entrance alongside a patient. My heart sank. It was sweet, anxiety-riddled Louise. *Was that how she had gotten him to agree to unsupervised leave? By promising to go somewhere with him?*

Louise was grinning from ear to ear, excitement radiating from her. A need to protect her overtook my anxiety. My maternal instinct reached out for her, and it was stronger than my fear. I climbed carefully back into the front seat, cursing the gear stick as I did so, and switched on the ignition. My phone had stopped ringing so I raised it to snap some pictures of Dr Rears and Louise together, trying to get the evidence Lucy and I needed. Dr Rears and Louise walked over to a new Audi parked right in front of the entrance. Dr Rears jumped into the driver's seat. I had expected Louise to join him, but to my surprise, she wandered off down the side path. It led off the hospital grounds and straight to the main road.

I had a split second to decide who to follow as Dr Rears pulled out of the car park. I knew Louise was safe if she wasn't with him, so I drove slowly after Dr Rears, staying well back. He turned right out of the car park, then right and right again onto the main road. The same way Louise had walked. He pulled off into a shop car park and unease hit me as I realised he was going to pick up Louise. She wasn't safe at all. I pulled over on the side of the road and waited. Sure enough, Louise came out of the shop a few seconds later and sat in the front passenger seat of the car. She was still beaming from ear to ear. Dr Rears must have promised her a nice day out. I felt sick at the thought of what he might do to her.

They left the car park, and I followed a few cars behind. Luckily, he didn't take many turns, so it was easy to keep up. We were in the busy city center, and there were lots of other cars to hide behind. The rain came back, which also made it harder for them to see me. I concentrated hard on his dark Audi for fear of losing them. Within a few minutes, he'd pulled onto the motorway. The unease grew deeper in my stomach as I realised they must be going to Edwinstowe. He was taking her to that creepy house. *How fucking dare he?* I prayed I was wrong, but they turned onto Coppice Court half an hour later. I didn't follow, choosing instead to park around the corner as I had before. I exited the car and stood behind a tree on the corner about two hundred feet away from them.

As she got out of the car, a look of uncertainty had replaced Louise's beaming smile. A furious rage bubbled within me which I pushed down. I didn't need unhelpful emotions right now. I needed to stay calm. I needed evidence. I snapped a couple of quick pictures of the two of them entering his house. I waited, checking the time continually on my phone. Two minutes passed. Then five. Then ten. It felt so much longer. Thoughts of what he might do to Louise agitated me, making my impatience grow.

After ten minutes, I strolled towards the property, searching up and down the street as I did so. Still, I saw no one, and the street was quiet. No cars drove down the potholed road. No feet walked the crumbled pavement. No one hid behind any cars. I took my chance and picked up pace to the house. I stooped and hurried up the drive, using the Audi for cover. It occurred to me that if anyone saw me, I would look ridiculous.

Once I reached the grimy front of the property, I peered through the grease-streaked window. I could make out the back of Louise as she climbed the stairs. I watched and waited. It wasn't much above freezing outside, but beads of sweat had gathered on my forehead. I couldn't stand at the window for too long for fear a neighbour would call the police, though I got the impression that the police were not so welcome on this particular street. I stepped to the front door and nudged down the handle. It wasn't a heavy door and easily clicked open. The cocky bastard hadn't even locked it. My phone was still in my hand, and I lifted it, pressing the record button. I wondered if what I was doing was illegal. I hadn't broken in, so I hoped it wasn't. The door groaned as it opened, and the stench of rotten food greeted me. I held my breath and pushed the thoughts about going to prison out of my mind.

Poised to run if I needed to, I stood at the threshold silently, and strained my ears for signs that one of them had heard me, that someone was coming to check the noise, but there were none. I could hear the low rumbling of a male voice upstairs, though the words were indiscernible. Louise's laughter floated down too. A voice told me to run. Had it not been for Joshua, I probably would have listened. Thinking of Joshua pushed my frozen legs forward into the hallway. The dark carpet underfoot allowed me to creep silently to the bottom of the stairwell. I left the front door wide open, though. I couldn't bear the thought of being closed in, not inside that house.

As slowly as possible, I crept up the stairs. I stopped at each step to check if the rumbling voices had stopped, ready to run if someone came to check the noises. They didn't. They were oblivious to my sneaking around. I reached the top and stood still, not daring to move. A narrow landing loomed in front of me. Tiny pinpricks of anxiety electrified my body, and the urge to run away was beginning to win.

There was an open door to my left and another further down the corridor. I quickly side-stepped through the closest door to catch my breath. I tried to remember the task at hand, but my head was spinning too much to think straight. I pushed the door partially closed and hid behind it, leaning my forehead against the wall, unsure what to do now that I was inside. I needed to catch Dr Rears in the act, or it would all be for nothing. I breathed in deeply, once again attempting to drown the anxiety that threatened to overtake me. It didn't work. I took my head away from the wall, needing to get out. I needed to run. But I realised as I turned to make my escape, that it was too late. Dr Rears was standing in the doorway, staring straight at me.

Summer

There was barely a metre between us. I tried to move back, but my limbs wouldn't listen. He didn't move, either. His eyes and mouth were wide open as he gawked back at me. Silence electrified the air between us.

"Hellooo?" A woman's voice cut through the silence, breaking the spell we both seemed to be under. I managed to step back and create more distance between us. He did the same as Louise appeared in the doorway. She put her arms around Dr Rears neck, but he shrugged her off and nodded his head in my direction.

"Look who we have here," he rasped at her as if it was hard to talk. Then he smiled, suddenly as cheerful as ever.

"Summer?" Louise looked over and spotted me standing at the back of the room with my phone still pointing at them. She grinned at me. "What are you doing here?"

I opened my mouth to speak, but no words would come. A stupid grin in her direction was all I could manage. I was stupid to have gone inside the house. My mouth was stuck together, too dry to operate properly. I looked around the small room. My vision focused better. An instinct to get back to Joshua took my panic over.

"Louise..." The word was barely audible, and I cleared my throat to try again. "Can you get me some water, please?"

Louise threw me a confused look at my strange request, but ambled off down the stairs without saying a word. She hadn't appeared scared of Dr Rears. I couldn't understand why not if he had been abusing patients, as

Lucy had suggested.

"Are you going to tell me what you are doing here, Summer?" Dr Rears looked at me smugly. "Breaking into my house?"

"I was going to ask you the same thing," I retorted. I couldn't believe the audacity that I could catch him with a patient alone in a random house, and he still made out like I was the one in the wrong. As if *he* was innocent. "This is not your house for one thing, and I saw you come in here from my friend's house. I saw Louise with you, and the front door was wide open, so there was no breaking in. If you'd like me to leave, I'd be happy to, but I caught it on camera." I raised my phone higher to make it clear I was still recording.

Dr Rears went pale, my words landing where I needed them to. He turned his back to me and stormed away. He'd turned left, so I knew he was still upstairs. I considered making a run for it. I listened with bated breath. I could hear clanging from the kitchen downstairs as Louise busied herself getting me some water, but nothing from wherever Dr Rears had gone. It occurred to me he might be fetching some sort of weapon.

"Hello? Yes, I'm at number twelve. I'll be back over in a minute. See you soon," I said loudly to nobody.

"Where are you going?" Louise appeared in the doorway, making my heart almost come through my chest. Jesus. I hadn't heard her coming.

"Oh, my friend is waiting for me." I quickly recovered.

She entered the room and passed me a tall glass of water. The glass was grubby as if it hadn't been washed for a while. I took it from her regardless and guzzled, the drum in my head subsiding.

"What's going on, Louise?" I whispered. Unsure now of where Dr Rears was and afraid of him coming back.

"Oh, this is Dr Rears' house." She was so blasé about the situation, not seeming to realise that what was happening was wrong. She beamed at me, her big brown eyes full of innocence despite the hardship she'd suffered at such a young age. This trip was an adventure for her.

"Okay, but why are you here, in this house?" I asked.

"Well, I'm on my leave, and you turned up!" She laughed loudly.

"Oh." I smiled at her. The haze in my mind was clearing now that Dr Rears was away from me. "I saw you guys from my friend's house and came round to say hi."

"Ohhhh." She nodded her head as if she now understood. Dr Rears appeared again at the doorway.

"Well, Summer, you shouldn't have walked into my house without permission." He sneered at me, once more his cocky self.

The haze reappeared, and I was unsure what to say at first. "Louise shouldn't be in your house," I blurted out and instantly regretted it. That wasn't my usual calm style of negotiation.

"No. She shouldn't be. And if you tell anyone, she will lose her leave," he warned, glancing over at Louise.

Louise's face dropped as he knew it would. "No, you can't tell anyone, Summer." Her eyes darted to me, full of panic and determination. I feared she would get angry with me if I caused her to lose her leave. Or self-harm, which was far more likely. I had to play along if I wanted her onside.

"Of course I won't tell!" I looked her straight in the eye. My mouth hung open as if in shock that she thought I was capable of telling on her.

"See?" A grin spread across her face as she turned to Dr Rears. "She won't tell. Summer helps me. She's my friend. We're okay."

Annoyance flashed across Dr Rears' face. He knew damn well I would tell as soon as I had the chance. Joshua flashed through my mind again. I needed to get away from this psycho.

"Go downstairs, Louise," he commanded.

Louise faltered and looked at me. I smiled and nodded, not wanting her to be caught in any crossfire. She turned back and walked away, her steps echoing on the stairs. Before I knew it, Dr Rears was in front of me, his face right in mine. His breath was shallow and tickled my face along with the stench of cigarettes.

"You couldn't leave it alone, could you, you silly girl!"

"Leave what alone?" The growl that came out of my mouth surprised me. My fear had evaporated, and every fibre in my body was on fire. I wanted him to attack me. I wanted a reason to lay into the son of a bitch, to snap my head back and headbutt him straight in the nose, to see him suffer.

"Never mind, you will pay now," he spat nastily.

I laughed. "What are you going to do to me? You're going to let me go anyway, so I'll walk myself out now. My friend is waiting for me outside."

To my surprise, his face changed. He laughed too, a deep rumbling laugh.

"Me? I will do nothing! You still don't get it, do you? I thought you were more clever than that, little Summer." He looked triumphant now, happy that he knew more than I did.

I squeezed my hand into a fist, digging my fingernails into my skin. It was taking all my energy not to lash out at him.

"No, it's not me! It's her!" he said.

"Who? Lucy?" I asked.

He laughed again. "For God's sake, child. Are you still bothered about Lucy? You're a mother, aren't you? A young boy?"

"Leave him out of this!" I roared in his face, spit landing on his nose. For the first time in my life, rage had overwhelmed me, and I was ready to kill.

"It's not what I would do! It's her, you stupid child! You need to think about your boy and leave this well alone. Do you understand?"

As much as I didn't want to admit it, his words brought me to my senses. What the hell was I doing about to pick a physical fight with a man twice my size and age?

"Fine!" I muttered. "I just want Joshua to be safe. Get out of my way and let me leave. I won't say anything."

He glared at me intently, his eyes inches away. My rage had subsided, but I glared back defiantly.

"You better," he finally whispered, "because if you don't, she will get your son too."

At Your Door

Summer didn't see me sitting in my car as she made her way to *my* house. I couldn't believe the cheek of her, the stupid fucking ugly bitch. White-hot rage pierced my skin, the familiar burn taking over. I fought the urge to run after her. I'd tried to warn her to stay away the last time she'd visited. I'd driven the car right at her. The memory of her running down the street, her arms flailing all over, made me laugh out loud. The burning cooled. The laughter was like medicine.

She thought she'd disappeared by hiding in that old cow's driveway, but I knew where she was. I let her live. It wasn't time. Yet here she was again, attempting to ruin my plan. I watched her open the front door and considered following her. Lucy tried to do the same thing by taking Summer away from me. Rage induced, I'd allowed my feelings to overcome my need to hold on to the plan. I broke my own rules and showed myself to that awful woman to get help to stop Lucy. I'd had no choice. Thankfully, she hadn't recognised me. She was always too drunk to notice me.

I won, though. Lucy was where she belonged, and I knew she wouldn't mention me. She was too scared that I wasn't real, and her own mind was fucking with her. I'd helped her along with that. A lingering burning remained, but I pushed it away. I couldn't follow her. It wasn't time. I needed to get Joshua first. I needed to get him whilst I still knew where he was. If she moved him and I couldn't find him, then he would no longer be mine. Someone else would take him once she was dead, his grandma or maybe his dad. The burning grew again. It started deep within my chest.

Joshua was mine. I couldn't bear the thought of someone else having him.

A thought occurred to me. If I took him, she would have to come to find him. And then I could kill her and keep Joshua easily. If they both disappeared, everyone would assume she took him away. Everyone would know how evil she was. But as I was about to drive off to get Joshua, Summer raced out the front door. Her steps were unsteady, and she kept looking behind her. *What the hell did he do now?* I grabbed my phone to call the blithering idiot doctor. I was going to have him for this. Him and that stupid patient he was fucking.

Summer

I stood for a moment, unable to move my frozen muscles. Mistrust made me slow. I couldn't tell if he was letting me leave or if it was some kind of trick. I forced my legs forward. It felt as though I was wading through thick mud. But he let me walk straight by him and out of the bedroom door. I stumbled downstairs, gripping the bannister, and searching for Louise, but I didn't see or hear her.

"I'm going now, Louise," I yelled but did not wait around for an answer. The urge to run was too strong.

I ran through the open front door and straight around the corner to jump into my car. My hands shook violently. I sat in the driver's seat cursing, wondering what to do about Louise, who I'd left behind with a supposed abuser. I started the engine first. There was no way I could think straight until I felt safe, and being able to make a quick getaway calmed me. I needed to help Louise, and I had to get back to Joshua, but I sat frozen in limbo. I was so sure coming here would give me answers, but instead I had more questions. I still needed to know who the hell *she* was. Then I remembered Mrs Timpson, and an idea formed in my mind. Not taking the time to think it through, I used my mobile to make a call and then got back out of the car. I half walked, half jogged to number 8, looking around me at all times. I didn't want Dr Rears or Louise to spot me still lurking around. Before I'd even reached her door, Mrs Timpson had opened it and stood beckoning me in.

"Hello, dear!" She seemed happy to see me.

"Hi!" I replied with a big smile to hide my agitation. "I was in the area, and I wanted to say thanks for the other day."

"Oh, no problem, love. Do you want to come in for a cup of tea? Oh, wait," she furrowed her brow, "a glass of water, maybe?"

"Ooh, yes, please." I feigned surprise that she'd ask me, despite knowing she would.

I once again walked into the living room, but this time I took a seat near the window amongst the plethora of clocks. Mrs Timpson took her time bringing the drinks. I assumed she was making a cup of tea for herself. All the while, I sat and stared at number 12. Nobody had left yet. I prayed they wouldn't. Not yet.

"Here you go, dear." Mrs Timpson returned with a glass of water for me. "Have you been feeling better?"

"Yes, thank you." I smiled and sipped my water, grateful my hands had stopped shaking. She eyed me suspiciously as if trying to decide whether I was indeed better. I must have still looked pale. "Better than I was, anyway." I tried to make my lie more believable. She nodded, sufficiently convinced.

"Horrible thing, anxiety. Our Betty used to suffer terribly."

She continued to tell me about Betty as if I knew who she was talking about. Despite the seriousness of the present situation across the road, I inwardly smiled. She was the perfect stereotype of a sweet, elderly lady. Though I didn't remember my own grandma, I'd always imagined her to be like this Mrs Timpson. I nodded and smiled for about ten minutes through her monologue about various people I'd never heard of, keeping one eye on the window at all times. I struggled to keep up with her, impatience pulling my attention away. Still, nothing happened at number 12.

The sharp noise of the house phone ringing made me jump. I laughed to make light of my nerves. Mrs Timpson threw me a sympathetic smile and patted my shoulder before picking up the house phone, explaining that she was waiting on her son to call. She wandered off into the kitchen to talk to the person on the line. It amazed me she had a phone modern enough to be wireless.

"Hello? Is that you, love? Speak up. You're talking too quietly," she said to who I assumed was her son as she walked away.

I stood up under the pretence of stretching my legs and turned my full attention to number 12 through the window, willing something to happen. And finally, it did. The noise was faint at first, and I strained my ears to make sure I hadn't imagined it. As the seconds passed, it gradually got louder. I noticed a car down the road pull away suddenly as if spooked by the noise. Eventually, the sirens were unmistakable, and two police cars came into view. They pulled up outside number 12. Two officers jumped out of each car, three men and one woman. I sat back down so they couldn't see me watching. One man approached the door and knocked loudly whilst another looked through the window. The woman and the other man stayed well away. Their heads were bent back, looking at the upper floor windows for any signs of movement. I didn't recognise any of them from the previous day.

I'd expected to be nervous, but the electricity running through my veins was pure excitement. He was going to be caught, Louise was going to be safe, and so were Lucy and all the other patients.

Dr Rears answered in less than a minute. The officer who had been looking through the window joined his colleague to talk to Dr Rears, and the pair went inside with him. I had an itch to join them, to tell them what I knew, though I'd placed the call anonymously. I heard footsteps behind me. Mrs Timpson had returned from her phone call.

"Ooh, I thought I heard sirens. What's happening over there?" The drama immediately excited her.

"I'm not sure!" I lied, feigning the same interest she displayed. "Let's take a look, shall we?"

We both stood at the window. I didn't think anyone could see me, but I stayed back a bit. Fifteen minutes went past with Mrs Timpson concocting many potential scenarios. Maybe someone was hurt, maybe the doctor had been robbed, maybe he was involved with fraud. I marvelled at her creativity. I tried to ignore her for a moment as I noticed Louise leaving the house with one of the police officers. Her eyes were wide with fear. She slowly entered the back of one of the police cars, and after a couple of minutes, it drove off. I hoped they would take her straight back to the hospital and not the police station.

Five minutes later, Dr Rears left the property with the other officers. Annoyance flew through me as I saw he was not in handcuffs. *Surely he needed to be arrested straight away?* He climbed into the back of the police car by himself. I could imagine the charm offensive he was unleashing on the way to the station. I breathed a sigh of relief. Today did not go to plan, but I was one step closer to Joshua and I being safe. It was time for stage two.

Summer

It was afternoon by the time I left Coppice Court. The nerves stayed with me as I drove, and I made sure to keep an eye on all cars around me. I was positive I wasn't being followed. It was lunchtime and hunger cramps gripped my empty stomach. I visited the motorway services on the way home to order some food. The excitement of the morning had given me a tremendous appetite.

People milled in and out of the service station in a steady flow. Families dawdled inside chatting to each other, probably on their way to somewhere exciting. Business travellers ate alone or rushed around as if they were too important to smile or make room for other people. I didn't seem to fit in with any of them as I made my way to the fast-food outlet to order a burger and chips. I sat alone at a table in the corner with my back to the wall, where I could see all angles.

The burger and chips were delicious. I managed half of the meal before I couldn't wait any longer. I had to make the second call. The one I'd been putting off. I made my way back through the service station to the peace and quiet of my car. Once in the driver's seat, doors locked, I took out my phone and scrolled to the top of my contacts list to find Aaron's number. The phone kept ringing until it went to his voicemail. I rang again, but still no answer. I threw my phone to the side in annoyance. I'd expected him to be waiting for my call. I considered calling Swanson. He had said to call if I needed anything, I wanted to know what was happening with Dr Rears, what Lucy had told the police, and what Aaron had said. If I could get more information, I could figure out who had been following me. That was stage two of my plan. Swanson was probably too clever to let anything slip, but it was worth a try. I had nothing to lose by calling.

Butterflies took flight in my stomach as I found Swanson's card in my glove box and entered his number into the keypad. I paused before connecting the call, trying to figure out what to say to him, but nothing came to mind. Fuck it. I'd wing it. The phone rang long enough for me to consider hanging up before Swanson's deep voice finally answered.

"DI Swanson speaking."

Shit. Why did I think I'd wing it?

"Hi, DI Swanson." I used my best business voice to speak to him. The same sharp tone I sometimes used with hospital social workers or lawyers if they didn't give me what I needed to assist a patient. "It's Summer Thomas."

He paused before answering. I wondered what was going through his head. *Was he happy to hear from me?*

"How can I help, Miss Thomas?"

"I wanted to see if you had any further questions for me." The words came out without thinking. Thank God I'd actually found something to say.

"Yes, we do. I'm in the station right now if you'd like to come down?"

"Yes, okay." I could ask him about Aaron and Dr Rears while I was there. I could gauge his reaction better face to face. It's harder to say no to someone in person, though I doubted it would make a difference to the seasoned detective. We said our goodbyes before I pulled away from the service station and back onto the motorway. Twenty minutes later, I was walking into the cool reception area of the police station. I hadn't realised yesterday how modern it was, but I noticed it this time. The area had the smell of fresh paint. The walls were a cold blue colour, broken by random blocks of white. Fresh posters about crime rates and support groups dotted the walls, and a long counter took up the whole left side of the room. All the receptionists were behind thick safety glass.

I tentatively strolled up to one receptionist and told her I was there to see DI Swanson. She smiled at me and told me to take a seat to the right.

She was the kind of jolly person who was instantly likable. Life must be much easier if you have that kind of ease around people. I'd probably be a better advocate if I was, and Joshua might still have a proper family. I was so lost in my thoughts that I was surprised when Swanson appeared before me after a minute or two. I briefly wondered if he was eager to see me. After saying an awkward hello, he led me into a room similar to the one we were in the previous day. I was glad to note that the rude DI Hart was nowhere to be seen.

"So, Miss Thomas, shall we continue our previous conversation?" Swanson asked.

"Call me Summer." I smiled. *Was I flirting?* I stopped smiling. "And before we do so, can I ask if Aaron is still in custody?"

"Without your full statement, we had little to charge him with. So he was released yesterday with strict instructions not to contact you." He tried to smile reassuringly, but it looked more akin to a grimace.

"Right. And what did he tell you?" I asked.

"How about I ask some questions first, and then we'll go over what other people have said?"

I sighed, but nodded my agreement.

"So start from how you know Aaron, please."

"From work. Well, actually, I used to know him a few years ago when we were both at university. He was a friend of a friend. I didn't know him too well."

I stopped and studied the foreboding figure before me. His serious brown eyes stared down at his notepad. His large hand made the pen look tiny as he scribbled notes. He gave off the impression that he could protect anyone from anything. I tried to stick to the plan, to work alone and find out the truth. Yet, for some inexplicable reason, a powerful urge to tell him the truth overtook me. Before I knew it, I had told him much more than I'd planned. I told him everything I knew. All about Lucy, except for my dream. All about Aaron, except for the sex. I told him all I knew about Dr Rears, apart from my earlier visit, and that I believed Lucy when she accused him of abuse. Someone had helped her to escape, and it must have been someone on the inside. It had to be someone who wanted something from her in return for getting out. He raised his eyebrows at some parts but didn't interrupt me once. He allowed me to keep talking, and the more I talked, the harder it was to stop. It was like verbal diarrhoea.

"There's the other woman, too," I said tentatively after I'd finished discussing Dr Rears and his misdeeds. "I keep seeing her everywhere. I thought Lucy was following me, but she can't be now. She's back in the hospital, and I still saw the woman yesterday at the emergency room."

His head shot up at these words, and I looked away from his gaze. That was the part that concerned me the most, where he would accuse me of being crazy, of seeing things.

"Has anyone else seen this woman?" he asked his first question since the onslaught of my verbal diarrhoea.

"Aaron was with me once, outside a cafe near my flat, but he denied seeing her." I noticed his eyebrow raise. "But my mum has seen her," I added. "She went to my mum's house yesterday to tell her I had been taken. She must have seen it happen. So she must have been following me then, too." I remembered the bang at my flat door. Had that been her? Was she trying to scare me?

My face flushed as he continued to look at me. Tears stung the corner of my eyes, threatening to flow any second. I blinked them back. I hadn't confided in anyone for so long.

"I was scared she was after my son. He's six. I sent him to his dad's last night." I shrugged. "I don't know what she wants, but I don't think it's a friendly stalker. It's the way she looks at me. She could have been the person calling you, trying to make me look crazy."

"Okay," he said, "here's what I'm going to do. I'm going to interview Dr Rears and find out about this mystery woman. Then I'm going to call you and update you. Okay? I'm going to help make sure you're safe, Miss Thomas."

I smiled gratefully at him, though I was irked that he didn't call me Summer. My small smile wasn't enough to convey the appreciation I felt, but it was all I could manage. Exhaustion had hit me worse than the blow Lucy had given me yesterday. "What do I do now, though? Wait?" I asked.

"Yes." He replied in an authoritative manner which half made me want to argue with him. I had never been good with authority. "Go home, sit, and wait. My job is to help you, and that's what I'm going to do. No sneaking around by yourself, okay?"

I thanked him, and he walked me back to the reception area. Before walking away, he told me again to sit at home and wait for his call. I think he knew I would not listen. I would go home, but I would not sit and wait. This woman knew where I lived. Where Joshua lived, and I couldn't bear to be apart from him any longer.

I made a plan on the short drive back to my flat. I would make sure Mum knew to continue to stay with her sister, and I would collect some things for Joshua and me. I was already off work for the week, and he could pull a sickie from school. We would go to a hotel, but not the one down the road. We'd go away on a holiday, alone. The way we worked best. I planned for all the items we would need as I walked from the flat car park and through the front door of my building. We would need a phone charger, Joshua's tablet, some books, clothes—but my planning was cut short when I reached my flat and found my front door wide open. Someone was inside my flat.

Summer

The familiar anxiety prickled at my body. I slowly backed away, as if the door itself would attack me if it heard me moving. I reached the corridor door and yanked it open. My footsteps echoed loudly as I ran down the marble staircase and out into the fierce October wind. I didn't stop until I got to my car, jumped in and locked it. I started the engine, but I wasn't sure where to go. I grabbed my phone with shaking hands. It took me a few tries to unlock the screen with my thumbprint.

I had four missed calls from Aaron. Was it him in my flat? Trying to make sure I was okay? I hadn't spoken to him since the complete debacle with Lucy. Maybe he was worried enough to break in. I called him back, desperately hoping I was right despite the unlikeliness of it being true.

"Summer?" Aaron answered on the second ring.

"Yes, it's me. What the hell has been going on, Aaron?"

"Look, it got out of hand, okay. I didn't think she was going to hurt you! She's so paranoid. And I'm in a bit of a situation—"

"You are?! I've been knocked out, kidnapped, tied up, caught trespassing, and now someone's broken into my flat!"

"What?? Are you there now? Are you safe?"

"I didn't go inside. I'm out in the car park now. I was kind of hoping it was you. If not, I'm going to call the police."

"What? Why would I break into your flat?"

"I don't know what you're capable of after yesterday."

"She hit me too, Summer. Knocked me clean out, and when I woke, she'd tied you up. I'd never hurt you. Look, don't call the police. I won't be able to come help then, they've told me to stay away from you, but I need to see you. I need to tell you some things."

"Oh, I wonder why they've said to stay away from me?" I rolled my eyes, even though he couldn't see me.

"Okay. I deserved that. Now sit in your car and be ready to drive off if you see her. She's dangerous."

"If I see who?" I demanded, sick of not being told the full story.

"I'll be there in five minutes." He hung up. I cursed him loudly, despite being alone.

I sat in my car, waiting and looking for any signs of the mystery figure. Whoever she was, she scared grown men half to death. It was nearing dinner time, and the sky was changing to a dark blue. It was going to be a night sky soon, and I prayed for Aaron to hurry. I did not want to be sneaking around in the dark. I wanted to get our things, get Joshua, and get the hell away from Derby while Swanson did his job. True to his word, I spotted a tall figure darting towards the car park after a few minutes. I waited until he was a hundred feet away before getting out of my car to greet him.

"Hi," he said breathlessly as he reached me, his face blotchy and sweaty.

"Hi." I was curt with him, still angry from the danger he had put me in the day before.

"Look, give me your keys and stay in your car. I'll check it out for you," he said after a few seconds of trying to get his breath back.

"No! I'm coming with you." I knew I was being stubborn. A part of me would have preferred to pass him the keys and stay away, but I was already embarrassed that I wanted his help. I couldn't take any further rescuing or indebtedness.

He motioned for me to get behind him, and we carefully walked to the front door. I passed him my keys and he let us in. There was no one in the grand entry hall. The chandelier loomed over us as we made our way up the staircase once again. Friday night's antics with Aaron came back to me as we walked, and I felt a pang of regret for the first time. We entered my corridor and made our way slowly to the flat door. It was closed. I looked up at Aaron, wondering if he was going to accuse me of making it up.

"It was wide open, I swear." I whispered, despite no one being around us. He nodded and put his finger to his lips.

I pointed at the right key for him to use, and he unlocked the door as slowly as he could. It was impressive how silently he managed it. I grappled with my urge to grab the keys from him and throw open the door. Still silent, he manoeuvred the handle down to open the door. It didn't squeak, but it rubbed noisily against the thick carpet. We stood looking in, listening to the silence. Nothing moved. Nobody jumped out at us. It looked completely normal. Aaron moved forwards to the entry hall and stood still to listen again. Still silent. I followed him into the hall. *Had I been seeing things? Was the door even open when I got back?*

As soon as we reached the lounge, my fears of hallucinations were silenced. My laptop lay on the floor, the screen smashed. Someone had thrown papers and books all over the room. They had taken pictures of Joshua and me from the wall and thrown them on the floor, shattered and unrecognisable.

At first glance, it looked like nothing had survived. The TV was cracked. The coffee table overturned. Tears stung my eyes, and I let them come. I didn't care if Aaron saw. I looked around for Joshua's things, wondering how I was going to afford to replace his tablet and all of his toys.

A small wave of relief washed over me as I remembered his tablet was with him. He'd brought it to Mum's and then to Richard's. That was the most expensive *toy* he had and his favourite item. Everything else I'd have to replace bit by bit. As I looked around to find his broken toys, I realised none of his toys or books had been thrown on the floor, but neither were they in the place they usually were. Panic gripped my stomach as if someone had punched it.

"We need to talk," Aaron said. I'd actually forgotten about him.

"Where the fuck are Joshua's things?!" I shouted at him. I didn't care at all about what he had to tell me. I cared about one thing.

"What?" Aaron looked at me with a confused expression.

"Joshua's toys, his books, they're not smashed on the floor. Where the fuck are they?"

His face changed as he realised the implications of what I was saying. I grabbed my phone out of my jeans pocket. My entire body was shaking, but I refused to lose my calm completely. I could not fail Joshua. I got Richard's number up and pressed dial.

"Hey, Summer. You on your way?" Richard's easygoing voice made me want to reach down the phone and slap him.

"Richard, is Joshua okay?" I yelled down the phone.

"What? Yes, he's fine. Why wouldn't he be?" He took a defensive tone.

"Look, can you see him right now? Is he with you?"

"Yes, he's eating his dinner." He sounded confused. "What's going on? Are you okay?"

"I think so, but someone has broken into the flat."

"Oh shit, have they taken anything?"

"Yes, Joshua's things. They've smashed all my stuff up."

Richard was silent then as he tried to take in what I was saying. "Why would they take a child's things?" he asked eventually, caution in his voice.

"I don't know for sure, but I feel like we need to go away, Richard, for a few nights on a little holiday. You don't mind, do you? I've told the police. They will catch whoever this is, and then we can come home."

"He could stay here," Richard suggested.

"He could, but I think he'd be happier on a holiday. It would be exciting for him. He won't know anything is wrong." I didn't say it out loud, but Joshua hated being away from me for more than a night or two, and he'd already been away since Friday. It would devastate him if I didn't spend tonight with him.

"Yeah, okay," Richard agreed. "I won't tell him yet. When do you think you'll be over?"

"Well, I need to speak to the police, so it might be an hour or two," I said. "Can you look at last-minute hotels and B&Bs for us, please? Anywhere child-friendly. Maybe near a theme park or something, someplace far away."

"Okay, that's fine. Keep me updated." He hung up the phone.

"Summer, we need to talk." Aaron tried again to get my attention. I was ready now that I knew Joshua was safe.

"Yeah, we do," I spat angrily at him. "My child is in danger and no one will even tell me who from! Who the fuck is this mystery woman all of you grown-ass men are so scared of? Because I'm telling you now, if I get my hands on her, I will go down for fucking murder."

I shook with the same rage that had come close to winning me over at Dr Rears' house. I needed someone to blame for this mess, and Aaron was right in the firing line.

"Sit," Aaron ordered. "Let's talk."

"Tell me what to do one more time, Aaron, and I swear to God you will regret it. You fucking sit and tell me what's happening." I knew I sounded petulant, but I couldn't help it. The rage was winning. My instinct to protect Joshua was trumping any kind of fear or anxiety.

Aaron stood still. "Is Joshua at Richard's?" he asked.

I nodded. "Now answer my fucking question, Aaron. Who the hell is doing this?"

"Wait, we need to get somewhere safe. She could be back any minute."

"Who though, Aaron? You're not talking about Lucy, are you?" I waved my hands in the air. Aaron shook his head. "Then who? For fuck's sake, tell me who is doing this?"

For the first time that evening, I stood still and looked at Aaron. I noticed the fear in his eyes. Whoever this was had him spooked big time, like with Dr Rears. I knew I should be scared, too. I needed to calm down before I did something stupid, but every instinct I had was pushing me to defend Joshua. Before having a child, I never thought I could hurt anybody. But I'd known as soon as Joshua was born, I'd kill for him. I don't even think I'd even feel guilty.

Aaron appeared to be considering what to tell me, and I tried to reach the placid, gentle, collected me. The normal me. But anger had consumed that version of me with a rage born of maternal instinct. I was more dangerous than the average psychopathic murderer. Then, someone else appeared who I could aim that rage at, the same someone that scared all of these grown men. Someone who had never left the flat.

Summer

The figure stood in the doorway, blocking any exit from the lounge. Her black hair was scraped back into a ponytail. She wore dark trousers and a dark jumper. A large kitchen knife glinted in her hand. This was the same woman that had knocked on my mum's door and the one who had been following me. The monster that was a danger to Joshua. For once, she didn't hide or run away. She stood silently, her entire focus on me. A slow grin spread across her face, showing her yellow teeth. Her skin was patchy, not burnt like Lucy's, but she looked like a patchwork doll who had been stitched together with different fabrics. From afar, the two women certainly looked similar. It was seeing the skin close up that finally enabled me to recognise her. A gasp escaped me as I pieced together bits of what had been happening over the last few days.

"You?" It was all I could say at first. The woman before me laughed in such a deep voice it sounded like a growl.

"Yes, dumbass, it's me. Didn't even recognise me, did you? Walking around the ward, telling us all what to do, and being besties with the patients. Do you recognise me now, Summer?"

I nodded and felt my resolve harden. The shock had allowed my rage to subside. I was calmer, and I could think straight. If I could think of a plan, then I could get out of this without being hurt and without hurting anyone else. I recognised Emma now, the lead nurse from Bluebell Ward. The same Emma who had been off sick yesterday afternoon. In all my time on the ward, she had never looked me in the eye. She was always monitoring the patients, too busy to talk to me, or so I had thought. All that time, she had been keeping her distance so that I wouldn't recognise her. Her name wasn't Emma at all. She didn't even have blonde hair. It must have been an excellent wig.

"You…look well." I couldn't think of anything else to say. She had lost a lot of weight since I had last seen her, well before she became Emma. My response once again set off her deep laugh.

"Not that I need you to tell me, but yes, I look good. Your brother helped me along." She grinned again.

"What is going on, Marinda? Have you hurt somebody?" Using her actual name was a gamble. I was unsure if it would provoke or calm her. It didn't seem to do either.

"You have no clue what's going on, do you?" She rolled her eyes as if I was an idiot. "It's not me who hurts them. It's the good Dr Rears!" she said as if this was obvious to anyone with half a brain.

"Dr Rears let me go. He said it's you I have to watch. You're the dangerous one," I said with a shrug.

She lost her smile, her eyes flashing with anger. I'd never seen her like this. Marinda was always the calm one. She helped my brother as much as she could. They'd been together for an entire year before he attacked my mother. She was training to be a make-up artist so she could support them both after he lost his job. She used her make-up well on the ward. I hadn't had any inkling it was her.

"I'm not the one who hit you." She shrugged. "I went to get help."

"Why did you get help if you're so angry with me?"

"So I can hurt you now." She laughed. "I've been watching you and Joshua. I came here to get him. But he isn't here. Where is he?" She smiled again, knowing her words would rile me.

She was right, but I *knew* Marinda. Or at least I used to know her. I remembered watching her and my mum talk and laugh. Before Dad's death, Mum would help her with her skin in the summer when her pityriasis versicolor flared up around her left eye and cheek. A flaky skin condition that also caused discolouration. It was made worse by humid summer temperatures and Marinda had hyperhidrosis. After Dad died, she would take me to the shop and buy me sweets when Mum was comatose on the sofa. She looked after me the night Eddie lost his battle with the devil. I'd even tried looking for her once, whilst searching for Eddie. I couldn't fathom why she would hate me.

"Why are you following me, Marinda?"

"Payback time." She cocked her head to the side and watched my reaction, still grinning at me.

"Payback for what?"

"For what?" She mocked my voice in a whiny tone. "You know what. You're the reason Eddie went away, and I was left alone. Your statement put him in the hospital. Don't play mock innocent with me. You feel so guilty that you haven't even visited him once. You haven't even apologised to him! And all this time, he's been in that awful place, drugged up to the eyeballs for no reason. I've hated you ever since you opened your big fat mouth to the police. And then you walked on to the ward a few months ago like nothing had ever happened. Imagine my horror when I found out that while he is trapped in there, you've been swanning about pretending to care about patients! Thinking you're clever with your degrees and your supposed awards. I can see lies, remember? You are a *liar*."

Of course, Mum always thought Marinda had her own mental health issues because she could see colours when people spoke. Synesthesia is not a mental health concern, but Marinda interpreted these colours as truth or lies, good or evil. I remembered her telling me after Eddie had been taken away that his aura had changed to an evil colour since she met him. Red or black, I couldn't remember, but it had terrified me. I noticed Aaron moving slowly from the corner of the room. He was watching Marinda. She was completely focused on me. I couldn't tell if she knew he was in the room or not. She had surely seen him when she entered. I didn't look at him, keeping my gaze on Marinda.

"I didn't know where he was," I told her. I didn't feel guilty about what I'd done. I was a child. Eddie was ill, and he'd needed help. Something else she'd said had caught my attention, though. "What do you mean, drugged up for no reason? Eddie was severely ill."

She rolled her eyes. "What do you even know about Eddie's so-called illness?"

"Not much. He heard voices a lot. He saw the devil telling him to hurt people. Telling him to hurt Mum. I assumed he was a paranoid schizophrenic."

"Your mum was a pain in the neck, Summer. She was always pissed on vodka or gin. She even had the cheek to call *me* nuts once because of my gift! She tried to get Eddie to break up with me! But I saw through her. She was a waste of space. I wanted her gone *and* I wanted the house. It would have been my first, proper home." She waved her hands as she spoke.

"What do you mean?"

"The house would have gone to Eddie." She smirked at me.

"So what?"

"Soo... Eddie was mine. The house would have been mine. He didn't hear fucking voices. I needed him to see what your Mum was really like. She was the one who needed to go, not me."

"I don't understand?" My fight was leaving me as the repercussions of her words hit me. "He didn't hear voices. He lied? Is that what you mean?"

She shook her head slowly, a smirk still lined her face. "The only voice Eddie heard was mine."

"Bullshit," I snapped. "And if it is true, then you need to be in the fucking hospital."

"I'm not ill, Summer. I'm in charge of an entire ward of fucking nut jobs. How did I get there if I'm so ill? Your mum started it all. Plus I had fun pushing Eddie and seeing how far I could take it. It wasn't too hard, to be fair, thanks to Daddy dying. I wanted to see how far I could push him, and I wanted that house all to myself. I wanted Eddie all to myself. I would have stopped once your interfering bitch of a mother was out of our lives. And I nearly did it too. If it wasn't for you hiding under that fucking table and snitching up your own brother. You ruined it for me, Summer. I could have had that house, with Eddie doing everything I needed, maybe even our own family. My *first* proper family. But now your boy will have to do."

Her words made me feel sick. I couldn't listen to her anymore. I needed to change the subject and keep her distracted so that Aaron could get to her.

"How did you get in here?" I tried talking about the physical acts she had accomplished to stop her from talking about my family.

"I've been in here a few times." She smirked. I bent over and heaved, unable to hold it in anymore. "I took your keys from your locker, had it copied in twenty minutes at a shop down the road."

"Have you been in here at night?" I remembered my dream.

"Yes." She smirked again. "I watched you as you slept. Then you suddenly screamed and jumped up like a fucking lunatic. I shut the door and ran off."

"What happened to Lucy? Did you help her escape?" I changed the subject again while I tried to regain some composure and ignore the bile in my throat.

"Oh, for God's sake, you always needed to know every little detail, didn't you? Yes, I took Lucy off the ward to be a good girl for Dr Rears. She wasn't supposed to fucking run off. I also told her that you'd said you didn't want to see her." She laughed.

"A good girl for Dr Rears?" I didn't want to know any more, but I had to keep her talking as Aaron inched his way over to her.

"Yes. Those stupid girls at the hospital are worthless," she spat. "I have my fun and then let them go. It's not like I've killed anybody."

"Your fun?"

"I just scare them a bit. They'll do anything for me. For their leave or to get out of that fucking hell hole of a hospital. Once we're at the house, they do what they're told. Or should do. Lucy was an idiot. She was supposed to clean up, and then she could have gone shopping. I never saw her again."

My brain was faltering from trying to process what Marinda was telling me. I couldn't focus. Nothing made sense.

"Jesus, Marinda. What do you mean, they do as they're told? What do you tell them to do?"

She smiled and leaned towards me. "Whatever the fuck I want from them." She emphasised each word as if she got a kick from it. "Aww, do you think I'm bad? You should see what I caught Rears doing last year! It was he who gave me the idea. He made me realise they would do whatever we wanted. I don't shout at them or beat them. They behave, and they continue to get leave. It's simple, really. They've all been through far worse!"

"What did you catch him doing?"

"Fucking!" She laughed again. "Fucking! Can you believe it? I knew he wasn't right, like you. I followed him all the way out to some field with Aaliyah. She was barely sixteen. I lost them down some country road and the next minute found them fucking. He had her bent over the bonnet, his lily-white arse sticking out!"

"So, instead of reporting him, you help him?" My stomach churned again.

"God, no. He begged and begged me not to say anything. He said he loved her, for fuck's sake. Pathetic. How could anyone love that? Anyway, that's when I realised we could work together. We could cover each other's backs. I had no interest in helping him. I wanted to see what the patients would do for leave. I don't have sex with them like he does. I'm not like that pervert."

"You don't sound much better." The words were out of my mouth before I could stop them.

"They look after me in other ways because I look after them. There's nothing wrong with it." She looked at me defiantly, clearly believing her own bullshit. "Everyone was pleased. Well, until you turned up and Lucy ran away. She wasn't even supposed to be on leave. I couldn't very well say she'd run out of the locked hospital, could I now? I couldn't admit I'd taken her out, regardless. What was I supposed to do?" She shrugged her shoulders.

"Why not call the police?"

"So Lucy could talk to them? If I lost Dr Rears, who would I have to help? The idiot is terrified that I will tell someone what I saw, what I know. He does everything I need, and I'd rather the police didn't take that away from me. Then you had to stick your nose in like you did with Eddie and that sold it. *You* have to go."

"You'd never have gotten away with it even if it wasn't for me. What about the other staff? Other patients?"

"The patients were easy enough to keep quiet. Tell them they were hallucinating the dead ghost of Lucy. They soon asked for more meds and shut the fuck up. Staff were harder, but luckily most are bank staff anyway, and I know how to keep the ones that aren't quiet. Don't I, Aaron?" She turned to look at Aaron, and alarm crossed her face.

Everything that happened next was a complete blur. Aaron ran towards her in an attempt to tackle her. Something shiny and silver flashed before I'd even moved to help him.

"No!" I screamed, but it was too late. The blade slid into Aaron's body. He looked winded and fell to the floor, gasping for breath.

"You next, bitch." Marinda barely flinched as she removed her knife from Aaron's gut. She rushed towards me. I turned to run, but she was coming from the only doorway. I was trapped.

Summer

"Summer?" A nervous call came from the hallway. I knew that voice.

"Kelly, run!" I yelled as loudly as I could, running to the other side of the lounge to get Marinda to follow me.

If she followed me away from the door, then I could make a run for it and get Aaron some help. Horror flooded me as Marinda turned and ran out into the corridor. She was heading straight for Kelly. I ran after her as fast as my legs would allow, yelling over and over for Kelly to run, dreading what I was about to find. Immense relief flooded me to see Kelly standing in the corridor alone, though she was white as a ghost.

"What the fuck, Summer? Who's the crazy bitch?" Kelly's mouth was wide open as she stared at me.

"Where is she?" I demanded.

"She ran out the door." Kelly shrugged and pointed over her shoulder.

"Look, I haven't got time to explain, but lock the door and call an ambulance." She still stared at me in confusion. "Kelly, now! Aaron's been stabbed," I said breathlessly.

I made sure she was moving to lock the door before I ran back to check on Aaron. He lay on his left side, gasping in short, quick breaths. Blood leaked from his shirt and covered his hands. I knelt next to him and took off my cardigan to bind the wound. My first aid training brimmed in my mind, recovery position, hold the wound, stop the bleeding. Aaron looked up at me, eyes wide with terror. He made a gurgling sound as he tried to form words.

"Shh, it will be okay." I tried to soothe him. "She's gone. The door is locked. We're safe. An ambulance is on its way. It will be here any minute."

"No," he mumbled, "my mum…Mum…"

I ached to hear him calling for his mum. His eyes closed.

"Aaron!" I said sharply. His eyes flickered back open to look at me. Kelly was next to me now, but I barely heard what she was saying. "You need to stay awake for me. Can you do that, Aaron? Can you stay awake for me? Your mum's on her way." I lied. "Stay with me, Aaron,"

I kept talking the whole time, rambling about going for a drink soon. About stupid memories of us as students. Anything to keep him awake. Kelly had gone outside to wait for the ambulance. She finally returned with two male paramedics five minutes later. Thank God they were so fast. By then, Aaron's skin reminded me of the wax models in London's museum, and his eyes had rolled to the back of his head.

"Hi, Aaron, I'm Ben. I'm going to help you, okay? I'm going to cut your top so I can reach the wound, then I'm going to give you some pain relief. Try to stay awake for us, Aaron." They talked constantly. I could finally step back and let them take over.

They got to work straight away, trying to give him gas and air, but he wasn't able to breathe it in. They injected something, but I couldn't tell if it was to clean the wound or give him pain relief. I didn't know how they could be so calm. They sealed the wound with all sorts of bandages and kept up a one-sided conversation with him while they worked.

I stood beside them, feeling helpless. Then I remembered Marinda. Where the hell had she run off to? *Was she looking for Joshua?* He'd be waiting for me at Richard's. Richard would think it was me knocking on the door, like I had the other day. I stepped into the kitchen and grabbed my phone to call Richard. He answered abruptly.

"Hey. Look, something has happened." I wasn't sure how to tell him.

"What now?" He didn't sound angry, more surprised.

"Well, it turned out the patient who hit me yesterday was running from someone else. It is the same someone who turned up at my flat today and smashed the stuff. I'm okay, but she's dangerous. I wanted to make sure she doesn't know where Joshua is. You haven't seen anyone, right?"

"No, nothing. Look, don't worry about Joshua. He's fine with me, and my brother is here, too. Make sure you're safe and then call me. Maybe stay at your mum's?"

Shit. My mum. I couldn't be sure if she was still at her sister's or back at home. Marinda knew where my mum lived. She hadn't moved house in thirty years. I didn't know if Marinda blamed Mum, too, but at least she hadn't hurt Mum or Joshua when she had the chance yesterday.

"Okay, I have to go." I hung up on Richard and dialled Mum's number. No answer. I called again and again, but she didn't pick up.

I felt eyes on me and looked up. Kelly was standing in the doorway, watching me. She was still paler than I'd ever seen her. "Who are you calling?" she asked.

"My mum. That crazy bitch knows where she lives. She isn't answering."

"Try calling your Aunt?" She suggested.

"I don't have her number saved." I tried one more time before pushing past Kelly to check on Aaron.

The paramedics were putting Aaron onto a stretcher. I couldn't believe he'd risked his life for me. "I'll see you at the hospital," I promised as they carried him away.

I looked back at Kelly. I'm going to my mum's. I need to make sure she's safe."

"I'm coming too. You can tell me what the fuck is going on while I drive." She took my keys out of my hand.

"Kelly, she's crazy! Stay here and tell the police where I've gone. They'll be here any minute."

"No fucking way. I'm coming too." She walked past me and waited for me in the communal hallway. I was secretly glad she was so stubborn.

We walked out together, side by side, but as she drove off, my heart sank. Maybe if I had opened up to someone else in the first place, Aaron wouldn't be on a hospital stretcher fighting for his life. Maybe this was all my fault. I prayed that Mum would be okay.

Summer

I called Mum's mobile multiple times on the drive over to her house, but there was still no answer. I was furious with her.

"Call the police. They'll be on their way to yours. We might as well tell them where we think she might be," Kelly said.

"Actually, I know who I can call." I checked the numbers I had called earlier that day and found the unsaved number that I knew must be Swanson's.

"DI Swanson." He finally answered after letting it ring.

"Hi, it's Summer Thomas. Look, I need help. That stalker has just stabbed Aaron, and I think I know where she's going next." I was far more blunt than usual, but my mind was racing. I'd never considered a life without Mum before. Joshua would be devastated. I had to make sure she was safe.

"Where?" was all he said. I gave him my mum's address.

"Don't go there. We will check on her for you. You go somewhere safe." He hung up before I had time to tell him I was nearly there.

Kelly glanced at me. "I'm still going," I said. She nodded.

It usually took twenty minutes to get to Mum's house. Kelly did it in twelve minutes flat. As we drove up to Mum's house, I looked for any sign that she was home. There was a lamp in the lounge window, but she always left that on in the evenings. Although it was dark by then and difficult to see, I searched the shadows for Marinda and told Kelly to park past the house in an attempt not to alert Marinda if she was inside. We got out and closed the car doors as quietly as we could before jogging quickly back to Mum's. There was nothing to hide behind on the drive as we approached the house. We were out in the open and needed to be quick. I looked through the bottom corner of the living room window, bent down, trying to make sure I couldn't easily be spotted if anyone was in there. I saw a shadow in the far corner, but I couldn't tell who it was without standing to look. I rang Mum's phone one more time and heard the ringtone blasting out from inside the living room, but the shadowy figure ignored it. I couldn't hear any voices. Maybe Mum was in there alone. Maybe Marinda had already killed her. My heart skipped a beat.

I looked at Kelly and nodded my head towards the front door, gradually pulling the handle down.

"Stop." The loud command came from behind us. I nearly jumped out of my skin. I felt Kelly startle too. A frightened look passed between us as we turned around simultaneously.

Swanson and Hart stood at the end of the drive. They made a strange pair standing side by side with such a size difference. Hart was even shorter than me.

"Are you going inside?" I ignored Hart and looked at Swanson instead. My hand stayed on the handle.

"We're going to wait for the armed response unit. They'll be here soon," Swanson reassured me in his smooth, calm voice. Soon? I didn't feel reassured.

"Don't open that door, Miss Thomas!" Hart insisted. She could clearly see me considering my options, but I was sick of talking.

I opened the door and ran inside. The detectives had ruined the element of surprise, so there was no point in sneaking around anymore. I ran straight into the living room with Kelly quick on my heels, loyal to the end. I spotted my mum first. She sat at the far end of the dining table. It had been her shadow I could see from the window. She was sitting at the table eating fish and chips from a cardboard box as if nothing was happening. As if I hadn't just been threatened in my own home and a crazy person hadn't stabbed Aaron for protecting me. My worry turned to the usual resentment. She was never there for me when I needed her, not since Dad had died. She stood as I ran in, almost choking on a chip in the process.

"What the hell, Summer?" she shouted as she got over her coughing fit. "You scared me half to death. What's wrong?"

I ignored her because I had spotted the second person in the room. My mum hadn't touched a man since my dad had died. Yet sitting next to her was a man sharing her fish and chips. Dr Rears.

Summer

Dr Rears once again looked as shocked to see me as I was to see him. "You know each other?" he asked incredulously.

"Oh, this is Summer, my daughter," Mum said, "and her friend Kelly. Hi, Kelly dear."

"Hi," Kelly said, looking confused.

"Mum, what are you doing with Dr Rears?" I asked.

"Oh, do you two know each other? Well, we met last week on the bus." She smiled at him as I threw him a dark look. "We had lunch together yesterday, and we were supposed to go for a walk today. But Albert got held up, so fish and chip supper it was instead."

"Albert?" It took me a moment to realise that must be Dr Rears' first name. "Held up? He got arrested today for bringing vulnerable patients to his home and fucking them!" I spat. Mum's face dropped, and guilt grasped me. I could have worded it better. I hadn't noticed the detectives entering the room behind me. The sudden voice of Swanson made me jump yet again. He moved quietly.

"Mrs Thomas, I'm DI Swanson, and this is my colleague DI Hart."

Hart gave a strange, brief wave in my mum's direction before turning away. She was looking around the room, taking in every nook and cranny. I fought the urge to tell her to get out.

Swanson continued. "Has anyone been here today to threaten you?" He looked at me. "A woman, I believe?"

Mum looked even more confused now. Her day was getting stranger and stranger. "No. I only got home a couple of minutes ago. I was telling my daughter that my friend, this gentleman here, and I were supposed to go for a walk, but then we got fish and chips instead." She pointed towards the half-eaten food in front of her.

"So there's no one else in the house?" Swanson asked. "Can we look around to check? To make sure you're safe?"

"Yes, go ahead, but you won't find anyone," Mum waved towards the direction of the hall.

Swanson walked past us and set off to check the rest of the house, starting with the kitchen. Hart stayed behind but went to the window to look outside.

I turned back to Dr Rears. "Why are you with my mum? Did Marinda put you up to this?"

"Who is Marinda?" Dr Rears' brow furrowed as he looked at me.

"Marinda?" Mum asked. "Marinda Tanda?"

"Yes, Mum, I'll explain soon." Mum's mouth gaped open, and I turned my attention back to Dr Rears. "You know her as Emma Fahy. Her proper name is Marinda Tanda."

Dr Rears shifted uncomfortably in his seat. "I don't know what you're talking about," he said.

"So you happened to bump into *my* mum last week and hit it off?" I rolled my eyes.

"Yes, as it happens, I did." He stood up. "Well, I'm going to get going. I have a prior engagement."

"You're not going anywhere. Sit down," Hart commanded. Dr Rears did as he was told without a word.

"Summer, Marinda Tanda is dangerous," Mum looked over at me.

"Yes, Mum. I know that now. She tried to kill me!" I threw my hands in the air in exasperation. "Wait, how do you know she's dangerous?"

"She egged Eddie on the night his demons got too much," Mum looked away. "She told him to make sure he did what the devil said or you would die too. She made him so much worse.."

"Jesus, Mum. You never told me that. She looked after me that night at the police station. She told me not to tell the police anything."

"I didn't know, Summer. I was unconscious. I made sure you were safe as soon as I woke up."

I looked away and didn't respond. There were too many eyes in the room listening to us. We could talk when everyone had left. At least I finally knew why Mum hadn't wanted me to look for Marinda or Eddie.

"Ms Thomas?" Hart directed her attention towards me. "If the woman isn't here, then where is she? We need to make finding her a priority if she's dangerous and armed."

"I don't know." I willed my brain to think harder. Then it came to me. "He knows." I pointed towards Dr Rears.

"I do not!" he protested.

"Sir, if you know where this lady might be, and you aren't telling us, you could be in serious trouble. Especially if she hurts someone."

Dr Rears fell quiet for a moment. He appeared to be weighing up his options.

"Don't you think you're in enough trouble as it is?" she asked him.

He sighed sadly as if he was giving up. "Try 12 Coppice Court, Edwinstowe." He put his head in his hands.

Sirens wailed outside as two police cars pulled up. Hart got on the radio as Swanson returned from checking the house. He shook his head at her. He had found nothing.

"Redirect ARU to Coppice Court, Edwinstowe," she said into the radio. "You," she pointed at Dr Rears, "are coming to the station for more questioning. You clearly didn't tell us everything today, did you?"

He nodded weakly and stood to follow them out the front door. He avoided my mum's gaze as he left with the detectives. All three of them went outside to speak to the officers on the drive. I walked over to the window to watch them. One of the officers helped Dr Rears into the back of the car and climbed into the front seat. Another officer followed a minute later into the front passenger seat before they drove off.

The other two officers approached the house as the detectives walked to their own car. I saw Swanson climb into the driver's side of a dark Audi. I turned away from the window as the front door slammed shut behind the officers. I recognised one as PC Townsend. He had a different partner today who introduced herself as PC Middleton.

"We would like to ask you all a few questions." PC Townsend smiled around at us. "Starting with you, Miss Thomas. If that's okay?"

Swanson

Hart and Swanson arrived in Edwinstowe thirty minutes later, with their siren blaring through the cold evening air.

"Turn that noise off," Hart instructed as they approached Coppice Court. She took out her radio to check how close ARU was. Five minutes.

The Coppice was as quiet as they pulled up to number 12. Someone had abandoned a FIAT Punto on the drive and left the driver's door wide open. Hart checked to ensure the car was empty, whilst Swanson crept up to the front window, straining to see through the murky nets. He walked over to the front door and tried the handle. It was unlocked. The door creaked as it opened and the smell hit him as soon as he opened the door—dirt, rotten food, dust. He turned on his torch to check it out and noted bags of rubbish lining the kitchen at the far end of the property. A shiver ran down his spine. There was something not right about this house.

He could see the stairs and a door to his left. Careful to remain silent, he crept inside with Hart hot on his heels. He checked the door and found the living room. Empty. He continued to the stairs, the quiet feeling oppressive. Hart moved past him to check the kitchen. She came back seconds later and nodded. They ascended the stairs together, Swanson going first, straining to hear any signs of movement. The pair were silent as they moved in and out of each upstairs room. In the last bedroom, they looked at each other in frustration. The house was clear. Marinda was nowhere to be found.

"Any other ideas?" Hart asked.

Swanson walked over to the window of the bedroom, stroking his beard. He studied the street below.

"Tell ARU they may as well park close by," he said. "With that car on the front, she must be around somewhere."

Hart walked out of the room, barking orders into her radio. Swanson continued to stare out of the window, his mind working through the puzzle. He spotted a lone figure on the driveway of another property, not too far down the road. The figure was female and wore a baseball cap, which struck him as strange in the grey winter evening. She looked around as if searching for someone and then hurried away. She was walking away from number 8 Coppice Court.

Swanson kicked into gear and yelled for Hart as he ran down the stairs. She appeared in seconds.

"Where are ARU?" he demanded.

"Parked outside," she yelled after him as they reached the bottom corridor.

"Tell them down the street. The woman coming from number 8."

Hart did as he asked without question, using her radio to reach the ARU. As the pair approached the front door, they saw ARU jump out of their dark van parked across the street. The woman noticed them too and broke out into a run. The ARU shouted for her to stop, but she ignored them. She was fast but no match for ARU or the detectives. Two of the ARU officers reached her first and tackled her to the ground. She screamed and kicked out like a wild boar, but they were far bigger than her. She was handcuffed within a few seconds. The ARU officers dragged her over to where Swanson was bent over, close to number 12, gasping for air. He wasn't built for speed. The woman no longer appeared to have a weapon, but she did have blood spattered on the front of her top. She was breathing heavily, and tears streamed down her face.

"Marinda Tanda?" Swanson asked.

"My name is Emma Fahy. I have no idea who Marinda Tanda is, but you've got the wrong woman!" she spat at him through anguished tears.

Her eyes looked all around as if trying to plan an escape route.

"Care to explain the blood on your top?" Hart asked her.

The woman didn't answer. Instead, she stopped sobbing and focussed her gaze on Swanson. Her eyes were wild, and spit foamed at her mouth. Swanson instinctively took a step back. Getting spat on wasn't fun.

"What were you doing in number 8?" he asked her. Questioning would usually be reserved for the police station, but he needed to know if she had an accomplice or if she'd hurt someone.

"I wasn't in there," the woman answered far too quickly. "I heard a shout and knocked at the door, but nobody answered."

Hart shared a look with Swanson. "Take her to the station," Hart commanded the ARU officer. The woman started shouting and kicking again as the officer dragged her away.

Swanson hurried towards number 8 Coppice Court, with Hart once again following closely behind him. He made his way up the cobbled driveway and past the grey car parked there, checking inside the vehicle as he passed. It looked as though it hadn't been driven in a long time. He reached the door and knocked loudly three times, waiting for a response. Hart peered through the front window for a moment.

"Inside now!" She yelled.

Swanson kicked open the front door with one large boot and ran inside with Hart right behind him. He ran up the short corridor and burst into the living room, familiar adrenaline pumping. It didn't take him long to see why Hart had yelled for them to go inside. On the floor, right in front of the window, lay an elderly lady, her clothes soaked with blood. Swanson knelt next to her and checked for a pulse. Silently, he looked up at Hart and shook his head.

Summer

I put the phone down, tears stinging my eyes. It made no sense. Why the hell would Marinda hurt Mrs Timpson? Did Marinda know she'd helped me? Mrs Timpson didn't even know she'd helped me. So how would Marinda? It's not like the old lady knew anything about her or Dr Rears. Unless Marinda thought Mrs Timpson had called the police earlier that day. Maybe she had seen us watching through the window.

I was sitting outside my mum's house. The key was in the ignition, but the car was off. I was on my way to see Aaron before picking up Joshua. He was still at his dad's and was so excited to be coming home.

I needed to check on Aaron first. I wasn't sure I would be allowed near him, but I needed to try. I willed myself to move and finally turned the key. My legs were like jelly, but I compelled them to spring into action anyway. *Left foot down, push the car into gear, right foot down.* I talked to myself in the same manner all the way to the hospital. *Just get there. He will be okay.*

I spent ten minutes trying to find a place to park. Parking made me nervous at the best of times, but the hospital car park was always so busy. I finally found someone pulling out and I took their space and rushed to the reception of the A&E department to explain who I was looking for. The lady behind the desk was kind and plump. She led me to a small, empty waiting room and explained someone would be with me shortly. *You're here now. He will be okay.* After a few long minutes, a doctor appeared. She introduced herself as Dr Jasani.

"Are you related to Aaron?" she asked.

"I'm his girlfriend, we live together," I lied. I'd lied so much it was coming easily to me.

"Oh. Well, he was in pretty terrible shape when he arrived. He was stabbed in the abdomen, but we have stemmed the bleeding. He was lucky, and the knife didn't hit any organs. We've sutured the wound, and he is stable for now."

"Oh, thank God." The tears flowed. I hadn't realised how close they were.

"He isn't awake yet, but do you want to see him?"

"Yes! Yes, please."

She took me on a short walk down the corridor and into a private room on the left. Aaron was lying on the bed with his eyes closed. The machine next to him beeped steadily. His phone and wallet were next to him on the bedside table.

The doctor left me to sit with him and told me to call the nurses if he woke up. There was a stack of two small plastic chairs in the room's corner. I took the top one and placed it next to Aaron. His chest rose and fell rhythmically, and the machines beeping periodically. I placed my hand on his, unsure what to do or say. Scenes of people on TV talking to people in comas swam through my mind.

"I'm sorry, Aaron." It came out as a whisper. "I'm so sorry. You're safe now."

I watched him for a quarter of an hour. His eyes twitched now and then, but they didn't open. I didn't want to leave him, but I needed to get Joshua.

"I'll be back tomorrow," I told him and kissed his cheek.

His skin was warmer than I thought it would be. As I reached the door, I heard a ringing noise. His machine? I spun around and walked back to him. The sound was coming from his phone. I grabbed it, hoping it was a relative calling, and suddenly remembered my promise to call his mum. The number flashed up, so it wasn't a number he had saved in his phone. Disappointment hit me, but I answered anyway, in case it was important.

"Hello?" I sounded businesslike and in no mood for sales calls.

"Hello, this is DI Swanson. I'm looking for Aaron Walker."

"DI Swanson? It's Summer."

"Summer? Why are you answering this phone?"

"It's Aarons'. He's in hospital. He's the friend Marinda stabbed, remember? Why are you ringing him? He's not able to talk yet."

He was silent for a moment. "Well, I shouldn't say. I'll explain when we see you."

"No, please, I can't take anymore waiting. We aren't meeting until tomorrow. I can't wait until then. Please." My voice verged on hysterical.

He sighed loudly. "Look, we're trying to find Mrs Timpson's relatives. This number was written on a piece of paper next to her house phone. I thought it was her son's number. There are pictures of her with him all around the house."

The realisation hit me hard. *My* m*um...Mum.* I heard Aaron's voice in my mind as he called out to me, lying bleeding in my doorway. He'd known exactly where Marinda was going. Mrs Timpson was his mum.

Summer

Two days later, I was in the hospital with Aaron. He sat propped up in his bed, still in the private ward. I sat next to him again in the plastic chair. Some colour had returned to his cheeks, and his hair fell in a mess around his face. He was doing better now that the police had caught Marinda. Though, he was devastated about his mum, as was I. He could finally talk about what happened. A couple of weeks ago, he had spotted *Emma* taking Lucy out even though she had no approved leave. He'd asked Emma about it. He had always liked Emma and got on well with her, so he was shocked when she got nasty with him and told him to mind his own business. She initially threatened to tell the police he'd raped her.

"But you didn't!" I stupidly said. He smiled sadly at me.

"Of course not, but I was scared. Even with no proof, an accusation like that can destroy a man's life. I would have been sacked, regardless."

"Christ," I muttered because there was nothing else to say. He was right.

"The same day you asked me about Lucy, Emma had come to speak to me." His eyes were glazed over, as if he wanted to get the words out but didn't want to feel the emotions attached to them. "She showed me a picture on her phone. It was my mum in the garden. She said nothing, but smiled at me. I asked her what the fuck she thought she was doing. She said 'Lucy never existed no matter who asks' and then she walked away."

"I'm so sorry I didn't try to call your mum after you were stabbed. I was so worried about getting to my own mum that I didn't even think."

"It's not your fault, Summer." He squeezed my hand. He sniffed, and a lone tear fell from his cheek. "Emma, or Marinda, whatever the bitch's name is, would have gone missing and turned up later to do it. They caught her thanks to you." He paused before adding, "I'm so sorry I lied to you. I didn't know what to say or what to do. I knew if you asked too many questions, she would threaten you too. At first, I thought she'd hurt Lucy. Killed her or something."

"How did you know where Lucy was staying?" I asked.

"Lucy found me. She followed me home one day and turned up at my door. I nearly had a stroke." A stilted laugh escaped him. "When you said you had seen her, I assumed it was because she wanted to know where you lived. I didn't know if it was to hurt you or what." He tried to shrug his shoulders but winced at the pain.

"Did she try to hurt you?"

"No. She said she needed help." He looked away guiltily. "I told her to fuck off at first. I was so worried about my mum. But a bit later she put a note through my door with a mobile number on it. I rang her eventually. I told her I'd help her. She didn't trust me then, though. She said she would only trust you."

I nodded. I knew he was finally telling me the truth. I wasn't even annoyed anymore that he'd lied. I understood. Lucy was back in the hospital now, although I hadn't seen her. I'd told my mum the whole story. Dr Rears had been arrested again and was no doubt loudly protesting his innocence. He had admitted Marinda ordered him to get close to my mum, though she never said why. I assumed it was to threaten me. He'd worked with Marinda because of her threats to tell everyone about his affair with Aaliyah. I didn't actually see him do anything to Louise, and with so little evidence, he could easily walk free. Thankfully, he wouldn't practice again. Like Aaron had said, the accusation alone would ruin him. At least we could get Marinda on an attempted murder *and* a murder charge for stabbing Aaron and his mum. She should be put away for a long time. I hadn't yet told Mum what she had said about Eddie not actually being ill, but I planned to soon.

"How are you feeling?" I asked him, feeling silly but unsure of what else to say.

He grinned at me with his uneven teeth. "Been better physically! But now I'm free of that psycho bitch. At least I know no one else will get hurt. I wish I'd said something sooner or got Mum away somewhere safe."

"I should have realised what was happening sooner," I said, on the verge of tears. I looked down to hide my welling eyes. "I'm handing my notice in. I'm no advocate."

"Summer, look at me." Aaron leaned over and raised my head with his hand. "You did exactly what you were supposed to. More even than most people would have done in your position. You were Lucy's confidante, her voice. You were there for her when no one else was and when she was at her lowest. Ill, terrified, and alone. Even after she bopped you over the head and knocked you clean out! You are an amazing advocate."

**

Later that day, Joshua laid on the sofa with his head in my lap. I stroked his head gently, never wanting to move. Toy Story played on the TV as we cuddled, and I finally felt safe. Until a knock at the door made us both jump. Anyone wanting to visit needed to press the buzzer on the outside door before gaining access to the building, so who the hell was knocking on my door? I stayed still. Joshua turned and looked up at me.

"Who's banging on the door, Mummy?" His bottom lip pouted in annoyance at the interruption.

"Not sure, baby." I smiled despite the terror which gripped me like a vice. "I'll go check."

He sat up and moved over to lie down on the other side of the sofa. I rose and walked out as if everything was normal, and stood in the hallway to survey the door. The possibilities ran through my mind. Lucy was in the hospital. Marinda was in custody. Aaron was in the hospital. Mum never visited. Kelly would have called. There was no way I was opening it. I could look through the peephole, but to be frank, I didn't want to. I tugged my phone out to see if I had any missed calls from Kelly. There was nothing, other than a notification about the weather. *Knock. Knock. Knock.*

"Mummy, get the door!" Joshua whined from the living room.

"I'm on my way," I lied as I stared at my phone, wondering who to call.

A buzzing noise from the phone almost made me drop it to the ground. I checked the number, unknown.

The familiar anxiety came creeping back into the pit of my stomach. I was unsure whether to answer, until I realised I recognised the number after all. I quickly accepted the call before they hung up.

"Hello?" I said warily in case I was wrong.

"Hi, Ms Thomas. DI Swanson here."

Relief washed over me. I'd been right. "Hi," I said as I gathered myself. I put my hand to my chest, trying to calm my pounding heart.

"Er, I've just knocked on your door. Are you in? Someone let me through the main door when I arrived. I realised after knocking twice that I should have called first…" He trailed off.

I didn't answer him. Instead, I walked forward and finally swung open the door. There he was. The top of my head barely grazed his chest now that I was bare-footed. I was so relieved I actually laughed, much to his perplexion.

"Hi," I repeated. "You scared me half to death."

"Er…Hi. I'm sorry. May I come in for a moment?"

"Sure." I stood aside to let him in and closed the door behind him. I led him through into the kitchen. "Would you like a drink?" I offered, cursing myself for not picking up milk. He'd probably want tea like everyone else in this country.

"Water, please. I don't drink hot drinks."

"Oh! Really?"

"Yes." He looked sheepish. "Bit awkward when everyone you question offers you tea."

"Yes, I know the feeling. I don't drink hot drinks either." My heart said this was another reason we were well suited. My brain told it to shut up.

"Oh." He looked surprised.

"I don't like them, other than hot chocolate with cream and marshmallows." I made a mental note to get some milk so I could make me and Joshua hot chocolate later. We could drink it before bed, whilst watching yet another film or playing a board game. As if he read my thoughts, Joshua came flying into the kitchen right at that moment. He stopped dead in the doorway and positioned his big blue eyes directly on the intimidating Swanson, who suddenly looked like a rabbit caught in headlights. I suppressed a giggle.

"Hi, little fella," he eventually said.

"I'm not little. I'm big." Joshua huffed, eyebrows knitted, bottom lip out.

"Joshua, this is Detective Swanson," I told him, emphasizing the word detective. His grumpy face lit up, and he was all smiles suddenly.

"Detective? Do you catch bad people? Like…bank robbers? Or people who take toys? Or cars? I heard sometimes people take cars. Mummy said so, and she said people also take things from cars, so I must not leave things out on the seat. And what about chickens?"

"Chickens?" Swanson gave me a baffled look. I laughed out loud, as did Joshua.

"Joshua, give me a hug." I diffused the situation before he chased Swanson away. He came running to me and squeezed me tight. I kissed his soft hair. "Now go watch the film while I talk to the detective. I'll bring you a snack, okay?"

"Okay, Mummy." He ran off again to the lounge.

"Chickens?" Swanson asked again. I shrugged my shoulders as I poured a glass of water. I had no idea what the kid was talking about.

"Who knows?" I passed him the glass of water. "What brings you round?"

"Well, it's a little awkward, which is why I came in person." He paused and looked at me, looked *down* at me, I should say.

"Go on..."

"If you don't want to know, that's fine, you can say. It's no skin off my nose, but I thought I'd offer." He raised his hands as if in surrender.

"Go on..." I repeated, wishing he'd spit it out.

"I know where your brother is," he finally said.

"Oh."

"But like I said, only if you want to know?"

"Well, yes, of course. Thank you. How come you know where he is?"

"We need to know if he has seen Marinda. She's blaming him. Saying that he told her the devil was after her and she needed to kill his family."

"Oh."

"You're saying that a lot." He smiled at me, and I smiled back. I didn't know what else to say. "Well, maybe think about it and let me know if you want the address."

"Is he in a hospital, still? Or is he out?"

"He's in a hospital."

"Oh."

Swanson laughed. "You need to expand your vocabulary."

I laughed too because I didn't know what else to say. Did I want to see my brother? Someone had to deal with the mess Marinda had created. He needed to know what she'd told me about his hallucinations. If he didn't know already. But did I want to open up more wounds and get deeper into this mess? Part of me wanted to be selfish for once and let the police deal with it.

"I'll think about it," I said.

"Sure, call me when you're ready."

"Has Marinda said anything else about why she wanted to hurt us?"

"No, she seems to be playing ill."

"Well, I would say she thought it all through pretty well!" I scoffed. Marinda was not ill. She knew right from wrong.

"I agree. We can catch up about it soon, but I'd better go, lots to do."

"Sure." I smiled, though I wished he'd stay.

I walked him to the door, and we said our goodbyes. He would be in touch soon regarding the case, anyway. Then I grabbed a packet of biscuits and went back to sit with Joshua again. He curled his skinny body right into mine as we lay on the sofa watching the film, eating biscuits, and thinking about getting milk for hot chocolate. A normal family again, doing normal things. That was what I needed from life, what Joshua needed. My brother stayed on my mind, and I knew I had to help him. He needed me, too. Not today, though. I curled around Joshua even tighter. At that moment, the two of us were enough. Tomorrow, though, who knew?

II

Mother... Liar... Murderer?

'The truth you must tell,
To all who you know,
Or you'll end up in hell,
Where you'll never grow."

Eleven years ago, Astrid Moor got away with **murder.** *Now, someone wants to make her pay.*

Astrid turns to Alex Swanson for help, except he's a big shot DI now, and isn't prepared to help her again.

But even though she's alone Astrid doesn't take kindly to threats, and when she finally realises who is terrorising her she makes a decision she will never recover from.

A decision with far worse consequences than any secrets from her past.

Prologue

Summer didn't know why Eddie was so upset with Mum. The door sounded like it would come off the hinge any second. She looked around, desperate for somewhere to hide.

'There, Summer!' Mum pointed to the table at the back of the lounge.

Summer rushed to the table, her legs wobbling like the jelly at Becky Smith's birthday party last week. She crawled underneath, bumping her head on the chair. A ten-year-old was far too big to climb under tables. This time was different, though; this wasn't a game of hide-and-seek. She regretted pulling a sickie from school now. Even putting up with the nasty jeers of Patty Whileman would be better than this. Mum ran to the table too and yanked down the checked tablecloth to cover the gap between the legs.

'Come and hide, Mum!' Summer raised her voice over the shouting coming from the other side of the front door. She couldn't quite hear what Eddie said, but he definitely wanted Mum to answer the door — that much was clear. Mum's pretty face popped under the tablecloth.

'Listen, Summer. Whatever happens, you stay there and you stay silent.' They had only just eaten lunch, yet her slurred words and blotchy skin showed she'd already drunk a sizable amount of vodka.

Summer nodded so hard that her head ached when she stopped. She put a hand to her forehead, closed her eyes and wished for Daddy to come back. It was silly. People didn't come back from the dead. Even so, it might happen if she wished hard enough. None of this would be happening if he hadn't died. She would be in school. Mum wouldn't slur her words. Eddie wouldn't be trying to kick in the front door.

Mum slid something hard along the floor to Summer and disappeared again behind the tablecloth. Summer looked down as the thing bumped her leg. Mum's mobile phone lay there, a quiet voice coming from it. She reached out, but just as her fingers tightened around it, Mum's face appeared again. Summer dropped it. She should never touch Mum's phone.

'Here!' Mum whispered. Summer snapped her head back up, hoping she hadn't been caught trying to pick up the phone.

Mum held something out to her. 'Take this and stay on the phone.' Mum was breathless now. She'd stopped slurring; her eyes were wide.

Summer didn't ask questions as she took the large kitchen knife. She wanted to but Mum's eyes scared her. Her face disappeared again. Summer held the knife with the blade facing away, like Daddy taught her when he showed her how to chop vegetables. She could still hear a voice coming from the mobile phone. She picked it up with trepidation.

'Hello?' she whispered.

'Hello, who's this?' The woman's voice sounded surprised.

'Summer. Who are you?'

'Well, Summer, I'm Suzie. I'm going to get you some help, OK?'

Summer nodded, feeling a bit too scared to answer. She didn't see why they needed help. Eddie was mad again. She knew he would just punch a wall or something and calm down.

'Summer, are you there?'

Oops, Summer had forgotten Suzie couldn't see her nodding. 'Yes,' Summer whispered into the phone. She wasn't sure why, but it seemed right to whisper.

'How old are you, Summer?' Suzie asked.

'Eleven in two weeks.' Summer refused to say she was only ten. She basically was eleven already.

'OK, sweetie. You're doing great. Where are you and your mum?'

'I'm hiding under the table. I don't know where Mum is.' Summer listened for a sign of where Mum was. She could hear her shouting to

Eddie to calm down. It sounded like she was by the front door, which he was still kicking ferociously. 'She's talking to Eddie.'

'Eddie? Is that your brother? The one who is unwell?' There was a nervous edge to the lady's voice that hadn't been there before.

'Erm... yes. Eddie is my brother. I don't know what's wrong with him,' Summer whispered, 'Mum says he's poorly, but he doesn't seem sick; not even a fever. He just acts weird sometimes.'

'Is Eddie inside the house?' The lady sounded calm again.

'No, but he's trying to get in. I think he'll break the door down.' The door really sounded like it was going to splinter any minute.

'OK. Don't panic, sweetheart. The police are on their way. They'll be there in about five minutes, OK?'

Summer nodded again and kept listening out for Mum. She wanted the lady — she'd already forgotten her name — to stop talking so she could listen and see what Eddie was so mad about. Why did they need the police? Eddie would shout and bang and hit the wall and then go away. She couldn't see why the police needed to come this time. Maybe he had hit someone else's wall. That would get him in trouble. He had been hitting things since Daddy died. Summer's heart hurt at the thought of her dad. She wished hard again for him to return.

Her eyes flew open as the door splintered. Mum screamed and ran through the living room and into the kitchen. Eddie's shouts were a lot louder now.

'Summer, are you still there? Summer?' The lady on the phone was talking, but Summer couldn't speak. Her body tingled with something. Not the sadness she'd felt when Mum told her Daddy was dead. An unfamiliar feeling that made her want to run away or scream. A terror she'd never experienced before.

'Mu-um! Where are you?' Eddie's deep voice laughed as he sang for their mum.

'She'll be in the kitchen, Eddie,' Marinda said. She was inside, too.

Summer filled with hope. If Marinda was here then maybe everything would be OK. She could see Marinda's white trainers by the living room door. Summer shifted forward, ready to dash to Marinda and ask her to make Eddie OK again. But then she spotted a larger pair of trainers. Eddie's black trainers. He crossed the living room floor, still calling for Mum. In seconds he was standing right next to Summer's hiding spot, and the police were nowhere in sight.

Astrid

It's a terrible thing to grow so accustomed to fear that it becomes a friend. When its welcome shadow reminds me to triple check I locked the door every time I leave the house. Or to look over my shoulder every three minutes to make sure nobody is following me. Or to text Harry at 11:55 a.m. every day, to check he's OK. A day without this shadow would be so strange. I wouldn't know what to do. Where would I go? What would I say? And if I didn't hear those constant warnings, what would keep us safe?

But on this particular Tuesday, my fear was far worse than usual. It wasn't the same nagging anxiety which kept me on my toes and ensured young Harry and I were safe. No. My friendly fear had manifested into full-blown terror because of a simple piece of paper. My trembling fingers made the scrap of paper shake, as if it was scared too. *Scared of me? I wouldn't blame it.*

Pushing the unhelpful thoughts away, I opened my fingers and watched the paper spiral to the marble table, which took centre stage in the kitchen. I picked it up again and threw it on the counter, where it sat ominously, a white warning against the dark quartz worktop. I stepped back, not wanting to be too close. My boots were loud against the porcelain floor. I stared at it from a distance, just to make sure it was real. Sometimes I saw things I knew deep down weren't real. Dark shadows who haunted me. Creatures that visited my nightmares. Quick flashes of movement in the corner of my eye, or a familiar face lost in a crowd.

I resisted the urge to move the paper a third time. Evil emanated from it, though I knew that was ridiculous. I was unsure why I had appointed human feelings to a piece of scrap paper. Where did it come from?

The note was waiting for me when I returned from the school run. Like flowers from a murderous stalker. The morning had started off normal enough. I'd walked Harry to school as usual and said goodbye with a quick hug before he crossed the main road. He sauntered the rest of the way alone, one shoelace trailing behind him and his black school bag slung over his shoulder. I rushed back due to rain drops breaking through the grey sky. I counted the seconds as I walked and checked behind me every time I reached one hundred and eighty. Sometimes I cheated and looked earlier, but one hundred and eighty was the magic number.

I used to walk Harry all the way to school, but he was fighting for independence lately. Eleven years old was far too grown up to be seen walking to school with his mum. At least it was in his mind. Not that you'd think we were mother and son. He didn't have my red hair or freckles, and he was already almost the same height as me. He looked like his dad, though Harry had never met him. His dad had been tall, with brown hair. Just like Harry. He had unblemished skin which tanned every summer within minutes of the first day of sunshine. I was grateful Harry didn't look like me. At least he wouldn't get bullied for being pale and ginger.

The walk back from school had been normal, too. I stopped off at the local shop for milk and made my way back to our traditional red brick home on Rose Way, a beautiful street on the outskirts of the small city of Derby. Tall oak trees lined the pavement, and each detached house had its own private gateway, surrounded by tall fences or trees. Privacy was the reason I'd been so eager to move into this house eleven years ago. The owner allowed us to move in with no credit checks or paperwork, thanks to a mutual friend. With four bedrooms and two bathrooms, the house was far too big for Harry and me. Nonetheless, I loved it.

Nothing felt different that morning. I thought I had such *good* instincts because I was always on edge. I would know if Harry and I were in danger again and I could prevent anything bad from happening. Yet my instincts must be waning after eleven years of being safe, because everything felt so *normal*. That was the worst part.

It didn't feel normal for long, though.

As I pushed open the front door, something underneath made an unusual swishing noise, like letters on the mat. But the postie always used our beautiful wooden postbox at the end of the garden path. I hadn't locked the front gate, though. I never did for the school run. It took less than ten minutes and even I wasn't that paranoid.

I closed the door, bristling at the thought of the postie missing the postbox. I gently placed my costly handbag on the coat rack and glanced at the mat. It wasn't the post. It was just a lone piece of white paper.

Even then, I assumed it was some sort of advertisement, which made me bristle further. We had clear signs on both the gate and the front: 'No Cold Callers' and 'No Unsolicited Mail', yet the odd flyer still made its way through. It wasn't until I picked up that seemingly harmless scrap paper that I finally realised things were absolutely not normal. Nor would they ever be again.

Summer

I parked in the furthest space possible to make sure no patients could see me through the barred windows. I never liked patients to see my car if I could help it. Far too many of them had boundary issues.

I'd been waiting for this moment for almost twenty years, and yet I couldn't move. I wished my younger brother, Dylan, was with me. He was the only other person who would understand how I felt, though he would have talked me out of it.

I stood next to my car. The driver's door was open in case I ran away instead. But the previous month's events proved I couldn't run from the past any longer. I had to face it at some point. *Why not now?* Marinda had pushed me to this moment, regardless of what I wanted. I had no choice other than to seek Eddie out; I had to know the truth about him after what she'd admitted. I just hoped I wasn't putting my family in danger.

The autumn sun shone between the dark clouds. I covered my eyes to take in the vast building that stood before me. Sunlight sparkled on the raindrops which clung to the bricks after the recent downfall. It made the building less ominous, at least. I couldn't imagine this facility looking inviting in the dark. The council responsible for building the hospital years ago had buried it deep in the Derbyshire countryside. Field after field surrounded it in all directions, with various animals dotted around inside them. The countryside had never attracted me. It was pretty enough, but it bored me too quickly. The fields, trees and hedges all looked the same. A ten-foot wall barricaded the building inside a nine-acre space. A large sign read 'Welcome to Adrenna Hospital'.

It looked more like a prison.

Butterflies took flight inside my stomach as I made up my mind. I slammed the car door; the noise echoing through the silence.

After grabbing my handbag and laptop from the boot, I crunched over the gravelled car park to find the entrance. To start with I had to figure out how to get inside. These places were never easy to get inside on the first visit. I never knew why, but the entrance was never where you'd expect it to be. There were steps leading to the front entrance of the building, but the doors were barricaded with aged wooden boards. So I walked down the side and spotted a door with a cracked sign above it saying 'Welcome'. The butterflies got worse as I reached it. Another sign on the door informed me to press the doorbell. I squeezed my eyes shut. The image of the doorbell danced around on my eyelids, taunting me. *It isn't too late to drive away.*

'Can I help you?'

I whipped open my eyes at the sound of the crackling voice. 'Er... yes... hi...' I stumbled as I turned to see who had spoken, still jumpy even with Marinda locked away and awaiting trial. Nobody was there. It took me a moment to realise the voice came from the intercom system above the doorbell.

'I'm Summer Thomas, the advocate?' I said.

'Have you got your ID?' the woman replied.

'Er... yes.' I grabbed the ID card hanging around my neck and held it out to the intercom.

'Turn to your left, please.' Her voice made it clear she was getting agitated with me. I did as I was told.

Seconds later, a loud buzzing noise rang out and the lock clicked open.

'Please open the door and make your way to reception.'

I eased open the door as if something might jump out at me. As soon as I entered the hallway, my breath caught in my throat. That hospital smell of medicine, bleach, and disease hung in the air. An open stairway greeted me to the left, and a corridor stretched out in front of me. The decor didn't help my breathing. Deep red walls encased the entrance hall and the wooden floor was almost as dark. Everything you'd expect from such an old mental institution. Which was everything it shouldn't be in modern times. Dark, and sad, combined with a feeling of being watched at all times. My eyes flicked over the walls but I didn't see any CCTV cameras.

There was a door at the end of the corridor. I took my time to reach it, stepping carefully to quieten the heavy thud of my boots. Through the door, I easily found the reception desk to my left. It was as out of place with the old-fashioned decor as an iPod would be at an antique teapot display. It was such a bright shade of white that I had to stop myself from shielding my eyes after being in the darkness of the corridor. An authoritarian receptionist sat behind thick safety glass. She looked me up and down as I walked over to her, her lips pursed. She was clearly the same chirpy character from the intercom.

'You're not the usual advocate.' She clipped her words, as if she'd had enough of advocates already today, despite me being the only one. She raised a perfectly plucked eyebrow over her sizable glasses. Red lipstick smudged above her top lip. I tried not to stare at it.

'No. She's off sick.' I gave a friendly smile to win her over.

'Well, she usually comes on a Friday. Why don't you come back then? The residents don't like their routine being disturbed.'

My smile hadn't worked.

'I can't make it on Friday, I have my own visits to make.' I kept smiling and hoped she believed my lie. Sweat beads formed on my forehead. Christ. This battle-axe must scare the more anxious patients half to death.

'Well, it's only 9:30, most won't be awake yet.' She sighed. 'Sign in here, please.' She rammed a register under a gap at the bottom of the safety glass.

I did as she asked and pushed it back through the gap. My hands trembled. I cleared my throat loudly to divert attention away from them. She peered at me over the rim of her glasses and snatched the register back from the gap.

'Here are the keys.' She handed me a black pouch and a belt. 'And here's a locker key. No phones, handbags, laptops or lighters. You can have a pen and paper, but keep the pen out of reach. Don't put it down anywhere. Put everything in locker twelve please.' She pointed to the lockers behind me.

I nodded through her speech — I'd heard it all before at many other hospitals — and picked up the key and pouch before she changed her mind or asked more questions. I was lucky she didn't call my employer to check Becky wasn't off sick. I just hoped they assumed it was a daft mix up.

Once I'd put my belongings inside locker twelve, I turned to her, awaiting further instructions.

She said nothing, but stared back with one eyebrow raised again.

'Where are the patients?' I asked.

'Up the stairs, you'll find three doors. One for each ward.' She pointed back down the corridor I'd just come from and turned away to face her computer.

Without another word, I returned to the staircase and made my way up each step, gripping my pen and notepad as if they were weapons. I supposed they could be in the right circumstances. Especially a pen. The landing at the top had three doors, just like the old grouch had said. One door led to the left, one straight in front and one to the right. They were modern, with thick glass panels so anyone could see what was going on before opening the door. I peered through the first door on my left and saw another long corridor. It was the same through the second door. Through the third door was a large room with light walls and a white floor. Sofas and chairs were dotted about the middle of the room and a large TV was attached to the far wall, encased in a protective cabinet.

Close to the door a man in a white coat stooped over someone sitting in a chair. I fumbled with the keys, trying to find the right one to get into the room and wishing I had more of a plan. I hadn't really thought I would go through with it; expecting the hospital would turn me away. Or I'd run away myself. Yet here I was. *What if Eddie recognised me? What would I do if he didn't recognise me?*

Once I'd finally found the right key, I creaked open the heavy door, attempting to be inconspicuous. The man — I assumed he was a doctor — whipped around. He smiled at me, revealing blinding white teeth.

'Hi!' He was so cheerful I had to fight the urge to turn and run.

'Er... hi. I'm Summer. The advocate.' I smiled back.

'Oh! No Becky this week?' he asked.

'No, she's off ill.'

'Oh, nothing too serious, I hope. I'm Dr Randall. Has anyone shown you around yet?'

I shook my head.

'OK. So this is ward C. This is Damon.' He pointed to the large man in the chair. Damon didn't move. He stared at the floor in front of him, ignoring us both. 'But... he isn't feeling too well today. I'll be back in a few minutes, Damon.'

He moved over to the far side of the room and motioned for me to follow. 'This ward is for the patients who are new to us and are very ill. Ward B is the next one along, and those patients have settled in nicely and are doing better. Ward A is for people getting ready to leave. So, just be most careful in this ward, as there are a few people you shouldn't be alone with. Avoid one-to-one with anyone in here today. I assume you know what you're doing.' He smiled again. His friendliness made him instantly likeable. I was always a little jealous of people who found it so easy to talk to people. I didn't even want to lie to this guy. But I had to.

'I think Becky had a meeting with one patient in particular today... Eddie?' I said.

He scrunched up his face in thought. 'Erm, Eddie... Eddie...' he muttered. 'No, we don't have an Eddie in this ward.'

'It could be because his birth name is River.' The words came out too fast. Shit, I was forgetting my play-acting in my rush.

'River?' His eyebrows raised. 'I'd definitely remember that name. Nope, sorry, not in this ward.'

'What about the other wards?' I said.

'There's definitely no River in them either. Or Eddie anymore, for that matter.'

'Anymore?' I asked.

'We had an Eddie Thomas. He wasn't one of mine, but I do know we released him about six weeks ago,' Dr Randall said.

'Released?' Fear twisted around my gut. If they had already released him, he could be anywhere. He could know where Joshua and I live. He could pay a visit to Mum and finish what he started. She still lived in the same house he'd attacked her in all those years ago.

'Yes.' The doctor smiled. 'I believe he's in a low security unit now. I don't think I'm allowed to reveal which one to an advocate?' He posed his question with his head cocked to one side.

I looked away from Dr Randall, as if surveying the ward. It always annoyed me how little doctors knew about advocates. Could I lie to him? I needed the information, but I already might get sacked if Becky found out I visited and mentioned it to her supervisor.

'No. Not without the patient's permission.' I decided to tell the truth.

'Ah, fair enough. I assume Becky will be back shortly?'

'She will. She may even be in on Friday. I'm covering today, just in case. I'll have a chat with some patients. I'll stay in this area seeing as I don't know them very well.'

He nodded and walked back to Damon.

I wanted to leave straight away, but it would seem suspicious. And I couldn't leave without taking my things from locker twelve, right in front of the witch downstairs. She would definitely suspect something if I rushed off.

So I wandered away from Dr Randall and looked around the open living area of the ward. I wished I'd taken my suit jacket off and left it in the locker. My nerves were already making me sweat more than usual, and the warm air exacerbated it further. The room smelled of sweat and something else I couldn't quite put my finger on, bleach maybe. There was one large window on the far wall, but it was firmly closed and, most likely, locked. As stifling as the air was, the atmosphere was colder than most of the hospitals I visited. Or maybe that was just my mood.

But an idea came to me. If the doctor couldn't tell me where Eddie went, maybe one of the patients knew.

The living area was quiet, though. If I was going to find someone who knew Eddie, then I needed patients who were less catatonic than Damon. There was an art room to my left, and a corridor leading off to what was probably the bedrooms. The only two patients I could see other than Damon were sitting on the sofa watching TV. Maybe they could tell me where Eddie went. I walked over to sit on the sofa across from them. They both eyeballed me as I sat down.

'Hello,' I smiled, 'I'm Summer, an advocate. I'm here to chat with patients. If you need anything…'

Their eyes were distant and unfocused, and they said nothing in response. The tall, slender one closed his eyes and rocked back as he fell asleep. I noticed purple bruising around his neck. The other man was short and stocky, with thick glasses and a bandage around his head. He stared in my direction though he didn't appear to see me, never mind hear my introduction. Christ, what drugs were these guys on? They were clearly not going to tell me anything. But I continued to sit and watched the ward instead.

A couple more patients appeared as the morning progressed, and I moved over to another seating area to introduce myself again. But after an hour of the same distant look from every patient, I decided it was time to leave. Maybe Swanson could help me find Eddie. It would be a good excuse to call him, seeing as I hadn't heard from him in a couple of weeks. My butterflies returned at the thought of his voice. I silently shooed them away.

I headed over to the nurse's station to let them know I was ready to leave the ward. The station was a small room at one end of the ward, which was surrounded by thick glass. I peeked through the glass to see who was inside, and a friendly face stared back at me.

Aaron Walker.

Finally, someone who could help me.

Astrid

The sun struggled to shine as I sat in the back garden surrounded by plumes of cigarette smoke. My finger repeatedly tapped against my cheek as I allowed the burning smell to envelop me. I hadn't smoked for six months, but the note scared me more than the risk of lung cancer, despite my mum's slow death thirteen years prior. Not that I stuck around to watch her die.

I'd tried to ignore the note. I binned it and sat in my studio corner of the living room to concentrate on work instead. There was an editing job I needed to finish, as well as an illustration job. I had to stick to deadlines tightly, with word of mouth being my primary source of advertising. My high standards meant customers must book at least four months in advance and brought in more high-paying jobs than ever before. As I stared at the letters on the page, I knew I wasn't editing to my usual high standards. The note twisted around in my mind and swallowed any other thoughts like a dark mist. *Where did it come from? Who wrote it? What did they mean?* I needed a break.

So now it was early afternoon and the note was back in my hand. The corner stained a deep orange from old spaghetti bolognese. At least my hand no longer shook. The nicotine had calmed my nerves. I inhaled another lungful of the harsh smoke. It felt good as it hit the back of my throat. I held it for a moment before blowing out one long stream of smoke into the cool air.

Despite my fear, I couldn't stop looking at the note. It was like watching a horror movie. I wanted to look away, yet I couldn't. I *needed* to see what damage it caused. Except this was real life, our life, and I couldn't turn it off if it got too scary. I could throw it away again, but what would come next?

The paper wasn't big. It was torn, plain white paper. The writer had been in a hurry, judging from the scrawl. It could have come from my printer. *Maybe it did.*

I shivered even though there was no evidence that the sender had entered our home. Yet they *had* been in my garden. They knew where I lived.

I couldn't understand how. Nobody knew where Harry and I lived now. I had been in Rose Way for over a decade, so the odd person had visited. My landlady… although I saw her all the time as a friend, and she had no reason to threaten me. I discounted her. Alex Swanson… he had always protected me. I hadn't seen him in years, and he had no reason to threaten me. I discounted him.

A couple of Harry's school friends and his school records, I supposed. Then there were companies like the bank, the doctor. But nobody truly *knew* who I was. They knew me as Astrid Moor, with no knowledge of my past. Except Alex.

The note contained thick, black letters in sprawling handwriting like a child's. Four short sentences. The words were simple, yet they surrounded me with a dark fear. Which I guessed was the wordsmith's aim.

The truth you must tell,
To all who you know,
Or you'll end up in hell,
Where you will never grow.

No one in my current life could have written this. They didn't know my truth.

I had worked hard to seem like a normal, straightforward person with no secrets in my past. Nothing to hide. A single mother; young, but not too young to raise an eyebrow. No dad in the picture. A decent income from reputable sources; paid her bills on time.

Only one past event could be connected. One event which changed my life and defined it in a way that I didn't realise a single misfortune could do.

And that was the mystery of my missing husband, Benjamin Bates.

Sophie - May 2007

Sophie forced a cough to shift the burning at the back of her throat. She loved the high. She usually enjoyed the burn, too, but this time it was stronger than normal. Where the hell had Mel got this cocaine? The thought didn't linger. As long as she got high, it didn't matter where it came from.

It was lunchtime and Mel *still* wasn't home. She disappeared with some random guy last night, after the club kicked them out at closing time. Luckily, Mel was coherent enough to give Sophie her house keys so she had somewhere to sleep. She'd have been fucked, otherwise.

Sophie stretched out on the sofa and wrapped the itchy blanket around her bare legs as she waited for the high to kick in. She preferred the sofa to Mel's spare room. Bedrooms were too personal. They were safe places for treasured possessions, or cuddles, or sex.

Mel's disappearance wasn't unusual, so Sophie didn't worry. But she was running low on the free gram of cocaine Mel had given her. She scrolled through her phone contacts, searching for someone who might have more drugs. It didn't have to be coke. She wasn't picky, just no heroin. As long as she didn't go that far, she'd be fine. Guilt twinged at her, but she knew she would survive long enough to sort out her shit. One day she'd be clean with a good job, a husband and some kids and she'd say a big 'fuck you' to Mum and stupid Greg.

That day wouldn't be today, though.

Three loud bangs on Mel's front door made Sophie jolt up. She ran her fingers through her long hair, trying to get the knots out whilst attempting to gather her thoughts. Should she open the front door? It was Mel's house, not hers. Another bang at the door. *Shit.* Annoyance flashed through her as she wished they'd fuck off and leave her in peace.

Although it might be someone with more drugs.

She stepped around empty beer cans to the front door, wearing only her t-shirt and underwear. She smiled to see she had left the keys in the lock the previous night. Or that morning, whatever time she made it home. She opened the door a crack. A tall, skinny man stood there in dark tracksuit bottoms and a baggy t-shirt. His jaw swung from side to side. Sophie dropped her smile as she realised his jaw swinging was him chewing gum, and not the effect of drugs.

'Hey. It's Ben, right?' Sophie had met Mel's older brother a couple of times. He was a plumber or electrician or something like that. And quite sexy in a wiry way, at least compared to all the drug addicts around town. He had muscular arms for a skinny guy, and eyes which were almost grey. Sophie noticed his hands more than anything else. Big hands that would make anyone feel safe.

She smiled up at him and hoped she didn't look too rough. Mel had mentioned he'd asked about her. She'd told him to fuck off and leave Sophie alone,. Actually, Sophie didn't mind his attention. She opened the door wider to show him what she was wearing. Or, more accurately, what she wasn't wearing.

'Er... hey, Sophie.' His eyes flicked down to her bare thighs like she'd hoped.

'I guess you're here to see Mel? She's not in yet from last night. I'm not sure where she went, so I don't know when she will be back.'

'Oh. Er... OK.' He didn't move, but stood and stared at her instead. She couldn't tell whether his eyes were actually grey. His gaze flicked down to her loose breasts. Her nipples had hardened from the cool breeze blowing through the front door.

'She probably won't be that long. Do you want to come in and wait? We could have a drink together? I just took a line and need someone to party with, anyway.' She winked at him and immediately regretted it. Winking was never sexy in real life. What the fuck was she doing? She laughed. A buzz was flowing through her brain, messing with her thoughts.

He grinned, despite her lame wink, and nodded in return. Sophie walked away, taking her time so he could look at her arse. It was her best asset; the only part of her body she liked.

The cocaine swelled her confidence and she swayed her hips as she avoided the empty beer cans strewn across the living room carpet. Not the sexiest atmosphere. It would have to do. She turned as she reached the kitchen. He whipped up his head with a guilty look.

Sophie pretended she hadn't caught him staring at her arse. 'What do you like to drink?' A wave of excitement flowed through her.

'Er, anything. I'm not picky.' He threw his phone and wallet down on the kitchen table.

Bet you're not, she thought as she bent over to open the fridge door.

'Do you prefer Carling or John Smith's? Or Mel might have some vodka knocking around somewhere.'

'Carling is fine. I don't do bitter and vodka makes me angry.' His jaw twitched.

'I know a few people who say that about vodka. I don't think any alcohol makes me angry.' She took her time to grab a four pack and smiled as she passed him the beer.

'Break me one off,' she said as she walked back to the living room. There was only one sofa in the small room. She sat in the middle.

She eyed him as he lumbered over. He had a strange way of walking. It was as if his legs had grown quicker than everything else and he was still getting used to them. She enjoyed the vulnerability of being half naked while he stayed fully clothed. There was something sexy about being so exposed, and the possibilities of what might happen next.

Greg had always liked it when she was naked and he wasn't.

She tapped a chipped fingernail against the small bag of white powder on the table and raised one eyebrow at Ben.

'No thanks, beer will do me. I don't do drugs.' He eyed the bag as if it were a bomb. Ben's strong South London accent made even simple

SOPHIE - MAY 2007

things he said sound cocky. He exuded confidence, even without drugs. It intrigued Sophie, maybe even made her a little jealous.

'Suit yourself.' She flicked on the TV to remove the possibility of an awkward silence. On the news, a reporter showed an image of a nearby street where a teenage girl was raped. That was not the sexy atmosphere Sophie was looking for. She switched to the music channels. Music was always easy to talk about.

'Leave this one on!' He took a seat next to her. The song was a heavy rap song Sophie had never heard of.

She laughed as he attempted to rap along, losing the pace within seconds.

'Stop laughing at me. I bet you can't do better.' He continued his attempt to rap, nodding his head in tune with the music.

Sophie laughed harder.

Over the next hour, they finished their pack of beer and attempted to sing. Ben gave her a disapproving glance but said nothing as she snorted another small line of white powder. Sophie felt the heat from his body as they moved closer together.

The drug coursed through her body, her confidence rising, and her inhibitions falling away. A need to touch him overtook her. She placed her hand on his thigh. A slow smile spread across his face, and he leaned forward to kiss her.

His tongue was rough in her mouth. Sophie didn't mind. She needed him to be rough. She needed him to take control so she didn't have to think anymore. He pulled off her t-shirt and pushed her down onto the sofa. His large hands cupped her breasts and squeezed hard, just like she'd been imagining since he sat down. It hurt more than she expected, but she didn't care. It was a nice pain. His stubble scratched against her neck as one hand pulled down his tracksuit bottoms. She was barely wet when he pushed himself deep inside her and moaned into her ear.

Five minutes later, it was all over. Sophie lay naked on the sofa in his arms. She would be happy with her accomplishment until the drugs wore off. Ben's heavy breathing drowned out the noise of the quiet music coming from the TV.

'I'd better go,' he told her ten minutes later. 'I don't think Mel would be too happy if she saw me here, lying naked with you.'

'Oh, OK.' Sophie smiled and rolled away from him to grab her t-shirt and underwear from the floor. 'I need a shower, anyway.'

'Yeah, you do!' he grinned. 'How old are you? You never said.'

'I'm eighteen.' It wasn't exactly a lie. It'd be true in a couple of months.

He picked up his jacket and phone, and threw her an awkward wave as he strode out of the front door and slammed it behind him. Sophie lay on the sofa, grabbed the scratchy blanket, and went back to scrolling through her phone. She would find someone more fun than Benjamin Bates. It was the only way she knew how to stop the loneliness from winning.

Astrid

I struggled to concentrate on an illustration for a children's book. It crossed my mind that a run might clear my head more thoroughly. I hadn't run for three days, and it was a necessary evil to stop the fear from growing too big. The darkness struggled to keep up with me when my feet hit the ground until they ached and my lungs almost burst from my chest. It always returned soon after I stopped running, but as a smaller, manageable darkness instead of the intense demon it sometimes became.

Even so, I wasn't in the mood for running, and I needed my fear with me today. I had a reason to be scared, and I needed help to deal with it. The fear would keep me alert. I couldn't forget that.

At 2 p.m. I gave up working and sat in front of my new laptop. The sun disappeared altogether and the grey sky made the day even more depressing. I sat in the garden with the laptop, regardless of the weather, hoping it would clear my head. And I sank into the hanging egg chair that Harry had made me buy the previous summer. The fresh air felt cool against my skin. It was a welcome refreshment.

At three grand, the laptop was an expensive treat, but one I needed for work. Then I spent another thousand on Harry's new laptop to bring him out of his recent pre-teenage funk. I regretted the spend because it depleted my emergency fund, which I usually made sure totalled at least five figures.

I never knew when we would need to disappear.

Still, just under eight thousand was enough to escape should we need to, though hopefully it wouldn't come to that. I pulled the elastic band around my wrist and let it go. I snapped it again and again. My anxiety lessened with each snap of pain. I stopped and counted to ten before snapping it another three times. I needed to get stronger. That *poem* was going to force me to do something I hadn't needed to do in years: check up on my relatives.

My usual work-related social media account popped up. It displayed happy pictures of a young woman I'd never met. A stranger I befriended on social media, then stole her photos and blocked her and her entire friend list. She could still catch me, of course, but she hadn't found me out so far.

But that wasn't the account I needed to use. I logged into my other account. This time a man around my age smiled at me from the profile pictures. He was attractive, whoever he was. I had created the fake male profile after Harry and I left our old life, when Harry was only a few weeks old. I'd added over two hundred strangers as friends. Then I added the people I wanted to monitor. People who could make my life very tricky if they wanted to.

I had three prime suspects for the sender of the note. They were not the most intelligent people in the world. So I prayed that whoever had sent the note was a social media over-sharer. I genuinely hoped to see 'Haha put this note through her door today.' written on somebody's account.

By relatives, I didn't mean my blood relatives. I didn't know any of my own relatives. I'd only known my mum, and she'd died before I got married. Not that she would have been welcome at the registry office. She'd chosen Greg over me a long time ago, and I hadn't seen her since I was 15. That was sixteen years ago No, by relatives, I meant Ben's family. My in-laws, though I supposed they were nothing to me since his disappearance. It took a couple of tries to remember the password. Once I'd logged in I searched for my sister-in-law first, Mel Bates. Her round face smiled as her profile picture pinged up. Yellow hair fell limp around her shoulders, hiding most of the tattoos covering her arms. Like most profile pictures, it was about as far from the truth as you could get.

Anger bubbled inside me as her blank eyes stared out. I felt a petty urge to write something unpleasant beneath her picture. I snapped the elastic band against my wrist three more times. *Stay calm.*

Other than her marriage, Mel's life had changed little in the last decade. We last saw each other just after our friendship fell apart, when she was a single mum to baby Jayden. Since then, she had married and given birth to another son.

I scrolled down through her last few posts. They were mundane and mostly food related. I stopped scrolling on the fifth image. It was a picture of *three* young kids with the caption 'mummy luvs you more than anything xxxxxx'. Jayden was about Harry's age, and the younger boy looked about six. The little girl looked no older than a toddler.

I continued to snap the elastic band. I could never understand how someone like Mel could create child after child, whilst I would never have another. She shouldn't be allowed one child, let alone three.

Still, nothing about a note or any ominous statuses that could be about Harry or me.

Fear gripped me before I'd even finished typing the next name in the search bar; I knew what I was about to see. She hadn't changed her profile picture in years. As her profile popped up, I came face to face with the very person who haunted my sleep. Julie Bates stared out at me with an enormous smile and wispy brown hair, but it wasn't my mother-in-law I was afraid to see. She wrapped her arms around a teenage version of my ex-husband, Benjamin Bates. Ben, who I had loved more than life itself, and who now lived in my dreams as an emaciated and rotting figure.

Julie had been my second biggest enemy, ever since Ben and I moved away to escape Mel's attempts to break us up. It was Ben's idea to move. I'd have done *anything* for Ben. Yet Julie had always blamed me. She didn't realise it was her own clinginess and Mel's lies that he needed to get away from.

Julie hated me enough to want to scare me, or worse. If she knew where I lived, she'd be straight round banging on the door and causing trouble with her big mouth. But she wasn't clever enough to figure out where I was, or to write a threatening poem. I doubted she could even spell after so many years of alcohol abuse. I scrolled through her profile. There were no posts, just game notifications filled her feed.

I moved on to the last candidate. I'd left my enemy number one until last because I needed to build up to it. To remind myself he wasn't the little boy I'd fallen in love with anymore. Ben's oldest son, Kai Bates, would now be about twenty years old. A well-timed breeze made goosebumps appear across my arms as I opened Kai's profile. I slammed down the laptop screen before it could load, delaying the moment I might see his face.

I sat for a minute before meandering back inside to the warmth of the house. I poured a glass of water on my way to the living room, procrastinating as much as possible. Eventually, I curled up on the Arlo & Jacob sofa in the far corner of the living room. I wished I had wine instead of water but pushed myself to focus. There were no harboured bad feelings from me towards Kai, although I couldn't imagine he was a pleasant person after being dragged up by his awful mother. I did know he would blame me for taking his dad away, thanks to his mum and grandma telling him their version of events.

Once curled up, I couldn't delay it any longer. I held my breath, and pulled open the laptop screen. Kai's profile showed nothing. The profile picture showed some random singer or rapper, and the banner was a black logo I'd never seen before. I released my breath, and scrolled through his feed. He had posted nothing for months. Harry told me kids these days only used certain social media apps, and others were for 'old' people like me. It was funny, I didn't feel old. I felt like my early thirties was a weird age category: neither young nor old, but not middle-aged either. Though to eleven-year-old Harry, I may as well have been one hundred years old.

Kai remained my best guess. His youth suggested an awareness of technology that made him more likely to know how to find me, despite how careful I had been. At least if Kai wrote the note, Harry was safe. He wouldn't want to hurt his younger brother, who was innocent in the whole thing. Harry didn't even know Kai existed, and I was going to make sure it stayed that way. There was only one person I knew for sure had not written the note, and that was Ben himself.

Because I murdered him eleven years ago.

Swanson

Detective Inspector Alex Swanson poured over the thick file at his desk. The pounding in his head had increased, and the fumes of fresh white paint did not help in the large, open office. The peeling, grey walls had been fine as they were in Swanson's opinion.

There were more urgent things to spend time and money on. A third sexual assault had taken place in the city centre within six months, and they needed all the possible funding to find the depraved arsehole.

The office buzzed with activity, with more officers roaming around than Swanson had ever seen, and the noise was making his head worse. He rubbed his eyes and blinked hard at the file in front of him.

The victims had all given a similar description of the rapist. He was white, about six foot with dark facial hair and a prominent nose. No tattoos or anything of much use, and no DNA so far. The first victim, nineteen-year-old student Lu Chen, had showered before arriving at the station the day after the attack. She said the attacker smelled of petrol and had a foreign accent, though she didn't know where from.

The second twenty-one-year-old victim, Donna Bradway, got away by kicking him hard in the balls and screaming *'fire'*. She'd read somewhere that people are more likely to pay attention if you scream 'fire' rather than 'help'. To be fair to her, it worked. A couple came running to help her, but the suspect had disappeared by the time they arrived. She said the attacker smelled of paint and his accent was like a mixture of Russian and French.

The third victim was still being interviewed by a specially trained officer.

A TV appeal with a facial composite would go out on tonight's news. It was going to be a long week of looking into the plethora of mostly useless leads from the public. The first attacks both happened in the depths of the picturesque former mill village, Darley Abbey, on the west bank of the River Derwent. The third took place close to the university grounds. Swanson was waiting on the interviewers to confirm exactly where.

Footsteps moved towards him, and he smelled a puff of sweet scent as DI Hart flopped into the chair on the other side of the desk. She sighed.

He didn't look up, so she cleared her throat. 'I can see you grinning to yourself about ignoring me, Alex Swanson,' she said in mock exasperation.

'I'm busy.' Swanson dipped his head further, though he still grinned.

'Uh huh. We will be after tonight.' Hart sighed again.

'You not looking forward to the prank calls?' Swanson finally looked up at her sharp face, which was expertly painted as usual.

'Shut up.' She rolled her eyes. 'We'll hopefully get some sort of lead. I've been thinking about petrol and paint. Why would he smell of both?'

'Well, could be anything really, couldn't it? He might have filled his car up recently and spilled a bit. Like when you spilled some on your shoe.' He laughed at the memory of her panicking about catching fire.

'Oh, fuck off,' she mumbled.

He stopped laughing. 'What's up?' he asked. Hart was usually quick with the banter. Just telling him to fuck off was a failure in her eyes.

'Nothing other than this rapist.' She put her head in her hands. 'He's ruining my comeback game.'

'We'll get him.' Swanson's tone was serious.

She looked up at him in surprise.

'Yeah, we will.' She smiled. 'I need a wee.'

'I didn't need to know that.' Swanson shook his head as she got up and walked off.

She had a point about petrol *and* paint. Were there any jobs or hobbies where you might smell of both?

He closed his eyes, but the noise of everyone milling around and talking drilled into his skull. He needed to get out and away from the mess. Quiet spaces were far better when he was working through a problem. He crossed the office, dodging DCI Murray's view, and climbed into his black Audi in the rear car park. He could go home for an hour and have a working lunch there, although it would be a late lunch as it was 3 p.m.

He weaved in and out of the mid-day Derby traffic and onto the A52, heading four miles east to his home in Ockbrook. He felt the tension ease as he left the A52 and drove along the quieter roads of the small village. His cottage was behind a Moravian Church, one of very few Moravian settlements in the UK.

He pulled up in his driveway and kept his head down, not wanting to catch the eyes of any neighbours as he hurried to the tired front door. Moving away from his mother would be best. It was only stubbornness that kept him in the village. Why should he be the one to leave? He had moved away for a bit, but that didn't turn out well. Now he lived right behind the highly religious Moravian settlement his mother was a part of. Not that he had anything to do with her or the church. Atheism was more his style.

His cottage had no entrance hall, and the front door opened straight up into the wonky living room. It was his favourite room in the house because it had everything he needed. His telly sat on top of a modern oak TV stand, with a PlayStation underneath that Hart ripped him mercilessly about on the few occasions he had allowed her in his home. A mini fridge that housed energy drinks and chocolate sat next to the ancient sofa. The previous occupants had left the sofa, and it was the comfiest sofa Swanson had ever owned. It was covered by the blanket he slept under when he couldn't be arsed to go upstairs to bed. His weights sat in the adjacent corner, though he hadn't used them in a week. And if he needed anything else, the kitchen was only a few feet away and had a small toilet squished in under the stairs. Other than using the shower, he barely needed an upstairs. The only problem with the living room was the low ceiling when he was working out. Either his fist or his head was going to go through it one day.

He sat on the sofa and pulled out a notebook and pen from underneath. He made notes on what he knew so far and what he didn't yet know. After shaking and scribbling the pen to get it to work, he noted the suspect's description, accent, and the distinctive chemical smells outlined by the victims. That he legged it as soon as the second girl fought back showed he was a wimp and likely to be some sort of social outcast. But it wasn't definite. People had easily fallen for Ted Bundy's charm, including the judge who sentenced him to death. This guy hadn't killed his victims, though. Not yet. So the major concern was escalation. If they didn't catch him, his confidence would grow and the level of violence would probably escalate.

It was unlikely that the first victim was this guy's first crime. He probably started off with something far less risky. So what was he doing until the last six months? And where? What if he had been doing this in another location? Swanson grabbed his phone to call Hart.

She didn't bother with 'hello'.

'Er, why are you calling me? Just come and speak to me. I'm still in the office,' she said.

'I came home for a bit to think.'

'What the?' He could hear Hart moving as if she was looking around for him. 'Oh, that's why everyone is much happier than usual.'

'Hart, listen. I think this might be someone who just moved into the area. We agree these aren't likely to be his first victims, right? He probably started off smaller.'

'Right,' Hart said slowly.

'Well, what if he's just moved to Derby?'

'From a different country?'

'Well, I was thinking from a different town, though I suppose given the strange accent it could be a country.'

'I'll ask Murray what we're doing about cross-referencing similar crimes nearby. I'm sure she's got some guys on it already. Are you coming back in?'

'Yeah, yeah. I'll be back soon.'

He hung up and admitted defeat to the pain in his head. There was an old box of paracetamol in the also-wonky kitchen. He downed a couple of pills dry, then sat back down and closed his eyes, waiting for the pain to go away, but his mind glazed over. And he never made it back to the office as promised.

Astrid

My ex-husband didn't disappear. I murdered him after an argument. Then I hid the body in such a wickedly clever place that nobody would ever find it, and cleaned the scene so comprehensively that I left zero evidence. All while looking after a newborn baby. It really was a miracle. At least, if you asked Ben's family, that's what they'd tell you. But there are many sides to every story, and you should never listen to just one if you want the truth.

My phone vibrated in my pocket. I took it out and threw it on the black glass table in front of me. I would have been in trouble if Harry saw, after telling him to be careful with the glass table many times over the years. The sun returned once again, and shone through the window to bounce off the screen of my laptop. Typical autumn weather. I shifted my position on the sofa to face away from the window and continued to scroll through social media.

All that appeared were the usual self-serving and attention seeking statuses. I never understood why people are so desperate for attention and 'likes'. It all seemed so fake. Harry wanted to be a scientist when he was little. Thanks to *influencers* he now wanted to be a millionaire YouTuber. Personally, I'd prefer to stay in my own world and speak to nobody except Harry ever again. I stopped scrolling and slammed the laptop screen down before throwing it to the other side of the sofa.

I perched on the edge of the seat with my head in my hands and eyes closed. Someone was fucking with me, and I needed to find out who. I was so lost in my thoughts that I didn't think to check my phone. Fear gripped me as the noise of someone yanking on the handle of the front door filled the hallway. I froze, listening for further noise. There was only silence. I shook my head; I was hearing things.

Then the banging started.

Someone was trying to get inside my house.

My heart thudded as I jumped off the sofa and ran into the corridor, stopping dead in the doorway to the hall. Nobody *ever* visited us unannounced. Nobody knew where we lived. So who the hell was banging on my door?

I pulled at the band on my wrist, hoping it would help to stop my panic from spiralling. It didn't work this time. The door handle rattled again as someone pushed against the door. I stepped away and backed up until I was in the kitchen. *Should I get a knife? Should I call the police?*

The darkness began in the corner of my eye. It always started there. I needed to calm my anxiety or the darkness would creep out into the room, seeping into the ceiling next. That's when the fear Arracht would appear. My very own monster. But I couldn't lose myself in the darkness today. I had to find the person who wrote the note, and I couldn't do that by hiding.

I pulled the elastic band harder, but the quick flash of pain wasn't enough to drag away the darkness. My panic had grown too quickly. The door banged again, and I ran to the far end of the kitchen. I crouched on the floor, nestled into the corner. It felt the safest place, and my legs were weak from fear.

The darkness seeped into the room as I knew it would. The corners of the kitchen ceiling turned grey at first. A fuzzy grey, like when an old TV loses signal. I closed my eyes and hummed. I didn't want to hear the guttural sound of the Arracht. It would reverberate off everything around me and stick in my brain.

Yet, through the darkness, a glimmer of determination reached out to me. I could not let the poem undo all of my hard work. That was what the sender wanted, and I refused to let them win so easily. I opened my eyes and forced my legs to stand. The movement made the blood rush to my head. My vision quickly went dark, and the kitchen turned sideways.

At first I thought the Arracht had arrived, silently for once. After a few seconds, the kitchen righted itself and my vision cleared. I stumbled to the kitchen doorway and leant against it, to flick the band against my wrist in quick bursts of three. This time it worked, and the pain absorbed my anxiety. I walked to the front door.

And then the yelling started.

Sophie - June 2007

It took three hours to decide on the little black dress from New Look, and now Sophie regretted it. It was far too short and men kept looking over, making her even more nervous than she had been on the walk over. She hoped she looked old enough to not be asked for ID in front of Ben. That would be seriously embarrassing. Luckily the bouncers let her straight in.

The smell of beer hit her the second she walked into the pub. It was more of a local drinking hole than a place to go for a proper night out. It surprised Sophie to see so many people inside on a Saturday evening. There were mostly groups of drunken men dotted around on various tables and bar stools. Some turned to stare at her, but she was careful not to return any looks so she didn't lead anyone on. There was only one person she was interested in seeing tonight.

The noise from other punters faded as Sophie spotted Benjamin Bates sitting alone at the table nearest to her. She'd never seen a cheesier grin than the one on his face at that moment. She grinned back at him and walked over.

'Hi,' she said, as she sat across from him and placed her bag on the chair next to her.

'Hey. I got you a beer.'

Ben pointed at the pint sitting in front of her and she took a sip, wishing she knew what to say on a date. What did people on TV do?

'So, have you been here before?' he asked. He looked down at his own pint and fingered the rim of the glass.

'Yeah, I've been here a few times with Mel and a few of the other girls,' Sophie said.

Ben's grin dropped as soon as she mentioned Mel. *Shit*. Had she just ruined her first date within the first five minutes? 'Have you been here before?'

'No, but I've heard Mel talk about it. She said it's one of the less shitty pubs.' He looked up at her and his grin returned.

'They make nice food,' Sophie said, her panic over and lesson learned. She wouldn't mention Mel again.

'Do you want to eat? I'll buy you something. What do you want?' He reached for his wallet.

'Oh no, I don't want anything. I was just saying.' She laid her hand on her stomach to stop it rumbling as he counted the notes from his wallet.

'No, no. If you want food, I'll buy you food. Do you want chips? Shall we share some chips? Yeah, we'll share some chips,' he decided for them.

Sophie laughed.

She studied him as he walked to the bar. His cocky stride and confident grin hid a sweet awkwardness. She tried not to think about Greg. That bastard had hurt her enough, and there was no way she would go back after he chose her mother over her.

'Cheer up, it might never happen.' Ben's voice shocked Sophie out of her trip down memory lane.

'Oh, sorry! I didn't see you coming.' Sophie tried to laugh it off.

'No seriously, what's wrong? Have I upset you?'

'No. Definitely not. I was just thinking about something.'

'Was it your mum?' Ben asked.

'My mum?' Sophie stared at him.

'Yeah… sorry, I shouldn't have asked. Mel said you haven't seen her in like a year. I was just being nosey, I guess. I'm sorry. You don't have to tell me anything.'

'No, no. It's OK. It's just that people rarely ask me about it. I think they find it awkward to ask.'

'I have a habit of speaking before I think. I hope I haven't upset you?'

'No. I'm fine. And no, I haven't seen her in a while. I moved out after she chose her boyfriend over me.' Greg choosing Mum over her would be more accurate, but she wasn't having Ben think she was a slut.

'Parents suck.' He reached over and took her hand. Her dainty fingers disappeared in his fist. 'I'll take care of you.'

She laughed. Ben didn't. His face was serious. 'I mean it, Sophie. I'll take care of you, if you let me.'

'I don't need taking care of, but if you're offering…' Sophie laughed and ignored the nerves creeping in, because she knew that within those opening minutes of their first date, she had fallen in love with Benjamin Bates. And love never ended well for her.

Astrid

'Muuuuuum!' Harry yelled through the door. 'Open the door for God's sake!'

In all my years of being a mother, I'd never been so relieved to hear him yelling my name in such a pissed off tone. I sprinted to the door to let him in.

'What the hell are you doing here?' I said, embracing him the second he got through the door.

'Er, school finished.'

I let him go and he grinned up at me, clearly finding the situation hilarious.

'Jesus, Harry, you should have called! You aren't big enough to cross that main road by yourself.' I couldn't help but raise my voice.

He laughed at my shock. 'You shouldn't be late then! I can't just stand across the road waiting for you like a five-year-old.' He rolled his eyes, as did I. He may not look like me, but he certainly had the same attitude I had as a kid.

'Just call me next time!' I said. I let him inside the hall and closed the front door behind him.

'Oh, so you're planning on forgetting about me again then?' He raised his eyebrows.

'What? No! Of course not. I'm sorry, baby. Come here.' I kissed his soft forehead and squeezed him tight again.

He allowed it for a second. I breathed in the soft scent of his shampoo and felt my anxiety dissipate. Then he shrugged me off like he always did lately. I looked away so the hurt didn't show on my face. He was growing up, and that was a good thing.

'It's OK, Mum. I enjoy walking on my own. I'm going upstairs to watch YouTube.' He kicked off his school shoes, leaving them a foot away from the shoe rack, and ran up the stairs to his room.

I didn't bother to tell him to put his shoes away properly. Instead, I watched him disappear around the corner on the landing, my heart still thumping. As soon as he left I pinged the elastic band on my wrist, closed my eyes and imagined the panic draining away. Harry was fine. I made one mistake after a terrible day, and I won't let him down again. I'll order his favourite Chinese food for dinner as an apology.

Feeling calmer, though still shaken, I locked the front door and pushed the handle down three times to make sure it wouldn't open. In the kitchen, I made sure I'd locked the back door as well. Again, I rattled the handle three times to calm the fear, even though cameras lined our front and back gardens. I returned to the living room to carry on my research.

Cameras lined our front and back gardens.

I slapped my forehead. How could I have been so stupid? The note had turned me into a gibbering mess. I grabbed my phone. Harry had texted me to say he was walking home and my guilt increased. I shouldn't have ignored it when Harry relied on me to be a good parent.

I opened the camera app and scrolled through the saved recordings, searching for this morning's visitor. The camera recorded every bird that flew by, every car driving past the front, and every cat that visited the garden. So there was a lot to scroll through to find the visitor.

I scrolled right down to 8:35 a.m. and watched Harry and I leave for school. A minute later, a boy not much older than Harry rounded the corner and stopped outside our front gate. He looked left and right before slipping through the gate and running up the drive with something white in his hand. I felt nauseous looking at this intruder on the drive, despite his young age. He disappeared briefly as the porch overhang blocked the camera's view, before he left the garden round the same corner he came from.

I rewound the recording back to where he stood at the gate, looking straight at the house, and I zoomed in on his face. His pale face was clear, as were the accompanying pimples and the scrap of paper in his hands. But I didn't recognise him at all.

The fact that it was a child made it somehow worse. I hadn't expected to see Mel or Kai sauntering down my drive with the note in their hand, nonetheless I had at least suspected to see an adult. A child surely wouldn't write such a threat and post it through the door. Then a realisation hit me that made the darkness rush at me once more. Maybe I was wrong, and the threat wasn't related to me and Ben. Maybe the note was for Harry.

'Never again will you grow.'

Summer

Aaron sat opposite me, sipping fresh coffee in a small cafe belonging to a farm, only ten minutes from Adrenna hospital. He ran his long fingers through his floppy black hair, as he often did when nervous. I fingered the glass of cold water in front of me. It had only been six hours since I'd seen him in the hospital. Apart from the drizzle of rain against the windows, and the chatter of a nearby family, the silence hung in the air between us.

Not that long ago our bodies were curled naked around each other. But we hadn't seen each other since his release from hospital just over a month ago. I wanted to give him space and time to heal after what Marinda did to him and his mother. I also didn't know what to say to him, and he didn't call me either.

'So, Summer Thomas.' He smiled at me. I missed his smile. His pale face lit up from even the smallest smirk. 'How have you been? How's Joshua?'

'Joshua is great. Cheeky as hell. He's at my mum's house at the minute. I'll pick him up when we're finished, seeing as I'm done working for the day. I'm OK, too.' I paused and smiled, not sure what to say next. Our eyes locked, and I cleared my throat and looked away. 'You have a new job then?'

'Yes. I couldn't go back to Derby. I know Marinda isn't there anymore, but still. Too many memories. And I didn't want her knowing where I worked. I've moved house too.'

'Where to?' I asked.

'Nearer to Adrenna.' He looked away.

I didn't push him further. Maybe he didn't want me to know either.

'So how long have you been working at Adrenna?' I asked instead.

'Not long. Two weeks now.' He slurped his coffee.

'Oh.' My smile dropped.

'What's wrong?' He put down his coffee and turned his full focus towards me.

'I was just hoping you could help me with something. It doesn't matter if you're so new.' I tried to hide my disappointment. He wouldn't have any idea where the hospital had released Eddie to. He probably didn't want to know anything about Eddie, anyway.

'Summer, you know I'd do anything for you.' He leant over the table and squeezed my hand, but caught himself and let go, clearing his throat.

I moved my hand back to my lap. 'Aaron, you've got a new job. A new home. You're still healing both physically and mentally, and I don't want to impede that. Anyway, I'm not even sure if I want to find him. It's feeling like all the signs are saying I shouldn't bother.'

'Find who?'

'Just a patient. It doesn't matter, honestly.'

'Another missing patient? I'm not going through all that again, Summer! And I definitely don't know anything this time.' He gave a hollow laugh.

'No! Not a missing patient.' I laughed too. 'Adrenna recently moved a patient to a low security unit. I'd like to know where he went is all. Just to see if we work with that unit. I wanted to check in on him.'

'Oh, well, that doesn't seem like a hard request? I'll just check the computer. It should say.'

'You're not allowed!' I protested.

'Who's going to know? I won't tell if you don't.' He shrugged. 'What's the patient's name?'

'OK. It's not *just* a patient, His name is Eddie Thomas.' I gave him an apologetic look.

His face paled. 'Eddie? As in Marinda's ex boyfriend Eddie?'

A protective instinct flared within me from somewhere. 'No. Eddie as in my brother Eddie, who Marinda fucked up so badly he nearly killed his own mother.' The words came out much harsher than I meant. I sighed and rubbed my face in my hands. 'I just wanted to see if he's OK. He's a victim too, just like you. He needs to know what Marinda did. He needs to know he didn't hear those voices, and that she was responsible for what happened.'

'He still tried to kill your mum, Summer!'

A few tables down, two children looked over at us. The parents tried to distract them with the menu.

Aaron lowered his voice. 'He's dangerous.'

'Yes, which is why I'm not sure I want to find him. But they've locked him away all these years, Aaron, and why? Because that evil woman took complete advantage of his fragileness after Dad died. He needs my help.'

'What about Joshua?'

'I won't let Joshua anywhere near him. I'll make sure of it.'

'Sorry, Summer. I can't help you. It isn't safe.' Aaron stood, his chair scraping against the floor. The family turned again to stare at us.

He walked away before I could reply.

I lowered my head to hide my flushed cheeks. Aaron's reaction wasn't a surprise. I couldn't blame him. There certainly wasn't much chance he would call me now.

I gave him a few moments to drive away and then walked out into the drizzling rain. I pulled up my hood, wishing I'd parked closer. Halfway down the street, I noticed Aaron was still in his car, engine on, staring out the window. He looked up and spotted me. Our eyes locked. His mouth opened as if he was going to say something, but he turned away and sped out of the car park instead.

I continued to my car, my heart heavy with guilt and annoyance. It was me who Marinda had wanted to hurt, yet it was Aaron who got caught in the middle and suffered the consequences. Him and his poor mother. But my brother needed me, too.

And DI Swanson was the only other person I knew who might help me.

Astrid

I tried to act as normal as possible that evening. I ordered Chinese food as a surprise and shouted at Harry to come downstairs once the food arrived and I'd set out his plate of chow mein.

'Look, your favourite!' I said, as I followed him into the kitchen.

His face lit up as I'd hoped. 'Thanks, Mum!' He grinned. He scraped the chair across the tiles as he sat down to eat. I winced, but clamped my mouth shut.

'How was school?' I asked instead.

'It was fine.' He shovelled the dripping noodles into his mouth.

'Careful! It's still quite hot.' I tried not to stare at him as I considered how to get him to talk. 'You do anything good at school?'

'It was school, Mum. Of course not.'

I tried a couple of times to get more than a few words out of him, but it was no use. He just didn't open up to me like he used to. We settled in the living room after our food, pulling out the recliners and watching the newest Ice Age film, sharing a bowl of sweet and salty popcorn. The film was one of a few favourites that he wasn't too old for yet. I glanced at him. He looked relaxed, lying back, his floppy hair hiding his forehead.

Yet there was something on his mind. We usually laughed and chatted together, and he had barely made a sound since the film started. Maybe he was mad at me for forgetting to pick him up but didn't want to admit it. Maybe he was just in a pre-teenage, sulky mood.

I could not mention the note. The words were far too haunting for an eleven-year-old to hear. I didn't want to scare him. But I had to find out if he knew that kid.

'Get up to much at break time?' I enquired, trying to sound light and carefree.

'What? No. Just a normal day.' He shrugged, still staring at the TV screen.

I tried again. 'What did you get up to?'

'Can't really remember.'

'It was only a few hours ago.' I laughed.

He shrugged again.

'Listen, when you won't talk to me it makes me think things *aren't* OK. You would tell me, would you? If you had any problems?'

'Of course, who else would I go to?' He gave me a look that asked if I was losing my mind. He was right. We had no one else, really.

'Well, there's Barb if you ever needed someone and I wasn't around. Do you have her number?' I suggested our landlady, my only friend.

'Yes, of course.' He looked away and back to the TV screen. 'I can't hear the film, Mum.'

I sighed but stopped talking. It was pointless. When he was smaller, I always knew what was wrong. It was me and him against the world after his dad's disappearance. I was honest with him and told him everything I could about Ben. Harry didn't seem too negatively affected by the whole thing, although it had to have an effect somewhere along the line. Now he was a pre-teen, it was becoming more and more difficult to know what he was thinking.

Could that note really be for him, though? The only thing I knew for sure was that I would not let Harry out of my sight until I found out what was going on.

The next morning, I got lucky and could put my plan into action straight away. Thanks to the pouring rain, Harry was happy to be driven to school and I didn't need to explain my sudden insistence that we drive there. We pulled up outside the entrance to the school.

'Want to stay in the car for a bit? It's still chucking it down out there.'

'Yeah, alright then.' He raised his voice over the rain hammering on the car roof.

'Want to play eye-spy?' My fingers drummed the steering wheel as I surveyed the school grounds in search of the boy who delivered the note. His pale face stuck in my mind.

'No, thanks.' His tone suggested he was unimpressed with my suggestion. 'Why do you still have the engine on?'

'So I can keep the windscreen wipers running.'

'Why bother?' His tone was still hostile.

'So you can see when your mates turn up,' I lied. I continued to survey the street, where everyone rushed by with hoods up and brollies open. It would be difficult, if not impossible, to spot the kid if he passed.

'Can I sleep at their house tomorrow night?' Harry asked, his tone lighter.

'Whose house?' I turned awkwardly to face him in the rear seat.

'The twins, obvs,' he said, giving me a big smile. It was amazing how sweet kids could be when they wanted something. 'Please?'

'OK,' I said after a moment's silence. At least if he was at the twins' house he'd be safe.

'Thanks, Mum.' He grinned at me. 'You're alright, you know!'

I laughed and shook my head. We sat quietly, each lost in thought, and a few minutes later the hammering stopped and the rain slowed to a drizzle.

'I'm off, Mum.' Harry pushed down the car door handle.

'OK, babe. Be careful, won't you?' I replied, watching him through the windscreen mirror.

'Careful of what?' He threw me another exasperated look.

'Oh, you know, just in general.'

'Erm, OK.' He began to leave the car, then stopped and looked down at his feet.

'You OK?' I asked.

'Yes... Love you.' He ran out of the car and slammed the door shut before I could respond.

I smiled as I watched him rush over to the school gate with his head down against the trickle of rain still coming.

Then I saw a figure by the gate, and my smile dropped.

I craned my neck to get a better look. It was a man, dressed smartly like a teacher. But it wasn't a teacher I recognised. He put out a hand to stop Harry as he reached the gate, and though I saw his lips move, I couldn't make out what he was saying.

Harry turned back to look at me with a befuddled look on his face. A cloak of fear grew around me. Something about this man wasn't right. I rushed out of the car. As soon as I opened the car door, the man hurried away. Within seconds, I lost him in a sea of faces. I ran to Harry, still stood at the same spot looking at me.

'What did he want?' I was breathless by the time I reached him, despite only running from across the road.

'He asked if I know somebody called Sophie Hunting.' Harry shrugged. 'Weird, eh?'

I felt the blood drain from my face, and tried not to show my shock. The street spun. I grabbed the gate to steady myself.

'Mum? You OK?' Harry's worried face looked up at me.

'Er, I don't feel too good, to be honest, babe. Dicky tummy. Run off into school and I'll get home quickly. Don't worry about that guy and don't leave the school without me. I'm picking you up from the playground today.'

For once, Harry didn't argue. He just nodded and walked off. Though he kept turning to eyeball me as he walked away.

I smiled and waved at him until he disappeared, but the edges of my world were darkening. The street spun again as I whirled around to find the figure, though I knew he was long gone. I closed my eyes and made sure the spinning stopped before I fought through the crowd of kids, parents, and teachers. I couldn't spot him anywhere.

I stood still, looking at the streets he could have vanished down. There were so many possibilities. He would be miles away if he drove.

Darkness encased my vision, and I needed to get home to safety. I flicked my elastic band as best I could under the sleeve of my coat and took deep breaths as I hurried back to the car. I could see other parents and kids staring at me. I didn't care.

Once in the car, I threw off the coat, closed my eyes and flicked the band properly. When I opened them again my vision was clear, and I knew what I had to do.

I rushed back home and sat in my car for a moment to make sure the kid wasn't around waiting to deliver anything else. My two neighbours across the street were chatting in their respective front gardens, so I didn't sit in the car for too long.

I listened for the sound of another note as I opened the door. It relieved me to hear nothing, and I rushed to lock the door behind me.

I didn't bother trying to work this time. Instead, I used my laptop to look up estate agents, both in the area and further outside. I had money saved to move away. The tricky part was that I needed to rent and remain anonymous. The two requirements rarely went hand in hand. I rented from Barb because she was happy for me to give her cash in hand. There was no contract, so she hadn't formally recorded our agreement anywhere. I've never been sure what Alex Swanson told her to convince her to let me move in, to be honest. But she'd only ever called me Astrid. She didn't know the name I was born with.

Yet that man at the school knew my other name. Sophie Hunting.

Ben and his family knew me as Sophie Hunting, though I became Sophie Bates not long after we met. A little too soon, according to his family. The strange man not only knew this, he also knew Harry was my son. He must have seen me in my car with him. This stranger knew I would see him talk to Harry, and he must have had an escape plan because he disappeared within seconds. But that man wasn't Kai. So who the hell was he, and how did he know who I was?

The name change was all done legally by unenrolled deed poll, which meant no solicitor involvement and no public record. I had proof if I needed it, though other than travel I didn't need to evidence it much. No one should have been able to find out via public record. Yet someone *had* found me.

Even so it didn't matter. I could move house and get away again. I'd done it once, I could do it again. And this time, I had spare money, and an older child rather than a baby. I had far more experience of being a mother and an extra decade's worth of life experience. We could do it properly this time. We could start a new life somewhere amazing.

I could tell Harry I was making more money and wanted a bigger kitchen or more rooms. Maybe a games room; that might convince him. We could move to the beach. Harry loved the beach. Or even Scotland—although I'd heard it was always cold there. I hated being cold. Moving south might be nicer. It was expensive down south, but I could afford it thanks to my illustrating business.

I drove to school at 2:45 p.m. to wait for Harry. They didn't finish lessons until 3:30 p.m. but I wanted a spot right outside the front gates. Despite the fact it would upset Harry. He could have more freedom once we moved. That could be another thing to add to the bargaining chip.

I studied the space around the school, watching for the man to appear again. Half of me wanted to confront him, the other half wanted to never see him again. I supposed the best thing to wish for would be him disappearing and everything just going back to normal. I had to face the fact that was unlikely to happen. He hadn't appeared when Harry sauntered out of the gates at 3:40 p.m., chatting to Tom and George as he walked. The same friends he was having a sleepover with tomorrow night.

He saw my car within a moment of leaving the school gates, so I waved at the three of them. His face dropped. He sloped into the car with his head down.

'I'm not that embarrassing, am I?' I smiled at him.

'Let's just go home,' he rolled his eyes.

I would have laughed if I wasn't so distracted, still searching for the guy from that morning. 'Anything else happen at school?' I asked in the most unassuming voice I could muster. I pulled off from the street and began the short drive home.

His head shot up from his phone. 'What do you mean?'

'Any more strange men asking if you know random people?' I eyed him through the front mirror as we stopped in school traffic, waiting for someone to let us out onto the main road.

'Oh yeah, forgot about him. That was weird!' He relaxed again.

'Yeah, it was. So, any more odd things happen?' It was like getting blood out of a stone. Something had made his head shoot up like that, though.

'Oh no. Just another boring day at school.'

'Why did you look at me so strangely when I asked then?'

'Because you're being weird and I didn't know what you were talking about!'

I couldn't disagree, so we drove the rest of the way home in silence. Driving was such a waste of time when it took less than five minutes, yet I felt safer in the car. It was a weapon, after all. More people probably died from cars than guns. At least in the UK. And I could put my foot down and just speed away at any moment.

A genius thought hit me: a camper van. It would be perfect! No one would ever find us. Would it be cool enough to convince Harry?

Once we reached home, Harry mooched up to his room again to watch YouTube while I made dinner. I practiced the conversation in my head.

The campervan was one idea, despite how expensive they were. We could move to the beach, or near mountains. We could have a games room if we had a house. Then I hit on something I was certain would work. I'd always refused to buy him a dog, not wanting the additional responsibility if we had to move. But a puppy had a real chance of convincing him the move was a good thing.

I made Padella's pici cacio e pepe for dinner. Pasta was another of Harry's favourite foods. Cooking was never my strength, until Harry reached six months old and I realised I needed to reduce his milk and feed him proper food. I taught myself healthy cooking through online videos and now I was proud of my skills.

I called Harry downstairs once it was ready. Excitement coursed through me at the thought of his smiling face when I promised him a puppy. I flicked the band on my wrist three times, just to rid the last speckles of anxiety.

'Hey baby.' I smiled at him and kissed his forehead. 'Made your favourite.'

He beamed as he sat down to eat his pasta. I sat opposite and gazed at him for a minute before picking up my fork and shovelling some pasta into my mouth. I tried to gauge his mood, though I supposed it didn't matter either way. My appetite was humongous. It was the fear that caused it, feeding off my anxiety and causing my appetite to become insatiable.

I swallowed my pasta and smiled over at him. 'Harry, I have some exciting news.'

He looked up with a grin, pasta spilling from his mouth as he spoke. 'You're pregnant?' He pointed to my stomach.

I laughed. 'Harry! This is serious.' It was nice to see him with his sense of humour back.

'Oh no.' He rolled his eyes in mock exasperation and flicked his empty fork around. 'Go on then, break it to me.'

'I've had a fantastic idea. I got a big job and came into some money, and I think... I think we should use it wisely. Maybe we should move.' I let my words sink in before continuing.

His face dropped. He stopped eating his pasta and stared at me. I couldn't tell if he felt panic or anger. 'What? Why?' he asked in a small voice.

I cleared my throat and looked down at my pasta. The black cloud grew in the room's corner once again, darkening my peripheral vision. 'Well, I thought we could go somewhere amazing! Like the beach?' I smiled as broadly as I could and hid my arms under the table to flick my band.

'I don't want to live on the beach. It's for holidays. I don't want to move, Mum.'

'I thought you'd say that. Look, if we lived near the beach we could get a puppy. Any puppy you want. We'd be in the right area for one. There's nothing around here for dogs, but if we moved to the beach...?' I let my trump card sit in the air and prayed it would get the reaction I needed.

The silence became uncomfortable before he spoke. 'My friends, Mum... I don't want to move schools. I don't want to be the new kid with no mates.' His fork clattered as he threw it down onto the table.

'You hate school.' My anxiety was rising and the dark cloud now covered the entire kitchen door.

'I don't hate my friends, though.' He pouted and folded his arms across his chest. 'I wouldn't see them anymore.'

'If we moved, you wouldn't have to go to school.' The words came out of my mouth before I had even considered them. 'You could learn from home and play the rest of the time. You could chat with your friends online and then see them on weekends. They could visit and you could visit them. It will be fine.'

'Why?' He looked at me, his eyes hard.

'I told you why. I just... it would be nice to live near the beach.'

'No. You've just promised me a dog and no school? You're desperate to move house suddenly. What are you not telling me?'

Sometimes I forget how grown up he was these days. Harry had spent his entire life in my company. He knew me better than anyone.

The shadow threatened to swallow me whole. I grabbed my skin and pinched, digging my nails in hard. Pain grounded me, and as long as I stayed grounded, the shadow would shrink again.

'Well, the big job I mentioned, it's in Cornwall.' I told him the first lie which came into my head. Anything to distract him. I was a good liar. I'd been lying about my identity for years.

'Ooh, so that's why you want to move. Just say that then, Mum. And I'll think about it.' He jumped off his chair and ran upstairs without even asking about dessert.

As soon as he left, the darkness shrank and I breathed a sigh of relief. The fear was often my friend, but when it grew too big, bad things happened. It had the power to take over everything, including my thoughts and actions.

I didn't bother to scold him for not putting his plate away as I usually would. I was glad he'd gone to think about it. He needed space to come to terms with what I was asking from him. I'd planted the seed. All I needed to do was wait.

After washing up, I retreated to the living room and spent an hour looking at properties in Cornwall, which was expensive compared to Derby. I wondered how to rent a house without exposing my identity. I couldn't go to a normal estate agent. Surely that would be traceable? After some searching, I found a website featuring private landlords with empty properties. Still, it was risky. I'd have to meet them first to make sure I could trust them, and I didn't have time for that. Harry returned downstairs just after I closed the laptop.

'Mum.' His voice was barely audible as he stood in the doorway looking at the floor and twiddling his hands. He looked so small. 'I was thinking about what you said, about moving.' He looked up at me with sorrowful blue eyes. 'I'd miss it here.'

My heart ached for him. The one thing I'd vowed to give him was a stable home, after my shit show of a childhood. And I was failing him. 'Come here, baby.'

He walked over to me, and I squeezed my arms around him. A steely determination came over me as I breathed in his scent. How dare this stranger upset my child's life. I'd felt this familiar determination before. 'It's OK. We aren't going anywhere.'

Sophie - September 2007

Sophie curled into Ben's chest as they lay on his battered sofa, watching one of the gangster films he loved so much. The ones she pretended to love just to spend time with him. She breathed in his heady scent and cuddled tighter into his chest.

'Are you enjoying our first night living together?' He kissed her forehead.

'I'll remember this day and night forever.' She smiled back at him. *Fuck you Mum, I am happy.*

'Day?' He raised an eyebrow.

'Meeting Kai!' She moved back and looked up at him. 'He's gorgeous!'

'He's cheeky.' Ben laughed.

'Yes, in a gorgeously adorable way!' Sophie said.

'I'll always take care of you, you know that, don't you?' Ben's face was serious.

'Yes.' Sophie looked away and settled back into his chest.

'What's wrong?' Ben asked.

She hesitated. 'I've heard it all before, Ben.' She looked back up at him. 'Promise me you mean it?'

'You've heard it all before? Do you mean you heard it from Greg?' Bens' face dropped. 'He was a paedophile, Sophie. He didn't love you. Not like I do.'

She tried not to react to the paedophile comment. She looked away, and her body stiffened. Greg wasn't a paedophile. They fell in love. The memory of Mum catching them having sex in the kitchen made her shiver.

Everything was OK until that moment.

Except that didn't matter anymore. Not now she had Ben to look after her.

'Listen, babe. Greg was an arsehole. He used you. Anyone in their forties shouldn't be anywhere near a teenage girl.' Ben pulled her face to his and kissed her hard. 'See? *I* really do love you.'

'I love you too, Benjamin Bates.' She uncurled from his chest and straddled him instead. She pulled off her top and looked down at him. 'See? I'd do anything for you.'

They made love right there on the sofa. And as they lay cuddling afterwards, Sophie knew at that moment they were going to make it. He would never let her go, she'd make sure of it. Whatever it took.

Astrid

Harry lay in his bed, with the duvet half off and TV still on. Faint snores escaped his lips as I watched him. An urge to climb in next to him grabbed me, just like I used to when he was younger. He'd sneak into my bed in the middle of the night most nights until he was nine years old, but one day he just stopped. I couldn't even remember the last time it happened, or the last time he'd kissed my cheek.

I pulled his duvet over him before creeping out and into my own bedroom. My wardrobe area was just big enough to walk into, with lots of shelves to store various items. Or hide them, if necessary. I reached up to the top shelf to pull down a box, the contents of which I hadn't seen in a long time. I moved the box to my bedroom drawer for ease and slipped a heavy weapon I'd hidden into my handbag.

Back downstairs, I triple checked every gate, door and window before climbing into bed just after midnight. I flicked the telly on and surrounded myself in the duvet, tucking every part of the duvet around my body like a swaddled newborn. An old re-run of a game show played on the telly as I closed my eyes, hoping to drift off into a dreamless sleep.

A clicking noise woke me, and my eyes flew open. *Click, click, click.* The telly had turned itself off, as it usually did in the night. I tried to sit. My body wouldn't move. I knew that noise, and it made me sick with dread. *Click, click, click.* The sound was coming from inside the room, and it was getting closer.

Panic built within me. I called out for Harry. My lips moved, yet no sound came out. My breathing came faster; the only noise beside the clicking. I tried again to move my arm, but something was holding it down. Something was holding my entire body down. My vision was clear. The shadow of fear was nowhere to be seen, yet my panic turned to terror. *Click, click, click.*

The far corner of the duvet moved. I couldn't turn my head, and from the corner of my eye I watched a lump under the duvet moving closer to me. It moved a few inches, then stopped. Then moved another few inches and stopped. As it shifted nearer, I saw it was the same size as a cat. Each time it stopped, it would click. *Click, click, click.*

The mobile phone beside me vibrated. Someone was calling me. I desperately tried to reach out to answer it, but the invisible force on top of me was too heavy. I still couldn't move. Sweat dripped into my eyes. The creature was now right next to my leg.

I felt a sharp scratch against my thigh and tried again to cry out. The noise died in my throat. The creature moved up the bed towards my head. I turned my face away as much as I could. It rubbed against my arm, then stopped. The *click, click, click* grew even louder.

I squeezed my eyes shut and willed my body to move. Blood pounded in my ears as I fought against the invisible pressure.

Finally, my arm pinged free. I rolled out of bed onto the floor with a thump and grabbed the phone.

'Hello?' I gasped. I was almost hyperventilating.

I flicked on the light and flung the duvet off the bed. Though I knew the Moralia would have left. It wasn't the first time it had visited me, and it wouldn't be the last. Even so, this was the closest it had come to reaching my face.

A raspy breath down the phone was all that greeted me.

'Hello? Harry?' I said again.

I ran towards Harry's room to make sure he was OK, but froze at the whispered growl at the other end of the phone.

'Tell Harry the truth about his dad, or I will tell him for you.'

The dial tone beeped and I threw the phone away from me onto the floor. My breath came in ragged, quick gasps. I turned to continue down the hall and into Harry's room, my pyjamas stuck to me with sweat.

Harry was sound asleep, still bundled up in his Minecraft duvet. I forced myself to breathe deeper and flicked my wrist. His snores helped to calm me. I closed my eyes and imagined the panic leaving my body. I stood there until my feet ached and I could stand no more. It might have been two minutes or two hours; I had no idea. But then the tears came, and I had to leave so I didn't wake Harry.

I stumbled back to my bedroom on numb legs and recovered the stash of cigarettes from my underwear drawer. It took four tries to light the cigarette with my shaking hands; I leaned out of my bedroom window to smoke it. There was no way I was going outside after that phone call.

The cool night breeze on my face felt good. I took deep, slow drags of the cigarette and watched the smoke as it weaved against the moonlight before fading away.

Tell Harry the truth, the voice had said. It sounded male. Could it be the man from the school?

However, I'd always told Harry the truth about Ben. The only people who accused me of lying were those who believed I was a murderer: Mel Bingham, Julie Bates and Kai Bates. My three suspects.

The Moralia plagued me for months after Ben's disappearance, but this was the first time it had visited me in years. It only visited when I was stressed or scared. I'd never seen what it looked like, but I had named it after a mythical Slavic creature called Mora. Mora was a part human, part animal monster that would invade your dreams and sit on your chest so you couldn't move. But Mora was a myth.

The Moralia wasn't.

At least, not to me. I didn't want to sleep again. The Moralia couldn't get to me when I was awake. I needed light and noise, so I made a coffee and sat in the living room with the telly blaring and the lights turned up to full brightness. But the night's events had exhausted me and, despite the coffee, I drifted off into a dreamless sleep. I woke to Harry shaking me.

'Come on, Mum. We've got to leave for school soon,' he whispered.

'What? What time is it?' My brain was foggy. I yawned loudly and fought through the confusion at being in the living room.

'About eight! Why are you on the sofa? Why are you still asleep?'

'Oh, I didn't sleep well.' I waved him away.

'Is that why the lights are on? Did you watch a scary movie again? You shouldn't watch them!' He smiled at me, knowing how much of a wimp I was.

'No, I just had a silly dream.' I gave him a big grin to prove I was OK.

'Aw, well come and wake me next time you have a nightmare and I'll make sure you're not scared, Mum.' He surprised me by wrapping his arms around me in a bear hug.

'Thanks, kid.' I squeezed him back and kissed his cheek. I'd missed this side of him. 'Now let me go, I need to get ready!'

'I can walk on my own...' He said as he walked into the hallway.

'No, you can't!' I laughed at his hopeful face. 'Maybe soon, though, OK?'

'OK.' He grinned and went into the kitchen.

I rushed into the shower and dressed in skinny jeans and a tight jumper to block out the cool autumn temperatures. I dragged a brush through my hair and attempted a smattering of makeup so my pale face didn't scare anybody on the school run.

Harry made us toast while I sorted myself out. He was terrible at buttering, leaving two large clumps of butter in the middle rather than spreading it around.

'Wow, this toast is the best I've ever had!' I exclaimed as I forced one bite down my throat. 'Come on, we'd better drive so we aren't late.'

'OK, can you not park right in front of the gates?' he mumbled. My pre-teen was back.

'I'll park across from the gates, that's all I can offer.' I shrugged.

We rushed into the car but I was calm on the drive to school. This was not the time to risk a speeding fine. I didn't even look back at the house as we left. I dropped him off across the road and watched him walk into the school rounds. I waited until the crowd cleared, and there was no strange man to be seen. Once the school gates had closed, I left.

It wasn't until my return home that I noticed something was wrong. It wasn't obvious. I don't even know what made me look over as I got out of the car.

Our front garden was small. The driveway took up most of the space to the right, with a grassy area to the left. Lipstick pink Nerines lined the end of the patch of grass. Orange chrysanthemums grew next to them. Someone, or something, had flattened both.

An animal could have destroyed my flowers, but… all of them? Only a massive animal could do that.

A human being sitting there waiting for me, however, would be big enough. The raspy voice from the previous night echoed in my ears. Was he watching me when he phoned? Did he run away when I opened the window to smoke?

I glanced around, my body on alert, but the garden was empty.

It relieved me to find the front door still locked. Nobody could be inside.

I slammed and locked the front door behind me and completed my usual checks. I stood in the hall and listened for noise or any sign of an intruder inside the house. Silence greeted me.

I didn't bother taking my coat or shoes off and instead walked straight into the living room. Perched on the sofa, I pulled my phone from my pocket and opened the camera app. The camera footage rolled in front of me as I scrolled through every recorded movement. Nothing suspicious came to light. I threw the phone away, watched it skitter across the coffee table and skid to a stop against a coaster. I couldn't deny what was happening any longer. Harry and I were in danger.

I needed help, and I had only one person to ask.

Swanson

Swanson swore as he narrowly avoided a driver swerving into his lane. He considered pulling the idiot over to scare him a little and make him drive slower in the future. But he'd overslept by an hour, and he was late for work. His mobile phone rang, distracting him.

He glanced at the car dashboard to check who was calling. Unknown number. He ignored it but listened as the call went to voicemail, hoping the mystery caller would leave a message. Instead, the line went dead. Fine. They would call back if it was important.

The sun broke through the clouds, and Swanson pulled down his sun visor to shield his eyes. He didn't want to wear sunglasses in October. And the sun could get lost as far as he was concerned. The grey sky suited his mood better. His head was pounding.

Less than a minute after it stopped, the shrill ring of his mobile phone began again. He looked down. It was the unknown number. He sighed and clicked the answer button on the steering wheel.

'Swanson,' he muttered. The idiot driver still played on his mind.

'Hi, Alex Swanson? It's me.' A woman's husky voice filled the car.

Swanson held back another sigh and fought the urge to ask who. It never went down well when he did that. Why did so many people expect him to remember them by voice alone? The huskiness awakened something in his memories, though. The female witness from last week, maybe?

'Er, hi.' He stalled for time.

'Hi, I'm sorry for calling, Alex, but I really need your help again,' she said, confusing him further. Nobody from work called him Alex. Even people in his personal life called him Swanson, other than Aunt Barb.

At the thought of Aunt Barb, the husky voice clicked in his memory. 'Sophie? Is that you?'

'Yes. I thought you already knew that?'

'No. It took me a minute to recognise you. It's been a long time. Sorry, what did you say you wanted?' Swanson kept his tone cool despite his surprise.

'I need your help.' She sounded on the verge of tears.

'Look, Sophie. I've given you enough help,' he replied calmly. 'You can't call me every time something goes wrong. We've talked about this. A long time ago.' He ignored the guilt which arose. It felt unnatural to push someone away who needed help, however he had no choice with Sophie Bates.

'I know, Alex. And I promise I tried hard not to call you, but someone is after me. I'm terrified.' Her voice wobbled again.

'Someone is after you? What do you mean?' Despite his reservations, his detective side couldn't help but ask questions. He spotted a shop and swerved into the car park, narrowly avoiding an old lady in a Nissan Micra.

'I got a note through my door the other morning. It told me to tell Harry the truth or I'll go to hell, and never grow. That's a death threat, right? I checked the camera and the person who posted it was some young kid. And then at the school run yesterday morning a random guy walked up to Harry and asked him if he knew me.' Her voice grew louder with each sentence.

'A child put a daft note through the door and then someone asked Harry if he knew you? It hardly sounds like someone is after you, Sophie.' He rubbed his beard and closed his eyes. He should have cut her off earlier. She always dragged him into her messes somehow.

'Yeah, well, my name isn't Sophie anymore, so why would they be asking for me under that name, Alex? And that's not it — if you'd let me finish. Someone called me last night from an unknown number and called me a murderer and when I woke this morning they'd been outside my house!

They had trampled all of my flowers.'

OK. Maybe she really needed his help this time. 'Did you see them?' Swanson asked.

'No. I've checked the CCTV and I can't find any recorded footage of them, but if it was dark and they were slow enough, it might not pick them up. It's not great in the dark.' Her voice had changed to little more than a whisper. 'Something weird is going on, Alex. I need your help.'

The guilt grew, yet he knew he couldn't get dragged in again. He could lose his career, and then he'd be no help to anyone. 'Well, notes and anonymous calls aren't my department, Sophie. Call the actual police. They will help you, honestly. It's nothing to do with me.'

'The death of a child would be your department,' she spat and hung up the phone.

Swanson winced as the dial tone filled the car. The dull ache in his head had increased tenfold. Sophie always knew just how to get him to do what she wanted. But it wouldn't work this time. He wasn't falling for it. He dealt with enough nutters as it was, and it became a bigger part of the job every year. It used to be that people were criminals or they weren't. Now everything was all convoluted. It was a good thing for people who were genuinely suffering from mental health issues and needed help, but certainly made things more complicated.

He turned up the radio. Maybe noise would drown out his headache. He pulled away from the car park and resumed his drive to the office.

Unless it got dangerous, Sophie needed to figure this one out for herself.

Astrid

A mixture of annoyance and longing curdled within me like a nauseous cocktail of beer and wine. I knew asking Alex for anything again was a longshot, but I thought he'd care enough to help us. He was a bigshot detective these days, and it seemed he thought himself too important for Harry and me. Still, it was nice to hear his voice after so long, if only for a minute. He recognised me instantly, though I'm not sure he felt the same way about hearing my voice as I did about his.

I pushed my feelings about Alex to one side and concentrated on the next steps. If he was unwilling to help, then I needed another plan. Ensuring Harry's safety was my biggest priority. I didn't know if this person was a physical threat to Harry, but if they threatened a woman, it wasn't a stretch to assume they'd hurt a child.

I texted him and asked him to go straight to Tom and George's house after school for their sleepover. I knew their parents wouldn't mind giving him dinner. It was only a few doors down from the school and he'd walk there with his mates, so he would be safe.

Next, I called Barb. She was the closest thing I had to a real friend. I closed my eyes and prayed for her to answer the phone. She didn't work other than being my landlady, so she was often free unless getting her hair done or a facial. My prayers were answered after only three rings.

'Hey, Barb, how's things?' I stood up from the sofa and circled my living room as I spoke.

'Oh hello, beautiful,' she replied in her exaggerated, clipped accent. 'I was thinking of you earlier. I just picked up a *gorgeous* GG Marmont

Matelassé mini bag. You would love it! It would go great with your lovely leather jacket.'

'Oh, wow! Maybe I could come round and look? My car is in the garage though, so I might be a while since I'll need to take the bus.' I dropped my bait.

'The bus? Oh gosh, no, I wouldn't dream of it. Borrow the Audi. And next time you have an issue you must use my garage, dear. They always give you a courtesy car. I'm getting my nails done this morning, but I'll come by and pick you up at lunchtime and you can drive the Audi back home.'

'Oh, that would be great!' I feigned surprise. 'Thanks so much, Barb.'

'What's wrong with the car, anyway? Actually, don't bother telling me, I won't remember. Just whether it is serious?'

'Oh no, it's only in the garage until tomorrow. I'm not sure what they said. It won't take too long or cost much, so I'm happy.'

'Ah. Well, that's good. Still, it's too long to go without a car. I'll see you at lunchtime!' She hung up the phone. I smiled, I could predict Barb's actions perfectly.

I busied myself with looking presentable while I waited for Barb. My pale face or barely brushed hair wouldn't do. I applied a full face of makeup and curled my hair. For most of my youth I wore it blonde, and only gave in to my natural red after Ben disappeared. Maybe it was time for a change. Although I loved the red, it made me easier to spot in a crowd.

When I looked more like myself, I moved my car into a small car park around the corner where Barb wouldn't see it. Adrenaline kept the fear at bay. The darkness was lurking just out of sight, but it didn't make itself known. Not yet.

Barb arrived at lunchtime just like she'd promised, to my surprise. Barb was an hour late to her own wedding. There was no dramatic reason. She just wanted more time with her bridesmaids. Not that her husband was still around. A car crash had taken his life fifteen years ago. He'd owned a local company which Barb sold for a lot of money after his death. Her deep blue Maserati Quattroporte glinted even in the weak November sun. It was the most comfortable car I'd ever had the pleasure of being a passenger in. I slid into the front seat, feeling like a movie star.

'Hello darling,' she smiled over at me, baring bright white teeth.

'Hi,' I smiled back, showing my own white teeth. I'd always been a little embarrassed about my teeth after not looking after them as a child. I had other things on my mind back then. As soon as I had enough money to be frivolous, I'd asked Barb where she had her teeth whitened.

'How is my sweet little Harry?' She shifted into gear and pulled off from my street.

'Not so little.' I laughed. 'Or sweet. He's acting like a teenager.'

'Oh dear! I suppose it's inevitable,' she said with a grin.

We made small talk all the way to her house. I kept it together, despite wanting to blurt out the plan to her. She was the closest thing I had to a proper mother. But I knew Barb. She would make me go to the police. And other than Swanson, the police were the last thing I needed.

It took less than ten minutes to reach the leafy village of Darley Abbey, where Barb's grand home sat on the outskirts of the abbey itself. She reversed into the driveway as she chatted about what she'd bought for Christmas and who she had left to buy for. She had a lot of friends. Certainly more than I would ever want or need. A few minutes later, I had the key to the Audi in my hand.

'Thanks so much, Barb. I owe you one.' I smiled. Though we both knew there was nothing she would ever need from me.

'You're welcome. Anytime. You know that, don't you?'

'Yes, of course.' The worried look in her eyes aroused my suspicion that Alex had told her something. 'Barb, do you ever speak to Alex?'

'Oh.' She crumpled her brow. 'Not recently, no. He's a detective now, you know.'

I nodded, happy she was telling the truth. 'I just wondered how he was doing.'

'Fine, as far as I know. Sandra told me he's been seeing someone.' She waved a manicured hand around as she spoke.

Despite how long it had been since Alex and I were romantic, a pang of jealousy stabbed at my stomach. 'Who's Sandra?' I tried not to let my disappointment show.

'My sister. Alex's mother.'

The thought of Alex having a mother threw me for a moment. He'd never spoken of her, only his Aunt Barb. The only reason I knew Barb was because she had a spare house when Harry and I needed a new home.

'Are you OK, dear?'

'I just didn't realise he had a mother.' I laughed as soon as the words were out. It sounded ridiculous.

'Oh, yes! Sandra and I don't speak much, mind you. Alex gets his broody ways from her, shall we say? They don't speak much either.' She winked at me.

I smiled and thanked her for the car, then drove back home. I parked across the street and jumped into the back seat where the windows were tinted and I would go unseen to passers-by.

Alex crossed my mind again as I sat there. If he *was* seeing someone, it would explain why he was so off with me earlier. He risked his career for me all those years ago, and now he wanted to forget all about me. Maybe it was for the best. The last thing I wanted to do was get him in any trouble.

It was only early in the afternoon, yet I didn't want to get out of the car and risk the man seeing that I was in the Audi. So I'd stuck some cans of pop and snacks in my handbag so I could eat while I waited. I'd also put in my phone charger, though I could see now that Barb's car had wireless charging installed.

Patience wasn't usually my strong point, but I would have sat there all night if that was what it took. All I needed to do was wait.

The only problem with sitting still was that the Arracht liked to visit when I wasn't preoccupied. Sometimes I didn't mind. He kept me safe, afterall. At other times — when I needed to focus — he drowned out the light too much for me to do so. I was still in control as long as he didn't completely take over my sight. Whenever the corners of my vision darkened, I flicked the band on my wrist and focused on the house. It was difficult, but it worked.

People came and went, walking down the street past my house. My heart stopped each time I saw a man I didn't recognise. Nerves flew around in my gut, making me nauseous. The darkness fell by 5 p.m. with it being so close to winter.

It was barely 6 p.m. when I watched a tall figure emerge from the right-hand side of the street. I didn't take too much notice at first. Then he caught my eye as there was something familiar about him. He sauntered towards my house on long gangly legs. I strained my neck to see his face, but his hood half-hid it.

I had left the gate unlocked and partially open. He stopped as he reached my front gate, and looked around.

As he turned, he looked straight at the Audi. I thought he'd seen me in the back, but the tinted windows were too dark in the evening gloom. I shifted in my seat, leaning towards the dark glass to get a better view. As he turned to walk into my front garden, his hood shifted to reveal his face.

A familiar face.

A face I once loved.

I stared into the face of Benjamin Bates.

All the air rushed from my lungs at the sight of him. I fumbled with the car door trying to get out to reach him, forgetting I'd locked it. It took a couple of tries to pull the lock and push the car door open. My legs were heavy as I stumbled over the road.

My driveway was short, and by the time I reached the gate, Ben was nearly at my front door. I tried to call out but my voice sounded strange and breathless.

He turned just as the motion sensor lights illuminated the garden. We stood only a few feet away from each other for the first time in eleven years. I expected elation. Yet I stumbled backwards, fighting the sudden urge to run from him.

The sensor light bathed his face in a yellow glow.

As I stepped closer I realised that, although I saw Ben's gangly legs, oval face and strong nose, he looked younger than I remembered. His eyebrows were more prominent, and his nose hooked.

'Kai?' I asked, my voice a whisper.

He ran towards me.

I was too shocked to move.

He was fast. I raised my hands to my face to protect myself. His hands were on me in an instant. I felt his anger as he pushed himself into me with all his might. My head smashed against the ground as I fell, and pain shot through the back of my skull. I kept my hands raised and waited for the attack.

All I could think about was Harry. *Please let me survive for Harry.*

Swanson

Swanson sat back at his desk, once again surrounded by a crowd of other officers. His mobile vibrated in his hand, and an unknown number flashed up. It better be someone with good news. He swivelled around in his chair to face the wall and put a finger in one ear before answering.

'DI Swanson,' he said.

'Alex, it's me.' He knew her flustered voice straight away this time. *For fuck's sake.*

'I told you not to call me.' His voice was as calm as he could make it. Sophie's presence in his life only meant one thing for him: trouble.

'Alex, please, I'm desperate. Kai's just been around my house. I saw him this time. I was watching from a car across the street. He knows where I live. I need to move. I need help.'

'What, like a stakeout? And who the hell is Kai?' He was losing his calm edge. Damn headache.

'Ben's oldest son. He thinks I murdered Ben, like they all do. And now he knows where I live. Even if he does nothing violent, he will at least tell the others where I am. Please, Alex. I don't know what to do. It will take time to move, at least a few days. I just want to make sure Harry is safe until then.' Her voice shook.

'What makes you think he would hurt you or Harry? You don't know if he thinks you're a murderer.' Swanson thought about how he would feel if he believed Sophie had murdered his dad.

He decided Sophie had good reason to be worried.

'It must have been him in my garden before. Tonight I caught him about to break into the house. When he saw me, he pushed me to the ground and ran. He'll be back. I don't think he would hurt Harry, but if he thinks I murdered his dad, why would he *not* hurt me?'

'Fine, text me his full name and everything you know about him, and I'll check him out. That's all I'm doing, Sophie. Then we're done.'

He swivelled back around and threw the phone down on the desk. It landed with a thump.

Bloody Benjamin Bates. He'd always known that case would come back to haunt him.

Swanson didn't get scared often. Fear wasn't useful in any situation. Adrenaline was far better. But Benjamin Bates was not a case he wanted anyone else to look into.

He felt a shadow hanging over him, but didn't move. Maybe if he kept his head in his hands they would disappear. A faint whiff of flowery perfume hit his senses.

'Yes, Hart?' He still didn't look up.

'Stop being an arse. We've got a lead, come on.' DI Hart slapped his shoulder. Her perfectly manicured fingernails scratched his neck.

'Watch your claws.' He raised his head to give her an annoyed look. 'What lead?'

'Remember the second victim said the rapist smelled of petrol? Then the third victim said he smelled of paint?' She grinned like a maniac, the bright red lipstick making her look far too happy for the subject matter.

'Yes?' Swanson wished she'd get to the point.

'Well, we thought that might mean he was a painter, or worked in a paint factory or something, right?'

'Uh huh.'

'Well, there's that massive car manufacturer like five minutes outside of the city, isn't there?' She perched on his desk and held her hand out in front of him, inviting a high five for her big revelation.

Swanson thought out loud. 'So… someone who works in multiple departments. Therefore, someone experienced, someone who knows what they're doing, and has been there a long time. It's a possibility.'

Hart lowered her hand. 'A strong one, right? Well, I mean, maybe not *strong*. I know it's still a long shot. But we have nothing else at the minute. Come on. Let's go because they're open until 8 p.m and for fuck's sake take some paracetamol. I'm sick of that miserable look on your face.'

She rummaged into the depths of her faux leather handbag and, eventually, threw a box of pills at him. How the hell do women fit so much stuff into such small handbags? He ignored the pills, downed the glass of water in front of him, and grabbed his suit jacket from the back of his chair. 'Come on then, Robin.'

'You better stop with that Batman stuff or I'll report you to HR for bullying.' She backhanded his chest hard, making him grunt and laugh. 'So that's what it takes to get you to smile, is it? A slap? I'll remember that. Come on, let's go find this bastard. I've got a good feeling about this.'

'You always say that,' Swanson said as they left the office and entered the claustrophobic corridor that led to the back exit.

'Well, one of us has to be positive, Krypto.'

'Krypto?'

'Superman's loyal dog,' she gave him a sideways glance and smirked.

Swanson drove. It didn't take long to reach the car manufacturer. Although the vast area it covered was like a maze to anyone who didn't work there. They found the reception eventually and walked in to face two young receptionists staring at them with big smiles and white teeth. They were both impeccably dressed, with no blonde hairs out of place.

'Good evening. How can I help?' said the one on the right. She looked at them, her head cocked to one side.

'Evening.' Swanson walked forward. He introduced himself and Hart and showed her his ID. Her smile never faltered. 'We need to speak to someone in charge, please.'

'Sure, I'll be back shortly. Please take a seat.' She stood and gestured to the group of grey, egg-shaped chairs behind them. He smiled but didn't move, and watched her walk away. He took a few steps back to stand with Hart.

'I'm not going to fit in one of those fucking chairs,' he whispered.

She grinned back at him.

A few minutes later, the receptionist returned with a stocky man. He introduced himself as Gary in a thick Derbyshire accent. He gestured for them to follow him through to his office.

Gary, in Swanson's opinion, was a bit of an arsehole. He was grey-haired, short and plump. But he walked with the confidence of someone who was used to people moving out of his way, and he *expected* it to happen. He talked a lot as he led them to a plain office just big enough for a desk, with chairs either side. Swanson and Hart sat and explained to him they were looking for someone.

'So you can't tell me what this bloke has done?' His cocky look changed to one of bemusement. He seemed to enjoy having their attention. They were a new audience for him to show off to. He was clearly not pleased that they wouldn't give him the full story.

'We're just following a line of enquiries, that's all,' Swanson said, using his calm interview voice. He'd dealt with a lot of Garys before. 'There isn't much to say yet. When we know more we'll let you know. If it's pertinent, of course.'

'Of course,' Gary nodded. 'But there really isn't anything I can think to tell you at this stage. There are over a thousand people who work here. We have many tall, white men with facial hair. No one stands out.'

'The man we're looking for also has an accent, though it couldn't be placed. Possibly Russian or French,' Hart said.

'Well, I mean, that doesn't help much if I'm honest. A lot of those white men I mentioned have an accent.'

'OK. Could you possibly get us a list of white men over six feet tall who started working here in the last six months and have an accent?' Hart asked.

'Er, I suppose so. That narrows it down. I'll still need some time.'

Swanson and Hart said their goodbyes to Gary and made their way back to Swanson's car.

Hart waited until they were in the car before voicing her opinion. 'I still feel like this is a lead somehow.' She tugged on the sleeve of her suit jacket.

'Yeah, maybe,' Swanson said, 'I guess we'll wait and see.'

'You don't agree with me,' Hart stated.

'Maybe.'

She turned to look at him as he began driving. 'Well, what ideas have you got?'

'It's nearly 8 p.m. I'll drop you at the office then go back to mine. I have an idea in the making, OK?' He stopped at a red light and gave her a sideways glance.

'Such a team player, Swanson.'

'I know, it's my greatest skill.'

Sophie - January 2008

Ben towered over Sophie as she perched on the sofa. She didn't know what to do.

Tears threatened to fall. She choked them back. Crying would make things worse but tears blurred the edges of her vision, anyway.

She could see two Bens floating in front of her. She didn't blink. It was easier when he was blurry.

This Ben was a different person entirely. Not *her* Ben. Her Ben would never get this angry. Only fuzzy, double Ben did sometimes.

'Do you promise?' he asked her.

'Mel's my best mate, babe. I don't really have anyone else,' said Sophie. Her voice shook thanks to the stupid lump in her throat.

'You've got me!' he raised his voice. 'Don't I give you everything you need?'

'Yes! Of course you do.'

'So what do you need her for?'

Sophie said nothing. She wiped her eyes with the back of her fist.

'Who gave you a home, and food?'

She sniffed. 'You.'

He smiled now. His voice calmed. 'Who got you off drugs?'

'You.'

He broadened his shoulders, seeming larger than usual. 'Exactly. I saved you. So you agree? I give you everything you need?'

Sophie nodded, though she had a sinking feeling in her stomach as if she was walking into a trap.

SOPHIE - JANUARY 2008

'Then why would you insult me and everything I've done for you by spending time with someone who is bad for you? Hey?'

She swallowed the bile gathering in the back of her throat.

'How could you throw it all back in my face like that?'

Sophie lowered her head and blinked once. She stared at the floor until her vision blurred again before returning her gaze to Ben.

She knew that if she could hold her eyes open, the edges of her vision would go black, like a shadow creeping over anything she didn't want to see.

Just like it did when her mum got mad when she was little.

'You're right. She was bad for me before, but I won't touch drugs, babe. It's just nice to have a girl to talk to. We can both have friends.' She tried smiling at him. Her vision was so blurry she couldn't tell if it had any effect on his anger.

'I don't need anybody else, and I thought you felt the same way. We've been together for an entire year. Am I still not enough for you?' He was quieter then, and guilt tugged on Sophie's conscience. The angst in his voice broke her heart, and she hated herself for causing him pain.

'It's just different, you know, girl talk,' she tried to explain, 'I can't talk to you about makeup and hair dye. Or periods!' She chuckled quietly, desperate to lighten the mood.

'You think this is funny?' He didn't raise his voice, but there was a threatening edge to his calmness.

'What? No! Of course not. I'm sorry, Ben. Really, it isn't funny. I was just trying to explain...'

He bent down, his nose an inch from hers. 'Are you going to stop talking to that bitch or not?' He clenched both fists at his side.

Sophie's breath stuck in her throat. She'd never seen him this angry. 'OK, I won't talk to Mel anymore.' She allowed the darkness to take over her vision. She couldn't see Ben at all now. 'Anything for you, babe.'

Before she could duck out of the way, he grabbed a fistful of hair to yank her head back and kissed her hard on the lips. He pushed her onto the sofa and pulled up her dress with his free hand.

Sophie kissed him back and closed her eyes. It would be over soon, and he would be her Ben again.

All she had to do was lie back, keep her vision dark and make the right noises.

Everything would be fine.

Astrid

I walked the fifteen steps from the back door to the front door, back and forth between them. The shadow followed me, always close by. Every time I checked each door handle three times, and each time it was locked, of course. It was a pointless waste of time. But walking back and forth kept the anxiety flowing around my body as I walked, rather than it building up if I sat in one place.

I stopped in the kitchen after I lost track of time, and noticed the pretty bottle of Isle of Wight gin on the counter. Grabbing a gin glass, I poured myself a double serving and perched on the edge of the sofa in the living room.

Alex was going to search for Kai. I just needed to wait for him to call me.

I doubted Kai would come back tonight. He must have waited until he thought I was out, when my car wasn't parked in the drive.

I held the citrus gin on my tongue for a moment before swallowing, concentrating on every sip. After a few minutes my hands no longer shook, and my mind was calmer.

I thought about the situation. Kai could have hurt me if he wanted to. He had the perfect opportunity while I lay helpless on the ground, too shocked to move. Instead, he ran off as quickly as he could. Did he intend to push me, or was it a mistake? I saw his eyes as he ran towards me, wide and fearful. I supposed standing in front of a murderer would scare me, too.

I'd expected to feel elation if I ever saw Ben again. Yet, terror overcame me when I thought he was standing in front of me. The worst part was the relief when I realised it *wasn't* Ben. Maybe it was a relief that it wasn't a stranger, though Kai was little more to me than that, really.

The gin numbed my tired body. I lay down on the sofa and pulled a thin blanket over me, listening to the silence for any signs of Kai trying to break in. I closed my eyes, just for a moment.

It didn't take long for the Moralia to come. *Click, click, click.* My eyes flew open, and a dark shadow scuttled across the floor of the living room. It was as quick as a spider and moved in the same directionless way. *Click, click, click.* I felt invisible hands all over my body, weighing me down. I saw a flash of movement again, and a lump appeared under the blanket by my feet. It moved up, stopping at my knees, then my hips. It clicked every time it stopped.

As it reached my breasts, I felt its weight on my chest: it climbed onto my body. I couldn't breathe. There was a sharpness against my chest. Claws tore at my skin. Silent tears ran down my face. The pain intensified. My body jerked backwards as I fought the force holding me down, but I couldn't free myself from its claws.

It ripped more flesh from my chest and I could no longer bear the pain. As the world turned to darkness, I finally screamed.

I rolled off the sofa and my face smashed against the hardwood floor. More pain shot through my nose and lip. I ignored it. I got to my feet and stumbled as I ran to the other side of the room to flick on the light. My hands rubbed my chest. There was nothing there. No blood. No gaping hole from the Moralia's claws or teeth. I heaved deep breaths and let the tears come. The blanket had fallen off the sofa with me and lay crumpled on the floor, empty. The Moralia was gone.

I flicked the band on my wrist and closed my eyes, but the panic would not fall away. The pain of the band barely reached me. I ran to check the back door, pulling the handle three times. Then the front door, the back door, the front door. I don't know how long I ran between them, my breath ragged in my throat. Eventually I calmed enough to collapse at the kitchen table in tears. I needed a coffee. A soothing hot coffee always helped.

But by the time I'd made a coffee, daylight had forced its way through the kitchen window. My head ached. I loved waking to natural sunlight on my face, but that morning the powerful light was unwelcome. It was also a signal that it must be nearly 8 a.m.

I jumped up from the kitchen table, spilling my coffee in my rush upstairs to get Harry ready for school.

He didn't respond to my knock.

I opened his bedroom door and his empty bed confronted me. A fear far worse than the Moralia gripped every inch of me.

'Harry!' I yelled. There was no response. Where the hell was he?

I fell to the floor and tried to catch the vague memories of the previous day. My thoughts were like jigsaw pieces which didn't fit together. I clamped my eyes shut. Did I pick him up from school? No.

Was he at a friend's house? Pieces of our conversation came back to me. I scrolled through my phone to check the last texts we sent to each other; he was at the twins' house. Relief flooded through me.

But I had to get a grip. I needed to go for a run. It was the only thing that didn't fail me when the darkness caught up. I threw on some exercise gear, I tucked my phone and key into the phone holder and ran straight out into the morning air. Everything was going to be OK.

Swanson

Swanson drove to the hotel first thing the next morning, hoping a young lad like Kai wouldn't be awake and checked out of his room by 7 a.m.

It hadn't been difficult to find Kai. All he had to do was call some local hotels last night. Derby was a small city with only a few main hotels. Swanson found him on the third call, at a hotel chain in the city centre.

The hard part was getting away from the team in the middle of the biggest serial rapist investigation Derby had ever seen, though Hart had finally given him some peace once he said he had an idea brewing. His best ideas always came to him when he was surrounded by silence and his own company. Swanson had pored over all the facts again last night and came up with nothing. The press team had released the facial composite and leads were being collated. A special team had been set up specifically to review the leads and put them into an order of urgency. Hart would let him know when they got something to investigate, which probably wouldn't take too long.

Swanson pulled his suit jacket tighter around his chest to ward off the cold air as he crossed the car park. The purpose-built hotel loomed over the east side of the city, with over two hundred rooms. Inside, the reception area was bright and modern, and far too purple. A well-groomed man stood behind the counter with a broad smile on his face. A handful of guests wandered to and from the breakfast area, but none waited at the counter other than the receptionist.

'Welcome, Sir. Are you here to check in?' Mr Well-groomed asked as

Swanson strode up to the desk.

'No. I'm Detective Inspector Alex Swanson.' He flashed his ID. The man's smile faltered as he looked at it, and then back up at Swanson. 'I'm here to see a guest of yours and I need the room number.'

'Oh, erm... OK.' He looked around, spluttering. 'Sure, I think that's alright. What's the guest's name?'

'It is OK. The man's name is Kai Bates.' The ease of the conversation surprised Swanson. There was normally at least a little questioning on whether they could just give him a customer's details. But the man sat down and typed into his computer with no further hesitation. He threw a few nervous glances at Swanson as he searched.

'Kai Bates. Room one-thirty-eight.' He smiled again, bigger than ever.

'Which is where?' asked Swanson.

'Oh, sorry!' the man laughed. 'Up those stairs there, and turn left.'

'Thank you.' Swanson could feel the receptionist's eyes on him as he walked away toward room one-thirty-eight.

It wasn't hard to find. He knocked loudly three times, then heard a mumbling noise and a thud. At least someone was inside.

'Who is it?' a deep voice called.

'Room service,' Swanson shouted back.

More fumbling noises and the door finally opened to reveal a shirtless, skinny young man yawning and running his hands through dark hair. 'Young man' was right: his face showed too much bum fluff for him to be considered a man yet. Three ugly tattoos marked various places on his chest, and even worse ones covered each arm.

'Hi, sorry for the disturbance and the joke. I'm obviously not room service. I'm Detective Inspector Alex Swanson.' He flashed his ID again. The man's eyes widened. 'I'm looking for Kai Bates?'

'Who is it, Kai?' a woman's voice called out.

Swanson looked over Kai's shoulder. A young woman lay in the bed, facing away.

'Nobody, babe,' he called back.

Swanson raised an eyebrow.

Kai moved into the corridor and pulled the door closed behind him.

'Great, so you are Kai Bates then.'

'I ain't done nothing wrong.' The words rushed out as if he'd said them a million times before.

'OK. That's good to know.' Swanson smiled and leant back against the wall. 'So, Kai. What are you doing in Derby?'

'Visiting a friend.'

'Oh!' Swanson feigned surprise. 'A friend you couldn't stay with because…?'

Kai's mouth opened, then closed again. He shrugged. 'Don't see how that's anyone's business but mine.'

'No… maybe not. Do you know where Rose Way is, by the way?' Swanson raised an eyebrow.

'What about it?'

'Do you know where it is?' Swanson said again.

'Nope.' Kai didn't miss a beat.

'Oh, that was a fast answer. Don't need to think about it for a second? Rose Way?'

'Nope.' Kai shook his head.

'Well, there's been a report of you attempting to break into a house there last night.' Swanson lay out the details with care, revealing as little as possible.

'She's lying!' Kai raised his voice. He was becoming more on edge by the second.

'OK. No need to shout. You clearly don't want your friend in there to know I'm here and that's fine. Keep your voice down, and maybe she won't find out. You said *"she's* lying"? Who is *"she"*, exactly?'

'Whoever reported that I broke into their house.' His voice quietened to a loud whisper, but he still waved his arms around in frustration.

Swanson got the feeling that Kai was one of those people who was always loud, no matter how hard they tried to whisper. 'I didn't say a *"she"* was involved, Kai.' Swanson was enjoying himself.

Another look of panic crossed Kai's face. He was an easy nut to crack.

'I didn't say "she", I said "they",' Kai said.

'No Kai, you said *"she"*. And by *"she"*, I assume you mean the lady who lives there. The same lady who supposedly killed your father, right? The one you've been sending notes to and calling in the middle of the night?'

From the expression on Kai's face, Swanson was suddenly unsure.

'Notes?' Kai had already proved he wasn't a good liar, and now he appeared genuinely confused.

'Yes, notes. Phone calls. Breaking and entering. Threatening behaviour,' Swanson said.

'I haven't threatened no one. All I did was push her out of the way! If I'd wanted to hurt her I could have done it. It was dark, and no one was around. But I just wanted to see my brother, Harry. There's no harm in visiting a relative.' Kai smiled in triumph and reached into his pocket. 'I don't even have her phone number. You can check my phone actually.'

'So, you expect me to believe that you didn't send a kid to put a note through her letterbox?' Swanson tried again.

'What kid? I don't have any kids. And I definitely don't know any kids around here, other than Harry. Well, I don't even know him,' he shrugged. 'I just wanted to see Harry to make sure he's OK. Dad would have wanted me to make sure. I've never been to her house before yesterday.'

'Tell me then, Kai. How do you know where they live?'

Kai leaned against the door, folded his arms, and clamped his lips shut.

'Kai, I need to make sure she's safe. Harry too. I need to know how you found them. I need to know who else knows where they are. If you really didn't put the note through their door, then tell me so the police can keep them safe, because someone is threatening them. If it isn't you, then who is it?'

Kai sighed and uncrossed his arms. 'I got a note, too. They pushed it through my mum's door at home. I dunno who it was from.'

'You got a note too? What did it say?'

'Yeah, it was weird, to be honest. Here, I've got it with me.' Kai disappeared into the hotel room and came out less than a minute later. He handed a crumpled piece of paper to Swanson.

'Murderer, murderer, lies in wait,
Murderer, murderer, has your brother,
Murderer, murderer, take her fate,
Murderer, murderer, blow her cover.'

'Is she a murderer?' Swanson looked at Kai.

'We found no body. But if you ask anyone round my way, they'll tell you she murdered him,' Kai was strangely calm. No one would guess he was talking about his dad's murder.

'This doesn't tell you the address?' Swanson held the note up between them.

Kai grinned. 'Turn it over, *detective*. It's on the back.' His grin dropped when he saw the look on Swanson's face. 'Look, I've done nothing, OK? I got the note, I drove up, booked into a hotel, and yeah, I panicked when I went round and saw her. Then I went to the pub, met... her.' He jerked his head towards the door. 'And we had sex all night. That's all that happened.'

'OK. How long are you in town for?' Swanson's headache had returned with a vengeance.

'I dunno.' Kai shrugged and looked away.

'Well, for now, stay here. If you need to go home, call this number.' Swanson handed him his own card. He didn't want Kai ringing the station. 'What's your vehicle registration?'

'I don't see why you need that. I just told you I've done nothing wrong.' Kai was getting animated again, throwing his hands around like a stroppy teenager.

'Kai, just make it easy on yourself and tell me.'

'Fine.' Kai muttered his registration plate, went back inside his hotel room and slammed the door without a goodbye.

Swanson cursed, trust Sophie to drag him into a messy situation at the worst possible time. He turned to walk back to the reception. It was even quieter now that the guests were seated for breakfast in the restaurant. As he walked through the exit, Swanson bumped straight into Mr Well-groomed receptionist.

'Oh, sorry, sir!' The receptionist jumped backwards as if Swanson had given him an electric shock, then looked down at the floor. 'Actually, I'm glad I ran into you.'

'You are?' Swanson resisted the urge to tell him to fuck off. He didn't have time for random issues.

'I don't have to provide my name, do I? If I give information?' He looked back up at Swanson, and pulled at the collar of his shirt.

Swanson eyed the receptionist's name tag. James Farrow. 'No. What would you like to tell me?'

'It's about that man on the TV who hurt all those women.' The man fiddled with his hands and continued to look down.

'Oh?' Swanson's interest piqued.

James motioned for Swanson to follow him, and they walked outside together. There was no one around, and James continued to grin as though he was having a normal goodbye chat with a guest. They strolled over to the empty smoking area.

James looked over his shoulder. 'I know a guy fitting the description I heard on the news last night. He stays here sometimes. He's... rough. And he always brings a different woman with him. I think they're prostitutes. Anyway, we got a noise complaint last time and security said there were some weird things going on in the room when the man opened the door.'

'Weird things? Can you elaborate, please?'

'He tried to block the security guy's view, but he'd already seen the girl's arms tied above her head to the bedpost. We see a lot of strange things. The guard assumed it was consensual and did nothing about it. He saw her leave an hour later, and said she looked fine. But when I saw the image last night... well, it looks a lot like him.'

'OK, please get me his name, address, etc. We'll look into it.'

'OK. Give me five minutes.' James's nerves had disappeared, replaced by a giddy excitement that Swanson had seen a thousand times before, though it didn't get any less annoying. James rushed back into the hotel and returned within a few minutes carrying a piece of paper.

'Is there a reward?' James asked.

'Not for anonymous tips. Thank you, Sir,' Swanson said before turning to walk back to his car.

Swanson drove back to his office through the usual rush hour jams. Luckily, he was in no hurry. It was only 7:45 a.m. and he didn't need to be in until the 9 a.m. briefing about the rapist following the press release.

He knew what the briefing was about already. They finally had DNA from the latest victim. He passed the information from James Farrow onto the newly formed team to process and add to the other tips. Looking at everything they had collected so far, it would be a long day but the DNA gave him hope. Maybe, once examined, it would link to someone who was sitting at home waiting to be arrested and it would all be over. A man can always dream.

Astrid

I ran until my legs were so heavy I could barely lift them, and then I ran all the way home. I pushed through the pain with every step, fighting for breath and thinking of nothing other than my aching chest. The fear Arracht didn't leave me, it was a constant shadow on my back.

It was mid-morning by the time I reached home, and my mind was calmer. I was capable of straight thought again, and that was all I needed. If I could think my way out of this, then the Moralia would leave me alone, as long as I could stay calm. I stopped in my front garden, bent over and gasping for breath. Sweat dripped from every pore, but the cool breeze felt amazing against my skin. I wasn't ready to enter the warmth of the house, so I pulled out my phone to text Harry. The voicemail icon flashed up.

'Hi, it's Swanson. Kai got a note, too. It had your address. Call me.'

I tutted loudly at his message. It was as short and sweet as ever. When it came to information, Swanson was a taker and not a giver. Which was the opposite of how he was in the bedroom.

So Kai said he got a note too… that didn't mean anything. What if he was lying? The only thing that made me think it might be true was that I couldn't imagine Kai writing poems to threaten me. I didn't know him well these days, but if he was anything like either of his parents, there is no way he would act that way. His mum has no brains at all, and as much as I loved Ben, poetry and threats were not his style. He was brutally honest. It was one reason I loved him so much. I'd always hated confrontation as a teen, though I had changed a lot since then.

If Kai was telling the truth, then the person writing these threats knew both Kai's address and mine, and also knew how Kai and I were connected. I needed to know what his note said.

I dialled Alex's number. He didn't answer. I fiddled with the phone holder, grabbed the key to unlock my front door, and shoved it inside the lock.

Yet the key wouldn't turn.

I pushed down the handle, and my new calmness disappeared. The door opened easily.

I hadn't locked it. I'd been too preoccupied with getting out for a run. I edged the door open.

'Hello?' I called out and took one step inside. Silence. I took another step inside, frantically opening up the camera app on my phone to see if anything had happened.

'Close the fucking door, Sophie. Or I'll scream about you murdering my dad so loudly the entire street will hear.' Said a deep voice.

My phone dropped to the floor.

Kai appeared from behind the living room door. *Shit.* He stood still. I swallowed my fear. I could run, but couldn't risk this street thinking I was a murderer. If they called the police, they could take Harry from me. I closed the front door, keeping my face towards him.

'I didn't murder your dad.' My voice shook as I spoke.

'I know.' He still didn't move, though his face softened. 'I just said that so you didn't run. Look, I'm sorry I pushed you yesterday, OK? I just panicked.'

A memory swirled in the back of my mind. Fuzzy thoughts of hands, and pain, and apologies.

'Are you OK?' Kai's voice brought me back to the present.

'Yes. I'm fine,' I snapped. I tried to reach the memory but it had disappeared.

'Can we sit in the living room?' He gestured towards the room behind him.

'I'd rather we didn't.' I stared at him.

'I just want to talk.' Kai looked away. He seemed more sad than angry.

'What about?' I asked.

'My little brother. I have a right to see him.' His face was so solemn. Guilt tugged at me. Maybe Harry had the right to know about Kai, too. I sighed and pointed at the living room.

He walked into the room first, and I waited until he stood at the far side of the room before entering the doorway. There was no way I would trust him because of one measly apology.

He whistled as he reached the far corner of the room and spun around in a slow circle, taking in the expensive decor and large TV.

A mixture of pride and guilt curdled in my stomach. I could have raised Kai here, too.

'Nice place!' he said. His voice was loud, just like Ben's. You'd always hear Ben before you saw him.

'Yes,' I said. There was no point in being modest. 'Harry isn't here.'

'I know. Figured you wouldn't talk to me if he was.'

'I loved your dad.' The words were out before I could stop them, and regret hit me. I didn't want to reminisce. I wanted him to go away.

'I know. I remember.' Kai looked down at his feet.

'What do you remember?' I asked, my curiosity overriding my desire for him to leave.

'When I was a kid, you told me how much you loved him and me. How you wanted me to come and live with you. You never came to get me though.' He raised his head. A small smile lined his face.

'Is that an accusation or a statement?' I couldn't help being defensive. I'd tried so hard to convince Ben to take Kai away so we could raise him together.

'It doesn't matter. My mum needed me anyway so I wouldn't have come.'

I gritted my teeth and fought the urge to say something negative about his mother's parenting skills.

'I just want to see Harry. He's my little brother. He's all I've got left of my dad. Does he even know I exist?'

I shook my head. 'I planned to keep it that way. I thought you all believed I'd murdered Ben. I don't want him getting any thoughts in his head.'

'No. I know you didn't murder him. I believe you,' he paused. 'Harry has a right to know I exist. He has a right to make his own decision about whether to meet me.'

My heart ached looking at his blue eyes. Harry and he looked so alike. They were both the spitting image of Ben. I cleared my throat and looked away.

'I'll think about it.' I stepped away from the living room door to allow him to pass. 'I think you should go now.'

'Fine.' He crossed to the living room door, but stopped when he saw the canvas I used for illustrating.

'What are you doing?' I asked.

He picked up the pencil. 'Giving you my number.' He scribbled something on the paper before leaving the room. He turned to me as he opened the front door. 'But if you don't tell Harry about me, I will.'

'You fucking won't.' I didn't raise my voice. I didn't need to. My intention was obvious. I wasn't letting him near Harry.

'Then I'll be back tomorrow night to tell him myself.' And with that, he closed the door behind him and walked away.

Swanson

Swanson had escaped Hart, and the rest of the team, by hiding in a disused side office that was really more of a storage room these days. He cursed and roughly massaged his forehead with one hand, trying to rub away the painful tension in his brain, as he considered his options. Why did he get involved with Sophie again, when he needed to concentrate on the scumbag getting away with raping women?

He needed to figure out what to do. He'd always known Sophie would need help again one day, and had hoped she wouldn't call *him* when she did. What Swanson really needed was someone to talk it through with, but he couldn't talk to DI Hart this time. She was one of the best detectives he knew, and he didn't need her to figure out the biggest mistake of his career.

There was one person who could help, though. Someone who would understand a fragile mind like Sophie's, and it was the perfect excuse to call. He picked up his mobile and called Summer Thomas. She answered as quickly as she usually did.

'Hey, Summer. It's me.' Swanson cleared his throat and told himself it was a business call, just like any other call he would make for work.

'Hello, DI Swanson.' Her voice was soft, and business-like. Summer was quietly spoken — the kind of person you can't imagine ever losing their cool. But he knew her words would cut through most people like butter if needed.

'Are you free for some lunch? I could do with your opinion on something. Professionally, of course.' *Shit.* Why had he added that?

There was silence for a moment before Summer answered, 'Yes, OK. If you can meet me close by. Barbara's Baps maybe?'

'Barbar's Baps?' That did not sound like a place he wanted to go.

Summer's soft laugh came down the phone. 'Barbara's! It's just a little cafe round the corner from my flat. They make amazing toasties. Trust me.'

A grin spread across Swanson's face as he hung up, but he made sure he wasn't smiling when he left the oversized cupboard-come-pretend office. He didn't need people asking if he had a lead on the case. He'd barely walked a few feet down the hall when he ran straight into Hart.

'Where the hell have you been?' She eyed him up and down.

'Having some peace and quiet away from you.' He continued down the hall. She rushed after him, her short legs and high heels putting her at a disadvantage.

'You know you love me, really. Where are you going?' She called after him.

'Jesus, you're nosey,' he said.

'Just stop for a sec! Bloody overgrown sunflower.'

'What? Sunflower? Is that an insult, or...?' Swanson stopped and turned to her.

'It was the only tall thing I could think of,' she shrugged. 'Look, Ops ran that information you gave about the hotel guy. He lives half an hour away. They can't get him on the phone. It's a dead line. Someone's gotta chat with him.'

'Why? Did we pull anything relevant? He doesn't work at that car place, does he?' Swanson inwardly cursed Sophie again for dragging him into her mess and preventing him from focusing on the case. He hadn't even looked at the name or address that James Farrow provided.

'The first time he stayed in the hotel was six months ago.' Hart smirked as if she was revealing something massive.

'So?' Swanson wished she'd spit it out.

Hart being Hart, she stood and smirked until it hit him.

'Around the time of the first rape?' he said a second later.

'Yep, and there were similar rapes in his area prior to that...' She tucked her hair behind her ear, a sure sign she was about to launch a full-scale explanation or theory.

'Was there any DNA from those rapes?' he interrupted her.

'Nope.'

'So, I take it you've asked if we can chat to him?' he asked.

Hart nodded.

'When are we going to see him?'

'Once we have the DNA from victim three through, we'll have more to talk about. But we could check him out, at least.'

'OK. Give me one hour.'

He ignored her confused look and stalked off down the corridor and outside to his black Audi. He sped out of the car park and ten minutes later he was sitting in Barbara's Baps waiting for Summer. She'd texted him to say she was running later than expected.

A family sat on the other side of the cafe and four builders sat in front of him. He trusted Summer's cafe choice and ordered two cheese toasties and a jug of water. In fairness, it seemed like the kind of place to not skimp on the cheese.

Summer arrived a few minutes later. She glided into Barbara's Baps in a world of her own, not noticing anything around her, a small smile on her lips. The bell above the door jingled, and all four builders stopped talking for a second to look at her. *Arseholes.* He bit his tongue and stood to welcome her.

Her smile widened when she saw him.

'Hi!' She passed the builders without even glancing in their direction. They quickly turned away and carried on with their conversation.

She took a seat across from Swanson and he sat, too.

'I ordered two cheese toasties in case you wanted one... feel free to order your own thing, though. It's not a problem.'

'Oh! Thanks. That's fine. I often order the cheese toastie here. They're amazing.' She ran her fingers through her hair, getting it out of her face. Swanson pushed away thoughts of his own fingers in her soft hair.

'Great,' He smiled awkwardly and, as if on cue, the greying waitress brought over a toastie each and plopped them down on the table with a smile.

'There you go, ducks. Enjoy.' The waitress trudged back to the counter.

Swanson cleared his throat. Summer didn't hesitate to dive into the toastie. He followed her lead, happy she wasn't shy about her food.

'So,' she said between mouthfuls, 'how can I help the great DI Swanson? God knows I owe you one.'

'You don't owe the police anything. It's my job.' Fuck's sake. Why did he act so awkward and stoic around her?

'Fair enough, but I'd like to help if I can?'

'Well, I... we... could use your expertise.' He wished he'd thought more about how to word his request.

'My expertise?' She looked confused.

'Yes. In mental health,' he explained.

'Oh, I see. Don't you have your own guys for that? I'm not a forensic psychologist until another 18 months of supervision have passed.'

'Yes, I know. We have some experts, but it's rarer than you'd think.'

'OK.' She gave him a look that seemed able to see through any bullshit. 'So, what do you need to know?'

'It's about a little-known case. So this is just between you and me.' He kept his voice low.

'Go on.' She put down her toastie and waved at him to continue.

'On your unit visits, have you ever come across someone who completely forgot committing their crime?'

She furrowed her brow. 'Erm, I've had patients say it. Whether it's true is anyone's guess.'

His voice became more urgent. 'Can it be true, though? Is it possible?'

'Well, yes. It's possible for people to forget traumatic events or black out. It's called dissociative amnesia.'

'Don't people remember eventually?' Swanson asked.

'Often, yes. Not always.'

'Does it cause any further problems?'

'Problems? Mentally?'

Swanson nodded.

'Well, it's not like anterograde amnesia, where the patient suffers an inability to make fresh memories. It's usually retrograde amnesia, so they *can* remember new information and therefore make fresh memories. The majority don't even realise they've had amnesia until someone makes them aware of it. Their brain might even fill in the details with new fake memories. But dissociative amnesia is associated with several things. Personality traits, genetics, previous psychological trauma from a young age and yes, other comorbidities such as personality disorders.'

'Like psychopaths?' Swanson asked.

Summer smiled. 'No. Psychopaths aren't an actual thing. Psychopathy can be a *symptom* of a personality disorder, such as antisocial personality disorder. But that's not related to dissociative amnesia. If a murderer suffers from amnesia it's probably because they're so traumatised by their act that their brain has forgotten it. Unlike your average psychopathic murderer. The dissociative amnesia here would more likely be linked to avoidant or dependent personality disorders or obsessive-compulsive disorder.'

'Hmm. I didn't realise you knew so much,' Swanson said.

'What are you trying to say?' She looked away as she laughed, once to the side and then down to the floor. As if her own laughter embarrassed her.

'Just that I'm impressed.' He smiled, and noticed her cheeks colour.

'Thanks.' She took another bite of her toastie and swallowed. 'I know a lot because of my brother, I suppose.'

'Did you visit him at the hospital address I gave you?' Swanson picked up the last bit of his own toastie. It was as good as Summer said.

'Yes. He isn't there anymore. They wouldn't tell me where he's gone.' She still smiled, but the sadness was clear in her dark eyes. Swanson felt an urge to make it go away.

'Oh, you should've said. I can look into it for you.' The words were out before he considered them. Shit. Another favour amid everything else?

'I didn't want to ask… but I'd be grateful.' She smiled over at him. Fuck it.

'Want to grab a drink later? We can talk some more?' Swanson asked.

She looked at him, her eyes widened. She looked away again before answering. 'I have Joshua tonight. But I'd love to another time.'

'Sure, just let me know. I have to get back to this case now, though.' Swanson felt his own cheeks colour. 'See you.' He stood and rushed out of the cafe before she could say goodbye.

That was the last time he was asking someone out. This lunch had been useful, though. He knew something was off with Sophie, and maybe Summer would help if he did her a favour and found her brother.

Sophie - September 2008

The two-bed semi loomed in front of Sophie. Despite its peeling render and grey window sills, it felt like her own grand castle. Grass tickled her knees as she stood at the bottom of the paved garden path which led to the front door. They would need to buy a lawnmower, and definitely some weedkiller.

It had been over a year since they fell in love, and on their one-year anniversary they had celebrated in the registry office with two of Ben's friends as their witnesses. Mel had refused to come. She didn't think Sophie was good enough for Ben. Now they had their very own home. Not a room in someone else's house or in a tiny flat, but their own house to live in together, alone.

She was Mrs Sophie Bates, and this house was their fortress to keep out any enemies. Though any enemies — or friends — now lived over one hundred and fifty miles away. The rent for a two-bedroom house in Ashfield cost the same as their tiny London flat. Here was somewhere they could *actually* start a family. Here, she would make Ben happy and give him everything he ever wanted.

He squeezed her hand, and she turned to look at him. He was staring at her with a sweet smile on his face.

'Look what I've done for us, babe. Our own home away from all of those arseholes.' He was so proud, and her heart swelled with pride too.

'I'm proud of you, babe,' she said. 'Come on, let's get inside.'

'It's me and you against the world now,' he replied as they walked hand-in-hand up the path.

'Yep. And maybe Kai, one day? He deserves so much better than Emmie as a mother.' Sophie wouldn't give up hope Kai could live with them.

'I've told you like a hundred times he won't be allowed. Emmie won't even let him visit. Best to leave him where he is. She can forget her child support money if she won't let me see him.'

Sophie pushed away the heavy feeling in her heart, and didn't share her thoughts. There was no point annoying him on such an otherwise perfect day. She would convince Emmie to let Kai visit, and she'd make sure he didn't want to return home. She could look after him the way a little boy deserved.

The front door emerged in front of her like a gateway to a calmer world. It was the cleanest part of the house, having recently been kicked in and, therefore, replaced. The owner had mentioned it to Ben during his initial visit the previous month. A domestic dispute, apparently.

'I hope the fella who kicked the door in doesn't think she still lives here,' Sophie said, 'he might come back.'

'Nah. They've locked him up. Besides, there's a cop living next door. I had a chat with him when I came to check the place out last week.' Ben squeezed her hand again. 'And you've got me. Men like that are cowards. They're scared of real men. Even if it *does* turn out to be a dangerous street, plenty of other places are affordable compared to London. I can work anywhere as an electrician.'

'And I can work anywhere as an editor, thanks to you. I still can't believe you paid for the course.'

Ben jangled the keys in front of her, his grin wide, and Sophie laughed as he unlocked the front door. He pushed it open slowly, but as she went to walk in, he stopped her.

'Wait, Mrs Bates!' He picked her up, making her squeal. She wrapped her arms around his neck, and he carried her over the threshold.

'Christ, you're heavier than you look!' He plonked her back down in the hallway.

Sophie looked around the tight space, up at the bare stairs and through the door to the empty living room. Tears stung her eyes, and she sniffed them away.

'What's wrong?'

'I'm just so grateful, Ben. You've got us this house, our jobs… I don't know how to thank you. You're amazing. I don't deserve you.'

'You've got the rest of our lives to make it up to me, Mrs Bates.' He swooped her up into his arms again. 'Starting right now.' He winked and kissed her.

Sophie was more than happy to oblige. She giggled as he carried her to the kitchen and sat her on the table. It was time to start their own family in their perfect new home.

Astrid

I sat on the floor after Kai left, flicking the elastic band on my wrist as the shadow enveloped me. I didn't bother to wipe away the tears. It was soothing to let them fall.

Only one thing could bring me out of the darkness when it was this bad: Harry.

I had to be OK for Harry, and I still needed help to protect him. Alex had helped me enough, so I called Barb instead. I held my breath for a moment to stop the tears and pulled out my phone to call her. She answered almost straight away.

'Hey, Barb. It's Astrid,' I said in the most neutral voice I could manage.

'Yes, darling. Phones do this wonderful thing now where the person's name shows up when they call you,' she said with a chuckle, 'are you OK?'

'Oh, yes.' I laughed too, glad she couldn't see my embarrassed face. 'Are you free? I could do with some company.'

'Sure, do you want me to come over?' Barb said. There was an edge of concern in her voice. Her accent was never as clipped when she was worried or angry.

'No, don't do that. I'll come to you. Be there in an hour?' I tried to make my voice lighter, as though I had no cares and no black shadow following me.

'Yes, perfect. I'll get some drinks ready,' Barb said, her accent sharp again.

I hauled my shaky body off the floor and stood for a moment, letting the blood return to my legs. One step at a time, I fought through the shadowy hallway. I'd kept my sanity together for ten years. I would not lose it now. Though last time I had Alex to help me through.

I flicked on the bathroom light and, to my relief, the shadow reduced to the size of a football. My anxiety eased, and my strength was building. I washed the sweat and tears away in a quick shower and reapplied foundation, blusher, and mascara before tying my hair into a bun. My hands still shook as I spritzed some perfume, but it would have to do.

I checked the back door and every window in the house before I pulled on my boots and left. I had to get out of the car three times in the drizzling rain to check I'd locked the front door. Eventually I drove away.

I reached Barb's house within ten minutes, and checked my face in the front mirror of my car, convinced I would look a mess. It surprised me to see a half-presentable face staring back at me. My boots thudded against the charming woodstone paving that led to her front door, and I used the heavy door knocker to let her know I'd arrived. It took her a minute to answer, but she opened the front door with her usual flourish.

'Oh, Astrid, darling! Come in.' She waved me inside, and I instantly felt calmer. A welcoming aura always surrounded Barb, which made me feel strange... in a good way. It was how I imagined normal people felt when visiting their mother. She didn't look the motherly type, though she had two sons and a grandchild. She wore her grey hair up in a graceful bun and brown Ralph Lauren boots to match a floral ankle-length dress.

I smiled and stepped into the entrance hall. She had decorated the walls in mustard yellow Farrow and Ball paint, which contrasted against a dark oak floor. And hung what I assumed to be *expensive* paintings on the walls.

I followed Barb to the living room, which was just as decadent, with antique hardwood chairs positioned strategically in front of a bookcase that spanned the length of the back wall. A luxurious Chesterfield sofa in the middle of the room stole the limelight. Over the fireplace hung a sizeable canvas picture of Barb, her late husband and their two grown-up sons. Both sons were the image of Barb.

What surprised me, though, was a well-dressed man sitting on the sofa.

'Oh, Charles, meet Astrid.' Barb beamed and walked over to the man.

He stood from the sofa and smiled. He was younger than Barb, maybe mid-forties. I stifled a laugh at Barb's sly wink behind his back and walked over to hold out my hand.

'Lovely to meet you, Astrid,' he said, in an accent almost as clipped as Barb's, though not as realistic. His hands were rough as he took mine and planted a kiss on the back of it. They reminded me of a builder's hands.

'You, too.' I smiled and took my hand away.

'Come on, dear. Let's talk in the garden. I'll put on the heater to keep us warm.' Barb grabbed my other hand and pulled me along like a schoolgirl.

Outside, the drizzle had stopped and the late afternoon sun once again broke through. It was still chilly, and I wrapped my jacket around me as we sat under Barb's gazebo. I hated that designer jackets were never warm enough, but after years of second-hand clothes, I cared more about showing my hard work than being cold. I could handle a few goose pimples.

Barb had already prepared a jug of lemon and water for the table, along with two empty glasses. She poured us a glass each before taking her seat across the table from me.

'So, tell me, Astrid. What's wrong?' She shifted in her seat as if getting comfy for a long conversation.

'Wrong?' I cocked my head to one side and focused on her.

'Yes, you sounded upset earlier.' She raised an eyebrow.

'Oh, sorry. No. Nothing's wrong. Just having an off day. Harry is out at the twins' house. He has been since yesterday. It gets lonely, eventually.' I did my best to throw her off. 'Tell me about Charles. Where did you meet him?' Her face lightened at the mention of Charles.

'Oh, there's nothing going on. We met about a month ago in Waitrose Cafe. It turns out we have quite a lot in common! But he's much too young for me. We went to the museum together this morning. He'll be off soon once he's decided which book to borrow.' She looked wistfully back at the house.

'Oh, I thought you'd met a nice toy boy.' I grinned.

'No, no. I have no interest in toy boys.' She waved her hand at me again. 'Now, Astrid. Tell me what's really bothering you and I'll see what I can do to help.' She shifted her focus back to me and gave me a serious look.

I sighed. I did trust Barb, yet I was unsure where to even start. 'When I came to Derby, what did Alex tell you about my past?'

'He said you had an awful ex-husband and needed a safe place to stay with your boy. That's it really. It was all I needed to hear.' She placed a hand on my knee and squeezed before removing it.

'My husband wasn't awful. But his family was. And when he disappeared they got a lot worse.' I paused. 'Well, Kai, my husband's oldest son, visited me today. He wants to meet Harry.'

Barb didn't exhibit the shock I'd expected. Instead, she leaned back in her chair and gestured theatrically for me to continue.

'The thing is, his family aren't the kind of people I want anywhere near Harry, and Harry doesn't even know Kai exists.'

'Why not?' Barb sat forward and raised an eyebrow.

'They're a hot mess, Barb. Jobless, dirty, mostly drug addicts or alcoholics.'

'Oh dear.' She looked deep in thought for a moment. 'Is there any other reason?'

'Like what?' I eyed her. What did she already know?

'I don't know, darling. It just doesn't seem enough that you'd be so concerned you would call me as soon as you'd seen him.' She waved her arms again.

Barb couldn't sit still... but then it was normal for her to talk with her hands. It didn't necessarily mean she was nervous or hiding anything. There was something off today though, and I couldn't put my finger on what the issue was. The atmosphere in the house was different. The welcoming aura was gone. I studied Barb, and she stared back at me with one eyebrow raised. This was Barb, for God's sake. The only friend I'd had for a decade.

'Well, they think I murdered him,' I said.

Barb shifted in her seat and looked down. She clasped her hands together on her knee, and took a breath before she looked back at me. 'Ah. I see. And did you?'

'Barb!' I stood as though she'd poked me with a hot branding iron.

'Calm down, dear!' She was as calm as ever. 'I have to ask. Sit.'

'I would never hurt somebody I loved.' I sat back down as she asked, though my glare didn't lessen.

'I know. But I don't know if you loved him. He could have deserved it, for all I know.'

'What? No! Like I said, Ben was amazing.' I blinked back more tears.

'Well, why do they think you murdered him? Was there a body?'

'No. He disappeared. His mum and sister think he would never have disappeared without telling them. They think I was some sort of control freak and I kept him from them. We moved away, but that was Ben's idea. When he first disappeared, they hounded me constantly, saying I was covering something up.' The words came out in a rush. I hadn't spoken to anybody about Ben or his family for years.

'And that's why Alex asked if I had a place for you to stay?' she asked.

There was something about her tone that I didn't like. Or was it the atmosphere still bugging me? I looked behind my shoulder at the house, and goose pimples prickled my arms. Coming here was a mistake. 'Look, I have to go.'

'No, wait. You just got here. Talk to me. Maybe I can help.'

I drained my glass of water and stood. 'No. I'm OK, honestly. Sorry for snapping. It's been a long day.'

'Call me when you get home.' She smiled, but her words didn't hold her usual warmth.

'Will do. I'll see myself out.' I walked away as quickly as I could manage and jogged through the house. The living room was empty. Charles was no longer there. I rushed to my car, dropping the keys halfway across the drive. My tyres screeched as I pulled off the drive.

Whatever it was, with Barb acting off and Alex not overly interested, it was up to me to protect Harry from Kai or anyone else that threatened our happiness. I checked my watch. He would finish school in two hours.

I pulled up outside the school to wait for him. I texted Harry and told him I'd be waiting in my car outside the school at pickup time.

I decided on one thing for sure. I had to tell Harry about Kai.

The weirdness with Barb had thrown me even more than Kai's visit. Or maybe the weirdness was *because* Kai's visit affected me so much. Had I caused the weird vibe with Barb? I couldn't tell. I sat in the car and stared at the school gates across the road. I stayed back a little, so I didn't look dodgy to any passers-by.

Knowing Harry was in there calmed me. My Harry. My reason for breathing and living through anything that throws itself at us. It was only a few minutes later when the school called me.

Harry had walked out of maths class an hour ago to use the toilet.

Nobody had seen him since.

Swanson

Swanson rushed back to the office to pick up Hart. She stood outside in the rear car park, waiting for him with a scowl on her face. Though that look was fairly common for her. Swanson was sure she specifically drew her eyebrows to look angry each morning. She had bruised his arm when he said that to her face.

She took a step forward as he slowed the car to a stop next to her. As soon as she opened the car door, she began her rant. 'Where the hell have you been? I've been waiting ages and had Murray in my face—'

'Hart! I had to see a friend. It's sorted now. Stop whining.' He laughed as her fist connected with his arm. 'Ow. You know I'm just winding you up. Tell me what you found out and where we're going then.'

'You're a prat. Look, his name is Peter Johnson. He lives half an hour away, or at least that was the address given to the hotel. His house is in Pinxton.'

'But if he lives in Pinxton, why get a hotel?' Swanson asked. 'That makes no sense. It's only half an hour away.'

'Hmm. Maybe he wanted to lie about where he lived, or have a drink?'

'Maybe, but you'd think he'd go further than thirty minutes down the road if that was the case.' Swanson pulled onto the A38 to Ashfield and put his foot down.

'Maybe he doesn't drive or have much money, and a hotel ate his travel budget. It is a terrible hotel he chose, so he's probably not rolling in it.' Hart scrunched up her nose, clearly disgusted at the thought of staying in a budget hotel.

'Hey, I always stay in that chain when I'm going away for a night or two.' Swanson gave her a faux hurt look.

'That doesn't surprise me.' She rolled her eyes.

Swanson laughed. 'We'll know more when we see his house.'

They fell quiet while Swanson drove for another fifteen minutes up the A38 and into Pinxton.

Hart fiddled with the in-car satnav and entered the postcode just before the Pinxton junction. Swanson followed the directions through the town and then turned left into a rat run of streets. Wonky gates, wheel-less bikes and gardens filled with rubbish flew by them. Swanson drove close behind a clapped out Fiat, which parked halfway down a small cul-de-sac just before the satnav alerted them that their destination was on the right.

They glanced at each other.

'Lovely,' said Hart, 'a really nice place to bring kids up.'

'Stop being judgemental,' Swanson replied. A teenager across the road spotted them, stuck his middle finger up and legged it. 'Or don't.' He muttered.

They found number eight Willow Gardens near the end of the cul-de-sac, cornered in by four other properties. None appeared to be very well looked-after, and number eight was no exception. There was no driveway. The compact front garden was a mass of knee-high grass and extensive weeds. A few ancient slabs were dotted throughout, and fighting to form some sort of a path to the front door. Swanson pulled up outside the house and the pair got out of the car and stood together, looking up at the house.

Hart sighed. 'Let's get this over with,' she muttered.

The smell of dog shit stung Swanson's nostrils. He held his breath and swung open the garden gate, which creaked in protest. The pair took their time to walk up to the front door, and deliberately stuck to the slabs to avoid any hidden surprises in the grass. Swanson knocked on the door, which shook despite him trying to be gentle.

He stood back to let Hart take centre stage. Men warmed to her more. Well, they did until she opened her mouth.

Footsteps approached, and the shadow of a person got closer through the frosted glass. A large man opened the door and towered over Hart. He looked about sixty, and was holding a yapping Yorkshire Terrier in his arms.

'Peter Johnson?' Hart asked. She had a smile on her face, Swanson noted. It would be the dog. Hart loved dogs.

'Yes?' The man smiled back but looked surprised to see two people in suits who knew his name.

'I'm Detective Inspector Hart, this is my colleague Detective Inspector Swanson.'

The man nodded to her introduction, shushing the terrier. It stopped barking, thankfully. Dogs with small man syndrome were the worst. Swanson didn't understand why anyone would want one.

'We were hoping you could help us with something. Could we come in, please?'

'Oh yes, of course, love. Come in out of the cold.' The man waved them in and the dog growled. 'Don't mind him, I'll put him in the kitchen.'

They followed Peter into the tiny hallway and he gestured to the left, telling them to sit on the sofa and that he'd be back in a minute.

The living room was full of pictures of the same five or six people. Family, Swanson assumed. One kid looked familiar, though Swanson couldn't place him. It looked clean but a musty smell hung in the air, like it often did in an older person's, though Peter Johnson wasn't that old really. Hart sat on the beige sofa and glanced around, no doubt taking everything in with her sharp eyes.

Peter returned in less than a minute with a plate of biscuits. 'Here you go.' He smiled at them both, 'Please, take a biscuit. Would you like a cuppa?'

'Oh. No, thank you,' Hart said.

Swanson sat next to her on the sofa. He sank into the old cushions a bit too easily. The weights would have to come back out soon.

Peter took a seat in the armchair opposite them. He moved slowly, as if he was in pain. He didn't look like he could attack anyone. 'How can I help?' he asked.

Hart leaned forward. 'Well, we wanted to ask you about a recent hotel stay—'

'Hotel stay?' Peter interrupted, looking confused.

Swanson thought he'd better say something or he might just look like the muscle. 'Yes, in Derby.'

'Oh dear, I haven't been to Derby in years.' Peter shook his head, 'Sorry, but I don't think I'll be able to help.'

'Oh, right. Only, the hotel gave us your name and address,' Hart said.

'*My* name and address? They must be mistaken, love. I can't travel too far. I'm not in the best of health. My son has to come round most weeks just to check I'm alive.' His chesty chuckle suggested he smoked a pack of cigarettes a day despite his poor health.

'So, you haven't been to Derby at all? Or stayed in any other hotels recently? Say, over the last few months?' Hart tried again.

'No, dear. I wish I had. It would be nice to get away. Even if it's just to little old Derby.'

Swanson and Hart glanced at each other.

'Do you know how the hotel might have gotten your name or address?' Hart asked.

'I have no idea, love. Something to do with them computers maybe?'

'Computers?' She asked.

'Yes, them computer things they use now, the iPods and such. They make a lot of mistakes, don't they?'

'Not this kind of mistake.' Swanson interjected.

'Ooh, well. I really don't know what to say.' The man looked down at the floor, deep in thought, but he said nothing further.

'OK, Sir. Sorry for wasting your time,' Hart said. 'Could you give us a call if you do remember something that might be useful, please?' She stood and stepped closer to Peter.

'Of course, lovey.' Peter took the card Hart handed to him and hauled himself out of his chair to walk them out.

The pair stepped carefully down the driveway again and climbed back into Swanson's car.

'What do you think?' Hart asked him once he'd started the car.

'I don't know, to be honest.' Swanson tried to assess his feelings. He did not get the impression that Peter Johnson could hurt anyone easily. 'He actually seemed to be telling the truth.'

'Yeah, I think so, too. If not, he's one of the best liars I've ever spoken to.' Hart looked out of the window and chewed her lip.

Thirty minutes later they reached the office car park and Swanson pulled up in a space at the back.

'Why do you always have to park at the back?' Hart moaned.

'So you have to walk further.' He replied without missing a beat.

She tutted loudly and opened her door to get out. Swanson grabbed his things to do the same but the phone buzzed as he picked it up.

'You go in, I'll be in soon,' he called after Hart.

She waved a hand, slammed his car door shut and walked off.

Once alone, he unlocked his phone and opened the new text message. It was from Summer with an address. *Eddie.*

He cursed. Another place he didn't have time to be.

But there was no way he would let her go alone.

Sophie - August 2009

Ben didn't say a word the entire drive home from the hospital, and Sophie didn't dare say anything either. A ball of devastation curled up inside her, one she knew she could never recover from. It would stay there as a shadow on her heart. Just like the last time.

Now, leaning against the kitchen counter for support, she sobbed silently, trying to hide her crying from Ben.

'Look at me,' he said.

She turned to face him but could not stop the tears from flowing this time.

'I'm sorry,' she whispered.

His nostrils flared.

The fear overcame her sadness. She took a deep breath and held it, controlling her sobs. 'I'm sorry, Ben,' she said.

'Sorry?' he whispered, 'that doesn't help. All I've done for you, and you can't give me the one thing I want in return. Maybe I should have listened to Mel. She said you were useless.'

The familiar dread sat in the pit of her stomach as she swallowed back more tears. She never used to upset him this much.

'We can adopt?' She instantly regretted her words. *Why was she so stupid?* They would never allow them to adopt with his criminal record after the fight with Emmie. It didn't matter that it was Emmie who had attacked him. And now, they would suffer because of it.

'Who would let a former drug addict like you adopt a child?' His face turned a pale shade of red and he turned away.

'I... I... don't know. I'm talking rubbish. I'm sorry. I'm upset too.'

His fist connected with her face and pain exploded through Sophie's eye. His hand was around her throat so fast she didn't even see him move.

'*You're* fucking upset? You're a waste of fucking space.' His voice was a low growl.

Sophie's breath stuck in her throat. Her head throbbed. She tried to raise her hands to pull him off her neck, but his body got in the way. The edges of the room turned a fuzzy black as a shadow enveloped her.

Her eyes bulged and, in the shadow oozing across the ceiling, she saw a face. A gaunt face, too decrepit to distinguish as either man or woman. Wisps of dark hair trailed from its head, and she watched in horror as its emaciated body emerged within the shadow. An aged hand reached out to her from the ceiling. Skin had fallen from some fingers to reveal grey bone underneath.

Ben released his grip just enough to allow her to breathe, and leaned his face so close that she could smell cigarettes on his tongue. She took a painful deep breath. The shadow, and the thing within it, disappeared. Had she seen death?

'You will be fucking sorry,' Ben whispered.

He let go of her neck and she breathed deeply again. A second later he grabbed her shoulders and wrenched her around. She stumbled. Ben grabbed her and forced her to stand. He grabbed a fistful of her hair and bent her body over the kitchen counter, pushing her face hard against the ice cold countertop. He reached up her dress and pulled down her underwear.

Horror hit her as she realised he wasn't just going to punch her this time.

'Please, Ben. No,' she tried to say, but her words were mumbled against the countertop pressing against her cheek.

He pressed her head harder into the kitchen unit. She cried out, her ear was being crushed.

'Shut the fuck up. This is the least you owe me,' he growled, 'we're going to do this every day until you get fucking pregnant, you hear me?'

SOPHIE - AUGUST 2009

Three loud bangs echoed around them.

Ben let go. Someone was knocking on the door. His eyes were wild with panic.

'Don't move,' he told her, his voice a rushed whisper.

She froze, still bent over the icy counter with her dress above her hips. The person at the door knocked again, louder this time.

'Fuck's sake, go into the living room.' Ben buttoned up his trousers as Sophie pulled up her underwear and ran into the living room. She knelt on the floor and half-closed the door so she could hide behind it and look through the crack. Her body shook, and she took deep breaths to try and calm herself.

At the front door Ben yelled: 'Who is it?'

'It's me, from next door,' a deep voice called back.

Ben swore under his breath before opening the door and smiling widely.

'Hi. How are you, mate?'

Sophie could only see Ben, but their neighbour's voice was loud and clear. She couldn't remember his name.

'I'm good, thanks. Thought I heard shouting. I wanted to check if everything is OK?' The neighbour took a step inside the hallway.

Ben stepped to the side and blocked the path inside the house. 'We're fine, mate,' Ben said, still smiling. 'What did you hear?'

'Shouting, crying, banging. Is Sophie in?'

'Must have been the telly. She's not in, she's at a mate's. Thought I'd watch a film while she was gone,' Ben shrugged. He was a good liar.

Sophie's heart quickened as she hid behind the door. She could see the man's outline through the crack and felt an urge to reach out to him. But then, what would Ben do? The sweet Ben that she knew and loved? Where would she go without him?

'Oh, great. I thought some arsehole had broken in or something,' their neighbour said.

'Yeah, I bet, mate.' Ben still grinned, yet his eyes were just as crazy as they had been in the kitchen.

'I'd better go.' The man stepped back and disappeared from Sophie's view. They muttered bye to each other, and Ben closed the front door.

Sophie stayed kneeling on the floor, she closed her eyes and waited for Ben to tell her what to do. To her surprise, he said nothing. His footsteps shook the ceiling as he stomped up the stairs. Then she heard their bedroom door shut.

She placed a hand on her chest and breathed. She was safe for now. He would say sorry soon and he would never do it again. There was no way he meant it. It was going to be OK.

The haunting face of the shadow stuck in her mind more so than Ben's attack. What the hell was that thing? Her phone lay on the floor next to her, where it had fallen from her cardigan pocket. She grabbed it and flicked open the browser to look up shadow monsters. Nothing came back at first: some stuff about a TV show, but eventually she saw an image of a starving, barely human creature with rotten skin staring back at her. She gulped, and continued to read.

'A fear Arracht is an abandoned corpse of an emaciated human which signals terror and death. It originates from Irish folklore and roughly translates to fear monster.

It is said that it appears when you feel fear so terrible that it is about to consume you, and it feeds from that fear to survive. When sucking the fear from a person, it will suck the very soul, too.

Leaving nothing but an empty vessel in its place.'

Astrid

I'd barely hung up the phone when I jumped out of my car and ran across the road to the school. The rotund headteacher, Mr Hardiman, stood outside the main entrance. His cherry red face was a deeper shade of red than usual. His mouth opened and closed when he saw me arriving within seconds of our phone call, but he said nothing.

'Where are the twins?' I said between heavy breaths, 'they'll know where he is.'

'They're in a lesson. I spoke to them before calling you. They don't know where he is.' He was far too calm for my liking. I wanted to grab him by the shoulders and shake him. Didn't he realise how serious this was?

'Then let me speak to them,' I demanded.

'I'm sorry, I can't allow it without their parents present.' He shrugged his large shoulders apologetically. 'But come in and we'll talk some more.'

I didn't have time for his bullshit. Before he'd finished his sentence, I'd pulled out my phone and dialled the twins' mum.

'Hi, Betty.' I turned away from the infuriating Mr Hardiman. 'Harry's gone missing.'

'What! No.' Betty gasped. 'What—'

'I need you to come to the school and speak to the twins. They'll know where he went.'

'Oh, of course! I'll be there in five minutes. Oh, gosh. OK. Five minutes, Astrid. Don't panic.'

I heard her rustling around with a coat as she hung up. I turned back and scowled at Mr Hardiman. His face was getting redder every minute.

'So, explain to me how my child got out of your school?' I asked.

'He went to the toilet in maths class, and he didn't come back.' His voice was weak.

'And no one saw him leave? What about the receptionist?'

'This is a secondary school, Miss Moor. It's a little different to primary. The small gate at the end is always open. Sixth form kids are in and out all day. We trust the kids not to walk out, and... well... they never usually do.'

'You have a duty of care to the children who attend your school. If anything happens to my boy, I will hold you personally responsible.' My panic was building, but I swallowed it down. The shadow was not going to stop me from finding Harry. He was the only thing that kept me sane.

'Why don't we go inside and get some tea? We can talk in my office?' he asked with a smile.

'No. We'll wait right here for Betty.' I was sick of talking to him. I turned away and looked at the gate.

Betty turned up a minute later, running over to me with a young baby in her arms. She was breathless by the time she reached us and wearing two different shoes.

'Show me where they are,' she demanded.

I liked Betty. She was a *proper* mum. She could sew, bake, and run anywhere with her baby in tow. Even if she didn't realise her shoes did not match. Not like me. I was the type of mum who felt out of her depth, constantly wishing someone more 'adult' was around. I felt a sense of camaraderie as soon as she arrived. She would back me.

'Come to my office and I'll call for them,' smiled Mr Hardiman. Why the hell was he smiling so much? It was getting harder with each passing minute not to punch him in the face.

We strode through the school corridors in silence, passing the odd teacher or child. Most were still in lessons. I hated the smell of schools. It was a sickly combination of sweat, deodorant, cheap food, and disinfectant. And it made me feel sick at the best of times, never mind when I was already so nauseous.

It didn't take long to reach the office, and Mr Hardiman's secretary went to collect the twins. Betty and I sat on two hard chairs across from the headteacher's desk. The baby on her lap stared at me with wide eyes.

'Are you OK?' Betty peered at me.

I tried to speak. I tried to say 'yes, I'm OK. I'm sure everything will be fine' but no words came out and tears threatened to fall, so I shrugged instead.

Behind her, the shadow had grown without me even noticing. It had taken over the entire wall. As I watched, the emaciated hand of the Arracht appeared. It was a shock of white against the dark shadow. Pale bones glistened behind dripping flesh.

Something grabbed my leg. I jerked away and looked down.

It was Betty. 'Astrid? Do you need some tea?' she said. Her voice sounded far away.

I shook my head and looked away from the Arracht. There would be no death today.

The twins arrived a few seconds later. The two ginger boys threw each other nervous glances and fiddled with their fingers as their mother tried to coax the truth out of them.

I forced myself to focus, but it was hard as there were so many fragmented possibilities running through my brain. I didn't know which one to focus on.

Was Kai responsible for Harry's disappearance? Or someone else?

Or was it nothing to do with Ben and related to something else entirely?

'Like I said, boys, you're only in trouble if you *don't* tell me what happened. I don't care what you've done, I only care that Harry is safe,' Betty was saying to them.

I clamped my lips shut and sat on my hands to stop the urge to shake the truth out of the boys.

'He didn't tell us where he was going today!' protested Tom, looking at George for backup. His brother nodded earnestly in agreement.

'Today?' I asked.

The boys' cheeks flushed. They wouldn't meet my eye and looked down at the floor instead.

'He's been gone other days?' I glared at Mr Hardiman, who looked more purple than red now.

The twins' faces dropped as they realised they'd landed their friend in it. 'No!' they said in unison.

'Boys!' said Betty sharply. 'Look at me please.'

The pair kept their heads low but peered up at their mother.

'There's a man he speaks to sometimes. In the gap next to the woods,' said George.

I tasted metallic bile in my mouth as my stomach lurched. 'What did the man look like?' I asked.

The twins shrugged their shoulders. 'We haven't seen him. Harry just told us about him,' said George.

'What did he tell you about him?' their mother asked.

The boys didn't answer, but looked at each other with wide eyes.

'Boys, if you don't tell me everything right this instant I will throw every goddamn electronic device out of the window the second we get home, including your mobile phones!' she yelled so loud even I jumped.

'It's his brother,' the twins shouted in unison.

'Fucking Kai,' I snapped and stood up. 'I know who it is. I'll take it from here. Don't think I won't be back to discuss this with you, Mr Hardiman. And thank you for telling the truth boys.'

I stormed out of the office, leaving Mr Hardiman gaping like a fish. He was a stupid, weak man. I never understood how he got a promotion to head teacher.

I'd barely reached the end of the first corridor before I called Alex. His voicemail kicked in by the time I reached the gates of the school playground.

'Harry's gone. Call me urgently, please.' My own calm voice surprised me. I hadn't thought about the Arracht since the twins mentioned the man Harry was speaking to. Maybe I was finally becoming a normal, capable adult.

ASTRID

I will find Harry. We will move away. We will put this mess behind us. I had no time to sit around in fear, and the shadow didn't return.

Summer

Three hours had passed since Swanson and I left the cafe. I stood against the kitchen counter, though the white units were too bright for the headache that was starting at the base of my skull. I don't know why I'd mentioned finding my brother to Aaron. If he hadn't texted me, I could have given up searching for him. I wouldn't know if he was OK, but he wouldn't be able to hurt us. God knows Joshua and I deserved a quiet life after everything that happened with Marinda.

I'd finished at Anfield Hospital for the day, but Joshua was sleeping at his dad's house so I was alone. It was only 4 p.m., and I was looking at an evening of catching up on chores. I sighed, pulled out the kitchen chair, and placed my laptop and phone on the table. My tired eyes glazed over as I stared at the flowery welcome message, waiting for the ancient computer to boot up. The vibration of my mobile phone was a welcome distraction. My eyes flicked over to the phone as Aaron's name appeared on the screen. My interest piqued. I grabbed the phone and opened his message. It said nothing other than an address.

The laptop finally kicked into gear, so I opened Google as quickly as the old technology would allow and typed in the address. It was fifteen minutes away, on the other side of town. I replied to Aaron with one word: 'Eddie?'

His reply arrived a few seconds later: 'Yes.'

I jumped up and grabbed my purse, phone and keys, texting Swanson as I left to tell him I'd found Eddie and the address. As I ran down the grand staircase to the main exit, my phone rang.

Swanson didn't even say 'hello'. 'Are you going there now?'

The abruptness of his voice threw me. I froze halfway down the stairs. 'Yes.'

'I'm near your flat. Stay there. I'll pick you up.' He hung up.

What the hell was that about? As strange as it was, I walked outside and stood at the edge of the car park to wait. I supposed I'd prefer to go with a police officer, anyway. I raised my hood against the light drip of rain. Frizzy hair was the last thing I needed if I was going to meet Swanson.

A couple of minutes later, his black Audi approached along the main road, and he pulled up on the opposite side. The same feelings arose every time I saw Swanson: excitement and nerves. I jogged over to get out of the rain.

'Hello again,' I said, a little breathless from the jog. Jesus, I needed to run more often.

'Hey,' he flashed a quick smile, but did not appear to be in a good mood as he pulled away. He took a left at the end of my road into the main traffic.

'You OK?' I asked. It felt weird to ask him that. He always seemed so calm and collected.

'There's a big case at work...' he began, but paused as a driver swerved into our lane. He didn't speak for a few moments as he focused on missing the young driver.

'The rapist case?' I prompted.

'Yep. That's the one.'

'What are you doing here with me, then?'

He turned his head and gave me a sharp look. 'Well, there are a lot of excellent officers on the case. An entire team, in fact. And there's only one of you to help your brother. I can give you one hour tops, then I'm gone.'

I nodded, and we said little for the rest of the drive. Instead, I googled the hospital. Adrenna had transferred Eddie to a low security mental health hospital near Dale Abbey. The new hospital was for people getting ready to move back into the community, like a halfway house for patients rather than criminals. Well, some of them had a violent past like Eddie, but the doctors didn't consider them dangerous anymore.

I wasn't paying any attention to the road as I read my phone, so it surprised me when Swanson stopped the car. I glanced up. The street looked like any other upper-middle-class street. Rows of substantial, mismatched houses. Some were modern, and some were extensive period homes. Eddie's new hospital hid within a classical property that was larger than most homes on the street, thanks to a two-storey extension. There were no high walls or anything else to barricade the patients in. Nobody would know it was a hospital at all from the outside, except for the sign which welcomed you to *Bracken Tree*, with an accompanying NHS logo. Like most of these low security hospitals I've seen, there was a large drive and the house itself sat far back from the road, more so than many other houses.

'Are you ready?' Swanson's rough voice broke me out of my daydream.

I tore my gaze away from the hospital to look at him. 'What should I say?'

'Is Eddie here?' Swanson grinned at me.

'They aren't just going to let me in,' I rolled my eyes.

'No, but they'll let me in,' he flashed his ID card at me.

'Will that work?' I asked.

'Sure, it usually does.'

'OK. Let's go.' A strong breeze met me as I opened the car door, and I pulled my hood back up to protect my hair. As we walked up the long driveway, I kept my head down and tried to ignore my cocktail of emotions. I was nervous to see Eddie after so long, excited to help him, and scared of him being anywhere near me or Joshua all at once. We reached the front door and stood still. Swanson stared at me. I didn't move.

'Well, go on, then,' he said.

'Oh, sorry. I thought you were going to do something.'

He laughed. 'This is more your domain than mine. I hate these places.'

'OK, fine.' I relented and pressed the buzzer near the front door.

A young girl wearing a purple *Bracken Tree* t-shirt answered the door. 'Hi. Can I help you?'

I tried hard not to roll my eyes. She was little more than a child, and would not understand how to care for adult men with mental health issues. An underpaid and overworked kid, as usual. The bloody system was broken.

She smiled up at Swanson and ignored me. I didn't blame her. He had that authoritative presence. If he walked into a room, everyone turned to look. I was the opposite.

'I hope so. I'm Detective Inspector Alex Swanson.' He flashed his badge.

Her eyes widened, though her smile didn't falter.

'I'm looking for Eddie Thomas. Is he in?'

It took her a moment to speak. 'Er, I'm not sure. I'll check. Do you want to come in?'

I absolutely did not want to enter, but Swanson walked straight inside. I followed with a pounding heart. *Am I about to meet Eddie for the first time in twenty years?*

We stood out of place in the entrance hall as the girl wandered off down the corridor and through a door at the end. In contrast to Adrenna, the hall was lively and modern. Bright white walls complemented light wooden flooring. A notice board took up most of the wall, full of leaflets about different social activities. As we waited, a middle-aged woman descended the stairs in front of us. She took one step at a time, humming as she went. She didn't look up until she was halfway down, stopping abruptly as soon as she spotted us.

'Who are you?' she asked, her voice gruff.

'I'm an advocate,' I smiled up at her before Swanson could answer.

'Oh,' her voice was suddenly much lighter, 'are you here to see me?' She sounded like a little girl now and cocked her head to one side.

I shook my head.

She glared at me before stomping back up the stairs just as the young girl re-entered through the end door. She threw Swanson a nervous glance, as if scared of upsetting him. 'Eddie's not here.'

Relief flooded me.

'That's OK. Miss...?' Swanson said.

'Stacey Bean,' the girl twisted a strand of hair around her finger as she answered.

'Miss Bean.' He smiled. He could look super charming when he wanted to. 'We'll need to look around his room briefly.'

She nodded, glanced behind her and pulled on her hair harder. 'My manager is out with the patients. I just called her but she didn't answer. At the minute it's only me and one other patient who didn't want to go out. She's a talker. Has she seen you?'

'It will only take a minute. It's very urgent, though I can't explain why. You'd be helping us massively,' Swanson said.

The girl sighed and nodded. She walked back down the corridor and motioned for us to follow her. She led us through the property until we reached the rear door leading to the back garden. Across the patio were three self-contained flats.

She led us to the middle one. 'This is Eddie's room. Please be quick. If any patient sees you in there, then we'll be in all sorts of trouble. We need them to trust us, not think random people are searching their rooms while they're not here.'

She unlocked the door but clearly our visit didn't please her. Which gave me a small amount of faith in her, though she was still allowing two strangers into the room. I was pretty sure she could have refused us entry. Swanson hadn't been clear about whether he was allowed to do this or not.

We nodded and entered the room, closing the door behind us to lessen the chance of being spotted by the remaining patient.

I took in the room slowly. It was spotless. Not an item was out of place. There was a single bed, a miniscule kitchen area that was within the same space as the 'lounge', and another door off the back that must have been the bathroom. This was *my* Eddie's room, his private space. I wanted to simultaneously run away from it and explore it. Yet, I didn't move. It wasn't right, being in there without him knowing. I didn't want to see his things yet, not until he was ready to show me, if he ever was.

Swanson strolled around easily. I guessed he was used to looking through other people's things, both their lives and their belongings. He wandered to the end of the room and stood over a desk. He looked for a few seconds, then walked away. But something made him snap his neck back. He turned to me, mouth partly open.

'What?'

'Shit,' he muttered, reaching for his phone.

'Are you going to tell me what's wrong?'

'Voicemail. I need to listen to this.' He lifted his hand to show he'd be one minute, and raised his phone to his ear. I stood staring at him, and I watched his face whiten.

What the hell was *Alex Swanson* scared of?

Sophie - October 2009

Sophie stood in the middle of the living room. She didn't know where to turn, where to look. Ben sat on the sofa in front of her. His calmness made it worse. His betrayal caught in her chest and manifested into a deep internal pain. It was a heartache that would never go away. She couldn't even cry. Tears wouldn't help, anyway.

'I never thought you would do this to me.' Her voice was barely audible.

'We haven't had sex in ages, Sophie. I *am* sorry, but what did you expect? She threw herself at me and it was over in like one minute. It was stupid.'

'I know we haven't had sex lately. I just thought you felt bad, you know, after what happened. I thought you'd let me know when you wanted it.'

'Felt bad?' he looked confused.

'Yes, because the last few times we had sex, you... were kinda rough,' She couldn't think of the right words to use.

'I thought you liked it rough! Fucks sake, Sophie. If you didn't like it, just say. That's not my fault.'

Sophie said nothing. She didn't mind rough sex. She didn't mind that he lost his temper sometimes. Everyone had flaws. She hated that he hadn't touched her in weeks. Being ignored and not understanding why was far worse than any other punishment. But now she understood why. He'd been with someone else.

'Was it just one time, with you and this woman?'

He answered instantly. 'Yes.' He looked away and rubbed the back of his head. He always did that when he lied.

The room spun. Sophie closed her eyes. She knew what was coming.

SOPHIE - OCTOBER 2009

'Please, Ben, tell me the truth.'

'OK. It happened twice. The first time, I don't even know what happened, babe. I'd just turned up to do the job in her kitchen. The next minute she was all over me and it had happened before I knew it. And it happened again before I left.'

'And that's it?'

'Well, I had to finish the job the next day, and I said no, babe. I didn't *want* to hurt you. But she got naked and begged me. It was honestly all Kathy.'

Sophie barely listened. A shadow had grown on the wall behind Ben. The Arracht had returned and was reaching its bony hand out to Ben. She stared at it as he prattled on with his excuses, and a strange calmness overcame her. It was like a river. It started at the top of her head and ran down to her toes. The calm quenched the pain in her heart like a painkiller. This emaciated demon of death should terrify her, but he was on her side. She could see that now. The article she'd read was wrong.

The Arracht hovered over Ben, the bony hand near his neck, and she smiled.

'What are you smiling at?' Ben turned to see where she was looking.

'You won't see her again, will you?' Sophie's voice was normal again.

'What? No, of course not,' Ben looked at her and looked behind him again, trying to follow her eyes. 'Er... are you OK?'

'If you do, Benjamin Bates, I will leave you. I'll be out of here faster than you fucked her. Do not fucking test me,' It was the first time she had stood up to Ben in a long time, and it felt good.

He let out a stifled laugh. He stopped when he saw her face. She had felt unsure of herself for so long, but the Arracht was on her side.

She wasn't alone anymore.

Astrid

It had been three hours since Harry went missing. The sky had turned black and the wind howled, shaking the living room window. I stared through the glass, praying Harry was somewhere safe and warm.

It wasn't lost on me that the first 24 hours were crucial in a missing person case, and I should be out looking for him. Yet I'd looked everywhere I could think to look. I'd checked his friends' houses, the football field and the youth club where we practiced Taekwondo. I rang Kai over and over. Harry's phone was now switched off.

It was so different from when Ben went missing all those years ago. I remembered little about his disappearance. I just *knew* he would not come back, and I was unexpectedly calm about it. It seemed strange to admit it now, but it hadn't felt unusual to me.

I lost a part of me that day, and the Arracht became a new companion, always with me. That was the day it grew into a dark force that would stay by my side.

Maybe I was calm then because I had Harry to concentrate on. He was just a tiny baby, and he needed me. I had to be calm and together for his sake. Now, I had no one to focus on. Without Harry, I would be lost forever.

The pain in my heart was too much to bear. I had to find him and make sure he was safe. There was no other alternative.

The only good thing about it being likely that he was with Kai was that I genuinely didn't think Kai would hurt him. God knows what sort of lies

Kai was filling Harry's head with, though.

I stood in my living room, just staring. Staring at nothing.

The sound of the door handle made my head snap around.

'Harry?' I rushed to the door and flung it open.

It didn't cross my mind to check the camera.

I saw Harry first and relief flooded me. His tear-streaked face looked up at me and I reached out to comfort him, but he pushed me away and turned away.

It was then that I realised another person was standing next to him. Harry pointed up at him.

'This is my brother, Kai.' Harry's voice cracked as he looked at me accusingly. 'And now I know you've been lying to me my whole life.'

I tried to grab Harry's hand, but he pushed me again. 'Not until you tell me the truth!' he shouted.

'Harry, that is not your brother,' I whispered.

The man let out a stifled, short laugh. His half-hidden face was familiar to me, though I was certain it wasn't Kai.

Harry's face flushed with anger, more than I'd ever seen before. 'Stop lying to me!' he fumed.

'I'm not lying. You have a brother. He looks just like your dad, Harry. He was here yesterday to ask me if he could meet you. Look at me, Harry. *This* man is not your brother.'

The man finally spoke. 'She's lying.'

'I am not!'

'You lied to me about having a brother, Mum! How can I believe you now? Why would you lie to me in the first place?'

'Lying and omitting information are not the same thing. I will call your brother right now, Harry. It is not this man.' I pulled my phone out of my pocket. Stupid mistake.

The man grabbed my phone from my hand and pushed Harry through the doorway, straight into my stomach. He winded me hard, and we both sprawled on the floor.

He rushed inside and slammed the front door behind him. I jumped up and pulled Harry up off the floor. My hands shook, but I ran down the corridor into the kitchen, dragging a stunned Harry with me by his hoodie.

The man took his time following us.

Harry pulled away from me and turned to face him.

'Harry, come on!' I yelled.

He ignored me and spoke to the man. 'Hey, why'd you push me?'

'To get you inside. You wanted the truth, didn't you? Sorry if I hurt you, mate,' he replied.

I now stood by the back door, but Harry was a couple of feet away, between the man and I.

'We're leaving,' I demanded to Harry, turning to unlock the back door.

'No, Mum.' He turned to face me. 'I need to know the truth.'

'Let's go somewhere to talk, then!' I said.

'No! I want you to tell me here in front of Kai. No more lies.'

'That isn't Kai, Harry! I don't know who the hell he is. Probably the person who's been terrorising me with notes and calls!'

Harry's face dropped. 'That wasn't Kai. I just called once. I only wanted the truth. I wasn't terrorising you.'

'What are you talking about?' I stopped fiddling with the back door and turned to him.

'The call? And the note. That was me.' Harry looked up at me. 'I'm sorry if I scared you. I felt so guilty after the call. Kai doesn't want to hurt us Mum. I just wanted you to tell me the truth.'

'That was you? Did this man put you up to it? Did Kai put you up to it?' I remembered Harry made me breakfast the morning after the call, and told me he loved me before running into school.

'He asked me to put the note through the door. I got an older kid at school to do it for a fiver.'

I choked back tears, determined not to let the stranger see me cry. 'Jesus, Harry. I've been worried sick about that damn note.'

It all slotted together. I'd known for a while something was wrong with Harry. Then it hit me where I knew the stranger from.

'Yeah, well, you shouldn't have murdered my dad and hid my brother from me.' Harry looked so small suddenly, his bottom lip pouted out just like when he was a toddler. My precious baby still, even at eleven years old.

'I did not murder him. This man has been filling your head full of lies. Which is why I didn't tell you about Kai in the first place. Not that this man is Kai. His name is Charles. He's been sniffing around Barb. Kai knows I didn't murder your dad.'

'OK, it is true.' The man shrugged. 'I'm not Kai. But my name is not really Charles either. Harry has a brother called Kai, though, yes?'

'Yes. I've established that already,' I said shortly, 'are you his friend?'

Harry finally took a step towards me. I reached out and pulled him closer to me, wrapping both arms around him.

'No. I'm Harry's friend.' The man took out a large carving knife from his sleeve. 'Because you murdered their father, Sophie, and it's time to admit it.'

Sophie - June 2010

What began as Sophie's worst nightmare became a dream come true. At least for a bit. The tiny newborn boy curled up in a Moses basket next to their bed.

It took five grand to pay off Kathy in the end, but it was worth it. She had wanted an abortion. It was Sophie's idea to pay her to keep it. An unofficial surrogate was better than no baby. Now, Sophie and Ben's life was complete. It was the perfect plan.

And eight months later, the plan came together. Sophie's editing qualification turned out to be quite lucrative. She'd earned over two thousand pounds from one gig and a few hundred from some others. She had never seen Ben so happy.

Harry was two weeks old, and the deal was done. She was finally a mother. It was difficult to stop looking at his tiny nose and tiny fingers. Most new mothers online were moaning about how tired they were, yet Sophie lay awake at night staring at him, wishing he'd wake up so she could have another cuddle. She was desperate to get to know him. *Would he be funny, or shy, or loud, or cuddly, or a good eater?* He would definitely eat his vegetables and love reading, she'd make sure of that.

Ben was so helpful. He knew what to do since he already had Kai. Though he told her not to pick Harry up when he cried at night so he didn't get too spoiled. She picked him up anyway. Ben was fast asleep, so he wouldn't know.

That night, it was 2 a.m. by the time Harry stirred. His tiny arms and legs kicked out, and his eyes and mouth scrunched up. Sophie grabbed him just as he opened his mouth to wail. She snuck into the spare room where the mini fridge and bottle warmer sat, and settled in the armchair to feed him back to sleep. Ben said she needed to stop night feeds after six weeks, as that was best for Harry. Otherwise he'd be reliant on her at night time. She didn't agree, but Ben was hard to argue with. He'd probably forget what he said anyway. Just in case, she wanted to make the most of such special moments. Maybe she could convince Ben otherwise.

She stroked Harry's tiny hand as he suckled on the bottle. His fingers curled around her little finger and her heart swelled. She'd been worried she'd see Kathy in him, but he was Ben's double, and she would do anything to protect him. No harm would come to Harry under her watch.

Thirty minutes later he was still feeding, and an uneasy feeling crept over her. Ben wouldn't be happy if he woke up and she wasn't next to him.

A creak came from somewhere in the house. Sophie froze. *Was Ben awake?*

She stopped breathing as she listened. Yet the only noise was the quiet suckling of Harry's feeding. Her heart hammered and she willed it to be quiet. She looked down and noticed Harry's eyes were closed and he was suckling in his sleep. Gently, she pressed her little finger into the corner of his mouth to detach him from the bottle teat and stood as quietly as she could. She stood still for a moment, listening for any movements in the bedroom. Nothing.

She snuck across the hall to the bedroom. Ben liked to sleep with the door open, so she didn't have to worry about it making a noise. She placed Harry back in the Moses basket and turned around. Fear slapped her in the face as Ben's eyes stared back at her. His nostrils flared. His eyes flashed with anger.

'Where the fuck were you?' he asked, not even trying to be quiet. He was going to wake Harry.

'Harry woke up,' she stammered, 'he needed feeding. I didn't want him to wake you.'

Ben flung the covers off and stood.

Sophie took a few steps back to ready herself for whatever was about to happen. To her surprise, Ben walked over to her and put his arms around her in a hug. She shivered under his arms, unable to hide her fear. They had been happy for months now, waiting for little Harry. But it had been stressful for Ben.

'Why are you shaking?' he let go of her and stood back to look at her face in the moonlight glow. 'Are you scared of me?'

Sophie didn't know what to say. She knew it made him angry when she showed fear. It was silly when he was just hugging her. She looked up at him. Words strangled in her throat.

'I said, are you scared?' he said again, quieter this time.

Still, she didn't answer.

'I gave you a baby, even tell you how to look after it, and you *ignore* me, then think *I'm* the bad guy?'

'No... no... I'm sorry Ben, really. I'm just new to being a mum. I'm excited. I just wanted to cuddle him. He looks just like you. He's gorgeous.'

'Yeah, well. He wasn't going to look like you, was he?'

Sophie felt an ache in her heart stronger than any pain she'd felt before. It wasn't pain; it was anger. A rage she'd never known before seeped through her. She knew she wasn't perfect, but she'd tried so hard to make Ben happy. If a baby wasn't the answer, then what was?

Before she knew it, Ben grabbed her by the hair. She yelled out in pain, and he slapped her across the face, one hand still full of her hair. Her legs buckled as she tried to stay upright while he yanked her.

'Shut the fuck up,' he growled, 'you'll wake him. Stay silent.'

He bent her over the mattress by her hair and pushed her face into the bed. He spat in his hand before forcing himself inside her. She bit the duvet to keep silent. Harry's perfect little face looked at her from the other side of the bed, between the bars of the cot. His eyes closed. *How could he do this in front of Harry? What was wrong with him?*

Then she looked up. The Arracht had arrived. It had grown bigger than she'd ever seen it, and it's ugly face was enraged.

A calmness ran through her, as it had the day she'd found out about

SOPHIE - JUNE 2010

Kathy. She barely felt what was happening. *She* wasn't the problem. Ben was. And she was going to make sure Harry's eyes never opened to his dad hurting his mum. Harry was going to be better than this.

The Arracht circled the ceiling, bits of his rotten flesh dripped down to the bedroom floor. The stench was strong, Sophie couldn't believe Ben couldn't smell it.

Ben was ready to finish and grabbed her hair to drag her to the floor. She obeyed as quickly as she could and opened her mouth like she knew he wanted. Darkness covered the room. The Arracht turned and flew straight towards her. Sophie screamed as it flew inside her. It's dark presence engulfed her. It gave her a new strength born from a manic rage which consumed all other thoughts.

As Ben forced himself into her throat, she bit down hard.

He screamed louder than Sophie had ever heard anyone scream in her life and backhanded her across the face. She released her jaw and turned to grab the nail scissors from the bedside table before launching herself at him.

She threw her arm back and felt the scissors enter his flesh. Then everything went black.

Astrid

'Get under the table,' I ordered, though Harry didn't move. I pushed him instead over to the left of the kitchen, away from both of us.

'Stay where you are,' Charles growled.

Beams of autumn sunlight shone through the kitchen window and lingered on the edge of the knife. It was almost pretty. I laughed.

Charles and Harry both stared at me.

'What's so funny, Sophie?' Charles asked.

'Haven't you wondered why I'm not shaking in my boots? Here you are, a big six-foot tall man with a knife in his hand, and yet I'm not scared at all,' I said, as smugly as I could.

He faltered, his arm sagged. His confidence disappeared.

The Arracht hovered above him, flesh dripping to the floor.

'Why do you think I'm not scared, eh? Take a guess.'

'You're not well. The knife is to protect me, not to hurt you. The last time someone tried to get you medical help, you stabbed him to death.'

'Oh, really? Please tell me where you heard such a ridiculous story?' I asked.

'A friend.'

'A friend. Really? Well, they're lying. For your information, I'm fine. I have never been mentally unwell, but I can be dangerous when it comes to protecting Harry. Now, get the fuck out of my house while you can still walk.'

'If you're so dangerous, why not just kill me now? Because it would prove me right? That you are a murderer.'

'Because I'd rather *not* in front of my child. Unless I have to. And I'd rather not have to move another body.' I shrugged. I felt Harry's wide eyes on me, but I didn't take my stare off Charles.

'So you did kill Ben, then?' His eyes glinted with satisfaction.

'Who said I was talking about Ben?' I laughed again. I was quite enjoying fucking with him.

His eyes squinted in confusion or anger, I wasn't sure which.

I primed every part of my body in case he moved forward. I knew if I could throw him off-guard then I'd stand a better chance of winning in a physical fight. I've won plenty of sparring matches at Taekwondo. I'd already worked out which hand to hold his knife away with and which foot to swing around his head.

'Have you ever actually killed somebody?' I asked, trying to fuck with him further. 'Have you felt their last breath leave their body? Their death rattle will stay with you forever.' I did a raspy breath to show him what I meant. I tried not to think about the fact that I was terrifying poor Harry, who cowered at my side. Instead, I concentrated only on the monster in front of me.

His face was pale. This wasn't playing out how he wished.

I kept going. 'Have you tried to move a dead body? They're heavy, you know. I'm sure you've heard of 'dead weight'. And then there's the CSI stuff. You've probably left hair all over already.'

The man looked around him as if he would see any hair that had fallen from his head.

'They can tell how tall the attacker was from the blood splatter, whether you're right or left-handed,' I said.

He gulped. 'Shut up! I don't want to kill anybody. I want to help. You just need to tell the truth.' He was losing it. I had to be careful he didn't attack us out of fear.

'Just leave now and I will move away. Then we can both forget this happened,' I said.

'No. You just admitted you killed him. I know you had issues, but you need help to face up to it. That isn't an excuse to hurt people. You have to pay.' The man's eye twitched.

'Do you deserve to go to prison?' I asked.

'Why?' he looked like he might cry.

'Because you will if you don't put the knife away and get out.' I gestured towards the knife. 'Either that, or you'll die.' I ran to Harry and grabbed my handbag on the counter, reaching inside.

'Stop!' yelled Charles.

But I couldn't stop. My body moved without me telling it to.

I had no control.

And my vision was going black once more.

Summer

'We need to get back in the car,' Swanson said as he turned and ran out of Eddie's room.

I rushed after him, slamming Eddie's flat door shut behind us without a second look. I was glad to leave, though God knows where the hell we were rushing to.

'Where are we going?' I asked as we reached the main house's corridor.

'I'll explain on the way.' His urgency must have been obvious as we reached the front door, because Stacey opened it as soon as she saw us running. Swanson ran through the open door without saying a word.

'Thanks for your help.' I smiled at her as we ran past.

She said nothing in reply and just stared at us.

We reached the car, and I fell into the front seat, trying to keep up with Swanson. He sped off down the street, still not telling me what the emergency was.

'What's spooked you?' I asked.

'I don't know where to start.' He sighed. 'It's a bit of a long story. A woman I know just left me a voicemail. She rang me the other day too. Someone has been accusing her of things. Leaving her notes and calling her in the middle of the night. Now, her eleven-year-old son is missing.'

'Oh no.' I gasped, and my hand flew to my stomach. The thought of Joshua going missing made me feel instantly sick. 'Do you want to kick me out while you go to her? I can get a bus back.'

'Nope. I think I'm going to need you with me.' He threw me a glance as he sped around a corner.

'What? why?' I wish he'd just spit out the complete story.

'I've just seen pictures of this same woman, and her missing son, in your brother's room.'

It's a good job I was sitting already, as I felt my legs go weak. I opened my mouth to speak but only a strangled noise came out. No. It couldn't be true. I turned to glare at Swanson.

'He's not dangerous anymore. That's why they transferred him there. He wouldn't hurt her son,' I snapped. I knew it was weak. I'd worked in low security places as a support worker before I became an advocate. I knew some patients there were absolutely still dangerous. Even so, I didn't care. My brother was not dangerous to random children.

'Summer, you don't know your brother. I know what Marinda said about him not actually being ill, but perhaps he is now. He's been locked away and told he was crazy for twenty years. That's enough to drive anyone nuts.'

I kept my mouth shut at his use of the word 'nuts'. He was right about Eddie though. I didn't know him at all, other than some vague childhood memories. The most vivid of these was him trying to kill Mum.

'Why would he take a child?' I asked. 'It makes no sense.'

Swanson said nothing in reply.

It took ten minutes to reach the destination, a beautiful detached house on Rose Way. Swanson abandoned the car across the street and ran up the drive. He banged on the front door. I followed him and stood awkwardly at the end of the drive.

Nobody answered the door. Swanson knocked again.

'She's probably not in. I'd be out looking for Joshua if it was me. Let's go.' I looked over at Swanson. I hadn't seen him like this before. He seemed to be in a world of his own, agitated yet zoned out.

Just then, a bang ripped through the house, so loud that the front door shook.

'Shit! Get down, Summer!' Swanson lifted his mobile to his ear but I couldn't hear what he said.

Someone screamed inside the house.

An image of Joshua appeared in my mind and I ducked behind the driveway fence in an attempt to move to safety. I had to stop getting into dangerous situations.

Swanson put the phone back in his pocket. 'I'm going in. Go to the car.' He ran into the house without waiting for my response.

But the pictures Eddie had flew through my mind. If Eddie was in there hurting somebody then I needed to help.

Swanson

Swanson jumped back behind the front door. He poked his head around the frame to see who had the gun.

A man stood in the kitchen doorway at the end of the corridor, blood splattered across his shirt. Behind the man stood Sophie.

The man spotted Swanson and instantly he raised his arms in the air. Swanson heard a clatter as something hard fell from the man's hand.

'Help!' Sophie screamed. Tears streaked her face. Her eyes were wild.

Swanson moved into the house and stayed low behind the stairs. 'Where is the gun?' he yelled out.

'It's here. I won't shoot. Just please help.' Sophie was inconsolable and barely got the words out. She was even worse than the night Ben had gone missing.

Swanson stuck his head around the base of the stairs. The man blocked the kitchen doorway with two empty hands held in the air.

'Move,' Swanson said to the man, pointing to the far end of the kitchen. The man did as he was told.

'Eddie?' a voice asked in a whisper.

Swanson startled; he hadn't noticed Summer sneak in behind him.

The man's neck snapped round to look at her. His pale face whitened further. His mouth half opened, and he took a few steps forward.

'Move!' Swanson was more threatening this time, and the man instantly stepped to the side of the kitchen.

Sophie dropped to her knees, sobbing over a silent small figure on the floor. Harry. Thick blood seeped from his side.

'I shot him, I shot him,' Sophie continued to wail.

Swanson ran over and pushed her away from Harry. He knelt over the boy. There was so much blood it was hard to tell where the wound was.

'I already called for an ambulance. Where was he shot?' Swanson said.

Sophie shook her head through her sobs. The pool of blood was mainly to Harry's left side, so Swanson set to work finding the wound and applying pressure.

'Eddie?' Summer repeated as she entered the kitchen.

'Summer,' Swanson snapped, 'come here and help me hold pressure on the wound. It's his arm.' He pointed at Eddie. 'You stay there.'

Summer startled as though she'd only just noticed the injured boy. She immediately dropped to the floor to help. Harry wasn't fully conscious. His eyes flickered open and closed. His small body shook. Sophie ran back over and sat above his head to stroke his hair.

'I'm sorry, baby. It's OK. It's OK. You're gonna be OK.'

Swanson could hear distant sirens, and it wasn't long before paramedics ran inside the house. Summer and Swanson moved out of the way and let the specialists work on Harry. Swanson turned to find Eddie, but he was nowhere to be seen.

Summer

I ran outside to look for Eddie as soon as the ambulance crew arrived to care for the boy. It had only taken a few minutes for the ambulance to arrive, yet Eddie was gone.

Swanson followed me out. My whole body shook as I turned to him, and I put a hand near my mouth as I felt the nausea rise.

'There,' Swanson pointed to a drain.

I ran over and threw up. I lifted my hands to wipe my mouth. The child's blood was all over them. Blood covered my trousers, too. The pavement spun. I grabbed the kerb for support.

I didn't hear him coming, but Swanson's powerful hands lifted me up and sat me down properly. 'Put your head between your knees. You're in shock,' he ordered.

I did as I was told without question. I heard commotion and sirens but took no notice of what was happening. Seeing Eddie had shocked me, but that poor boy covered in blood would stay with me forever. His mother's screams would never leave me.

'He's in the best place now, Summer.' Swanson was looking down at me. 'Come on, let's get you home.'

Swanson gave me a lift home, much to Hart's disdain. She'd turned up just as the ambulance arrived and wanted to question me straight away. Swanson and I didn't speak much on the drive. He helped me up to my flat and promised to call as soon as he knew more about what had happened.

I showered and sat in my empty flat to wait. The telly was on in the background. The noise was comforting, though I didn't watch it. Joshua was still at his dad's house for the night, and would be meeting his baby sister. I thought I'd feel jealousy, or at least a little emotional. Yet the shock of the day's events clung on. It felt like a weird dream. Had I really just seen the aftermath of a mother who shot her own child?

After two hours of on and off dozing on the sofa, my doorbell finally rang.

'Hey, it's me.' Swanson's voice crackled through the intercom and I buzzed him through the main entrance. I opened my flat door to wait for him.

'Did you find him?' I asked as he stepped into the corridor. He shook his head. I moved aside to let him in. We made our way to the kitchen. 'Is Harry going to be OK?'

'We'll see.' Swanson leant against the kitchen counter. He never sat or accepted a drink, so I didn't bother to offer.

'And it really was Astrid who shot him?' I asked.

He nodded and rubbed his beard. 'Accidentally.'

'I guess she'll be in trouble whether or not it was an accident? I've had no one call me for a statement yet.'

Swanson looked away. 'I need to talk to you about that.'

'What about it? Will you take the statement?' I asked.

Swanson shook his head. 'There's something I need to tell you.'

Swanson - June 2010

Swanson woke covered in sweat, and his ears ringing. He jumped out of bed and flicked on the lamp. Either someone's screams nearby had woke him, or he was dreaming.

He stood still, listening out for any signs of trouble. A thud came from next door, but they were never quiet. Ben was always yelling, and now there was a baby added into the mix.

Swanson went round once after Ben invited him to a BBQ. His wife was nice, if a little quiet, but Ben was a cocky bellend. Swanson had only returned on one occasion since: a night when the shouting got so bad that he'd felt compelled to check on Sophie. She was out, or at least that's what Ben had said.

He didn't want to get too involved. He'd been there with his own parents. It never ended well.

He strained his ears. Could he hear grunting noises? *Christ, was he listening to Ben and Sophie having sex?* He rubbed his eyes and flicked off the light, ready to sleep again. Before he could lie back down, a deep scream made him snap the light back on.

Rather than the usual high-pitched screams, this time it was a man's yell. Adrenaline pumped through him as he threw on the jeans and jumper from the floor of his bedroom and ran outside to the front garden. Once outside he stood still and still peered over his fence at their house.

Was he overreacting? Were they just fighting again?

The hairs on his arms raised despite the unusually humid summer night. There were no more screams, but something wasn't right.

He walked up the path. At least if he knocked, he would know they were OK. As he raised his hand to bang on the front door, it flew open and Sophie appeared with the baby in her arms.

'Hey, Sophie. You OK? I heard a shout.' He looked behind her for Ben. She was shaking with tears, sobbing too hard to answer him. Fresh blood stained her nightdress.

'Come on. Come with me.' He put his hand on her shoulder and led her down the path into his house. There was still no sign of Ben. Swanson considered what he should do as an off-duty police officer. Call for backup? That seemed silly. It was just a crying neighbour. What would he say?

Once inside, he realised she was covered in blood. It was all over her top and even dripping down from between her legs. The situation was much more serious than their usual scraps.

'Sophie, what happened?' he spoke quietly and put his hands on her shoulders. She was shaking. 'Let's put the baby down.'

He made a space between cushions on the sofa for the baby and took him from her arms. She didn't fight him. He made her a glass of water as she took deep breaths and tried to calm down enough to tell him what happened.

'Here, sip this. Tell me what happened.'

'He just wouldn't stop. He wouldn't stop,' she said through gasping sobs.

'He hurt you physically? What did he do?' Swanson kept his voice gentle. He needed to coax the information out of her. Maybe he could get her to open up, and they could get a conviction for Ben. It was almost impossible if the victim didn't give a statement.

'He wouldn't stop. I had to. I had to do it to protect Harry. Don't take Harry from me.' She looked up and her pleading eyes burrowed deep into his.

Swanson gulped. 'Why would I take Harry from you, Sophie? Is Ben OK?'

She slowly shook her head. 'I had to stop him. I had to.'

'Wait here.' Swanson grabbed his house keys and locked the front door behind him as he rushed over to check on Ben.

He prayed Ben wasn't dead. Shit. He was a police officer, for fuck's sake. How could he let this happen to his own neighbour?

His feet crunched over the gravel path to their front door. His radio was at the station, so he had his phone in hand ready to call for backup if needed. He knocked on the front door quietly, trying not to wake any other neighbours.

No answer.

He pushed the handle down and the door popped open easily.

'Hello?' Swanson called out, adrenaline pumping through him. Silence greeted him.

A trail of blood led from the hallway and up the stairs. He snuck up the stairs one at a time, listening for any noise as he went. Once he reached the top of the stairs, he called out again.

It was still silent other than his own blood pounding in his ears. He followed the trail of blood to the main bedroom. Christ, what had she done to cause this much blood?

As he entered the room, the spatter continued along the floor at the bottom of the bed. He rushed to the other side, full of dread at what he might have allowed to happen.

But the dread turned to a rising panic as he saw what Sophie had done, and he fell to his knees on the bedroom floor. Benjamin Bates lay there, unmoving and freezing cold.

Summer

Swanson looked down at the floor as he spoke. It made no sense to me that someone like Swanson would bend any rules. Ever. He was always so stoic and straight-laced.

'So you helped her get away?' I asked.

Swanson nodded. 'It was stupid and I'll always regret it. I was young, and new to the job. The fear of another officer finding out what happened... it lives with me every day. I even cleaned up the blood in her house and let her sleep on my sofa for a couple of nights until his family somehow heard he had gone missing. Sophie told me he didn't speak to his family so I didn't think they'd be too much of a problem, to be honest. I thought he could just disappear. I called my aunt then. I knew she had a house that needed a tenant and I dropped off Sophie and Harry and paid their deposit.'

'Do you think she forgot what she did?' I asked.

'Well, it seems that way. My aunt had been in a similar situation with her first ex-husband, so I told her what happened. My aunt monitored Sophie for me, and they became friends. Yet Sophie tells everyone Ben just randomly disappeared and that he was amazing to her.' He shrugged. 'She seems to have no memory of either of them hurting each other at all. The family tried to find her. They were unsuccessful until recently.'

'Didn't the police look for her?' I asked.

He shifted uncomfortably. 'The police don't know. They were never told about any of it.'

'Never told?' I looked away, trying to process the web of what he was telling me.

'He wasn't officially reported missing by his family or by Sophie. She thought she'd reported it to the police via me, but obviously she didn't. I've just allowed her to think that because she seems fine otherwise. I didn't see the point in correcting her. So what if she can't remember what happened? As long as she and Harry are OK. I visited her all the time. We grew apart after... well, after...'

'You broke up?' I answered for him.

His face reddened but he nodded.

'Where the hell does my brother fit in?' I was more bothered about Eddie than any of this strange story, and didn't blame Sophie for forgetting. I already wanted to forget.

'Other than the photos, I have no idea.' He gave me a serious look. 'The photos were taken from far away, as if he'd been watching them.'

'Why would he be watching them?' I spoke more to myself than to Swanson.

He shrugged. We fell into silence for a moment. His mobile phone startled us both when it rang.

'Sorry,' he said, leaving the kitchen to answer his phone.

I sat alone, trying to figure out why on earth my brother would follow this random woman. Well, she was random to me. He obviously knew her somehow. Had they been friends? How could that be the case if he was released from the secure hospital only recently? It was difficult to make friends while locked away, though he must have had unescorted leave before being moved to a low security place.

Swanson returned a couple of minutes later, interrupting my thoughts. 'That was the same aunt I mentioned a minute ago. She needs to see me, something to do with Sophie. I'll call you later.'

I walked him out to the hallway. He turned to me as he was halfway out the front door. 'Be careful, Summer. We don't know how dangerous your brother might be.'

I nodded, thankful that Joshua wasn't around tonight. I just hoped my brother didn't know where I lived. *Unless he had been following me too?*

Swanson

The rain hammered down on the roof of Swanson's car as he drove to Barb's Manor. She hated him calling it that, but there were worse names he could think of for it. It was far too ostentatious. His phone rang and Hart's name flashed up.

'Yes?' Swanson answered.

'Where the fuck are you?' Hart's voice had that hushed urgency she always had when she was angry. Most people raised their voice when mad, but Hart was so loud usually that she seemed to do the opposite.

'I'll be back real soon. Something urgent came up.'

'Er… urgent like the mum shooting her own child that needs to be interviewed? Or urgent like the rapist we need to find?'

'It's to do with the mother, or the guy that was at the scene with her, anyway. I feel like this is all connected. Just trust me, I'll be back soon.'

Hart tutted loudly. Swanson tried not to laugh as he imagined her face turning red.

'Listen, arsewipe. I'm not going down with you. If anyone asks, then I don't know where you are and we never spoke.'

'Of course. Are forensics on the property?'

'The mum's house? Yes. They're nearly done. The bullet was lodged in the kitchen wall. Some blood splatter was in the same area. They've found some prints and hair samples to send off. Forest is at the hospital with the mum. There are a couple of guys out taking statements from neighbours, too.'

'OK, I'll be in soon. Don't interview the mum without me.'

'Call me if you need backup.'

'I'm only going to see a friend. See you soon,' Swanson hung up the phone.

The rain eased off, so he put his foot down to reach the Manor quicker. If he wasn't around to interview Sophie, then someone else might step in, and that was the last thing he needed.

He pulled up to Barb's a few minutes later and ignored the sweeping driveway, opting instead to park on the roadside for a quick getaway if Hart called again. He grabbed his phone and keys and hauled himself out of the Audi, cursing himself for not sticking with the weights. Dodging the larger puddles, he stalked up the driveway and rang her doorbell twice in quick succession. The door flew open seconds later.

'Alex, darling, thank you for coming so quickly. Come in now out of that awful rain.' She waved him inside with a flourish.

'Hi, Barb.' Swanson entered the hallway and she put her hand on his arm to lead him to their usual spot at the kitchen table. Her hands were the only thing which gave away her age. She never admitted exactly how old she was, but she was much older than his fifty-year-old mother.

'Thank you for coming so quickly,' Barb said as they sat on the cushioned marble-effect chairs. Barb had already laid out a water jug and a glass for him.

'Well, it sounded urgent.' ice clattered as Swanson filled a glass from the water jug.

'It's more strange than urgent, I think. I have a friend, Charles, who I met a few weeks ago in Waitrose. We have a lot in common. He dresses and speaks well, you know.'

Swanson sipped his water to hide his grin, though Barb was looking away from him and through the kitchen window.

She continued with her story. 'So we went out for dinner a few days later, and to the library a few days after that. Eventually I thought it would be OK to invite him back here. I had a book he wanted to borrow and he was so nice to me. Astrid called that same day, and she didn't sound too good, so I told her to come over.'

Swanson sat up in his chair and grabbed his notepad and a pen from his pocket.

'What are you doing, dear?' Barb asked.

'Just making notes. I have something to tell you in a minute, but go on.'

'Oh… OK. Well, I introduced them, and then Astrid and I went into the garden. When she left I found him hiding in here, watching her leave through the window. It was unnerving, if I'm honest. He didn't take the book he'd asked to borrow. Then he didn't call again until earlier today. He asked what Astrid had said and if she would be home today. Maybe I'm just being silly, but there are some strange people about, and the whole thing gave me the willies. I didn't want to call Astrid and worry her. So I thought maybe you could take care of it, darling.'

'Take care of it?' Swanson asked.

'Yes, you know. Look into it or something. He also asked if I knew someone called Summer.' She raised her eyebrows and put her palms to the ceiling.

'Summer?' Swanson's chair scraped across the floor as he stood.

'Oh, be careful with the floor there, dear.' Barb seemed unphased by his sudden movement.

'Listen, something happened earlier today with So… Astrid. I can't really go into detail. It involved a man in her home with Harry.'

The colour drained from Barb's face. 'Are they OK?'

'Well, Harry is in hospital, but we think he's going to be fine. Astrid is with him. We need to speak to her to establish what happened. It appears an intruder might have gotten into their home, and in her fight to make sure Harry was OK, she somehow hurt Harry herself. But we need to know who the intruder was.'

'Oh, God. Charles?' Barb put her face in her hands.

'Well, it sounds possible,' Swanson answered.

'Oh my God, I led him right to her,' she said through her fingers, her voice cracked.

'Do you know where he lives?'

'No… I haven't visited his house yet. I do have his number.' She raised her head and walked to the counter to find her mobile phone.

Barb fussed with the login screen on her phone. Christ it would take her ages to find the phone number. Swanson stepped over to her and held out his hand. She passed him the phone and he found the number and jotted it down.

'OK. I need to go, Barb. Thanks for calling. This could really help us. Don't speak to Charles again. If he comes over or contacts you, call me.'

Barb led him back through the hallway, much more subdued than she had been when she let him in. At the front door, she leaned up to him and kissed his cheek. 'Tell Astrid I'm sorry, please?' she said as she pulled away.

'She's OK, Barb. You don't need to be sorry. You've probably really helped us.'

She nodded, yet her face showed his words made her feel no better. Guilt tugged at him as he walked away, but he needed to make sure Summer was safe, and he needed to interview Astrid. His phone rang as soon as he pulled off Barb's street.

'Yes, Hart?'

'You on your way yet, or what? Murray said she'll put Walker on the interview if you're not here within five seconds.'

'For fuck's sake. Yes, I'm coming. Tell her to keep her wig on.'

'Shall I actually?'

'What?'

'Tell her you said to keep her wig on?'

Swanson laughed. 'You wouldn't dare.'

'Meh. You're probably right. It depends how much you piss me off in the next few minutes. The mum is at the hospital, anyway. How quickly can you get there?'

'I'm literally minutes away. I'll probably beat you.'

'Is that a bet?'

'Go on, then. Loser buys coffee.'

'You don't drink coffee.'

Swanson hung up and put his foot down. He tried to call Sophie, but the phone rang out. What the hell would he say to her? He needed to beat Hart to the hospital. He rang her again, but still no answer.

He reached the hospital within a few minutes and abandoned his car on a piece of grass close to the entrance. He'd deal with any parking fine later.

He walked through the smokers outside the entrance and checked out the reception area. It was far too busy to wait in line. An older receptionist stood reading some paperwork at the edge of the desk, not talking to anyone. He walked right up to her. She looked up, clearly annoyed at his intrusion.

He flashed his ID and asked where he could find Harry's ward. Her attitude changed and she was immediately helpful in telling him where to go.

Swanson followed her directions, walking through the maze of corridors and entering the lift twice to reach the correct floor. People milled about everywhere. Kids were running around tired parents and beds which were nearly as wide as the corridor were being wheeled about by porters. It was busy and noisy and everything else Swanson hated. The bustle brought him back to being a child, which was a time he'd much rather forget ever happened.

An ex had once accused him of being born as a grumpy old man. Hart had loved that.

Eventually, he found the correct ward with Forest sitting outside, just like Hart said.

'Forest.' Swanson nodded to him. 'Have you been here the whole time?'

'Swanson.' He nodded back. 'Yeah. Well, I'm trying not to get in the way.'

'OK. Have you got an update?'

Forest gave him a blank look. 'Well, I haven't been inside yet. I'm just making sure the mum doesn't go anywhere and the male suspect doesn't come back.'

'So, your update is that nothing has happened yet?'

Forest nodded again, his face very serious. It was almost comical to see him sitting outside staring at the door. He was older than he looked, but he was fairly inexperienced and not the sharpest tool in the box.

Swanson rang the ward bell to get the nurse's attention. She smiled and pressed the buzzer to unlock the ward door for him, waving him inside.

At the reception desk, he flashed his ID to the nurse. 'I'm here to get an update on the condition of Harry Moor, and speak to his mother.'

'Oh, OK. Harry's near the end of the ward. He's doing fine, just a nasty cut, really, but he's resting. I think the shock was worse than the wound. His mum is with him.'

Swanson nodded, ignoring the other nurses who edged closer to listen to their conversation. He smiled and thanked the nurse and headed in the direction she pointed.

He saw the back of Sophie's red hair before anything else, shining like a beacon.

She didn't move when he reached her and continued to stare at Harry instead. The boy lay fast asleep on his back in the bed, his breath steady and rhythmic.

'Astrid?' Swanson said, as quietly as he could. He placed his hand on her shoulder.

She whipped around.

'Oh, it's you. Why did you call me Astrid?' She turned back to face Harry.

'Well, I need to interview you with a colleague. It's best if we act like strangers, OK? But don't panic, it will be fine. Harry's fine, you're fine, everybody is fine.'

He fell silent. She didn't respond.

'Astrid? Did you hear me?'

'Yes, yes. We don't know each other.' She waved him away and turned back to watch Harry.

'I'll be back soon with another officer and we'll go somewhere to talk, OK?'

She nodded, but still refused to turn to him. Maybe she knew he couldn't help. After all, how could he if she admitted to shooting Harry? Where the hell did the gun even come from?

Swanson left the ward and called Hart. 'I'm outside the ward with Forest. Where are you?'

'Fucking lost in this bastard maze.'

'Well, I guess you're buying coffee.'

'Again, you don't drink coffee.'

'That's not the point. I won it fair and square, so I want coffee. I'll give it to Forest. Do you need directions?'

'Don't give me that pretentious shit that you do, just be nice and give directions like a normal person.'

Swanson laughed loudly, and Forest looked over at him in his nervous way. He gave Hart directions as nicely as he could manage and hung up to wait for her.

'Is everything OK in there?' Forest asked.

'Yes, they're both in there. The boy is going to be fine. It all seems like one big accident.'

'Oh, that's good then.' Forest stood and wandered to the window to look outside. He looked like a skinny child with bum fluff.

They didn't speak. Swanson couldn't be arsed with small talk. He went over every plausible scenario in his head. Could Sophie keep her mouth shut about them? He doubted it. She wasn't exactly on her game right now.

Hart bustled through the corridor doors a few minutes later. She held her head high, as if daring him to say something about needing directions. He wondered whether she could take a joke, but decided against it when he saw her red face. She was pissed.

'Alright?' he asked.

'No, I'm not. I'm sick of chasing you everywhere this week,' she snapped, 'and I've just been sent that list of names from the car place. Guess who's on it as a visiting worker? An electrician?'

'Peter Johnson?' Swanson guessed.

'Yep. So we need to pay him another visit first thing. In there, is she?' she pointed to the ward door.

'Yeah. Listen. I have to tell you something.' He pulled her to one side away from Forest, who wasn't paying any attention, anyway. 'I know the mum. We dated a few years ago.'

'Oh for fuck's sake, Swanson, and you wait until now to tell me.' Hart closed her eyes and put her hand up in front of his face. 'Nope. I didn't just hear that.'

'This is serious, Hart.'

'Forest.' Hart ignored him and walked away. 'You're coming with me, come on.'

She gave Swanson an annoyed look and pressed the bell to the ward. Forest joined her, looking so terrified that it would have been funny in any other circumstance. Poor Forest.

Swanson considered putting his foot down and insisting on going in, but actually if he wasn't there then Sophie was surely less likely to mention their past.

The nurse buzzed Hart and Forest into the ward. Swanson took Forest's seat and crossed his arms. He stared at the ward door, willing it to open again.

They should bring Sophie out of the ward to chat to her somewhere away from her son's sickbed, but as he waited, he realised they weren't going to. Many thoughts ran through his head. Has she refused to speak to them? Has something happened to Harry?

After thirty minutes, they came back outside and he jumped out of his chair to greet them. Forest looked much happier now, clearly relieved it was over.

'So?' Swanson asked Hart.

'Come on, I'll tell you on the way back down. Forest will stay for a bit longer.'

They walked down the corridor and headed towards the exit.

'So, she said Harry disappeared about 1 p.m., which we knew about as the school reported it. He turned up with a man at around 5 p.m. who looked familiar, though she wasn't sure where he was from. The man had a gun and forced his way inside. He wanted money, which she clearly has, but she had no cash on her. She led him to the kitchen to pretend to get some, grabbed the gun and it went off. Which is about when you arrived.'

'Right, well.' Swanson paused. 'I was trying to help a friend find someone.'

'You were trying to help Summer find her brother.'

'How did you know that?'

'I'm good at my job.'

'Meh. You're alright.' Swanson grinned, but stopped when he saw the sharp look on her face. 'OK. So, I think the man at the house was Summer's brother. He had pictures of the mum and the boy in his room at the hospital. So, I went over to check on her. That's what Summer and I were doing there.'

'OK. It's all making a bit more sense now you're finally explaining yourself. So how does he know Astrid?'

'No idea. That's the missing piece right now.'

'OK. Let's go back to the office. We need to sort through it all. What a fucking mess. I think forensics are finished sweeping the house though, so we should have the tests back pretty quickly.'

'I'll meet you there, I'm going to talk to Summer. If anyone can help us find Eddie, it's her.'

'Fine,' Hart said, though her tone suggested it was anything but.

They left in their respective cars, agreeing to meet at the office. Swanson didn't believe Summer would have any idea where Eddie was, but if he was as dangerous as Sophie suggested then he needed to make sure Summer was safe.

The last thing they needed was anyone else getting hurt.

Astrid

I've always hated hospitals, and avoided the doctor like the plague. I'd been lucky to have no emergencies until now, and Harry was lucky to be alive. It was just a flesh wound, yet it could have been so much worse. And it was all my fault. Other outcomes flashed through my mind. The sick feeling in the pit of my stomach would never go away. We would definitely move now. If Harry even wanted to stay with me.

Kai sat across from me as Harry slept, putting my nerves even more on edge. He'd turned up at the house just as we were leaving in the ambulance, but hadn't visited the hospital until much later. He looked so much like Ben. I knew now why I didn't like being reminded of Ben, why I'd gotten scared when I saw Kai. The memory of Ben's disappearance was too hard to relive.

'So you don't know who that man could have been?' I asked him for the millionth time.

He shook his head.

'I told you, I got a note with your address. I didn't see any man. And I wouldn't see Harry without your say-so. I know I can get angry and say things. But I want him to like me.'

I know I can get angry and say things. The blurred edges of a memory flashed through my mind. I pushed it away before it could form an actual picture.

'When he's better,' I answered.

Kai nodded. 'You'll let me know?'

'Yes. I'll call. He'll want to meet you. Now he knows you exist, and I need him to realise that man wasn't you. You can trust me.'

Kai left soon after. I sat with Harry, watching his rhythmic breathing until his eyes slowly opened. He looked around the room, still groggy from the painkillers.

'Hi baby,' I smiled at him, praying he wouldn't push me away. I blinked away the tears which threatened to fall.

'Hi, Mum.' He reached out for me and I took his hand. 'What happened?'

'Don't panic. Kai had a gun. The bullet hit your arm but it's just a graze. Nothing serious. You're going to be fine,' I said.

He groaned and closed his eyes. 'I don't feel fine.'

'I think you bumped your head on the way down.' I looked at his pale face and stroked his cheek.

'Yeah, I remember the nurse said. Where's Kai now?' he leant into my hand and closed his eyes again.

'He's gone. The police have him.'

He opened his eyes wide and looked at me. 'I'm so sorry, Mum.' His voice cracked and tears brimmed in his eyes.

I couldn't hold mine back any longer. 'Oh, baby. You have nothing to be sorry for. Can you ever forgive me for not telling you about Kai, Harry? I thought he was dangerous.' I sniffed.

He nodded. We hugged gently, though I wanted to squeeze him tight and never let go.

'What really happened to Dad?' his voice was so quiet.

'He really disappeared, babe. The police officer will tell you when he comes.' I kissed his head.

'What if Kai comes back?' he asked, fear in his eyes.

'I don't know, but don't worry. We're going to move for that big job, remember? We'll go to the beach as soon as you're feeling better. And we'll pick a new house, and a puppy. You don't even have to go to school.' I smiled at him. I'd always wanted to home school. 'And you can visit the twins whenever you want. It's all going to be fine.'

It didn't take long for Harry to fall back asleep. I wasn't sure if it was all the stress or the painkillers. If we were going to move, I needed to go home and pack. I flicked open my phone and booked a nice-enough hotel for two weeks in Cornwall. I wasn't staying in Derby a minute longer than I had to.

Harry's cheek was warm and soft as I kissed him goodbye. On my way out, I told the nurse I was leaving to collect some clothes. A police officer stood outside the ward, looking through the window. I buzzed open the ward doors and easily snuck past him.

I raced home as fast as I dared without risking a speeding fine. The last thing I needed was to draw unwanted attention. The driveway was empty when I reached the house, and someone had used the spare key to lock the front door. Luckily I'd instinctively grabbed mine on the way out of the house earlier in the evening.

It was 10 p.m. already, so I raced straight up the stairs to grab the suitcases, completely focussed on getting packed and getting out.

It wasn't until I walked into the living room to put down my first suitcase that I spotted him, sprawled out on the sofa as if already at home.

My husband, and the love of my life, was in my house.

Summer

I wound down the window to let the cold breeze wash over me as I drove. Sitting in the flat alone had made me overthink, so I was on my way to the supermarket. I needed to do the shopping before Joshua returned from his dad's house, anyway.

It didn't take long to reach the supermarket. The bright lights were welcoming against the dark evening sky as I pulled up close to the entrance.

I hated dark car parks.

As I entered through the open doors of the shop, my mobile phone vibrated in my jeans pocket. I fished it out and Swanson's name flashed up.

'Hey,' I froze in the middle of the supermarket, attracting filthy looks from shoppers as they tried to get by. I moved to the side of the entrance, trying to look apologetic.

Swanson's voice was more rushed than usual. 'Hey, Summer. Listen, I'm at my aunt's house. She made a friend recently. A man who became strangely interested in Astrid.'

'Whose Astrid?' I asked.

'Sophie — sorry, I didn't mention that she changed her name to Astrid,' He spat out the words as if that was an unimportant detail.

'Oh, OK. Wait… why are you telling me about this man?' my heart raced.

'Well, she has no photos of him, but I think my aunt's new friend might be Eddie. She has his phone number, but I haven't called it yet,' silence hung in the air as the question sat unasked. If he was going to call Eddie, I wanted to be there.

'Do you have time to meet?' I asked.

'Sure. Be at yours in less than half an hour.' He hung up without saying goodbye.

I abandoned my trolley and raced home in less than ten minutes.

I rushed to the bathroom, where a tired and pale face stared back at me in the mirror. I brushed my hair, slicked on some pink lip gloss, and applied concealer to hide the bags under my eyes.

True to his word, Swanson arrived ten minutes later.

I let him upstairs, and he stood awkwardly in the doorway with a half-smile on his face. I waved him inside with a nervous grin.

As we entered the kitchen, he handed me a piece of paper with a phone number and the name 'Charles' in tight, square handwriting.

'Charles?' I looked at him with one eyebrow raised.

'My aunt said that's the man's name.' Swanson shrugged.

'Charles was our father's name,' I said.

Swanson said nothing. I sat at the kitchen table and for once he sat too.

'Do you want to call him?' I asked.

'If you feel comfortable. I think he'd respond better to you.'

'OK, fine,' I said, although my anxiety was so bad I could have happily thrown the number in the bin and moved to Australia.

I dialled the number slowly, stalling. The phone rang out for some time. Nobody answered, and no voicemail kicked in. Phew.

'No answer,' I shrugged at Swanson.

'Did it ring?' He crossed his arms and leant back in the chair.

I nodded.

'Should I try?' he said, after a moment's silence.

'Feel free,' I passed him the piece of paper.

Swanson rang the number and stared at me for a moment with the phone to his ear. He shrugged.

'No answer. I'll call the low security unit tomorrow,' he said eventually, 'to see if he's been back.'

'Will you arrest him?'

'I'm not sure what he's done yet. We know he didn't shoot Harry, but Astrids accused him of bringing the gun into the house. We will need to at least question him.' He looked away to the kitchen door.

I nodded. There was nothing I could do if my brother had broken the law. Though how the hell he would know where to get a gun from or why he'd threatened Astrid with one was beyond me.

'Hart will probably wonder where I am. We're working late.' He glanced at the kitchen door again.

'OK. I need to go shopping, anyway.'

I led him to the front door, and he swept past me to get through, gently brushing against my shoulder. He mumbled a sorry and turned to look at me in the doorway. We stared at each other, just for a moment, and then he was gone.

I stared into the empty corridor, wishing I could call him back to stay with me. Usually, I welcomed being alone, but not tonight. Having Swanson around, even for a few minutes, had felt nice.

I shoved my feelings to one side and closed the door, and then went back to the kitchen to sit with my head in my hands. Tiredness stung my eyes but I knew I wouldn't be able to sleep anytime soon.

If my brother wasn't in the hospital, then where would he go?

Presumably, he had a plan before he went to Astrid's house. I just needed to figure out his next steps, which was nearly impossible without knowing why he went there in the first place.

Who else did Eddie know?

Panic flooded me as I realised where else he might go.

I jumped up and grabbed my bag and keys, and ran down the stairs to the car park. I tried to call Mum as I ran, but she didn't answer. There was barely any point in her having a mobile phone. I threw the phone on to the front seat and sped out of the car park.

Mum lived twenty minutes away in the old mining town of Ilkeston. I weaved in and out of traffic as much as I could, cursing the ridiculous fifty miles-per-hour speed limit and the roadworks on the A52. I called her again as I drove, yet still there was no answer. My legs felt like a dead weight as I maneuvered the pedals. *What would Eddie do to Mum?*

She still lived in the same house where he attacked her all those years ago. I'd begged her to move repeatedly — especially after last year. I tried calling Swanson instead, but he didn't answer. I left him a short voicemail asking him to call me ASAP.

I pushed on through Spondon, slowing for the speed cameras until I reached Dale Road and hit seventy miles-per-hour. Despite the roadworks and cameras, I made it to Mum's house in less than fifteen minutes. I pulled up in front of her small driveway and slammed on the brakes. Mum's front door was half open.

I grabbed my phone and left the car door open for fear of making too much noise. Sneaking out onto the pavement, I crept up the drive to the front door.

My body froze a foot away from the door. I felt eleven years old again, hiding under the table and listening to my brother break down the front door.

I shook the feeling away. There were no excuses as an adult, and I had to make sure Mum was OK. I took another step towards the open front door, but stopped when I heard an animated voice coming from inside.

'That's all I came to say. I'm sorry. I spend my life making other people say sorry now too, Mum, and I'm going to make you proud of me. Maybe one day you will forgive me.'

Eddie. Hearing his voice threw me. He sounded calm. He wasn't about to hurt her. Maybe he really was better.

Guilt tugged at me. Here I was calling the police on him just like I did all those years ago, when Eddie was just trying to make up for what he had done.

He didn't even know about Marinda's lies yet.

I heard Mum respond, but her voice was too quiet for me to hear her words.

Eddie responded to whatever Mum had said to him. 'No. It was my fault. I'm going now. *Don't* look for me. You're better off without me. I could get sick again at any moment.'

Footsteps headed towards the front door, and a jolt of fear ran through me. I ran to the left of the front garden and knelt by the tall fence which led to the back garden path. I wasn't ready to face Eddie, so I watched instead as the brother I'd spent twenty years looking for walked away.

He was shorter than I remembered, with thinning light hair. I hadn't realised that Eddie would be forty-one years old now, not the strapping twenty-one-year-old I remembered.

He stopped at my car with its partially open door, and craned his neck to look left and right down the street. My heartbeat quickened, though he didn't look behind him. He walked down the street instead and took a left turn.

I slipped down to the bottom of the driveway to watch him go; he walked to the end of the street and took a right.

A sudden urge to hug my big brother overtook me, and my feet pounded the pavement as I raced to the bottom of the street.

I bent over and sucked in deep lungfuls of air. I looked left, and saw nothing. I ran to the end of that street too, but he'd disappeared. Shit. Why didn't I stop him when I had the chance?

I ran back to Mum's, sweating and red faced by the time I reached her. The front door was still ajar. Inside, I found her on the sofa, tears streaming down her face. I rushed over and threw my arms around her.

'Are you OK? Did he hurt you?' I asked.

She shook her head.

'I'll make you some tea and then you can tell me what happened, OK?' I didn't wait for a response. My hands shook as I poured water into the kettle.

'Do you take sugar, Mum?' I called, feeling guilty for not knowing how she took her tea. I couldn't remember ever making her one.

She sniffed and sat forward in her chair, attempting to pull herself together. 'Two please, love.'

A few moments later, we had both stopped shaking and Mum was sipping her tea. It's amazing what a cup of tea can do for people.

'How was he, Mum?'

'He was... calm,' she shrugged, 'he didn't make much sense. He said he's sorry for hurting me and he just wants to help people get better by taking responsibility for their actions. I'm not sure what he was talking about. I guess he feels guilty.'

'I saw him earlier. In the kitchen of a lady's house. Her name was Sophie. She changed it to Astrid. I'm still not sure what he was doing there.'

'How does he know her?' Mum asked.

'I hoped you could tell me. She went through something years ago. Her husband abused her. She snapped and stabbed him. She seems to have forgotten what happened. She tells everyone her ex was amazing, as if she's blocked out all the abuse.'

'Oh, well, lots of women lie to others about domestic abuse. It's rare they broadcast it.'

'No, she apparently believes it. But I don't know her, so...' I shrugged.

'Was Eddie trying to help her to remember?'

'I honestly don't know.' I hoped Eddie was trying to help Astrid, but how on earth did he know about her or her past? He'd been locked away. It made no sense.

We fell silent as Mum drank her tea. Her hands looked frail against the mug.

'Does he know about Marinda?' I asked.

'I don't know. I didn't want to upset him, love. I suggested it was Marinda at fault and he told me no, it was his.'

'He needs to be told when he's in a safe environment.' I agreed.

My mobile phone rang, its shrill noise making us both jump. I pulled it from my pocket. It was Swanson returning my call.

My finger hovered over the 'accept' button, yet I clicked 'ignore'. The only thing I knew for sure was that I had to find my brother, and I wanted to do it alone.

Swanson

Swanson raced back to the office as fast as the speed limits and road works allowed. Hart would probably accuse him of disappearing again. Sure enough, her name flashed up on his caller ID a few seconds after he pulled out of Summer's car park.

She didn't even bother saying hello. 'Where the hell are you now?'

'On my way. I got stuck behind a slow truck. You know, the ones that spray stuff off the back. I wasn't risking a chip in my bonnet.'

'Oh. Well, be quick. The most recent DNA results are back in for the sick bastard that's been attacking these girls. We got a hit.'

'Shit, really? Who is it?' he sat up straight in the driver's seat, ignoring the tug of the seat belt.

'If you were here, you'd know.' Hart hung up the phone.

Swanson cursed out loud and put his foot down. He overtook an old woman in a Micra and sped towards the office. He knew exactly where the speed cameras were and how to avoid them. The rain pelted down now and mammoth puddles engulfed parts of the road.

He flew into the office car park a few minutes later and skidded to a halt in someone else's parking spot. *Fuck it.* He wouldn't be there long.

His phone rang again as he exited the car, and Summer's name flashed up. He silenced her call and sprinted into the office to find Hart. The Ops room was a whirlwind of activity and noise. Hart stared at him from her seat at his desk with a smug look on her face.

'Thought that would get you here,' she said, making no effort to move out of his seat.

'Yeah, yeah. You got me, Robin. Spill, then.' He took the chair next to his own and swivelled it to face her.

'Here you go.' She turned a computer screen towards him, and a profile of a man showed up.

Swanson stared at the picture with his mouth half open.

'You OK?'

Bile sat in the bottom of his stomach. He closed his mouth and swallowed hard to make sure it stayed down. He cleared his throat to sound normal. 'Yeah, fine. Where does he live then?'

'No idea. Last known address was 69 Mill Street, Ashfield. So what the hell is he doing around here?'

'Has anyone been to Ashfield to check on him yet?' Swanson asked.

'We're waiting to hear from the local guys. They're going to check it out. Murray's doing a brief in a minute.'

As if hearing her name, Detective Chief Inspector Murray walked into the office. DCI Murray was a secret crush for most people in the force, but not for Swanson. She was alright, but had the worst resting bitch face, and it suited her personality.

As soon as she noticed Swanson sitting in the middle of the room she strode straight up to him. He cursed himself for not being smaller. He could never bloody hide in a room.

'Where have you been?' She gave him a steely look with bright blue eyes.

Swanson felt his face redden.

Hart was going to take the piss for a long time.

'With Hart at the hospital, boss.' He looked at Hart, and she nodded once to confirm.

'Before that?' Murray raised an eyebrow.

'I got a call from someone who thought they had information on the shooting earlier today, boss.' He looked back at Murray, trying to meet her gaze. As if it couldn't cut through glass.

'And did they?'

'I think so, boss. Just checking it out. I'll update soon.'

'You can update me as soon as I finish this briefing and it will get passed on. I want to know what was worth disappearing from the worst serial rape case Derby has ever seen.' Her heels thudded against the grey carpet as she walked to the front of the briefing room. Hart stared after her, clearly looking at her arse.

'You fancy her,' Swanson said.

'I do not. You do! Oohh yes boss, let me in your pants please boss,' she whispered in a stupid voice.

'Fuck off. She's not my type. I prefer them *less* bitchy. Like you.' he stifled a laugh.

Hart slapped his arm.

Swanson didn't laugh for long. Over Hart's shoulder, the face stared back out at him from the computer screen. The sick feeling returned. 'I actually think... I'm gonna throw up.'

'You look white.' Hart gave him a strange look, 'Go to the toilet. Don't throw up here.'

Swanson snuck out of the room whilst DCI Murray had her back turned. He ran down the corridor to the men's toilets, and once he'd made sure no one was inside, he whipped out his phone and returned Summer's call. No answer. He sent her a quick text, and rang Sophie instead. His heart was hammering. She didn't answer either. Christ, how was he supposed to make sure they were OK if neither of them answered? He rubbed his face with his hands. He needed to get out and check on Sophie, first.

Because the face staring out from the computer was Benjamin Bates.

Astrid

Over the years, I'd imagined this very day in my head again and again. Ben and I reunited, at last. I would be safe again in his arms.

Yet instead of feeling safe, my fear towered over me, a vast shadow bigger than I'd ever seen it. I watched it grow over the ceiling, and down the rear wall. A cascade of memories flooded me as I looked at Ben, and terror hit me like a brick.

'Hi, babe.' Ben smiled at me. 'How have you been enjoying your life without me?'

Instead of running to him, as I had so many times in my dreams, I took a step back. My heart wanted to go to him. My body told me to run. I blinked hard, trying to stop the memories: fear, love, pain. Tears ran down my cheeks.

'Hey.' Ben stood and walked over to me. He was a whole foot taller than me. I tried to retreat further, but my back hit the side of the staircase. He reached me in seconds and towered above me. For the first time in so long, I could smell him again. My Ben. He reached out his thumb and wiped the tears from my cheeks. 'It's OK. I'm back now.'

I sank into his arms and let the tears flow. Too many feelings fought inside me, and I couldn't tell which ones to listen to. The shadow grew in each corner of the room and blocked out any light. Darkness surrounded me.

I needed to get out. 'This is too much,' I pulled away from his embrace and turned to walk away, with no clue of where to go. He grabbed my arm and pulled me back into his arms.

'Shh, it's OK. I've got you now.' His arms tightened further around me.

'Ben, you're hurting me.' I wriggled, trying to get out of his grip.

'It's OK,' he whispered, squeezing tighter, 'I just missed you. Didn't you miss me?'

I nodded my head, unable to speak. I struggled to draw a breath.

'You don't look like you missed me.' He released his grip a little and stuck out his bottom lip.

I said nothing, but took deep breaths. The shadow covered the entire living room. 'Do you see the darkness?' I asked him.

He laughed. 'All I've seen is darkness after what you did to me.'

'What I did?' My voice trembled. A memory of being thrown on a bed flashed in my head.

'Did you really think I would never find you?' he asked.

'What? I hoped you would find me. We looked for you for a long time.'

'We?' His face changed instantly. 'You mean the son you stole from me?'

'Our son!' I couldn't help but raise my voice. 'Officer Swanson and the police. Me and Harry, too.'

'Officer Swanson? Officer Swanson made me disappear!' He raised his voice. 'After you stabbed me, you ungrateful fucking bitch.'

'What are you talking about? I'd never stab you!' The room swayed. I leant back against the staircase and closed my eyes. 'Swanson looked for you for years.'

'Swanson found me after you stabbed me with those damn nail scissors. He drove me to the hospital and threatened to throw me in prison if I came back. Even though you were the one who attacked me! *I* was the victim and he treated me like shit.'

I shook my head. 'That's not true.'

'Are you calling me a liar?' His face darkened.

'No! How did you find me now? Has Kai seen you?' I asked.

'Easy. I found out where Swanson was based and followed him around for a bit. I was watching some old woman he knows, and you turned up at her house.'

'Old woman? Do you mean Barb?'

'Yep, think so. I followed you home weeks ago.' He grinned, 'Kai still lives where he used to, with that slut of a mother. I just left him a note. I thought he'd seen me when I was walking away but I'm not sure.'

'You left me that note?'

'I wrote the note and gave it to Eddie. He gave it to Harry. Harry didn't know what it said. But he knows the truth now thanks to Eddie!'

'Eddie? That's what that woman called Charles earlier.' Even in my panicked state, I knew I needed to keep him talking. Maybe the darkness would take him.

'Yep. My nuthouse friend. I met him doing a job at his place. He's not all there. Even so, he helped me. I told him you killed my friend and needed to pay. I've got friends everywhere, Sophie. Have you forgotten that?' He grinned, yet it was more menacing than a direct threat.

'He was with Harry earlier? You let someone who's mentally ill take Harry?' Flashes of blood and scissors and screaming ran through my mind.

'I was watching the whole time! He wouldn't have hurt Harry. Had to have someone watching you who you wouldn't recognise. At least until it was time for you to pay for what you did.'

'Make me pay? For what?'

'Don't act so fucking coy with me.' His face twisted into ugly rage and that was it, that was the face.

The memory flooded back to me and I pushed him away. 'You fucking rapist,' I spat.

My face exploded with pain as his fist connected with my cheek. The hard floor smashed against my face. His foot connected with my stomach, the taste of blood metallic in my mouth.

'Harry is my son, bitch. And I'm taking him with me. He knows all about you now, doesn't he?' he growled.

The thought of him taking Harry made me retch. The full memory of stabbing Ben overwhelmed me. Blood dripping all over our home came flashing back, and the panic that I'd felt as I ran away.

I thought he was dead. Swanson told me he was gone. Swanson lied.

'Leave Harry alone!' I shouted.

His hands wrapped around my throat in an instant. 'Harry will be well looked after and you'll never get the chance to hurt me again, bitch.'

He flipped me over as if I weighed nothing and his hand reached up my dress to pull down my leggings. He forced my head down onto the hard floor and his knee pushed my leg to the side. Every memory of him hurting me came back to me, and I remembered what I'd done. But with my face in the ground, I couldn't see the Arracht. I couldn't hear its guttural noise.

I was alone again, and I was going to die.

Summer

There was only one other person I could think of who might know something about Eddie, and that was Sophie. He'd been in her house, though I had no idea why. She must know something about him. Sophie didn't live far from me: she was just on the other side of the city. It didn't take long to get to her.

I pulled up on her road and got out of the car, leaning against the bonnet for a moment. I didn't even know what to say to her. *Should I admit he is my brother?* It was unlikely she would want to help him — or me — if she knew. She was probably still at the hospital, anyway, asleep with her son.

Fuck it. I crossed the road and readied myself to talk to her in case she was inside. But as I reached the front gate, I noticed her front door stood wide open. *Shit.* I snatched my phone from my coat pocket and dialled Swanson. Thankfully, he finally picked up.

'Look, I'm at Astrid's — or Sophie's — house… whatever her name is.'
'Why? It's a crime scene, Summer. You need to leave.'
'Don't interrupt! Her front door is wide open. I don't know what to do.'
'Jesus fucking christ. Do nothing. I'll be there in five minutes.'

I put the phone down and stared at the door. 'Astrid?' I called as loud as I could, hoping I would scare off any bad guys. *Like my brother?* I heard a shout and instinctively ran to the front door, but stopped in my tracks as I reached it. I turned to see if anyone else was around, and saw no one. So, instead, I peered through the front door. 'Hello?' I called.

'Summer!' a male voice called. A voice which made me want to run away from it and towards it simultaneously.

'Eddie?' I walked inside and immediately spotted Astrid sitting on the floor of the living room. Blood poured down her tear-streaked face. She turned her head towards me, but didn't appear to see me.

Eddie stood in the middle of the living room, and a man I didn't recognise lay on the floor. I looked up at Eddie. His face was a whirlwind of confusion.

'Jesus, Eddie. What did you do?' I stepped backwards.

'I…I… was trying to help,' he said. Tears streaked his cheeks.

'You saved me,' Astrid stood shakily, holding on to the wall for support. She looked at him, and then back at me. 'He saved me.'

'What happened?' I said to Astrid, but brought my gaze straight back to Eddie. This wasn't the reunion I had in mind.

'Ben came back. He came back,' Astrid muttered.

'He was hurting her,' Eddie pointed to the man on the floor.

'You stopped him?' I asked.

Eddie nodded. His hands were shaking. His eyes darted all over the room. He wanted to run.

'Hey, Eddie. It's OK. Look at me.' I smiled at him. 'Do you recognise me?'

He nodded. 'Summer.' It was barely more than a whisper. 'I'm sorry, Summer.'

'It's OK, Eddie. Do you know that man?' I asked.

'Yes. The electrician.' He pointed to Ben. 'He said she had his friend's son. He said she killed his friend and she was ill and Harry needed saving.'

'He's a liar,' Astrid said.

'The electrician?' I asked.

'Yes, he was doing a job at the…' He glanced at Astrid. 'At my house. He said he knew you, Summer.'

'He knew me?' I said. 'I've never seen him before, Eddie.'

Eddie smashed his fist into his own forehead over and over. I ran to him and gently took his hand, just as Swanson's large form appeared in the doorway. He surveyed the room and went to Astrid first.

'Are you OK?' he asked her.

She looked up and around the room. A smile spread across her face. 'The darkness.' She gave a short laugh.

Swanson glanced at me with worried eyes. 'The darkness?' He turned back to her.

'It's gone.' She laughed again.

'Good, I'm glad it's gone. Is your head OK?' Swanson asked her.

She nodded.

'OK, good. Help is coming.'

Swanson moved away from her and over to the man on the floor, he lifted his wrist to check his pulse. 'What happened to him?' he asked.

'He was hurting her.' Eddie had stopped punching himself and looked lost, like an overgrown child. 'I need to go now, Sir.'

Tears stung my eyes. My brother *wasn't* the bad guy. He was OK. He just wanted to help. Eddie moved to leave, and I pulled him back gently. 'You can't go, Eddie. The police will need to talk to you.'

He shook his head vehemently. 'No. No police.'

I looked at Swanson, who glanced at Eddie before turning to me. He nodded his head slightly. I took the hint. I leaned up to whisper in Eddie's ear.

'Run home, Eddie. I'll come and see you tomorrow.'

Eddie braced himself, took a deep breath, and ran.

Swanson didn't move. 'Too dangerous to leave this suspect alone with you two. Priority is ensuring he's OK, and then arresting him.'

I nodded and allowed hope for Eddie to replace the fear in my heart. Maybe we really could be one big happy family again.

The man stirred and groaned from the floor. 'Take Astrid away, Summer,' Swanson called to me.

I held a hand out to Astrid. Fresh blood still trickled down her pale cheek. 'Come on, we need to go,' I told her.

She didn't move. She stared at the man, and didn't seem to hear me at all.

'Easy, now,' Swanson said to the man as he tried to sit up.

I had to get her out before he saw her. What was her boy's name? I tried to rack my brain.

'Astrid? We need to check on Harry.'

Her head snapped around at the mention of Harry, and she grabbed my hand. She leant her shaking body against mine as we walked outside. A car pulled up once we reached the bottom of the drive, and DI Hart jumped out. A marked police car pulled up behind her. Thank God Swanson had let Eddie leave. Now, I just needed to hope he'd gone home.

Astrid

The next morning I was sitting in the hospital waiting room. Harry was being checked over before they released him. It wouldn't be long before I got to take him home, wherever home would be.

Ben was alive. The police had arrested him, but he was alive.

And I felt more scared than ever. Repressed memories had hit me like a truck. Except this time, I was a different person. As a mother for over a decade now, I knew I had to fight back for Harry's sake. I was more prepared after being a lone parent for eleven years. I was stronger; I had money, and I had a career that I could do from anywhere in the world. And Harry. What else could I ever need?

I had to hurry. The police would arrive to question me again as soon as they knew Harry was well enough to talk to them. God knows what they'd charge me with. I knew even Alex couldn't get me out of this mess. Blaming Eddie was wrong, especially after he saved me from Ben. Yet I would do anything to be with Harry, and if an innocent man had to go to prison then so be it. My ringing phone broke my trail of thought. It surprised me to see Alex's name pop up.

'Hi, So… Astrid,' he said.

'Hi, Alex.'

'Ben's still here. I'll let you know if he gets released,' he said matter-of-factly, as though I were a normal witness. My stomach flipped at the mention of Ben's name.

'OK. What has he said?' I wasn't sure if I wanted to know what lies he was spewing, but I needed to protect myself from whatever he said about me.

'Everything. Ben's singing like a canary, trying to get less time and blame everything on Eddie. He's accused Eddie of stalking Summer,' He let out a low, short laugh.

Good. If he was blaming Eddie, too, I might get away with it.

'Was he stalking her? She knows him, right?'

'Stalking Summer? Maybe a little. I haven't spoken to him yet. He's her brother.'

'Oh, I see. How did Ben know Eddie was her brother?' I grabbed a pencil from my drawing table and jotted down what Alex said.

'He doesn't. He saw photos of Summer on Eddie's desk when Ben was doing a job there. Ben had seen Summer and I together in a cafe so he knew Eddie and I were connected.'

'Oh. Are you two seeing each other?'

I heard a strange noise from his throat. 'Er, no. No, we're not. We're little more than professional acquaintants, really.'

He was lying. 'I think you'd make a nice couple. Do you think Ben will get away with it?'

'No. He... we got a DNA match for another crime. He will go away for a long time.'

'Another crime? What?' I noticed he ignored my comment about them making a nice couple.

'I can't say at the minute, but trust me, they will lock him up for years.'

'You lied to me. You said he was dead.' A memory played in my mind of Alex returning from the house all those years ago. He'd been gone for ages, and he had blood on his shirt.

'No, I said he was gone. I didn't say he was dead.'

We fell into silence. I heard his breathing down the end of the phone, then he let out a loud sigh. 'Do you know a Peter Johnson, by the way?' Swanson asked.

'Yes. Ben's Dad. They don't really talk. He came out as gay years ago and it embarrassed Ben,' I said, realising Ben was never the person I thought he was.

'Does Peter work as an electrician as well?' Swanson asked.

'No, just Ben, but he sometimes used Peter's name for cash-in-hand jobs. He was paranoid about being found out for his taxes or something,'

'I see. Look, I can't call you anymore,' Swanson said, 'the investigation… it all needs to be legitimate. No one can find out what happened before. I'd lose my job for not reporting it. Do you understand?'

'I understand. You've done enough for me. I won't land you in it, and I won't call you again, I promise.'

'If you need anything, call Barb. She will help you.'

'OK. I will.'

I put the phone down and immediately went back to Google. Harry and I were finally going to move away and forget this whole nightmare. Maybe a caravan, or our own motorhome. Then we could go where we wanted, and we'd always be able to get away.

Just Harry and I together, our little family would be safe at last.

Summer

Eddie had gone missing again. He didn't return to the hospital. Probably because he was too scared of being sent back to high security Adrenna after what he'd done. I didn't blame him, that place gave me the creeps and I was just visiting.

He was trying to help, but being violent meant he would get sent back regardless, and with Astrid saying the gun was his, poor Eddie stood no chance.

I could only imagine he was walking around lost somewhere. Swanson said the police would check with the homeless community, as they at least needed him for questioning.

Worry gnawed at me as Joshua and I ate jam sandwiches and played a game on his Xbox. It wasn't a good combination, and my fingers were sticky from the spilt jam on the controller.

'What do I do now?' I asked him.

'I told you, Mummy! Now you come out of creative mode and go to the nether and attack,' he threw his hands around, exasperated I couldn't get the hang of his game.

'Oh, I think you'll be better than me at that bit.' I played on his ego and passed him the control.

'Yes, I will be.' He nodded without a hint of modesty.

I laughed and walked over to the dining table in the corner of the living room to check my phone, which was sitting on charge. There was a message from Swanson waiting for me:

'We haven't found Eddie. Will let you know when I have more info.'

I sat at the table and considered my options again. I'd spoken to Mum a few times since yesterday to make sure she was OK and to see if Eddie had turned up. She hadn't seen him.

Neither of us had spoken to Dylan yet. You'd think we'd be closer than we were, growing up just the two of us with Mum, and the shared tragedy of losing our father and brother in different ways. Yet I saw Dylan only two or three times a year. Every Christmas, and some birthdays.

We tagged each other in the odd social media meme, but that was it. He lived forty minutes away in Mansfield. It may as well have been the other side of the country.

I scrolled to his number and let my finger rest there for a moment, not knowing what to say. I loved seeing him at Christmas, but it was so unusual for me to call out of the blue.

What would he think? He'd assume the worst and panic.

I pressed call before I thought about it too much and put the phone down altogether.

He answered on the second ring. 'Hello? Summer?'

'Hey, Dylan.' My anxiety eased now I could hear his voice.

'Are you OK? Is Mum OK?' he asked in a high-pitched voice.

'Yes, yes, we're fine!' I cut him off before his panic increased.

'Oh, good. Is it someone's birthday?' he asked.

'No. Dylan! Listen, I have something to tell you. It's about Eddie.'

'Eddie?'

I could almost see him scratching his brain. We never mentioned Eddie. It was an unwritten rule.

'Yeah. You know, our big brother,' I said.

'Yes, I know who Eddie is, Summer! I'm just surprised to hear you mention his name.'

'Yeah, well. He's sort of… back.' I put my head in my hands. This isn't how I should tell him.

'Back?'

'Yes. It's a long story, to be honest.' My fingers played with an elastic band that had been abandoned on the table at some point. How was I going to explain all of this?

'Is he there with you?'

'No, not yet. He's been following me, I think. I don't think he's dangerous now. Did Mum tell you about Marinda?'

'No. What do you mean he's been following you?'

'Oh, well, we have more to talk about than I thought,' I sighed.

'Right, I'm coming over. Text me your address.'

And with that, he hung up on me. I don't know what I had expected Dylan to say, but *not* that. I texted him my address and put the phone back on charge. A notification flashed up from Facebook as I was about to walk back to Joshua.

Charles Thomas wants to send you a message.

I gasped. Dad's name popping up on Facebook was not something I ever expected to see. I clicked 'view' and a message from Charles Thomas, a profile with no picture, popped up on the screen.

'I'm going to stay away. Nice to see you happy. Don't look for me.'

Eddie. I stared at the message as if looking at it would tell me what to do next. I needed to reply.

'Hi, Charles. It's OK, you don't have to run away. The police know it was all a big misunderstanding.'

But as I clicked send, the profile changed to 'Facebook user' and the message failed. He'd deleted the profile. I threw the phone down on the table and put my head in my hands.

'You OK, Mummy?' Joshua shouted from the sofa without taking his eyes off his computer.

'Yes, honey. Just dropped my phone,' I sat up to look at him, engrossed in his building game. A part of me still wanted to stay away from Eddie. That part grew when I looked at Joshua. I knew deep down that wouldn't happen. I couldn't abandon my brother.

Now I had seen Eddie, and knew how lost he was, I was no longer scared of him. But he could hurt someone else if a person like Ben Bates took advantage of him again. I needed to know where he was, and how his mind was.

He needed someone to look out for him.

Once Dylan was here, we could make a plan together. He could help me. We'd help Eddie together.

One big happy family for the first time in twenty years. We would keep Eddie safe together, as a family should do.

III

The Hospital

'The dogs always bark,
And the violets die a death,
When the devil brings the dark,
And when he gets inside my head.'

Summer Thomas is fighting for her life after coming face to face with the devil of Adrenna Psychiatric Hospital.

It's up to DI Swanson to find out the truth behind what happened to her, and he needs to be quick if he wants to save others from meeting the same fate.

But Swanson has his own health scare and past demons are back to haunt him. With the devil close by, he might not survive long enough to save anyone. As the history of the hospital becomes clear, he needs to figure out who he can trust to tell him the truth.

Before he ends up meeting the devil himself.

The Servant

The freezing breeze numbed the tip of my nose as I waited outside Derby Psychiatric Hospital, reminding me to pull up the thick scarf to hide the bottom half of my face. I made sure only my eyes were visible and pulled my hood further forward to block out the wind, though it still whirled around me, as if pushing me away from my dark calling. Every few minutes, a member of staff arrived in the car park. They yawned and stretched as they mentally prepared to begin their 6am shift.

But they didn't concern me.

Despite being over six feet tall, the prickly branches belonging to a smattering of unkempt bushes hid me well; opposite from the hospital car park. I was lucky it was the depths of winter, and the dark sky would stay that way for another couple of hours.

My cheeks flushed under the warmth of the scarf, and a tingle of anticipation ran through my skin. This was the day.

No more watching. No more waiting.

I knew Derby Psychiatric Hospital well from my stint there a few years back. The door I was staring at was the only exit and entry point that was used. A couple of fire exits allowed patients into the rear gardens for walking or smoking, but this was the staff door. The bushes were an excellent choice to watch the doors without being seen. I watched the staff come and go easily.

There was no way I could miss her.

The wind flew straight through the small holes in the cheap soles of my Chelsea boots. I moved from one foot to the other to prevent my feet from going numb, though it helped as the minutes slipped by, and nerves replaced my excitement.

I checked the silver face of the Rolex my father gifted to me years ago. It was 6:10am. The date was definitely the 1st of December. I was certain I had the right day. She needed to hurry. Time was not on my side.

He would not wait another day.

Why was she late today of all days?

I stopped moving and reached deep into the fleece-lined pocket of my hiking jacket. My fingers curled around the hard shape of an A5-sized notepad. The front cover emblazoned with 'Adrenna Hospital' in small white letters. I flicked through the last few pages, looking for any errors.

Wednesday November 24th
She worked the night shift. Arrived at 5:35pm and left at 6:09am.
Thursday November 25th
She worked the night shift. Arrived at 5:46pm and left at 6:11am.
Friday November 26th
She worked the night shift. Arrived at 5:43pm and left at 6:10am.

No errors. I definitely had the right day. She worked on Wednesday every week, and it was now 6:14am. Being tardy wouldn't do.

Maybe she wasn't even the right one for Him.

I chewed my lip and considered the reaction if I was to give him the wrong woman. *Was it worth the risk?*

The whirring noise of the doors opening made my head snap back up. And finally, there she was. She bolted through the hospital doors with her head high in the air, missing the usual exhausted look of someone finishing a night shift. She never seemed to look tired.

Though she gave a slight shiver as she crossed the road and pulled her dark winter coat firmly around her. I stayed well back, but wondered why she didn't zip it up.

I pushed away my doubts. She was the one. I felt it. Though at first glance there was nothing special about the young woman in her everyday blue jeans and plain brown boots. It was all in her haughty demeanour.

Her narrow eyes. She needed to be tamed. And He was the one to do it.

She had a proud walk as she made her way down the long pavements of London Road. I followed a suitable distance behind as we passed closed shops, old cafes, and Indian restaurants. Long blonde hair peeked out of her woolly bobble hat. I wanted to get closer, to touch it, to see how soft it was. But I forced myself to stay back.

A cotton scarf sat a little too tightly around her neck. She clearly wore it for decoration only, as it was too thin to be keeping anything warm against the cool winter temperatures.

I'd definitely gotten it right this time. I only needed to get the hard part over with and then I'd rest. The thought of sleep kept me moving, hands in pockets, tracing her footsteps as she continued down the last half a mile of London Road which led to the bus station.

I didn't rush. I didn't need to keep up because I knew where she was heading. She used the same route each time to get home after her regular shift at the hospital.

Though my legs were longer than hers, and so I accidentally caught up with her seconds before she reached the roundabout across from a large shopping complex and city centre market, which stood proudly on the edge of the cobbled city centre. She stood at the roadside and craned her neck, looking for cars coming from either direction.

This was my chance.

I pulled my scarf down and ran forward, spat on my hands and rubbed my eyes hard.

"Excuse me!" I yelled, my voice high and panicked.

Her head whipped around, dark eyes wide against pale skin.

"Please! Can you help me? It's my mother." I pointed to the car park of the kids' indoor trampoline play park, which sat behind us.

She stepped forward, but hesitated and looked around at the empty streets behind her.

"What's wrong with her?" She turned back to face me, and her face creased with worry. Though she didn't move any closer.

I'd have to try harder.

I scrunched up my nose as if holding back tears and shrugged my shoulders. "She just collapsed."

The woman took another look around. The streets were silent.

I could run at her.

"OK. It's OK, don't worry. I'm a nurse." She finally moved towards me and relief flooded me.

"Oh, thank you!" I turned and ran toward the secluded car park of the trampoline place. It was the only car park I found nearby which had no cameras.

She followed closely behind me and we ran to the road behind the shopping centre, pausing a moment and checking for traffic. It was strange, being so close to her after keeping my distance for so long. I breathed in the sweet smell of her perfume. Or was it shampoo? It was something flowery.

It was my favourite smell in a woman, and I hadn't expected it from her. A longing to touch her almost took over me, but I kept my hands firmly at my side and squeezed into fists.

It wasn't time yet.

And she wasn't mine to have.

One car drove by. A taxi. I put my head down as it passed, hoping my hood and scarf were enough to hide my face. But my concern was unfounded. The taxi driver was going far too fast to see anything much. I ran across the road once it had passed, and she followed right behind me.

"Over here." I led her to the side of the car park where I'd parked the large van earlier that morning.

She stopped on the other side of the van. *Damn.* She was still visible to the road.

I disappeared around the side of the van and stood with my back to it. I reached into my pocket, my fist tightening around the needle that lay hidden inside it.

"Mum? Can you hear me?" My voice came out strangled, and my heart quickened as I heard her boots getting closer to my side of the van. I stood firm, took a deep breath.

I saw the toe of her brown boot first and a flash of blonde hair a second later. I grabbed her hair and pulled her towards me. She cried out, her hands grabbed at mine.

Until I smashed her head against the van.

Her body went limp, and I plunged the syringe into her neck.

In an instant, it was over, and she lay on the ground, motionless. I peered around the other side of the van. No one was there. No one came running. Opening up the rear doors of the van, I dragged her by her feet and hauled her into the back. There was no need to be careful. She wouldn't wake for a while.

I climbed into the van and closed the door. I removed her shoes and woolly hat and put the faint scarf to one side. Her hair fell over her face, and I brushed it back. For the first time, I noticed the dark makeup around her eyes and tutted. I'd smudged it in the brief struggle. I'd have to remove it before He saw her.

I stripped the rest of her body, carefully placing her underwear into my pocket and the scarf back around her neck. I pulled it tight. Not enough to cut off her air supply. But enough that it wouldn't be hard to calm her in case it had to be over with quickly.

Once naked, I lay her on her back and stared. I wasn't supposed to touch her, but thinking about the way she walked, that narrow look in her eyes, and seeing her now.

She was helpless.

And it occurred to me it would solve my problem of whether she was good enough to be taken for Him. I'd *humble* her before He got to her. I had to make sure she knew her place. That was the answer to our minor problem.

I lay a finger on her shoulder. Her soft skin spoke to me. And I knew I was right.

This time, everything would be perfect. And I would make sure she was ready for her new beginning.

Swanson

The whiteness of the doctor's office closed in around Detective Inspector Alex Swanson. His breath stuck in his lungs. Why were the walls so bare? There was nothing to focus on. It was always the mundane things he noticed when in need of a distraction. Other people who had sat in this chair, and received the same news, might scream, or cry or swear.

Is that what he should do?

He stayed silent and tore his gaze away from the walls, focusing on the dulled floor tiles and trying to force air through his lungs again.

But the tiles weren't much help either, and his lungs ached to the point it was difficult to breathe. He needed to get out. It was too damn hot and stuffy in here, and the brightness was too much for his aching head. The room vibrated so hard around him he had to close his eyes and put his head in his hands to make it stop.

"Are you OK, Alex? Is there someone I can call for you?" Dr Nick Tiffin's voice rang through somehow. The city's top neurologist sounded far away and his voice echoed off the empty walls as if they were in a tunnel. Maybe they were in a tunnel, or even a dream, and none of this was real.

But Swanson rarely dreamed.

And if he did, why would he dream about cancer?

A hand on his shoulder broke his train of thought, and his head shot back up. Dr Tiffin had come out from behind his desk, and was bending over in front of Swanson, his large hand gripping his shoulder. Despite the man's considerable size, Swanson hadn't heard him coming. He ignored the deep throb in the base of his skull and stared at the dark five o'clock shadow on the doctor's chin.

"I'm fine. What are the next steps?" he heard himself say.

Dr Tiffin let go of his shoulder and walked back around to his side of the desk. He sat back in his chair, clasped his hands together, and eyed Swanson.

"Are you sure you don't need five minutes to yourself before we discuss this? It's a lot to take in," he said.

Swanson looked away and shifted in his chair, trying to make the dizziness stop. "I'm fine," he repeated.

"OK. Well, you need to be aware of the symptoms and what we can do to manage them. Headaches, nausea, even hallucinations can be possible, and you need to keep me informed. I know you've been having headaches of differing severity, so I'll prescribe some powerful painkillers and some mild ones. We need to figure out the type of tumour you have to determine the next steps, and in order to do that, we need to assess it. In the meantime, you can take these if you get any headaches." The doctor spoke slowly, and didn't take his eyes off Swanson once. He passed him a packet of pills.

Swanson reached over and grabbed them. The cheap plastic chair groaned as he did so. "Thanks. How do we assess it?"

Dr Tiffin looked away, searching for something on his desk. Eventually, he opened a drawer and rummaged through it. "I'll refer you for a biopsy. Have you ever had one before?" He pulled out a pad of prescription paper and scribbled something down on it.

Swanson shook his head. "I've heard of them, but no, I've never needed one."

Dr Tiffin leaned over the desk and gave him a sympathetic smile as he handed over the torn piece of prescription paper. Swanson fought an urge to tell him to stop fucking smiling.

"It sounds scary, but it's actually quite a simple procedure and nothing to worry about. We'll make a small hole in the skull and insert a very fine needle to take a sample. It's done under anaesthetic, so you won't feel a thing."

Swanson's hand flew to the top of his head. A hole in his skull sounded like something to worry about to him.

"OK." Swanson stood. He couldn't stand the whiteness of the room any longer, or the patronising smile on the doctor's face. "You'll contact me with an appointment?"

"Er... yes." Dr Tiffin stood too. "But please, sit and I'll go through the options of the biopsy."

"Sorry, I have to go to work." Swanson turned and stalked out of the office without another word, ignoring Dr Tiffin's calls to come back.

His legs were shaky as he closed the office door firmly behind him and ventured into the rowdy corridor. The noise hit him immediately and seemed ten times louder than usual. Plastic chairs lined the walkway on one side. They were full of people muttering to their friends or partners, or with forlorn faces waiting to be called for their own appointments. Preoccupied hospital staff stalked through the corridor. Nurses, doctors, porters everywhere. Their sharp footsteps echoed off the floor and imprinted on Swanson's brain. He leant against the wall and closed his eyes, trying to drown out the noise.

"Are you OK, Sir?"

His eyes flew open. A young nurse stood in front of him, her head cocked to one side. A small smile lined her plump face, and her round eyes creased with worry. He cleared his throat, stood straight, and forced a smile.

"Yes, sorry. Just have a bit of a headache." He turned and strode off down the corridor. The nurse didn't follow, but he felt her eyes on his back as he walked away.

His legs marched rigidly through the winding corridors. Anyone in his way soon moved to the side to let him pass, one upside of being too broad to hide within a room. He reached the open reception area and fixated on the exit on the other side. The winter sun shone through the glass doors in front of him like a beacon.

He barely noticed the other patients sitting in the cheap waiting chairs, most of whom turned to look up at him as he rushed past. He vaguely noticed one older lady in a pale blue suit half stand up from her chair, as though she wanted to check on him, but he shot her a look which changed her mind and she swiftly plonked back down in her chair.

Reaching the automatic doors was all that mattered to him. As he finally stumbled through the doors and into the ambulance waiting area, he put his head to his hands. The sun was deceiving, and a freezing wind whipped at his face, forcing him to suck in a deep breath.

A mother and child steered clear of him as they tried to enter the hospital doors without getting too close. The mother clasped the hand of her little boy and pulled him close to her whilst they manoeuvred around Swanson.

He stepped away from the doors and leant against the external wall of the hospital instead. Unlike the more modern parts of the extended hospital, the original entrance was made of cold, red brick which dug into his shoulders. He moved his head back and let the brick dig in further. The pain helped. His thoughts became more focused.

Something sharp dug into his stomach and he shoved his hand into his pocket to move the item. The pills! He grabbed them and broke two tablets out. They were like dust in his mouth, but he forced himself to swallow them down.

Now he needed to get to his car.

He looked over at the car park and tried to remember where he had parked two hours ago. A vague memory of being annoyed at how busy the car park was came back to him. He'd driven right to the rear of the colossal car park to find a space where his Audi wasn't likely to get another car door slammed into the side of it.

He stepped forward to start the long walk. At least the freezing wind might clear his head before driving to the office. He looked down at the ground as he walked and ignored his surroundings. A couple of cars beeped at him as he got in their way, but he didn't bother looking up. Let them get annoyed.

They'd live.

He might not.

It took him fifteen minutes to find his car, and another couple more to find his keys. He eventually dug them out of the same pocket he'd looked in first, cursing at his carelessness. The wind made his nose and cheeks numb, but he was in no rush to drive away. The large saloon car suddenly felt too small to climb inside.

He unlocked the door and clenched his fists, took a few deep breaths and pulled the door open to force himself into the front seat. The air had woken him up enough to at least be thankful that no one else had parked next to him. There was never enough space in these tight bloody car parks.

The thought of work made him want to drive to the other side of the country and never return. He could go home, curl up, and pretend nothing was happening. Or he could get out into the fresh air some more. Maybe he should go to Mam Tor, a beautiful Derbyshire viewpoint that stretched over Edale Valley to Kinder Scout. There wouldn't be many people there in this awful weather. It was perfect.

He pulled his phone out of his pocket. Three missed calls flashed up from his most intense colleague, Detective Inspector Rebecca Hart.

No surprise there. She seemed to treat chasing him as her part-time job. But *three* were a lot of missed calls, even for Hart. Something must have happened. Damn it, why had he left his phone on silent? He started the engine and used the in-car phone system to call her back.

"Oh, here he is," she said. He practically heard her rolling her eyes. "It's about damn time you called me back, Swanson."

He'd never admit it, but hearing her voice dripping with sarcasm made his world still again. The beginnings of a grin formed on his lips for the first time that morning.

"Alright, Robin?" he replied in his usual calm manner.

"I'm warning you, Krypto. You are cruisin for a bruisin."

Krypto. Superman's loyal dog. He laughed softly. "Who even says cruisin for a bruisin anymore?"

She huffed. "All the cool kids do. Obviously."

"Well, you're showing your age with that one. What do you want, anyway? I'm busy." He stretched back in his seat and relaxed a little, allowing his eyes to wander around the car park. It seemed brighter suddenly, though the wind still howled.

"Busy going to the doctor for those damn headaches, I hope."

He sighed as she brought his reality back in an instant. "Yes, actually."

"Oh," Hart paused, momentarily thrown by his words. She'd been going on at him for weeks to go to the doctor, and he'd never told her he'd had a scan. He watched an old man walk past his car, bent over in the wind, and wondered if he would ever have the privilege of reaching such an age. He'd always looked forward to getting old. An age where you can do or say as you please and no one bats an eyelid because you're old. You can sit in pyjamas all day, shouting at the telly and smoking a pipe with no concerns about consequences when you're already 90.

"What did they say?" Hart's voice shook his thoughts away.

"I'm fine. I'm done now, so I'll see you in the office shortly," he said, and hung up before she replied. He grinned to himself, knowing she would spit feathers at him for cutting her off.

Maybe going into the office wouldn't be so bad, after all.

Summer

Summer Thomas cursed her brand new winter boots as she tripped over the curb outside the compact cafe nestled amongst the terraced street. She righted herself at the last minute, just in time to prevent a fall on her backside in the middle of the pavement. She'd known the boots were too big but could not resist the faux fur lining in the cool temperatures, especially at half-price.

She pushed away a piece of hair that had fallen out of place and into her face. Thank god it was only two more weeks until her hairdresser appointment. Although she hated the small talk and awkwardness of a stranger touching her hair, it had been *way* too long since she last had it cut. And now it had grown down to the middle of her back.

Dylan Thomas stood outside the entrance to the cafe watching her. He let out a short laugh.

"Did you enjoy your trip?" he asked, grinning widely.

Christ, she remembered kids at school saying that whenever anyone tripped up in the classroom. She finished sorting her hair and looked up at him, returning his grin. He might have been her younger brother, but he'd been taller than her since he was 13-years-old.

"How old are you? Ten?" she retorted.

"Not as old as you!" He grinned even wider, his bright white teeth almost glinting in the sun.

She tutted as she stepped forward to reach him. "You're only younger than me by two years! You'll be thirty soon and it won't matter. Age is just a number."

She pushed past him and opened the door to the cafe named 'Barbara's Baps'. The bell above the door jingled as she entered, and the greasy aroma of chips made her stomach rumble.

"Is that why you cried at your 30th birthday bash?" Dylan asked, following her through the open door.

"No. That was because of the prosecco."

She walked over to a table in front of the window and gestured for Dylan to sit across from her. The cafe was small, but it served tasty food that was freshly cooked, and it never got that busy. Perfect for a private conversation, and she wouldn't have to cook later because 6-year-old Joshua was at his dad's house for the night.

"So, what have you done to your teeth?" she asked as they removed their coats and took a seat on opposite sides of the table. A cheap, green and white plastic cloth in a chequered pattern covered the table. The same grim colour scheme as the external front, and the old aprons the servers wore.

He grinned widely and gritted his teeth. "Do you like them?" he asked. He moved his head to the left and the right, showing off all angles of his wide smile.

"Yeah, to be fair, they do look good. Maybe a bit *too* white. As in, I think I've gone blind." She leaned her elbows on the table, but jumped back as it tipped suddenly.

Dylan quit his stupid grin. "There's no such thing as *too* white. Watch the table. I see you're as clumsy as ever." He shook his head and picked up a menu.

Summer didn't bother to argue his point. She had always been clumsy. A waitress with wispy grey hair came out from behind the counter and approached them. She held a pen and a pad of paper tight in her thick fingers.

"What can I get for you?" She gave a half smile and looked out of the window.

"I'll have a cheese toastie, please," Summer said, not bothering to look at the menu.

"One cheese toastie." The waitress repeated as she wrote on her notepad. She squinted at the paper as she wrote, then looked up at Dylan expectantly.

"Er…" Dylan's eyes flicked over the menu. "Cheese and ham toastie, if that's on here somewhere?"

"Cheese and ham." The waitress nodded and peered down at her notepad again. "Any drinks?"

"Coke, please," said the pair simultaneously.

The waitress chuckled. "Coming right up." She turned and lumbered off back to the counter without another word.

"So, now I know you're OK, other than tripping over everything and breaking perfectly stable tables." He stopped for a moment and waited for her reaction with a cheeky glint in his eye. She rolled her eyes but said nothing. "Do you have any news about our lovely Eddie?"

She sighed. "No, nothing yet. I don't know what to do next, really. I replied to him on Facebook, but he didn't get my message. That police officer or detective, Alex Swanson, came with me to speak to a few of the homeless people in the city twice now, and no one has seen him. Or at least they didn't want to tell me. I don't have any pictures of him, so it wasn't easy. I called you thinking we'd brainstorm together."

Dylan nodded. "OK, but I have no idea where to even start, to be honest. I barely remember Eddie. I was what, 8 when he got locked up? And work is crazy busy. Everyone wants their carpets fitted before Christmas. I'm working 12-hour days, including most weekends."

"I know. I'm busy, too. But he's our brother regardless of whether we remember him well. I want to know he's safe and not dead in a ditch somewhere with no one to claim him." She sat back on the hard, plastic chair and shuffled a bit to stop her backside going numb.

"Or make sure he's not hurting anybody?" Dylan raised an eyebrow.

"Well, yes, or make sure he's not hurting anybody. But Aaron checked out his record from Adrenna Hospital, which is where he was for a good couple of years, and he was *never* violent there with staff or patients. I really don't think he's a danger to anyone anymore. Other than himself, possibly. He's been in hospitals for so long, how would he know how to look after himself without someone always being there?" Summer kept her voice low. They were discussing a fugitive, after all.

"Yes, true. But if he's off his medication, he might be more of a danger to others. As in, maybe that's what kept him calm?" Dylan suggested.

"He wouldn't have needed medication in the first place if Marinda hadn't messed with his head, pretending to be some sort of demon. He was never violent before her, or before Dad died."

Dylan looked away as soon as she mentioned their dad, and she instantly felt guilty for mentioning their father's death. She'd only been 9-years-old when he passed and her memories of him were faint, but Dylan barely remembered him at all.

"Look, if they have medicated him for years for a mental disorder he doesn't actually have, he might actually be feeling a lot better *off* his meds." She tried to explain as Dylan didn't have the experience she had with mental illness.

"Oh, really? Is that what would happen?" Dylan turned back to look at her.

"Well, I'm not a doctor, but it sounds like a possibility to me. Those medications are so strong and have all sorts of side effects. They were literally made to mess with your brain. Doesn't it make sense to you that he would feel better off them? At least after the initial shock to his body." She leaned forward again, ignoring the tip of the table this time.

"I actually thought you *were* some sort of psychiatric doctor?" He squinted at her.

She tutted. "Why do you and Mum always say that? No. I'm *training* to be a forensic psychologist. I don't have a medical licence or deal with drugs, and I never will. Psychiatrists are doctors, psychologists do therapy. Plus, I still need a year of work experience to complete the qualification."

"Oh. So what do you actually do at the moment in the mental hospitals?" Dylan still looked confused.

She sighed. She'd explained it multiple times, but nobody seemed to understand her job at all. Even most of the hospital staff didn't understand it.

"I provide legal information about their rights and help support the patients in whatever they need. A psychiatric hospital is a scary place to be locked away in. Hell, it's a scary place to work in sometimes. And patients need support from an independent person who doesn't work for the hospital. Especially if they're paranoid, which a lot are."

"But everyone you work with is some sort of mentally ill criminal?"

"No, Jesus, Dylan. Stereotype much? Well, I mean, yes, a lot *happen* to have a criminal record, but that doesn't mean they're dangerous, and it certainly isn't all of them." She rolled her eyes.

"What kind of criminal records?"

"Some are bad, some are not that bad." Her lips shut tight. They were getting way off subject here.

"Are we talking like serial killer bad?" The vein on his forehead was bulging the way it did when he was worried.

"I don't think so. Well, I mean, I don't always know what they've done. I couldn't say no for definite. I only know the crime if they tell me or if I look at their file, which I can only do with their permission. It's all a bit complicated, really."

"Oh. It sounds like a dangerous job, to be honest, Summer. Especially after that one who escaped the other month."

"It's really not dangerous. Not usually. I've only had a couple of patients turn on me unexpectedly. It's the nature of their illness, sometimes. And they escape all the time when out on leave. That wasn't unusual, either. They usually get caught pretty quickly. The truth is they are far more likely to be a victim of crime than a perpetrator."

"Do you ever deal with psychopaths?" He picked up the butter knife and waved it in a stabbing motion towards Summer. He really hadn't changed since they were teenagers.

"That's... more of a symptom, rather than a diagnosis. But yes, I work with people who display psychopathic tendencies sometimes. Now, can we talk about Eddie?" She desperately tried to get the conversation back to their brother.

Dylan whistled through his teeth. They fell silent as they spotted the waitress leaving the counter with two plates of toasties. Each sandwich was bursting with golden melted cheese, and the smell wafted over. Summer's stomach growled.

"Here you go, ducks. Enjoy." She plonked a plate in between each of them and walked off.

Summer saw a pink slice of ham sticking out from the edge of her toastie. "Here you go." She moved her plate in front of Dylan and took her sandwich from his side of the table. She picked up the toastie and took a large bite, enjoying the burst of flavour. Cheese had to be one of the best foods ever. Definitely in her top five. Dylan bit noisily into his own sandwich and swallowed it in half a second.

He still ate like a teenager, too.

"Still. I'm dead proud of you, sis. You've done amazing with all that school stuff. But I'd rather you worked somewhere safer. Especially after all that stuff with that other patient," he said, his vein popping again.

Summer didn't respond. She wasn't ready to admit to anyone that she sometimes thought the same. A patient had turned on her only the week before, thinking she was out to get him. It had been a simple conversation that went from friendly to dangerous in a split second when he suddenly accused her of wanting to murder him. Maybe she needed a new job. Especially with Joshua relying on her. He still had his dad, but her bond with Joshua was special. She couldn't stand the thought of him having to grow up without her.

Dylan was lost in his own thoughts as he tore through his toastie, looking down at the table. Summer ate hers more slowly, savouring each mouthful. She watched a lone mother and small child in the opposite corner of the cafe. They were eating their food together, the mother unable to sit and eat hers as she was too busy making sure the little girl had everything she needed. An ache for Joshua tugged at her heart. Her eyes were pulled to the clock above the family. Damn. It was time for her visit. She ate the last bite of her toastie and took a big gulp from the glass of coke.

"I'd better get on with some work," she said.

Dylan took the paper towel from the cutlery and wiped his mouth. At least he had *some* table manners.

"Where are you today?" he asked.

"A high security hospital."

After the conversation they'd just had about safety, there was no way she was going to admit which one. She didn't need to cause him any more worry.

"Well, be careful." He grabbed his black parka coat from the chair next to him and shoved his arms through the sleeves.

"Honestly, Dylan, it's as safe as houses." She smiled at him as she grabbed her own coat and handbag.

They left a few quid each on the table for the toasties and waved goodbye to the waitress as they left. The bell jingled once again as they walked out into the fresh air and the wind ran straight through Summer's open jacket, making her shiver.

"I'll pop by at the weekend after work, and we'll try to come up with some ideas for finding Eddie, OK?" Dylan wrapped his arms around her and squeezed.

"Yes, please." She squeezed him back.

Dylan released his grip and crossed the road to where he'd parked his work van. Summer turned around to walk home, before remembering she had driven and she'd parked her car right on the road behind her. She heard a laugh and saw Dylan grinning at her from across the road.

She stuck her middle finger up with a smile and jumped into her car, blowing on her freezing hands and cranking up the heat as soon as the engine was running. Try as she might, she couldn't shake a strange feeling she'd had since speaking to Dylan about her job. Had she jinxed herself?

Was her job too dangerous, considering she had Joshua?

She drove away with an unsettling dread that suggested Dylan might be right.

The Servant

I'd delivered the woman to Him as promised, but the peace I longed for hadn't come. Instead, I lay back on my bed, hands tight over my ears. I knew He was coming. He was coming for me and I deserved it. I'd done it wrong.

Again.

I shouldn't have touched her first.

I was too weak to resist once she was naked, and He'd known as soon as he saw her. I'd raced home to beg for forgiveness. Soon enough, a stench filled the room which infiltrated my nostrils so completely that it forced me to hold my breath to stop myself from gagging. And the familiar black shadow stared from its corner.

Dark pupils bored into my own. The pale hair on my scarred arms rose as goosebumps tickled my skin. My toes curled and my stomach ached from the knots deep inside. Every inch of my being warned me. *Danger.* I was in terrible danger.

My body didn't know whether to settle on fight or flight. I knew fighting the shadow was futile. But I knew flight wouldn't work either. The shadow would follow me anywhere. So instead, the third, more cowardly option was the only one I managed. I froze.

I lay in my bed, hidden under the duvet cover. Naked. The soft blanket felt cool against my scarred skin. It was my only armour against the petrifying creature that was fixated on me. And I knew I must meet all demands. No matter what the cost, because the creature in front of me was not a creature at all, but a devil.

The devil.

And he was out for blood.

I knew what happened to those who defied Him. My lungs ached as breathing became more difficult. A rasping noise offended my ears so deeply it almost hurt. I felt my arms rise from under the blanket, as if someone else was controlling them, and shove a finger in each ear. But the rasp increased in volume. *Louder. Heavier. Deeper.*

Repeatedly, the noise cut into my eardrums. It was stuck inside my brain. I couldn't hear my thoughts as the rasp took over my mind until it was the only noise in existence.

"I see you." The rasping breath turned into a dark, gravelly voice. A whisper deep within my mind, but it wasn't my voice. No. It was the shadow. Though the shadow's thin lips never moved.

"Yes, Sir," I mumbled.

"You violated her," the voice said.

I nodded, knowing denial was futile. "I wanted to help, Sir. She needed to be more obedient."

"LIES! She was meant for me and you took her first."

I screamed and stuck my fingers deeper into my ears, though it was of no use against the voice in my head. "Sorry!" I shouted, "I will do better, Sir."

"I need you to *bring them* only. Choose someone you don't need to shape. You know what I need, bring them to me. I'll give you one more chance."

And with that, the shadow disappeared, and the room slowly brightened. Relief hit me, and I removed my fingers from my ears.

He was gone. Despite my misdemeanour, I had another chance. And this time I won't mess it up.

Because I knew exactly which woman to pick to make Him happy.

Swanson

An unusual sensation overcame Swanson as he weaved through the crowded main roads of Derby City Centre. His car was moving, as were the surrounding streets, yet he felt *still*. Lost in his own thoughts. He stopped at a red light and stretched one long leg to ease a creak in his knee. The glaring lights of a small roadside cash and carry caught his attention.

Fuck it.

He manoeuvred out of the stalled line of rush hour traffic and over to the pavement where the shop stood. He parked on the double yellow lines outside and ignored the glares from the other drivers. Let them look. Suspects glared at him every day.

He pushed open the heavy security door and marched inside the shop, heading straight to the counter. A spotty young man sat behind it on a tall, wooden chair. He dressed head to toe in a matching black tracksuit with two white lines running down the side of it. He barely looked old enough to sell the alcohol he sat in front of.

"Twenty of those and a lighter, please," he said to the boy, digging out his wallet and hoping he had some cash on him after noticing the 'no card machine' sign on the countertop. What kind of place didn't take card these days?

"Sure, mate." The boy barely looked up at Swanson before grabbing the cigarettes and tossing them over. "£9.59, please, mate."

Jesus. Last time he'd bought cigarettes they'd cost little more than a fiver. He tried to hide the shock on his face and threw a crumpled ten pound note on the counter. He marched back out of the shop without waiting for his change, his cigarettes and lighter in hand.

As soon as the frosty breeze hit his face, he pulled open the carton of cigarettes and dragged one out with his teeth. It had been five years since he'd last tasted the stale smoke of a cigarette, but his willpower was well and truly drained. What was the point in preventing cancer if he had a tumour already? Quitting nicotine clearly hadn't been worth the stress.

Although he certainly wasn't making it a daily thing at nearly a tenner a pop.

The first drag hit his throat hard as it swirled its way into his lungs. He blew it out immediately in one quick breath.

Urgh.

It did not taste as good as his memory allowed him to think it did. He sniffed deeply. It didn't even smell as good as he remembered.

Regardless, he took another drag and leant against the wall of the building next to the shop. The little buzz he got from each drag was worth it, for now. He scoped out his surroundings as he tried to get used to inhaling the smoke again. It took him a moment to realise where he was. He stepped forward, away from the wall, and looked around to double check. He was right.

Summer's flat was around the corner.

His feet moved before his brain connected with his body as an urge to be near Summer took over. He needed her calm. Her silly laugh. He rounded the corner and saw the cafe she liked was right across the road. *Barbara's Baps.* The cafe stuck out like a sore thumb on the residential street, an old, converted mid terrace house which someone had painted green and white. Though it had been a long time since a brush had been near it, judging from the chipped paintwork.

The windows were larger than the houses which surrounded it and as he glanced over, he instantly recognised Summer sitting near the left-hand window. A grin lined her lips, and she'd bunched her long brown hair to one side of her face so she could eat. She looked happy.

He hadn't often seen her happy. Between Lucy, Astrid, and Eddie, she hadn't had an easy couple of months. Her face lit up in a way he hadn't seen before.

Across from her, Swanson made out the back of a man's head, and he felt a heaviness in the pit of his stomach. The man clearly wasn't Aaron or Eddie. And yet he was the one who was making Summer so happy.

Good for her.

He stubbed out his cigarette and rounded the corner again to his car. Maybe work would be the best place to go after all. He needed a suitable case to get stuck into, and Hart clearly had something good to work on.

Summer

Summer felt the familiar anxiety in the pit of her stomach as she drove onto the winding dirt road that led to Adrenna Psychiatric Hospital. The hospital sat ten minutes outside of the city centre, the only one on her rota that she hated to visit. Though she hadn't pinpointed the reason why.

She put it down to knowing they wrongly incarcerated her brother there for so long. Being inside Adrenna was a secret glimpse into the lonely life he'd been living as a prisoner whilst she and Dylan lived freely.

That, and the fact Adrenna specialised in patients with personality disorders detained as criminals under a section 37/41. This included Narcissistic Personality Disorder, Antisocial Personality Disorder and Paranoid Personality Disorder, and essentially meant patients with a *violent* history inhabited it.

Her own brother had attempted to murder their mother in a fit of psychotic rage, but only after being tormented by what he thought to be a demon or devil for months. The only actual devil was his ex.

Surprisingly, no one had developed the land around Adrenna yet. So beautiful rolling fields still surrounded it. It would pose as the perfect, picturesque Sunday drive if looking at an image. But in person, it didn't have the usual peace of the countryside. Instead, the emptiness around the hospital contributed towards the unwelcome atmosphere.

The sun shone in Summer's eyes as she drove through the black iron gates of the hospital entrance. They had done little to update the decor since building Adrenna in the 1800s as an asylum for 'lunatics'. Few original asylums still stood in the UK, but Adrenna loomed tall as if proud of its dark history.

Maybe that was another reason for the creepiness.

From the old pictures Summer had seen online, it actually looked more foreboding now than when first built. It had been stunning at one time. The architect had clearly taken great pride in their work. But the gates no longer held their gothic prominence, welcoming visitors and patients alike. Weathering over the years had caused the iron to rust and become deformed, giving it a warped, crooked look. The red brick walls that surrounded either side of the gate were built twelve feet high originally, to keep the 'lunatics' inside. Though the walls still contained the hospital buildings, they now spalled from weather and lack of care, and the weaker parts crumbled with decay.

She sighed as her car crunched slowly over the gravelled car park to the right of the hospital. She'd jumped at the chance to cover Adrenna when her supervisor mentioned the previous advocate quit. Summer took it as a signal to keep looking for Eddie. Now he was missing it was the only way she'd be able to get to know him. There could be a clue here as to where Eddie was.

But that was before she'd found out the previous advocate quit due to stress from visiting Adrenna.

As with her previous four visits, Summer parked as far back from the grand building as possible. She needed no more patients finding out where she lived after Lucy.

She slung her old Radley handbag onto her shoulder and jumped out of the car, pulling the laptop bag from the boot before she headed to the entrance. The bracing wind was even stronger in the open space, and her hair whipped around her face. She pulled up the faux fur hood of her coat as far forward as possible. It might only be December, but bring on spring.

She took her time at first. The uneven gravel was tricky to walk on in her new, heeled boots, and she was in no rush to get inside. But a powerful gust flew straight into her hood, and she put her head down and quickened her pace to the front of the building.

The large entrance at the top of the stone steps was unimpressive compared to the rest of the building. Long ago, someone locked shut the old wooden doors with their peeling red paint, and nailed a wooden bar across them for good measure. The entrance had been unused for years. So she continued down the side of the building to a smaller door halfway down.

The dread grew in her stomach as she pulled down her hood to reveal her face and readied herself to press the intercom. She wondered if this was how Becky felt when pressing the intercom. If so, no wonder she quit.

A few seconds later, a loud buzzer rang out into the silence, followed by a clicking noise. She pushed open the door, entered the dark hallway and waited for the door to bang shut behind her. The bang of the door had almost given her a heart attack when she first visited, but she was used to it now.

The warm air in the hallway was stifling compared to the frostiness of the outside, and she wrangled her hand through the laptop bag strap to pull down the zipper of her coat. The grand staircase was adjacent to the doorway, but she ignored it and continued down the hall, her boots softened by the deep red carpet. As she reached the end of the corridor, she stopped, took a breath, and forced her face into a cheerful smile before opening the door.

The reception room was fairly small, but the bright white front desk immediately drew her eye to the left-hand side of the room. It was ugly and cheap, and far too modern compared to the other decor.

There were lockers on the right-hand side, and another corridor led around the back of the ugly desk. But the staff had never invited Summer down there. Which was unusual, as she should have access to the whole hospital as an advocate, but Summer didn't argue. The less she had to see of this place, the better.

"Morning," Summer said to the old bat behind the desk, which was encased in thick glass. The same receptionist was working every time she visited the hospital, yet she never revealed her name.

The woman looked up and smiled shortly. "Sign in here, please." She forced something A4 sized and hard through a gap in the glass window. It was the paper register and a black pen stuck to a wooden clipboard.

Summer took off her laptop bag and plonked it on the floor before she walked over and signed her name. She didn't bother saying another word to the woman, but awkwardly shoved the clipboard back through the hole, catching the corner on the top of the glass. The woman snatched it from her and threw her an angry look.

"Locker 16," she said, placing a ring of keys, an alarm, and a black belt through the hole.

Summer's face flushed, but she took the keys and belt with a 'thank you' and walked back to get her laptop bag. She removed her coat and placed it inside locker 16 with her handbag and laptop bag. The laptop wasn't allowed on the ward. Though it was a habit to bring it with her wherever she went in case she had to do research for a patient or write her notes before leaving.

She stole a glance at the old bat, who was looking down at her screen, and she snuck her phone into her pocket. Making sure it was well-hidden. She placed the belt that she'd given her around her waist with the ring of keys and alarm attached. The only other item she held was a notepad and pen, which she clutched close to her chest. She closed the locker door and left the room without a word, ignoring the sense of dread which built with every step.

Swanson

Swanson attempted to drive to the office, but found himself pulled over in the large supermarket car park nearby. The same place he'd first met Summer, right after a patient of hers kidnapped her. He remembered Hart struggling to calm the patient, and Summer swooping in calmly as anything to help. It was impressive. Most trained officers Swanson knew would have been far too traumatised to stay as calm as Summer had. Though it wasn't the most romantic of first encounters.

Maybe they were doomed from the start.

He wondered who the man was that made her laugh so much. She was clearly comfortable with him. He'd only spoken to her yesterday about finding her brother and she hadn't mentioned meeting anyone else. The police still officially wanted Eddie for questioning after Astrid had accused him of attempted murder. Though Astrid had also disappeared, which didn't bode well for her story's believability.

He got out of the car and leant against the cool metal as he lit another cigarette. His nose slowly turned numb in the cold air, and he rubbed his thumb against it absentmindedly as he smoked. People milled around him, mostly elderly people taking their time, or tired parents rushing around with a baby attached to them in one form or another. He should probably enter the shop and buy some mints to get rid of the cigarette breath. Hart would definitely smell it otherwise. He stepped forward to make a move to the entrance, but froze mid-step.

Two blank eyes stared straight at him. The eyes were clouded over with no visible pupil, but he felt their stare. They belonged to an old man, with a white beard and wispy hair, both running past his shoulders. His attire evidenced his need for a bath and a good meal.

But it wasn't the dirty appearance of the man which bothered Swanson. Why was a blind man staring straight at him?

Swanson shifted his feet and turned away to pull once more on his cigarette, but when he glanced back, the man hadn't moved an inch.

He stubbed out the cigarette and climbed back into the car. He didn't have time for creepy old men today. Or the headspace to even think about it.

He grabbed his phone and flicked through the random notifications. He had a message from Hart asking where he was, and he sent her a quick reply to say he was getting breakfast. That should stall her, and a bacon wrap would make her moan less when he finally had the motivation to turn up.

He threw down his phone on the passenger seat and looked up with a sigh.

And his heart nearly jumped out of his chest.

The man with blank eyes was right outside his window, still staring straight at him.

Summer

Summer walked back down the corridor and up the staircase she'd ignored when first entering the dim building. The staircase appeared as if it should lead to a grand landing area with an opulent ballroom waiting for her. But instead it led to a claustrophobic landing area with three doors.

The doors were out of place and didn't quite fit in with the surroundings. They were modern oak, and strong. A pane of thick glass ran through the centre of each door as a safety measure. It allowed you to look into the room ahead before entering.

Each door led to a different ward. Ward A was the first door leading to the left-hand side of the building. Her plan was to head into Ward A first, as some patients there were trusting enough to chat to her. It was a ward for patients who were responding well to treatment and were no longer thought to be a risk to themselves or others. They were less paranoid and didn't suffer from psychotic delusions anymore, and therefore easier to make relationships with.

It was also the ward where Eddie spent the last year of his stay. His patient file might still be saved on the computer.

She walked over to the door of Ward A and peered through the glass. Although this ward was less risky, she still had to follow procedure and ensure there were no patients close to the door before she opened it. Most modern hospitals had air locked doors between wards and even on entry, so it was almost impossible for a patient to escape. But Adrenna only had one locked door to get off the ward, and one other locked door to the

SUMMER

outside world. It wasn't much at all, really.

All she saw through the glass was an empty corridor. The coast was clear.

She pulled the keyring out of her belt and squinted at the peeling stickers on each one until she found the Ward A key. She double checked the coast was still clear, and opened up the door to a short corridor.

It was the opposite of the dark hallway downstairs, but far too cold to be homely. She strolled down the corridor and past the kitchen door, where a smell of burnt toast lingered. Patients living in Ward A were the only ones the staff trusted with their very own working kitchen, complete with a kettle and metal cutlery. Though they only allowed one patient in at a time. The room was small and difficult to supervise, and caution was still required. It wasn't always obvious if a patient suffered a relapse.

Past the kitchen, the corridor opened up into a spacious living area. This was also the only ward where the living area was a little more homely than the clinical corridor. They didn't encase the TV in a special protective case, they nailed it to the wall like people would in a lot of 'normal' homes. The sofas were all close together, and arranged in a U shape in front of the TV. There was an art room off to the right, where patients had access to art therapy on a Tuesday and Thursday, and they had a pool table in the far corner. Though the balls and cues were stored away in a locked unit, and only allowed out at certain times.

Another corridor led to the left and down to a locked gym. Patients had supervised daily access to the gym and to the computer room next door. The corridor to the right led to the bedrooms and isolation room; an empty room where patients stayed if they were trying to hurt themselves or others. There was a bed, a metal toilet, and a locked slip in the door for food. It was the last resort before forced medication.

Summer always stayed well away from that room. No patient in that room was in a safe enough frame of mind for her to talk to.

She scanned the ward and took in the current patients who were out of their rooms. A man Summer didn't recognise was walking away to the gym or computer room with a support worker. Bertie was sitting on the sofa. He was fairly new to Ward A, and his nervousness meant he didn't talk much, but she'd got the odd word out of him a few times.

Asif was sitting next to him, and Summer smiled when she saw him. He seemed to feel someone looking at him and raised his head to look around. His face lit up once he spotted her. Asif had taken to her straight away on her first official visit, and it was he who had given her a tour of the ward. Normally it would be the hospital manager or leading psychiatrist, but Summer was yet to meet the manager. She only knew her name was Glenda Kitching, and she was off sick. The leading psychiatrist, Dr Randall, was friendly, though. And had been far more welcoming than that receptionist downstairs.

"Hi, Summer!" Asif stood and rushed over to her as best as his limp would allow him to hurry.

Summer stepped forward to meet him. He was actually quite tall, but his bad leg caused a stoop that made him roughly the same height as her.

"Hi, Asif. How are you?"

"I'm OK. I could do with a chat. Is that OK?" Asif looked down as he spoke, a shy smile lined his lips.

"Of course we can. Where shall we chat?" She looked around the ward for a quiet space.

"Oh, here is fine. I have my ward round next week. Can you come in with me?" He spoke quickly, looked up, and wrung his hands together nervously.

The ward round was a regular multidisciplinary meeting where the different hospital specialists met with the patient to discuss their care.

She nodded. "Yes, I'd be happy too."

His face broke into another smile. "Oh, great, great. Thank you." He let out a short, much relieved giggle.

"You're welcome. Is there anything in particular you'd like me to do or say or do? Or do you want some moral support?" She imagined Asif being too shy to ask his doctor for something and needing her to ask for him, or maybe he wanted her to sit in whilst *he* asked for something.

He bowed his head, deep in thought. "I'll think about it," he decided.

That would be moral support, Summer mused. An idea came to her.

"OK. Am I allowed access to your file so I can prepare? No problem if you'd rather I don't. It's completely up to you."

"Oh yes, yes. That's fine." He nodded and gave her a big grin.

"Great." Summer gave him a moment to ask her for anything else, but he fell silent. His eyes flicked around the room. "Shall we sit on the sofa for a bit?"

He nodded, and they walked over together. A daytime talk show was playing on the TV. Bertie looked away from the show as they approached, and Summer asked him how he was doing. She made small talk with them both, counting down the minutes until she could reasonably disappear to look at the file. She waited about ten minutes to announce she had to do something and said goodbye to Asif and Bertie.

The nurses' station was a small room at the back of the open plan living area. It had a large window and was called the fish bowl by the patients. Nurses and ward staff could do paperwork there whilst still monitoring the patients in the living area. It was where the computer was, and all paper patient files, too.

As Summer walked over, she made a mental note of where the staff were on the ward. She saw a couple of nurses in the medication room, which had a door like a horse stable where only the top half opened. Ward A didn't have as many staff members as other wards, as no patients required two-to-one care or 24-hour supervision, and there were no other support workers around the living area.

She pulled out the ring of keys from the belt bag and selected the small black key with a sticker that said 'stations'. It was a strange, circular shape, and the same key opened each of the stations on each ward. Unlike the ward doors which had a different key for each. She glanced through the large window and made sure it was empty before letting herself in.

The room was small and stuffy. Cupboards lined the far wall from floor to ceiling. Summer knew that was where they kept the paper files for the patients, but she hadn't found Eddie's when she looked the other week. She wasn't actually sure what happened to the files once the patient transferred to a different unit. Maybe they followed the patient. That would make sense. They had sent Eddie to a different, low security unit right before he disappeared completely. It was like a halfway house, and easy for him to run away from once Astrid accused him of attempted murder.

In the corner nearest to Summer sat a computer with electronic files on each patient. And now, thanks to Asif, Summer had the perfect excuse to log in and review the files.

She checked her notepad for the password they had provided her with during her first visit to the hospital and logged in to the hospital's guest account. Her fingers drummed against the desk, and she glanced up periodically to look through the window.

She opened Asif's file first and briefly flicked through. His doctor diagnosed him with Narcissistic Personality Disorder and the court had convicted him for stalking an ex-girlfriend for six months, eventually attacking her in her own home. *Christ.* He was so sweet Summer couldn't imagine him acting like that.

She left his file open on one tab and used a secondary tab to flick through the names of each patient file looking for Eddie. There was nothing, but she fought away the disappointment. She wasn't giving up that easily.

She used the search bar on the file screen instead and typed in 'Eddie Thomas'. Hope gripped her as a folder in his name finally popped up. She double clicked on the folder with his name, and different files appeared in a list before her.

'Ward Round Record'

'Medication Sheet'

'Patient History'

She hesitated. These were highly private and personal to Eddie. It felt so wrong to even be this close to reading them. Would he be OK with her opening them up?

She thought about him being alone somewhere on a dark street in the freezing wind. He would be alone at Christmas in a few weeks. An ache tugged at her heart, and she opened the most recent file, which was a ward round record. It was the meeting minutes from his final ward round at Adrenna Hospital.

Summer skim read through the report with a smile. The discussion had centred around how well Eddie was doing, and how happy he was to be transferring to a low secure unit.

But a noise at the door made her heart thump. She quickly closed the file and brought up Asif's instead. She looked up, smiling at the nurse who entered the station and praying she didn't look as guilty as she felt.

"Hello." The young nurse smiled at her.

"Hi," Summer said with a big smile that she was sure made her look guilty of something. "I'm just checking a patient file. Do you need the computer?"

"Oh, no problem. It can wait," she replied, waving a hand away.

"No, no. Here you go." Summer logged off and stood up from the computer chair. "I'm finished, anyway."

The nurse gave her a cautious smile before taking the computer chair. The staff were always on best behaviour around an advocate like Summer.

She locked the nurse in the fishbowl room and threw a glance at her watch. She really needed to move on to the other wards. Ward B wasn't so bad. Their patients were midway and often super quiet. So it made sense to get Ward C out of the way. That was the most precarious ward.

The patients of Ward C were new and not yet responding to medication or therapy. They could be violent and difficult to manage. As an advocate, Summer didn't receive any kind of training in restraint or protecting herself. Despite many requests to her supervisor to be trained in defending herself safely, and Adrenna being home to some of the country's most dangerous patients, her concerns fell on deaf ears.

It wasn't the patients that bothered Summer, though. It was the staff. They were mostly young people who thought working at Adrenna would be cool. Or someone had told them it would be rewarding. But in reality, they were poorly trained, overworked, and disillusioned. Being on Ward C made her anxiety skyrocket because she had no faith in the staff to keep her safe if a patient had a psychotic episode or other violent outburst.

She got the feeling that they would be more likely to run away and save themselves. And she didn't blame them.

She took a moment to steel herself outside Ward C's door and peered through the glass section. There was no corridor in Ward C, and instead it opened out straight into the living area. She saw a few patients and staff, and the sense of foreboding made her feel sick. She unlocked the door anyway and closed it quickly behind her.

The ward was fairly quiet. Doctor Randall, the only senior member of the team that she had spoken to so far, had explained to her previously that these patients were on heavier medications, and they were often drowsier than the other wards as a result.

There was one patient wandering around with a vacant look, as if lost in his own world. Summer watched him for a moment. She'd love to know where he'd taken himself in his own mind. Hopefully, somewhere nicer than here.

There was another person in particular she had hoped to see, though. There were a couple of nurses on the ward and she walked over to an older lady she recognised, Beth. She'd been nice to Summer the previous week and actually struck up a conversation. She stood in the corner with a clipboard in her hand, looking down at it intensely.

"Hi," Summer smiled at her.

Beth looked up and gave Summer a warm smile. "Hey, Summer isn't it?"

Summer nodded. "I wondered if Aaron was around today?" she asked as casually as she could.

"Oh no, he hates earlies. He doesn't enjoy getting out of bed, the lazy sod." The nurse laughed.

Summer joined in with the laughter to hide her disappointment. She hadn't known Aaron hated earlies, though it occurred to her Aaron had mostly done the late shift at Derby Psychiatric Hospital.

"OK, I'll sit down for a bit and see if anyone wants to chat," Summer replied.

She strolled over to the sofas in the middle of the room and took a seat close to a patient named Andy, who sat in grey jogging bottoms and a matching jumper. He was looking at the floor, unblinking. Summer said nothing to him. He'd been the same last week and didn't appear to be a threat. She chose the middle of the room so patients could easily see her there if they wanted her help, and staff could easily see her should she need their help.

Yet a sudden chill reached her, and the hairs on the back of her neck stood up. She shifted uncomfortably in her seat and looked around. Two dark eyes were staring straight at her from around the ward corner. They disappeared before she had time to see the person's face.

"Who's that?" she muttered out loud.

"The Devil. You mustn't go near the Devil." Andy said.

Summer nearly doubled over in shock at hearing him speak. She turned back to him. He still stared at the floor.

"What was that, Andy? Are you OK?"

His head snapped up, his dark, narrow eyes stared into Summers. Her hand went to her alarm.

"The Devil is coming for you."

The Servant

The corridor to the dining area loomed before me. It was a pathway full of danger. People getting too close as they passed, or hiding behind doors. Corridors were plain dangerous. But I told nobody in Adrenna about that.

That was crazy talk, apparently.

I turned to face the quiet room behind me instead, but I still heard the low rasping of the shadow that laid within. I couldn't go back inside there unless I had what he requested.

I chose the wrong woman. I'd had to violate her to make her more humble, and I was not allowed to do that. But He had forgiven me. Well, He *would* forgive me. As long as I get it right the next time.

And I wouldn't sleep until I had.

So I was stuck on the threshold of the door. I had to choose between the wrath in my room or the unknown horrors of the corridor. A laugh trickled down the corridor. A soft, sweet laugh. One I knew.

The one the Devil wanted.

The corridor spun before me and seemed to get longer with each passing second. I kept my weapon in my hand and squeezed my fingers around it, not caring that it might cut my fingers.

I crept down the corridor, but stumbled and grabbed a hold of the wall. I took a deep breath and allowed the dizziness to pass.

I cursed myself and rubbed away the twitch in my eye. I needed to man up and make it to her. This was a risk for me. I had never killed before. But it was her or me.

And I would always choose myself.

The corridor righted, and I continued down the white tiles. My nerves were on edge, but nothing jumped out from behind any doors this time. I reached the end safely and peered around the corner to the living room of the hospital. A large room with huge, locked windows and sofas lining the edge of the walls, and dotted about the middle of the room.

There was an armchair in the middle of the room, near the TV, and there she was. Her long hair hung past her breasts. Her pretty face smiled at one of the other patients. The patient wasn't responding. Few of them did. They were fed too many drugs.

But that suited me fine.

I looked over to the far corner of the room to the nurses' station, a small room surrounded by thick glass. Two nurses were inside and chatting with each other. They smiled and laughed as if telling jokes to each other. They were probably joking about patients. I heard them joking inappropriately all the time. But I didn't care. I was glad they were distracted.

I surveyed the rest of the ward. One patient sat in the corner in an armchair. He wore the hospital's own grey tracksuit bottoms and matching jumper. Patients didn't have to wear them, but they were comfortable and handy for people who didn't have many clothes. Which apparently was most patients, in this ward at least. The most dangerous patients were on this ward supposedly, but actually they were so drugged up it was difficult for them to be dangerous to anyone. He stared at the floor. I watched him for a moment. He didn't blink once.

Another patient in the tracksuit walked around in circles on the left side of the room. He moaned to himself quietly and clasped his hands together. He was smiling, and clearly happy in his own world.

Two nursing assistants busied themselves with the last patient, trying to get him to stand so he could go for his nap. I made it a point not to learn their names.

They wouldn't be around long enough for it to matter.

I peered at the woman. I forgot her full name, but her first name was

THE ADVOCATE

Summer. Beautiful. If you ever thought about what the season of Summer looks like as a person, it would be her. It was her name that drew the devil to her at first. And her voice. Her soft, quiet voice. She walked as though she was afraid of nothing, but I saw fear in her eyes. It had interested me, and the devil saw her through me.

She was our new advocate. I'd tried to get the last one for the Devil, but it hadn't gone to plan. I'd only wanted to talk to her, but the Devil wanted more. Needed more.

When the patient did not respond, Summer looked around the room. She turned and spotted me, and I saw her eyes squint at me. My head snapped back around the corner, and I stood still for a moment. A few seconds passed, and I dared to look again. She wasn't looking, but the patient was talking to her, and he looked intense.

I stalked over to the middle of the ward, confident in my stride. My thoughts only focused on her because if I thought too much, I'd lose my nerve. I walked straight up to the pretty girl with the sing-song laugh who looked like Summer.

I unleashed the hidden razor blade from my fist.

And I gave her to the Devil.

Swanson

Swanson paused for a moment, his eyes closed tight, and allowed one last bitter breeze to wash over beads of sweat gathered on his forehead. His jaw clenched, he yanked open the entrance to the Derbyshire Police Station.

It opened straight into a bright room with a long desk lining the left-hand side. The powers that be, who were in charge of the wallet, recently gave the building funding to update the station decor. The sour smell of fresh paint still lingered. It wasn't a smell he could handle well. He took a deep breath and held it in his chest to keep the nausea at bay.

There were a couple of people keeping the two receptionists busy, so he kept his head down and walked straight through to the security door at the back, using his ID card to open the digitalised lock. Once safely in the corridor, he stood still and let out his breath in one big whoosh. He closed his eyes briefly to gather himself before he walked to the end of the corridor. There, the smell of paint lessened, replaced with the smell of cheap coffee from the nearby kitchen. Which wasn't too much better for Swanson's nausea.

Over the past few weeks, Swanson had sneakily commandeered a cupboard sized office to the left of the corridor. It was more of a storage area these days, but it was useful for the peace it provided him away from the primary set of open offices. They had designed the spaces to encourage 'working together' apparently. But they were noisy and off-putting. Ridiculous, really.

His anxiety lessened as he looked forward to sitting in silence at his desk and having some time to process the shit show that was his hospital appointment. But he opened the door to DI Hart perching on the edge of his makeshift desk. Her legs crossed. *Fuck sake.*

An open paper file was in her hands and she peered down at it. Her dark bob had fallen forward, partially blocking her face. But she looked up as he entered and shook her hair back. She didn't smile at him. Instead, her mouth set in a determined grimace.

"We've got a right one, here," she said.

"Hello to you, too," Swanson replied, still standing in the doorway. He thought about walking away, but didn't have the energy. She'd only run after him, anyway.

"Yes, yes. Hello." She waved her hand impatiently, snapped the file shut, and held it out for him.

Swanson sighed. "What now?" He ambled over to his desk and took the file from her. It was light. There wasn't much intel yet.

He squeezed past Hart, who made no attempt to move out of his way, and sat down at the desk. He opened it up and forced himself to focus, taking his time with the content. Hart would know something serious was wrong if he made even the tiniest of uncharacteristic movements. The first page in the file revealed a white-tiled floor, pristine apart from the large amount of deep red blood in the middle.

"Jeesh," Swanson said.

It reminded him of a recent incident with a young boy and his mother - the missing Astrid. He pushed the memory away and tried again to focus.

"Is that a hospital floor?" he asked.

Hart stood up and stepped away from the desk, turning in one smooth motion to face him. She folded her arms and nodded solemnly.

"What happened?" he asked.

"Do you know that big old hospital in the middle of nowhere? I think it's called Adrenna."

"I think so."

Swanson knew the hospital. He'd given the address to Summer to help her sneak in and look for her brother.

"Well, a member of staff was attacked a couple of hours ago by a patient. He was suffering from psychosis associated with paranoid schizophrenia. He sliced her neck and cut the hand of a doctor in the process. We need to have a chat with the doctor, and with the patient when possible."

"Why us? Is she pressing charges?" Swanson asked.

"Are you not awake yet? They have sliced her in the neck, Swanson. We might be looking at murder." She sighed and looked at him as if he was an idiot.

"Oh, yes, sorry. I didn't hear you properly. When was the last update?" He tried to keep his face normal, but what the hell expression did he normally pull anyway? It's not like he took note of his own facial expressions.

She uncrossed her arms and cocked her head, eyeing him warily. "A few minutes ago. She's still in surgery. Are you sure you're OK? I thought you were bringing breakfast like two hours ago?"

"Wouldn't be here if I wasn't. And yeah, I got distracted. I saw Summer and some weird old man nearly gave me a heart attack."

"What? Summer was with a weird old man?"

"No! I saw her for a moment in a cafe, and then an old man was being weird with me in the car park of the supermarket. He came right up to my car and stared. Nearly gave me a heart attack."

Hart erupted in a sudden belly laugh. He raised an eyebrow at her.

"Sorry, it's too funny thinking of you fearing an old man. What did he do?"

"Nothing. He didn't say a word, so I drove off."

"He was probably on drugs. I've seen you tackle worse things than a staring old man, Swanson! Have you lost your touch?" She laughed again before wiping a tear from one eye. "Have you asked Summer out yet?"

"Why would I do that?" he responded a little too quickly.

"Oh, OK. Sure. You be all surly and pretend you don't like her." She rolled her eyes. "You might smile more if you had a date lined up, and that would save *me* looking at your miserable face all the time. What did the old man look like if he scared you that much?"

"Some homeless guy with white eyes. It was weird. End of story." He waved his hand and sat up in the chair.

He'd driven away from the old man without checking if he was OK. Instead, he'd driven straight to a disused car park and slept for an hour.

"So are we going to this Adrenna place or what?" he asked.

"Alright, come on. You say that like I've *not* been waiting for you all morning." She turned and stalked out of the office, closing the door behind her.

Swanson stood a little too quickly. His vision blurred, and the room turned upside down. He closed his eyes, waiting for it to pass. After a moment, the dizziness stopped. He needed to eat something. He followed Hart into the corridor, but she'd disappeared.

He walked back through to the reception with his head down once again, and into the car park where he'd parked his Audi. He knew there was a Mars bar in the glove compartment. Just what he needed to get his blood sugar up.

Hart stood on the steps outside the entrance waiting for him. Her car keys swung in hand.

"I'm driving," she said, a determination set on her face.

Swanson scoffed. Hart rarely drove because he hated her erratic driving. He didn't know if he could put up with her lead right foot and angry braking today of all days.

"What? Why would I let you drive me?" he said.

"Because whether or not you want to admit it, you're ill." Her face softened.

Swanson immediately stood taller, his jaw set tight. "What do you mean I'm *ill*?"

"Don't insult me! I know you too well, and I can tell by looking at you that you're not well. You need to be at home, but you won't go, no matter what I say. So I'll allow you to stick with me on this one, but I'm driving, and you're going to tell me what's wrong."

She jiggled her car keys in front of him and turned to the red Astra to her left, which lit up as she pressed the key fob.

Swanson huffed. "I'm fine."

He wanted to argue, but a lack of energy made him follow Hart to her car. Despite his mammoth morning nap in the car, he'd woken up feeling worse. They got in the car and buckled up, and Hart swung them around in one effortless movement to pull out of the car park.

"So, what did the doctor say?" she asked as soon as they were on the main road which led to the city. They'd have to go through the centre to get to Adrenna, which was way out on the other side of the city in the quiet countryside

Swanson held his silence. *What was he supposed to say? He had a brain tumour? He needed a biopsy? What would she say and how would she react?*

He didn't want her sympathy; he wanted normality. "I don't really want to talk about it."

"Oh. It was that bad, eh? Hmm. We'll do this visit to Adrenna, then we'll go to yours and chat." She nodded as if agreeing with herself.

Swanson laughed at her unwarranted confidence. Though if anyone else gave him such orders, he wouldn't have had the same reaction.

"I said I don't want to talk about it."

"Oh, sorry. Didn't I mention that's not an option? You tell me or… I'm telling your Aunt Barb there's something seriously wrong and you won't tell anyone." Hart grinned at her own threat and glanced over at him.

"OK, OK. You win." Swanson leaned back in the car seat and rested his aching head.

He was enjoying being driven round for once, not that he'd ever admit it. He shifted in his seat. His whole body ached rather than just his head. So much for the painkillers working. It was strange having a tumour. Maybe he was aching from napping in a car, or maybe it was another symptom of his illness. How did people know? Worrying about it took more of a toll than the actual symptoms did.

His eyes were heavy with the gentle sway of the car. It felt good to close them for a moment as his head rocked against the headrest. Hart always cranked her heating way too high, but for once the warm air felt good. Cosy. The skies opened, and he listened to the gentle pitter patter of the rain on the roof of the car.

But a quick shake from Hart rudely awoke him.

"Sorry, but we're here," she said, peering at him with her head cocked to one side. "Either my driving has improved tenfold, or you're seriously ill. Which one are you willing to admit to?"

Swanson rushed to sit up. A deep heat filled his cheeks, and he turned away from her to look out of the window.

"I'm fine," he said, but the world spun again as the blood rushed to his head, and he closed his eyes until it stopped.

"Clearly you're not, though. Tell me what's wrong. You're worrying me now. Do you need some water?"

He heard her fumbling about, presumably looking for water. The dizziness passed, and he laughed.

"No! I don't want your mouldy old half-drunk water bottle. I sat up too quickly, is all. I haven't eaten. We can talk about my issues *after* we're finished here like we agreed. Come on." He unbuckled his seatbelt and gripped the door handle.

Hart didn't move.

"If you don't tell me now, I'm going to go into that hospital worrying about it rather than thinking about the case. I won't do my best job, and neither will you because you're totally off your game already, no offence. We'll miss seriously important details and the guy might get away with it and the woman might die with no justice and it will be all your fault Alex Swanson, so stop being macho and spit it–"

"I have a brain tumour," Swanson interrupted.

One thing he hadn't considered about being ill was the guilt he would feel at having to tell other people and watch *them* get upset. As soon as the words were out, he knew he'd done the wrong thing. As he watched Hart's shocked face a guilt settled within him, one that was going to stay for a while.

The Servant

I lay in my bed facing the ceiling. The rasping breath of the Devil was silent again. The bright bedroom light burned my eyes, even though they were closed. I made no move to turn it off. I liked the warmth of it bearing down on me.

The Devil always brought the dark with him.

Though I was grateful the Devil thought me good enough to assist him, I needed some sleep. I couldn't deny a slip of happiness at being able to sleep in peace for the first night in weeks. That's what He had promised me in exchange for doing his bidding.

As my mind quietened, I drifted off into another world. My favourite world. I was a small child again. Dad was sitting by the fire and telling me stories of grandad. Grandad cleansed the world, and Dad did too. Like I would grow to do the same thing. I would become a doctor, and work with those who saw things other people didn't.

Crazy people.

That's what the closed minded of the world called them. Some of them were ill and seeing things that weren't there, but sometimes Dad would find someone special. Someone special enough to be given to the Devil.

The Devil also liked women. He wanted the perfect woman and was on a constant search. Dad said Grandad had failed the Devil, but he wouldn't make the same mistake. He would find the perfect woman, and a protector for her so she wasn't a drain on the Devil.

But Dad did fail Him, like I almost had. Summer was the perfect woman, and now I needed to find her a protector.

Swanson

Hart froze mid-sentence, her mouth still open. She said nothing for a moment and simply stared at him. Their eyes met in the awkward silence. Swanson racked his brain for something clever to say. A joke. A noise. Anything.

They were never awkward with each other. The damn tumour was ruining things already. She shifted in her seat and looked away out of the windscreen.

"Oh. Well, that sucks," she said, her mouth finally closing.

Swanson didn't take his eyes off her. He wasn't sure what reaction he had expected, but not that.

"Is that all you have to say?"

She turned to face him again and shrugged. Her mouth opened, then closed as she found no words. A slow grin spread across Swanson's face.

"That sucks?" he repeated.

A deep need to laugh at her blank face built up. He held his breath and clamped his lips shut to keep the laughter at bay. The effort made his face turn a pale shade of red. But it was no use. As soon as he took a breath, he couldn't prevent the elongated snort of laughter that led to a deep, belly laugh when he saw Hart's eyes open wide. Though it only took a split second for her own shock to turn to a grin, and within seconds, they were both wiping away tears.

It took a few minutes for their laughter to fade away and silence to return. He felt Hart staring again and glanced over at her. She was giving him a strange look. Despite knowing her so well, it wasn't an expression he recognised. She spent most of her time either locked into a hard set grimace or laughing. Hart was not an in-between kind of person with emotions.

"You'll be fine, you know. It will take more than some stupid tumour to kick your fat arse," her face returned to its normal stoical glower and she looked away as she unbuckled her seat belt.

He nodded, though he knew she was full of rubbish. He still felt calmer as he reached for his own seatbelt and got out of the car.

The heavy pressure that had sat in his gut all morning eased somewhat at having admitted his problem to Hart. The light pitter patter of the rain felt cool against his cheeks, which also helped. Rain was the best weather. Memories of wet walks through the Peak District and Kinder Scout climbs danced in his mind. Maybe that's what he needed to do this week. Get out again and focus on walking. It was always better in the rain. The tourist walkers, mainly from London, disappeared. Leaving only the odd passerby to nod to as he hiked through the vastness of the Peak District hills, feeling unimportant in comparison. Lost. Peaceful.

And it wasn't often Swanson felt small. He'd always stuck out like a sore thumb in any room. Admittedly, the impressive Victorian building towering in front of him made him feel almost miniscule.

Hart had parked in the depressing gravel car park to the right of the building, and he was glad he hadn't brought his own car here after all. It would be far too easy to get a chip from a flying piece of gravel, and that stress was the last thing he needed.

"Jesus, look at that van." Hart pointed to a van in the corner of the car park. It was an old campervan which the owner had not kept well maintained. The large, rear windows were painted black, or black with mud. It was hard to tell.

Swanson scanned the area, but other than the hospital, all he saw were the tall grey walls which encased the hospital grounds. It was a shame the walls were so high. Surely the beautiful views of rolling hills would be far more calming for patients than brick walls.

Though Adrenna Hospital did not appear to be a peaceful place to rest and get better. There was a fierceness to the aura of the building that was distinctly unwelcoming. Swanson couldn't put his finger on what it was exactly, but abrasive came close to describing it. Or unnerving.

The building was shaped like a square U, with colossal stone turrets at each angle. Despite the grim atmosphere, it was a fantastic example of early Victorian architecture using once beautiful white limestone, though it had grown grey over years of weathering. He whistled through his teeth.

"It's bloody scary as hell. I dunno what you're whistling at," Hart said as she walked towards the hospital, her feet crunching over the gravel. "Can you imagine being forced to live here? I think I'd stab someone, too. I'd prefer prison."

"Well, no. That's actually a good point." He didn't disagree with her for once. As impressive as the building was, the atmosphere that surrounded it was suffocating. It was as if the ancient building had formed its own personality over the decades.

And it wasn't a nice one.

"Imagine the stories those walls would tell if they spoke. All those old stories you hear about how mentally ill people used to be treated," she threw him a grim look, "shackles and lobotomies and that."

"Well, hopefully it can tell us a thing or two about this poor nurse who was stabbed."

"Yep. Come on." Hart hurried to the front of the building with her head down against the rain. Unlike Swanson, she hated the rain and would do anything to avoid getting stuck in it.

Swanson followed at a much slower pace. A part of him hoped something would call him away, so he didn't have to go inside. But his long strides meant he arrived at the entrance at exactly the same time as Hart, whose head only reached his shoulder on a good day, depending on her choice of shoe. In front of them grey stone steps led to grand double doors, with no discernible handle or doorbell.

"What the hell? How do you suppose we get inside?" Hart looked up at him with a tilted head.

"Let's look around the side." Swanson strode over to the right-hand turret and continued around the corner. Hart hurried after him.

A deep scream echoed all around them and stopped them dead in their tracks. It vibrated off the high walls that surrounded them. They glanced at each other, and began to run.

The Servant

I was waiting next to the window when a red car pulled up in the car park. It wasn't a car I'd seen before, and it set my nerves alight. The driver parked quickly, but didn't get out. It was like they wanted to keep me waiting.

They wanted me to suffer.

I craned my neck to see who was inside, but the driver wasn't visible. I saw someone's legs in the passenger seat. So there were two of them. I guessed they were talking.

Were they talking about me?

I waited with bated breath to see what they did. It felt like aeons had passed by the time they left the car. I took a step back from the window, but observed them carefully.

A woman with what I can only describe as a hard face stepped out of the driver's side. She wore a fitted grey suit and her dark hair in a short bob. That wouldn't do for the devil. He liked more feminine women and longer hair. She stumbled as she walked across the gravel in heels to meet the passenger who had also exited the car. She had the grace of a caffeinated ape.

The passenger was a man, also wearing a suit. He hunched his broad shoulders as he walked and his eyes flickered everywhere checking out his surroundings. He was obviously the type who was always on high alert. Despite his size, he was far more graceful than the tiny woman. I recognised him instantly.

My escape from the devil had arrived.

I continued to watch as they approached the stone steps at the front of the building and stared up at the inaccessible front door with confused faces. So, they hadn't visited before, and they were wearing suits.

Police.

I backed further away from the window. I needed a distraction.

I glimpsed at the living area behind me. It was not quite lunchtime and most patients were still in bed. Bobby was quite close to me. He was on his own, walking in circles as usual and humming to himself. He was off his bloody rocker and had the mind of a child.

Well, a child who did terrible things. Though he'd known no other way after his own upbringing.

Bobby wouldn't notice a thing. Destined to be forever trapped in his own little world. But there were also two nurses in the living area. One was sitting on the sofa, trying to coax a small patient named Baz out of his pyjamas. Baz was ignoring her and turning away. The other was distracted by the narcissistic prick, Samuel. He was demanding his medication early. Samuel was a first class arsehole. The man was not ill. He was lying to get an easy time of it after murdering his wife. He said the Devil made him do it, but I knew that was a lie because I asked the Devil myself.

I noted Samuel was about to walk away, and he would walk right past Bobby.

My hand clasped around the razor blade in my pocket, and I timed my route. I turned towards the window and slashed my arm. Nothing too bad, a small gash, and then I stalked over to Bobby just as Samuel was passing.

What happened next was a blur. I pushed Bobby into Samuel and sliced Bobby at the same time. All three of us fell into a heap on the floor. Bobby screamed like a wild animal, followed by a roar from Samuel.

The nurses sounded an alarm and ran towards us. More of them appeared within seconds as the alarm rang out through the hospital and other staff appeared. One slipped on the pool of blood leaking from either Bobby or Samuel. The scene was fast becoming a blur, and I wasn't entirely sure which one I'd stabbed.

My legs shook violently as I stood and moved away and pointed at Bobby and Samuel so the nurses would run to them first and stay away from me. I'd sort my wound alone.

Bobby sobbed. I noted one nurse took off his jacket to inspect his wound, so it must have been him I stabbed. Good. That was the plan. Samuel shouted at Bobby for knocking him over, not daring to say anything to me.

More staff came tunnelling into the ward to help, and surrounded Bobby and Samuel. I looked out the window and no longer saw the detectives, but they wouldn't be allowed on the ward whilst a serious incident was occurring.

I relaxed.

There would be no police interrogation today.

But I needed to see that man again. The Devil needed him, and it was my job to bring Him what he wanted.

Swanson

Swanson's loafers thudded off broken concrete slabs as he sprinted down the side of the building, looking for a way inside Adrenna. He heard Hart panting behind him, hot on his heels.

The screaming stopped, but it was blood curdling enough to know somebody was badly hurt. Halfway down the building a steel security door jutted out from the grey brick. It was so out of place against the Victorian backdrop it threw Swanson for a moment.

He almost skidded on the escaped gravel as he reached the door. He pulled the handle, but it was locked and didn't budge at all.

"There," Hart pointed to the wall next to the door. Her breath came in short, sharp pants.

Swanson followed her finger and spotted a wonky intercom screwed on to the wall. He reached out and pressed the button. A buzzing noise blared out through the silence, but nobody answered. He waited a moment, then pressed again, but held his finger down for longer.

"Yes?" a crackly, female voice said through the intercom, obviously unimpressed with the interruption.

"Er... hello." Swanson threw a look at Hart. She waved at him to continue on. "Can you let us in? We can hear someone in distress."

There was a moment of silence before the voice replied.

"And you are?"

"Detective Inspector Alex Swanson, and this is my colleague, Detective Inspector Rebecca Hart. Is everything OK? We heard a scream?"

He heard a quick snort from the mystery woman, that sounded

suspiciously like laughter. Swanson stole another glance at Hart. She stared at the intercom, looking as confused as he felt.

"That was one of the patients acting up, I'm afraid. It's nothing to worry about. Not for you, anyway," the snotty woman responded.

"We're here about the earlier stabbing, actually, and just heard the scream a few moments ago. It really sounded like someone was hurt." Hart answered this time. Her forehead creased in a way which suggested she was about to lose her temper at any second. "Now please let us in so we can assess for ourselves what we need to worry about."

"Oh, of course you can come in to discuss the earlier stabbing." The woman sounded ultra polite suddenly. "I meant that the *recent* scream you heard is nothing to worry about. Nobody was hurt. Not physically, it was a distressed patient, and it is being dealt with."

"It?" Hart mouthed at him.

He shrugged in response. This place was worse than he thought. A buzzing noise came from the steel door, which was followed by a click to signal the lock opening. Swanson swiftly pulled it open and stepped inside. Hart followed so closely behind him she stood on the back of his loafer.

"Sorry, my bad" she mumbled and stepped next to him instead.

They stood inside the door, both hesitant to move any further into the building. Swanson had been in a few psychiatric hospitals as a part of his role and expected to enter some sort of busy reception area. But Adrenna was unlike any of the other hospitals he had visited.

The hallway was empty and silent. And if he'd thought the building was unwelcoming from the outside, the inside was far worse. The creep factor was exacerbated by dark red walls encasing the long corridor laid out ahead of them. To the left of the corridor was a staircase. There were no signs anywhere to show where the reception might be, though at the end of a corridor lay another door.

"Which way do you think? Stairs or door?" Hart's voice was much smaller than usual, which was strange considering usually she couldn't even whisper quietly.

Swanson shrugged. He strained his ears for any further screams, or any other noise, but heard nothing. His eyes searched the dark walls once more, yet there was no hint or direction anywhere.

"Let's try the door first. It seems the most likely place for a reception," he said.

Christ, if someone had been hurt they would never get there in time to help at this rate. He should've asked Summer to come. She'd been here at least once before; she might have been useful. Especially with patients. Maybe even the staff. He supposed they'd be nicer to her with her visiting regularly.

They stepped away from the door and it slammed shut behind them with a loud clunk. He saw Hart's hand fly up to her chest, but said nothing. He'd reserve the piss taking for when she was no longer freaked out.

And his own heart had stopped pumping a million miles an hour.

"Must be one of those safety self-closing mechanisms," Swanson said to himself more than anything. Having a heart attack on top of a brain tumour surely wouldn't be a good mix.

"If you say so. You first. It's bloody creepy in here." Hart pointed to the door at the end of the corridor.

Swanson stepped in front of her and treaded softly up the corridor, his feet quiet against the carpet. She followed behind him, close enough that he heard her slow breathing. The warm air clung to him from all angles and felt suffocating. Beads of sweat formed on his forehead. Fuck staying inside here too long. He already couldn't wait to get outside again.

A feeling of reluctance swept over him as he reached the door. Christ, what was wrong with him? He cleared his throat and threw the door open before swallowing a sigh of relief as it opened up into a reception room. A large and ugly front desk to the left gripped his attention immediately. It was bright white and a stark contrast to the older, much darker surroundings.

A grey-haired woman sat behind it sporting thick glass and an oversized, pale blue cardigan. She wore her hair in a tight bun and crossed her plump arms against her substantial chest. The woman eyeballed him through her large, oval specs with one eyebrow raised and no smile.

Swanson gave what he hoped was a warm smile regardless, praying she would lighten up if he showed her he meant no harm or drama. He may as well attempt to be friendly. Hart followed in behind, and the old bag looked her up and down, making no attempt to hide her disapproval. Swanson moved forward a few steps.

"Good morning," he said.

"Morning," she replied, her face still set in the same sullen grimace. "How can I help?"

"We're here to talk to a Dr James Randall?" Hart piped up. She returned the woman's surly tone.

Swanson cleared his throat and covered his mouth as he did so to hide his grin. Rude old people were one of Hart's many pet hates. And he knew she was going to whine about this woman for days.

"What about, please?" The old bag asked.

"We're not at liberty to disclose anything further, I'm afraid. Please tell us where to find him and we'll be on our way." Hart was staying firm.

The woman sighed, making it obvious they were inconveniencing her. "You need to sign in before you go on the ward."

"Oh, we're not going on to the ward. If you can find Dr Randall and tell him to come and meet us, please." Hart said.

The woman stared at Hart, her mouth set into a straight line. Hart stood her ground. After a moment, the silence was deafening. Swanson opened his mouth to interject.

"One minute, please," the woman said, saving him from having to think of something to say. She stood and left the office through a door behind her.

"Jesus christ. We're clearly not welcome," muttered Hart, rolling her eyes at Swanson. He raised an eyebrow in return.

"Don't you want to go on the ward to see what happened?" Swanson kept his voice low. He never knew who was listening, after all.

Hart shuddered. "I suppose we'll have to at some point, but I want that doctor with us before we enter. We might have arrested someone in there, for starters."

The door reopening made them both turn their heads. The woman had returned and ambled across the reception area without a word. She took her time in sitting down and sorting her chair into the correct position.

Swanson risked a glance at Hart. She was giving the lady an intense stare, her nostrils flared. He cleared his throat again and took a breath to suppress the laughter building up.

"Dr Randall isn't in, I'm afraid," the woman announced. For the first time, she smiled. A sickly sweet and sarcastic grin.

Swanson preferred her without a smile.

"Well, my colleague called earlier and was told he would be here to explain the situation that happened earlier this morning," Hart replied, struggling to keep her tone neutral.

"Oh, did he now? I'm so sorry you were told that. Which colleague was it? I'll make sure to have a word with them." She returned Hart's death stare easily.

"I'll find out the name when I get back to the station. If that was wrong, there must be another person here who can help? Another doctor?" Hart wasn't giving up easily.

The woman leaned back in her chair. She removed her glasses and breathed on them before answering.

"Not at the moment, I'm afraid. Dr Randall was on the ward at the time. He's our consultant psychiatrist. So it really is him you need to speak to."

"When will he be back?" Swanson cut in before Hart got any more agitated.

The receptionist wiped her glasses on her cardigan, and shrugged. "I'm afraid I'm not sure."

"Has he gone home?" Swanson asked.

"No. I believe he had to visit someone urgently. I don't know exactly where. He was in a rush."

"OK. We will return tomorrow morning and expect that will be enough time to allow you to ensure Dr Randall will be available to answer our questions," Swanson said politely.

He opened the door and waited for Hart to walk through first. She glanced at him begrudgingly but took the hint. Once they were back in the corridor, Hart looked up at him and gaped.

"What the hell was that about?" she whispered, but as usual, she said it in such a way that it seemed much louder than her normal voice.

"Let's not talk about it here. Come on." He pushed past her and led the way back to the exit.

But he stopped at the stairs next to the exit and peered up at them. The red carpet continued up the steps to an open hallway at the top. Two doors were visible from his viewpoint. He walked to the bottom of the stairs and leaned to get a better view.

"What are you doing?" Hart whispered. Again, far louder than her usual voice.

A man's shout came from behind one door. It didn't sound particularly distressed. Was that all they'd heard earlier? A patient making noise? Swanson turned back around to face Hart.

"Nothing," he said, stepping off the stairs, "come on."

He opened up the steel exit and the blast of cool, fresh air hitting his skin was invigorating after the stifling warmth of the hospital. Swanson breathed it in deeply, but regret hit him immediately and he coughed and gagged. The air might be fresh, but there was a powerful stench of cow shit.

Hart laughed, despite her grievance with the reception woman. The pair crunched over the gravel in silence, each one lost in their own thoughts. It wasn't until they were in the car, doors closed, that Hart spoke.

"So, that was…strange," she said, her eyes fixated on the steering wheel but her mind appearing to be much further away as she assessed what had just happened.

"Yep. Very. She actually reminded me of my old English teacher. I never liked her either. Horrible old bag." He shuddered and pulled his seatbelt across his chest.

Hart did the same, started the engine and cranked up the dial for the heating. "Yeah, she was a bit *matronly*, wasn't she? Any thoughts on why she would want to stop us investigating such a dangerous incident?"

"She's possibly just a jobsworth, I guess. But there's definitely a weird vibe to this place, and she didn't exactly help with that." Swanson rubbed his hand against his beard.

Hart looked away to check the coast was clear before reversing out. Swanson stole the opportunity to slide his hand over and turn the heating back down. She turned back, oblivious to his actions, and rolled out of the Adrenna car park.

"It's haunted," she said, her face dark.

Swanson snorted. "OK. And how do you know that it's haunted?"

"Because I'm a better detective than you. I did my research and read about the hospital before we came," she replied in a smug tone.

"Ooh, ouch. Bit low when I was in hospital getting diagnosed with a bloody tumour." Swanson threw her a mock look of hurt.

"Pfft. Excuses, excuses, Detective Inspector Swanson. Don't think I'm letting you off that easily because of something as small as a tumour." She gave him a sly side glance and grinned.

"So what makes you think it's haunted?" Swanson asked again as Hart pulled onto the dirt track that led away from the hospital and back to the city.

"So, for starters, look at the place." She waved a hand in the general direction of the hospital.

Swanson didn't disagree. The place looked like the perfect haunted psychiatric hospital from an old horror film.

"Plus, from what I read online there's been loads of reports of ghosts. And not only from patients but from staff, too," she said as if staff were more reliable than the patients.

A few months ago Swanson might have agreed, but that wasn't his experience recently. Summer certainly wouldn't agree.

Who was that guy she was having breakfast with?

"I didn't think you were the type to believe in ghosts," Swanson said, pushing Summer out of his thoughts.

"Oh, yeah. My aunt's pub was haunted. It was mainly in the spare room."

She shuddered. "The building had the *strangest* atmosphere, like Adrenna does. And she had all sorts happen. The lights would turn on and off-"

"Ooh, scary electrical faults." Swanson teased.

"-and so would the telly. They'd hear footsteps running up and down in the hall and heavy breathing," Hart carried on, ignoring Swanson's interjection. "Once a glass randomly smashed on its own. Just sitting there on the bar and it smashed!"

Swanson laughed. "Ghosts aren't real, Hart! Don't be a wimp."

"Uh huh, you keep telling yourself that. I'm gonna bring you to my aunt's pub one day and then you'll believe me. Did you not feel the creepy vibe at Adrenna?"

He shrugged. "It felt weird. Who are these ghosts that supposedly haunt it?"

"Well, the original doctor who ran the hospital was called Brian Stockport. He actually died *inside* the hospital itself a couple of decades ago. He took over the hospital following privatisation of the social care system in the eighties. A patient murdered him, according to Wikipedia anyway. This patient stabbed him to death."

Swanson whistled. "Ouch. Murdered by those he was trying to help, eh? So, now the good doctor haunts the corridors, does he?"

"So some people will tell you. But that's not the strangest part." her smug smile was back.

"Go on. Spit it out," Swanson said in exasperation.

"His son died there, too. He was stabbed to death by a different patient ten years later."

"What?" Swanson turned to look at her, but he could tell when Hart was taking the piss out of him. She was deadly serious.

She nodded as the car flew down the winding country lanes at sixty miles an hour. "That's weird, I know. But again, not *as* weird as finding out they were both murdered in the same room!" She gleaned at him, proud of her trump card. "Loads of patients and staff have reported seeing either the older doctor or his son walking around the top floor of the hospital."

Swanson didn't respond, but took a moment to gather his thoughts. He didn't believe in ghosts or anything else supernatural. But even he had to admit it was a strange story.

"It's probably not true. Anyone can write anything on the internet. We need the records," he thought out loud.

Hart shrugged. "I wasn't sure either, but now I've been inside, I believe every word."

"Do you still want to go back tomorrow?" he asked.

Hart was quiet for a moment as she handled the roundabout which led to the city centre. Swanson gripped the handle above the door.

"Yep. I want to see that old bag again. I miss her already." She grinned and Swanson laughed. "What about you?"

"Me? I'm not the one who's scared of the ghosts," he replied.

Hart was quiet for a moment. "I meant your head. Do you feel up to it?"

"Of course." Swanson said more snappily than he meant to. He regretted his tone instantly. An awkward silence descended, and the pair sat in silence for the remaining few minutes of the drive.

Swanson tried to ignore the ever-increasing burning pain in the back of his head. But by the time Hart pulled into the station and parked haphazardly in a corner space, he was desperate to take his pain killers.

"You hungry? I'll buy us some food," Swanson said as he rushed to unbuckle his seatbelt.

"I'm not hungry, but I accept your offer as an apology," Hart said, "you might want to set aside a food allowance though if you're gonna be even grumpier than usual while the doctors fix you up."

Swanson made a mental note to add on some sort of chocolate pudding for her as they left the car.

"Nice parking." Swanson nodded towards the vehicle, which was parked at a severe angle.

Hart glanced behind her at the car and shrugged. "Yep. I did it on purpose."

"Oh, yeah. Course you did."

"Yeah, I did. No one's going to want to park next to an idiot who parks like that." She pointed at the car and grinned.

"At least you admit what you are." Swanson shrugged and strode away quickly.

"Where are you rushing off to?" Hart called out.

"Getting away from you," he yelled back as he reached the station door.

Once inside, he rushed through the security door again and down the corridor to the bathroom. He ignored other officers nodding to him and slammed the bathroom door behind him. Thank god, it was empty. His head throbbed, and he grabbed the pills from deep in his trouser pocket. He swallowed two dry and leant against the wall. He took a deep breath and waited for them to kick in. Only a few seconds passed before the door to the bathroom swung open.

Swanson jumped off the wall and cleared his throat.

"Woah, everything OK?" Officer Graham Forest, a fairly inexperienced officer who was skinny as a rake, looked at him with concern.

"Yep. Great." Swanson nodded to him and walked back out into the corridor.

He did not need Forest to suspect anything was going on. The man wasn't known for subtlety. Though Forest was a nice guy and didn't mean to blab, he couldn't help it. He didn't have the brainpower to think through his thoughts before speaking.

But as Swanson left the bathroom, the corridor spun. The tiled floor moved upwards, straight out from under his feet and smacked him in the nose.

How the hell did the floor move?

"Swanson?" Forest's voice was far away, echoing in the distance. A drowned out ringing noise flooded Swanson's ears.

"It was the bloody floor. It smacked me in the face," Swanson murmured, "why did the floor move?"

"Stupid floor." Hart's voice cut through the ringing much louder than Forest's.

Swanson's eyes flew back open.

"Get up, Krypto. I need my sidekick. Come on. Up you get. Move your fat arse yourself please. I'm not superwoman."

With his eyes now open, Swanson saw he was lying on the floor in the corridor. The floor hadn't moved. He'd fallen somehow. Multiple hands were pulling at him, but he barely budged. Hart and Forest stood little chance of dragging his dead weight up off the floor. He took a breath, put his palms on the floor, and heaved himself up to his knees.

"Butt on floor, head between knees," ordered Hart. For once, he did as she asked.

"What's going on?" A sharp female voice cut through the noise.

Swanson took a breath, and the ringing decreased now he was sitting up. He looked up and spotted a blurry Detective Chief Inspector Murray striding down the corridor towards him. *Shit.*

"Why are you on the floor?" she asked in a neutral tone which didn't hint at either annoyance or concern. She probably didn't feel either.

"Er…" Swanson tried to say *'I'm fine',* but no words came out. His tongue felt thick in his mouth. He couldn't use it properly.

"He said the floor moved and hit him in the face, Sir." Forest piped up. Great, thanks Forest.

"What? Are you OK or not, Swanson?" DCI Murray asked.

He managed a nod.

"Good. Go home if you're ill. Let me know if you need anything else. Hart, sort him out." Murray walked off. "I don't want to see you back at work until you're better, Swanson. You're responsible for him, Hart," she yelled without turning to look back.

Swanson

The dizziness had passed by the time DCI Murray reached her office door at the end of the hall. Swanson waved Hart and Forest away and the pair stepped back. Yet they continued to stare at him as if ready to pounce any second. He put his hand against the wall. The coolness of the paint felt good against his clammy skin.

He leant all of his weight against it and pushed himself up, shaking off the instability in his legs. He felt their worried eyes staring at him, and his cheeks burnt.

"I just had a dizzy spell. Clearly I haven't drunk enough water," he said, though his voice came out with a strangled tone.

"Forest, get Swanson a glass of water, please," Hart commanded in a tone that warranted no arguments.

Forest turned and rushed off in the opposite direction to DCI Murray, heading towards the kitchen a few doors down. Two officers were chatting as they made their way by. They fell silent upon seeing Swanson leaning against the wall, though one swift glance from Hart sent them scampering by without asking questions.

"I'm not going to tell you to rest, because I know you're not stupid enough *not* to realise that yourself. But I am telling you I'm going to drive you home," Hart said once the two officers were out of earshot.

"I can't leave my car here," Swanson said, although thinking of driving himself home made him groan internally.

"That's what taxis are for, you tight sod," Hart replied.

The pair heard footsteps, and turned to see Forest rushing down the hall with a glass of water, drops spilling out of it everywhere. Swanson suppressed a laugh. He hadn't seen Forest's gangly form *rush* anywhere before.

"Here." Forest presented the half empty glass with a deeply concerned expression.

"Thanks, Forest." Swanson took the glass and downed it in three gulps. The water eased the shaking sensation enough so he no longer needed to lean on the wall.

"Do you feel better?" Forest asked and took the empty glass from him.

"He's fine, Forest. Give him some space," Hart said. She gave him one of her special death stares.

Forest nodded and moved back a step.

Hart continued to glare at him.

"Er, I'll finish going to the loo." He eventually got the hint and hurried back into the men's bathroom.

"Come on." Hart put a hand on Swanson's arm.

"I'm fine." He shrugged her away.

"Shut-up, you are not fine." She pulled at his arm again until he stepped forward. "Come on."

She walked off and motioned for him to follow her. Swanson sighed, but did as she asked. He contemplated driving himself home. He was more stable now the water had done its job. Maybe he really was hungry and dehydrated. *Did he have breakfast?* The day was a blur. He thought back to that morning, preparing for the hospital. His stomach had felt full of nerves about the appointment with Dr Tiffin. He definitely hadn't had lunch. That must be the problem.

"I can see what you're thinking, and it's not happening," Hart called out without turning to look at him. "I already took your key when you were sitting on the floor."

Swanson stopped dead in his tracks and shoved his hands in each pocket, searching for the key.

"Seriously, Robin," he yelled down the corridor to her. "The last thing a dizzy person needs is your erratic, bloody driving."

Hart stopped too and turned to face him. She was grinning. "You've survived one trip with me already today. You can survive another."

He didn't know if he was more annoyed at Hart taking his keys, or at the sense of relief he felt she had taken the choice from him. He'd rather not be stuck at home without a car, and not even be able to check if it was OK. But really any car would be safer in a police station parking lot than in the driveway of his cottage. And it was safer without him driving it whilst so unwell. At least until he ate something.

They snuck out of the building through the rear fire doors, an exit that led straight to the car park and was supposed to be for emergencies only. But Swanson figured Murray would rather they took the back entrance than him causing any further scenes in front of people.

The air was muggy compared to the freshness of the morning. Or did it feel that way because he was still hot and clammy? He crossed the car park once again to Hart's badly parked Astra. It was clear from the heavy air that more rain was on the way, and he wished it would hurry. Standing in the rain at that moment would have been lovely. He stood tall despite the tremour in his legs and forced each one to move in long strides.

Once in the car Hart reached out to turn up the heat, but glanced at him and decided against it. They fell into a comfortable silence this time. Hart didn't say a thing until she had to ask him for directions when they were a few streets away from Swanson's cottage. She'd visited twice before, but a sense of direction wasn't a strong point of hers, putting it mildly.

"Here you go, Sir," she said with a weird seated bow action as she pulled up on the curb outside of his home.

A calmness fell over Swanson at the sight of the wonky little cottage. He couldn't remember another time when he'd needed the silence of his own space more.

"Come on," Hart said, opening her car door.

Swanson's calmness dissipated.

"What are you doing?" he asked.

"I need to borrow your charger to make a call, then I'm gone, OK?" She raised her hands in the air as if being arrested.

"You're a liar." Swanson got out of the car too and headed towards his pale green door. It desperately needed repainting when he had a spare afternoon.

"No, genuinely, I thought I may as well get an update from the hospital on the woman who was attacked whilst I'm with you. It will save you the job of calling me later. You know, when you've tried to relax but got bored and decided to work again." She gave him a knowing look.

Swanson unwillingly agreed and let them both into the cottage, which opened straight into the cosy, misshapen living room with its ancient sofa and low ceilings. He stooped as he entered the room.

"Mind your head." Swanson looked down at Hart, whose head cleared the threshold by at least half a foot. She rolled her eyes at his sarcasm.

"I suppose you want a coffee?" he asked.

"Do you actually have coffee in?" Her face lit up.

"Nope."

She let out an exaggerated sigh. "You're actually even more infuriating when you're sick. Where's your charger?"

He pointed to an extension cable with a mess of wires in the corner of the room, half hidden by the sofa.

"That's a bloody fire hazard." Hart tutted. She walked over and perched on the edge of the sofa, reaching over the arm to grab the charger. She pulled it through a mass of wires, shaking her head and tutting some more.

"I'll give it a minute to charge," she said once she'd sorted the charger wire and plonked the phone on the arm of the sofa.

Swanson flicked off his loafers and sat on the barely used armchair across from her. She was in his usual space. He closed his eyes and allowed the annoyance of not being able to sit on his sofa spot to wash over him.

"Stop staring at me. I'm fine," he grumbled.

"Well, you're not though, you have a tumour," she said simply.

"Yes, well. Thanks for that reminder. It helped a lot."

She turned her body to face him and gave him a serious look.

"You're welcome. There's no point in it being an elephant in the room. You need to get used to it so you can beat it. I assume that's right, anyway. Sounds right, doesn't it? Spit it out. What are the next steps to make it go away?"

She wouldn't give up until she knew the full story. He'd seen her use the same technique with witnesses and criminals a hundred times. It was partly what made her so good at the job. He sighed and shuffled back in his chair, unsure how to get comfy on the unfamiliar piece of furniture.

"I need a biopsy first to see how it's growing. It might be benign, or it might be cancerous," he admitted. The words felt strange. Like he was lying, or dreaming, or as if someone else should say them.

She nodded. "So, when is the biopsy?"

He shrugged. "I don't know yet. They'll call me to let me know soon."

"You need to tell Murray asap so you can be available last minute for it." She fell silent and fiddled with a piece of hair. "Do you want me to come with you? I can take the piss out of you while you wait. It might make you feel better."

Swanson stared at her. "Come with me? To the hospital?" he repeated slowly, as if he misunderstood.

"Yes, Swanson. Come with you. Support you. You understand that, right? Actually, you might need someone to drive you home anyway with the anaesthetic and all that."

Swanson paused and looked out of the small window of his front room. It still wasn't raining. "I can get a taxi there and back."

"Pfft. Yeah right. You're as tight as a duck's arse! That would cost you a tenner at least and that's just for one way."

That *was* expensive. She had a point.

"I'm not even that tight. Just because I don't spend hundreds on one bloody dog handbag." He pointed to her leather bag with the little dog symbol that he knew indicated some sort of expensive designer handbag.

"Whatever. Let me know the date and I'll be there. I'm not giving you a choice." She crossed her arms like a stubborn toddler.

"Fine, if you insist." Swanson was too hungry to argue.

He stood back up and walked into the kitchen to see what snacks he had. He rammed a couple of pork pies and some ham into his mouth. Then pulled out a carton of chunky chicken soup and swiftly emptied it into a bowl. As he waited for the microwave to ping, he dug out the box of chocolates from his cupboard that he had meant to give to Summer a few weeks ago and went back through to the living room.

"Here." He shoved the chocolates onto Hart's lap, along with the rest of the pork pies.

She grinned. "Thanks!"

"Yeah, well, I'll need to keep your blood sugar up if you're going to keep fussing over me all the time. You'll be bloody intolerable otherwise."

"Soo, all I heard there was *thank you for being a great mate. I love you and appreciate you.*" She peered up at him, still perched in his favourite spot.

"Yep. That's what I said." He went back into the kitchen to fetch his soup and some bread.

He heard Hart through the open door which adjoined the living room and kitchen. There was no room for a hallway in the cottage.

"Hi, Forest. just checking for an update on the hospital worker who's… er… in hospital?" She fell silent as she waited for a response. Swanson dipped the butterless bread in the soup and thrust it into his mouth before drinking the rest of the bowl. Living alone meant no need for manners. He placed the bowl in the empty sink and made his way back into the living room to resign himself to the armchair.

"Want a sandwich?" he mouthed to Hart.

She shook her head. "Stable? OK," she replied to Forest.

"Is she a nurse?" Swanson asked in a loud whisper.

"Did we find out if she was a nurse or a doctor?" Hart asked.

Swanson heard the rumbling of Forest's voice, but not what he was saying. But as Hart's eyes widened, he realised it wasn't good news. She glanced at Swanson, but quickly looked away. Her usually peachy cheeks suddenly quite a shade lighter.

"She was a what? Are you sure? Get me her name, now. How do we not know it yet? OK, I need to go. Get that name to me asap." She hung up and continued to stare at the floor, as if deep in thought.

He almost didn't want to know. "Are you going to tell me what's wrong?"

She slowly raised her head. She was worryingly pale. "Have you spoken to Summer recently?"

"Yesterday. But then I saw her this morning having breakfast with… a friend. Didn't speak to her, though. Why?" Swanson asked. *Who was that bloody guy?*

He suddenly realised what Hart had asked him. *Why* she must be asking him.

His head snapped up. "Why, Hart?" he demanded.

She swallowed. "That woman who was stabbed… she was an advocate. A visiting one, not a usual member of staff."

Swanson tugged his phone out of his trouser pocket, his hands sweating. He ignored the new wave of dizziness rushing through him. His adrenaline pumping. He ignored all other thoughts and focused on dialling Summer's number.It absolutely could not be her. He'd just seen her, how could it be? But her phone went straight to voicemail.

Swanson

A grim mixture of panic and anger curdled and settled within Swanson's chest. He stood up, fighting away the dizziness that threatened to overcome him. His face hot with anger.

"It went straight to voicemail. How do we not know the name yet?" He tried to keep his voice calm, but he was sounding more panicky with each word.

Hart's own face paled. She stood to face him. "Someone will know. Wait one minute. Even if it is her, Forest said she was stable, OK? Stay calm."

She picked up her phone and quickly tapped something before holding it to her ear. Swanson went into the kitchen and redialled Summer's mobile. It went straight to voicemail again. His hands squeezed into fists as he walked back into the living room, his nails digging into his palms.

"Forest is going to find out the name of the victim asap. Apparently the nurse at Adrenna didn't know the name when they called it in because she was a new advocate to them, but they had it recorded in the visitor log and were going to let us know. I'll go to the hospital in the meantime. She's still unconscious, but if they've found it out then they'll tell us her name if we're face to face."

Swanson marched over to his shoes and shoved his feet into them. "I'm coming with you."

"Jesus, Swanson. Fine. I'll bloody find you a bed and leave you there," she muttered as she stormed past him to the front door. Swanson followed right on her heel and slammed the door behind them.

"Lock it." Hart jerked her head toward his front door.

"Shit, keys." He ran back inside to grab them and nearly tripped on the threshold on his way back out.

Hart was already in her car by the time he'd locked up. He rushed around to the passenger side to join her in the vehicle. The adrenaline made him feel more focused than he had done all day. He had Summer to focus on now. And he was on his way to help. It was going to be OK. The tumour could go fuck itself at that moment.

He hit redial and reached her voicemail again. All the times he could have asked Summer for a drink ran through his mind, and how silly it was that he didn't, just because she'd been busy the one time he'd asked.

They didn't talk on the drive. Hart knew him well enough to leave him alone with his thoughts. She pulled into the hospital fifteen minutes later and parked on the grass near the entrance. They jumped out and raced inside to the reception desk. People lined the waiting area, but moved out of the way as soon as they saw Swanson striding through. The young brunette on the reception desk watched him approach with wide eyes, not taking them off him once.

"Hi, high dependency unit, please?" he panted, struggling to catch his breath.

She pointed over her shoulder and belted out directions, clearly having said the same thing a million times before. The pair rushed down the corridor and arrived at the lifts breathless. A few minutes later they were on the right floor, and Swanson stopped abruptly, almost causing Hart to careen into the back of him.

Aaron Walker was sitting outside the ward. He wore his nurse's uniform still, and was leaning forward with his head in his hands. Swanson recognised his ridiculous, thick black hair and massive earring from interviewing him a couple of months back about Lucy Clark. Next to him was a lady in her sixties with sallow skin and thin grey hair which fell around her shoulders. It was Summer's mum. Swanson had met her once before. The man Swanson had seen with Summer in the cafe sat next to her. So whoever he was, he knew Summer and her mum well enough to be sitting here. His eyes were also swollen, though he looked more angry than upset.

"Jesus, Swanson," Hart said in between breaths. "Don't just stop like that!"

She came out from behind him, but fell silent when she saw Aaron and Summer's mum. Hart was with Swanson when he met both of them, and she knew what their presence outside the ward signalled. Aaron looked up at the sound of Hart's voice. Beads of sweat gathered on Swanson's forehead, but he wiped them away. He needed to focus.

"Officer Swanson?" Aaron stood, a confused look on his face. "Er... Not sure if you remember me, Aaron Walker?"

"Yes, yes. I remember you. I heard an advocate was attacked and Summer isn't picking up her phone?" He knew the likelihood of Summer not being in the ward was pretty much zero, but he asked regardless. He needed to hear someone say it.

Aaron nodded solemnly. He moved away from Summer's mum, who hadn't looked over once, and said in a low voice. "I was there. I saw the whole thing. A patient attacked her with some sort of glass or razor. They hit her in the neck. That's Summer's mum." He motioned towards the woman with his head. Swanson glanced over at her. She didn't look much like Summer. She looked as though she'd fall over if you breathed too hard near her.

"And that's her brother." Aaron nodded over to the angry man with swollen eyes.

A sense of relief hit Swanson at hearing the man was her brother, though it was short-lived when he remembered why they were all there. The man looked younger than Summer. He had her fair hair and a straight nose. He remembered her telling him about a younger brother. *Was it Dave? Declan?*

"Have you had an update on how she's doing?" Swanson forced his attention back to Aaron. His breath stuck in his chest as he waited for the answer.

"They've operated on her already and have closed the wound. They let us in to see her for a few minutes earlier. She's stable, but she's not awake yet. They wanted to check all of her equipment and stats so we came to wait out here."

Swanson closed his eyes briefly and let out the breath he'd been holding. "And where's Joshua?"

Aaron raised his eyebrows. Was he surprised that Swanson knew the child's name? How close were Aaron and Summer, anyway?

"He's at school," Aaron answered, "but his dad is going to pick him up."

Hart put a hand on Swanson's arm and interjected. "Thanks, Mr Walker."

Aaron nodded and hesitated as if he was going to say something else, but he walked off back to his chair. It was rare for anyone to not do as Hart asked straight away.

"I've got a missed call from the station. I'll be back in a minute," Hart said in a low voice and walked off down the corridor they had just come from.

Swanson leaned against the wall, his mind racing. Whilst he had been in the very same hospital, worrying about himself, Summer was about to turn up fighting for her life and he didn't even know it. Poor Joshua was going to be confused and worried. Then he realised what Aaron said.

He shot off the wall and stormed over to Aaron, who looked up at him in surprise and shrank back in his chair. A reaction Swanson was used to in response to him getting too close.

"You said you were there?" Swanson said.

Summer's mum still didn't look at him. She was staring into space. Her eyes were vacant. But he felt the brother's eyes on him, though he said nothing.

"Er... Yes. I work there now. It's my new job," Aaron said, "or was, anyway. It's a strange place. Not sure I'll stick around."

"Will you come and give a statement?" Swanson asked.

"Sure, do you need me now, though? I kind of wanted to stay here for now, with Summer." He pointed over to the entrance of the ward.

"I only want to know what happened. Let's talk over here." Swanson moved over to a quiet corner of the corridor away from Summer's family. Aaron followed closely behind him.

"So, talk me through what happened briefly now, and we'll take a proper statement later," he said in a low voice.

"Well, it was all a bit of a blur, if I'm honest. I walked on to the ward. I wasn't supposed to be in, but I was covering the early shift for a colleague. So I went to Ward C, straight into the living area, and a patient next to Summer jumped up and went crazy. He stabbed her in the neck with a razor blade he'd stolen from somewhere. There was blood everywhere. I set the alarm off on my belt and ran over to her."

"Why did he stab her?" Swanson asked.

Aaron shrugged. "No idea. He's a fairly new patient and still under supervision."

"Clearly not intensive enough supervision," Swanson said.

Aaron didn't respond.

"Did you notice anything else? Anything unusual?" Swanson asked.

"That's it, really. I held the wound and stopped the blood flow, and a different nurse called an ambulance." He rubbed his face with his hands again.

It was only now that Swanson noticed Aaron's eyes were bloodshot too, and blood stained the bottom of his top. Summer's blood. Swanson felt sick.

"I really thought she was a goner," Aaron whispered.

A furious rage sat within Swanson's chest. Someone was going to pay for hurting Summer. He heard the sharp tap of heels against tiles and turned away from Aaron. Hart was on her way towards them.

"That was the hospital. Dr Randall is back," she said.

The Servant

I watched out of the ward window and waited for the officer's red car to pull up. They didn't take long once I'd given the order. I watched the woman park up and leave her car in a slanted position in the middle of the gravel. And I repeated the registration number until I had it committed to memory.

I was pleased it was the same officers as earlier. They didn't stay in the car this time, and instead exited as soon as they'd parked up. The man strode over the gravel path, with the woman barely able to keep up with him, stumbling over the gravel again in her heels.

I'd been right in thinking she was no good for the Devil. He wouldn't like her demeanour at all. She wasn't worthy of Him, far too brash and common. But the man would do nicely.

He moved slowly, despite his big strides, like he had purpose to each step. His eyes scanned the area and took in every detail. His thoroughness was clear. The Devil would like that. It was a superb skill for a protector to have.

Plus, I knew he had a tumour. The Devil had told me.

So I didn't even need to feel any guilt about killing him. He was dying anyway. But we couldn't wait around. Tumours can make people weak. He needed to be strong like he was now. I had to weaken him enough to get him into the chamber. In a one-on-one fight, he would easily overpower me.

I'll explain to him why beforehand, maybe he'll understand. Maybe he'll think I'm crazy. Most people would. But the shadows of the Devil have not touched those people as they lay in bed. Most people think a simple duvet will protect them from any monsters.

You can't see the shadow looking at you in the dark. But trust me, it's there, and it can see you.

Swanson

Swanson was grateful that Hart had put her foot down and sped through the city. The heavens finally opened again as the city merged into countryside and he watched as large raindrops bounced off the bonnet. But it didn't slow her down. Instead, she reached Adrenna in record time. He'd always had the feeling that Hart didn't like Summer much, but maybe she cared about her more than he realised.

The building loomed before them in no time at all, looking even more depressing against the grey skies and torrential rain. Hart threw her car into a random spot on the gravel, and they stormed across the car park and down the side of the building to the steel door they'd used earlier that morning.

Swanson pressed the buzzer on the intercom and counted to three before pressing it again. His hands rolled into tight fists. He heard Hart's quick footsteps behind him. She'd caught up to him. He glanced over at her. She was giving him a wary glare.

"Let me do the talking," she said, pulling her hood up tight over her face.

He shook his head. "No way." He pulled his own hood over his head. His trousers were already sticking to his legs.

Hart leant right against the wall, trying to get out of the way of the colossal rain drops. "You're too angry, you know you are. You shouldn't be here, really. Murray would flip."

"I don't care. Nobody knows I have anything to do with Summer, other than interviewing her the other month. And to be fair to them, I don't.

Not really. The other times we met were to talk about her brother mainly." He turned away from her. "I can still be professional. Don't worry. I won't lose my temper."

"You will if they say something stupid," she muttered.

He raised an eyebrow and heaved his shoulders. "They better not say anything stupid then."

"Murray *is* gonna be pissed when she finds out you didn't go home. Plus, I'm pretty sure this level of stress isn't good for a brain tumour."

Swanson ignored her and pushed the bell again. Nobody spoke, but the buzzer sounded this time, and the steel door clicked to signal it was unlocked. Swanson pushed it open and stalked down the corridor into the reception area.

"Dr Randall will be with you in one moment," the old witch said from behind her reception desk as soon as he walked in. Hart was right behind him, with a face that said she was disappointed she would not get to argue.

"You can take a seat if your trousers aren't too wet," the receptionist continued, though Swanson swore she was hiding a smirk.

Neither of them moved. Swanson knew he looked surly, but he didn't care. He stood rooted to the spot and stared in the woman's direction. He wasn't taking any shit this time.

It only took a minute for a man to appear from behind the reception desk. Dr Randall, Swanson assumed. His height matched Swanson's six feet, though he was much skinnier with a bean pole figure and a head of floppy brown hair. He smiled at them both as he strode over, his teeth slightly crooked. At least he seemed friendlier than the receptionist.

"Hi, guys, hi. How are you both? I'm Dr Randall." He put forward a large and bony hand to shake Swanson's. "Lovely to meet you."

Swanson took the doctor's hand. "Detective Inspector Alex Swanson," he said curtly. He pulled his eyes away to stop himself from staring at the largest pair of glasses he'd ever seen. Dr Randall held the same hand out to Hart, who took it and introduced herself in the same curt fashion. Rain always annoyed her. She'd be in a mood until she was dry again.

"Follow me, please. My office is right down here and we can have a bit of a chat about the recent incident. Such a terrible accident." He shook his head and strode off back down the side of the reception desk.

Swanson clenched his jaw. It certainly wasn't an *accident*. Dr Randall unlocked a heavy wooden door and held it open as the pair walked through. Behind the door was another corridor which led round to the left of the building and followed behind the initial hallway.

"I'm sorry to have to bring you all the way down here because of a patient. I'm sure you have other criminals to catch that aren't safely cared for in a locked facility." Dr Randall threw them both an apologetic glance.

The pair said nothing. Swanson clenched his jaw harder. It might be harder to stay calm than he thought. They walked past a few more doors. Swanson glanced at the sign on each one. *G Randall. B Stockport. Store room. J Randall.* Dr Randall opened the last one and led them inside.

"This is me." He smiled, and once again held the door for them.

"Thank you," said Hart.

Swanson still kept his jaw clenched. This guy was way too polite. It was unsettling somehow. He surveyed the office. It was a mess. Boxes of books and paper files lined both walls, and a desk full of paperwork was positioned at the back of the room in front of a window. He glanced at the books.

Neuropsychiatry and the mind.
A History of Mental Health.
The Devil of Adrenna.

Dr Randall took a seat on the other side of his messy desk and motioned for them to each take a seat across from him. The window was behind his desk, with blinds that were half closed and prevented too much light seeping through. To the right of his desk was another door. Swanson stared at it. A door there made no sense to the layout of the building. Where the hell would it lead to? Dr Randall grabbed some papers and shoved them into a desk drawer. Swanson couldn't keep his mouth shut any longer.

"So where were you when we visited earlier?" he asked with no effort made to keep the annoyance out of his voice.

"Er... we had an incident on the ward, I'm afraid. A patient attacked another patient." He removed his glasses and wiped them on his white coat. "It's not been an enjoyable week, unfortunately. I had to declare the ward unsafe and couldn't allow any visitors."

"We were told you were out. Unreachable," Swanson said.

Dr Randall swallowed. His unusually large Adam's apple bobbing up and down. He recovered quickly, flashing another big smile. "Out? Oh no, I practically live here," he said with a nervous chuckle, "but I was busy dealing with the aftermath and making sure everybody was safe. Glenda must have gotten the wrong end of the stick."

"Glenda?" Hart said.

"Yes. The receptionist." He nodded again. Christ, he was like one of those annoying nodding dogs people used to put in their cars, the ones with the stupid big grins.

"Oh, I see. She didn't exactly introduce herself," Hart said.

"Oh, apologies. She can be blunt. The patients are very important to her. She means well." Dr Randall set his glasses back on his face and leant forward in his seat. "How is the advocate? Such a lovely woman."

"She's in hospital and might die," Swanson said. He felt Hart's eyes on him as she glanced over. She wasn't approving of his bluntness, then.

"Oh, dear! That is awful." Dr Randall sat back in his chair.

"For now, she's alive," Hart butted in before Swanson responded. "Can you tell me what happened, please?"

"Well, yes. Of course. I was doing my rounds, visiting the wards and making sure all is OK. Summer was sitting next to Andy when I entered Ward C. I thought I'd say hello, you know, like I usually do. I like to make everyone feel welcome. So I walked over to Summer and Andy and as I got there he jumped up and hit her—"

"*Hit* her?" Swanson interrupted.

"Well, that's what I thought he did. I rushed forward to restrain him and he cut my hand." He stopped to pull up a sleeve and show them a bandaged left hand. "I was quite close anyway, you see. I heard the alarms going off and saw blood. That's when I realised she'd been more badly hurt than I thought. It wasn't until a couple of other nurses came running over to help me pin Andy down I saw how much blood there was. I helped get Andy to the quiet room and locked the door. When I returned I saw the razor blade on the floor. I swiped it up and by this time sirens could be heard and a nurse, Aaron, was looking after Summer."

"Are you a qualified doctor?" Swanson asked.

Dr Randall frowned. "Sorry?"

"Are you a qualified medical doctor?" Swanson repeated through gritted teeth.

"Yes, of course. All psychiatrists study medicine, if that's what you're asking." Dr Randall looked perplexed.

"Why didn't you let the support staff handle the patient, like they're trained to do, and you, as a doctor, help the bleeding woman?" Swanson asked.

"I really didn't know how serious it was." Dr Randall's voice was suddenly much higher.

"Where's the patient now?" Hart butted in again.

"He's still in solitary confinement. He seems much calmer, but I have not deemed it safe to release him yet."

"Can we speak to him?" Hart asked.

He shook his head. "Not at the minute. He's really not very well and so he is still dangerous at present. Plus, he would need an appropriate adult at least. I'll call you as soon as he's calmed down. But I can tell you that when I spoke to him earlier, he said he couldn't remember the incident."

"He couldn't remember at all?" Hart asked.

Dr Randall shook his head. "Not hurting her. He remembered sitting next to her, and being thrown into the confinement room. But the attack is a blind spot."

"Do you have cameras on the ward?" Hart asked.

"Yes, but where this incident happened is also a blind spot, unfortunately."

"Can you at least show us the ward so we can see where the incident happened?" Swanson asked, standing up before Dr Randall could answer.

"Yes, of course." The doctor jumped up despite looking like he'd rather do anything but.

He stood and led them back through the corridor to a door at the other end. Swanson hadn't noticed there was another door here. It led into the initial hallway with the steel door. And the stairs to the first floor were in front of them.

"Just up here," the doctor said as he leaped up the stairs. He had an annoying way of bouncing rather than walking, with his shoulders hunched over. Swanson followed more cautiously, with Hart right behind him.

At the top of the stairs, there were three doors. Dr Randall led them to the one on the right. He peered through the glass and fiddled with a key ring that was attached to his belt.

"Before we enter, I need you to know that this is the ward where our most volatile patients live. This is the ward they enter when they first arrive, and we don't know them very well yet. You must be vigilant and stay with me. I have my alarm to call for help if needed."

Swanson glanced over at Hart in surprise.

"Thanks for the heads up, but I think we'll be OK with the three of us together, Doctor," she said.

The two of them entered the ward behind Dr Randall. They stepped forward as he made sure he'd locked the door behind them. Swanson squeezed his hands into fists to control the urge to storm around the ward. If he wanted answers for Summer, he would have to stay calm and investigate properly. As he entered the ward he saw one patient sitting on the sofa, staring into space. Another walked in circles, muttering to himself.

His heart sank. This was not the best place to be looking for answers.

But as he gazed around the rest of the ward, a bolt of recognition hit him in the gut. Because for the second time that day, two blank eyes of an old stranger stared straight at him.

Swanson

Swanson's stomach churned violently. He grabbed Hart's arm to get her attention.

"What?" she asked, craning her neck to see what he was looking at.

He turned to her. "That man with cataracts or whatever, white eyes, I saw him earlier, in the supermarket car park."

She turned back to him and frowned. "What bloody man with cataracts?"

"There!" Swanson turned to point.

But he was pointing at an empty space. The man had disappeared.

"He was right there." He glared at the wide open living area in front of him. The man was here somewhere. Dr Randall appeared next to them.

"Like I said, I'm afraid you won't get much out of the patients in this ward. I sent the staff who saw the incident home. You know, to rest." He gave them a solemn look.

"I saw an older patient with eye problems. His eyes were completely white. Who is he?"

The doctor paused and looked away, scratching his head.

"I... er... I don't actually know. I don't think we have any patients with such serious eye problems. Definitely no one who is blind. Unless we've had some sort of emergency admitted by another doctor, but even then I would be made aware."

"He was right there." Swanson pointed to the corner of the ward where he'd seen the man.

"Oh... er... Ok. Let's ask a nurse, shall we? This way, please."

The doctor led them to an office which took up the left-hand side of the ward. Most of the front wall was actually a large window that you could see directly into with ease. It must make it easy for nurses to sit there watching patients.

Dr Randall fiddled with his keys again. Swanson noticed his hand shook a little, and he struggled to get the right key. Swanson glanced around the ward before entering to check again for the old man, but he was nowhere to be seen. Dr Randall finally found the right key and held open the door to allow them to pass through.

"Wait inside here a moment, please," he instructed before closing the door and heading back onto the ward.

"Where the hell is he going?" Hart murmured and peered through the window to watch him. "I don't like being locked in small rooms."

"Hopefully to find the old man," Swanson said.

"Oh yeah, the one with no eyes?" She turned to face him. One hand on her hip.

"Not no eyes! White eyes."

"OK, OK. White eyes. It's still weird as fuck, Swanson. Do brain tumours cause hallucinations?"

"No." Swanson felt the heat in his face rising and clenched his jaw tight. Did they cause bloody hallucinations?

"OK. Don't get mad at me for putting it out there. You'd ask me the same thing if I was seeing weird things like that."

He turned away from her and looked through the glass to watch out for Dr Randall instead. He spotted him walking across the ward towards them with a nurse in tow. She couldn't have been older than 25. The top of her head only reached Dr Randall's chest. She looked up and her wide eyes met his. Swanson smiled and turned away, not wanting to intimidate her before he'd even said hello.

They entered the office a moment later with Dr Randall still wearing his ridiculous big grin. She followed behind him with her head down, playing nervously with her hair.

"This is Jenna Twiggs, one of our excellent nurses on shift today," Dr Randall announced, as if they were from a quality of care inspection team. "I'll wait outside and watch the patients for you, Jenna. Give me a shout if any of you need anything." He left swiftly, closing the office door behind him.

"Hi Jenna." Swanson swallowed and forced a smile again. It didn't feel natural, but she gave him a small smile back so he couldn't be doing too badly. "I'm Detective Inspector Swanson, and this is my colleague, Detective Inspector Hart."

"Hi," her voice was soft, not unlike Summer's.

"We're here because of the stabbing that occurred this morning," Hart interjected like a bloody foghorn. Swanson sighed inwardly.

"Oh, I wasn't here, I'm afraid. I wasn't on shift." Jenna continued to curl her hair around one finger.

"Have you heard anything about what happened?" Hart persisted.

"Erm... yes. That Andy got the advocate in the neck with some sort of razor." She lowered her head. "I really like her. She cares so much about the patients. Is she going to be OK?"

"She should be." Swanson nodded. "Can I ask, is there an older patient on this ward who has a disability concerning his eyes?"

She gave him a dazed look of bewilderment. "Disability concerning his eyes? Do you mean blind?"

"Possibly. He is around 70 or 80 years old, with a white beard, and has white eyes." Swanson watched as the colour drained from her face. Her head snapped round to look out of the window and into the ward.

"Where did you see him?" She demanded, suddenly standing to get a better look out of the window.

"In that corner." Swanson pointed to the far side of the ward. "Then he seemed to... vanish."

Jenna's shoulders relaxed, and she turned to him. "No. I have no idea who you're talking about. Sorry. Do you have any other questions?"

He shook his head.

"OK. I better get back to giving out the meds. It was lovely to meet you."

"Lovely to meet you too, Jenna Twiggs," Swanson said softly.

As soon as the door was closed behind her, he turned to Hart, who still stood with one hand on her hip. "Did you see her reaction?"

"She got up to look out the window, Swanson. She was trying to see what the hell you were talking about. Come on, let's go find the good doctor and get out of here. It's messing with your bloody head."

He opened his mouth to argue, but something about the look on her face stopped him. She'd already asked once about hallucinations. He didn't need her thinking that was actually true.

And he'd seen how the nurse had jumped up to look for the man. She knew who he was talking about, didn't she?

Swanson

Swanson huffed as he hauled himself into Hart's car and slammed the door. Visiting the ward had proved pointless. He'd not found one scrap of information, and could happily never visit that damn hospital again. Now all he could think about was the old man. The nurse obviously knew who he'd meant. The mention of him had terrified her.

"So, what do you think of the good doctor?" asked Hart.

"He's too…" Swanson racked his brain for the right word. He wasn't going to mention the old man again to Hart. He didn't need to give her any more evidence that he was losing his mind.

"Chirpy?" Hart suggested.

"Yes, definitely. But there's something else." He turned to gaze out of the window, willing his brain to focus.

"Happy?" Hart tried again. "You know how you hate overly cheerful people."

"Well, yes. If you were responsible for a patient that might have murdered an innocent woman, when you were standing right next to her, would you be *that* happy?" He glanced over at Hart, who threw her seatbelt on.

"He seemed more nervous to me, and overly friendly. Certainly nicer than Glenda. He doesn't seem the type to have dealings with the police often." She clicked the seatbelt into position, sat back, and chewed her lip. Her 'deep in thought' face.

"Yeah, maybe that's all it is."

"He was probably worried we'd shut him down or something." Hart shrugged and checked the empty car park was clear twice before rolling off the gravel. A remnant of her paranoia after hitting a bollard a few months ago while reversing out of a factory car park.

"Mmm." Swanson shuffled back in his seat and returned to gazing out of the window. He would've killed for five minutes of peace to think things through.

"Where am I going, anyway? Shall I take you home?" She asked as they reached the dirt road for the fourth time that day. He was sick of this road. Of Adrenna. Of not having any peace. He rubbed the deep throb at the back of his head.

"No. I'm feeling loads better. Let's go back to the station. I'll drive home." The call of his quiet cottage was too hard to resist.

"Are you sure?" He felt her eyeing him suspiciously.

He nodded. "I'm sensible enough to pull over if I need to, Ma'am."

"You look better. Not as deathly grey as you looked this morning. Still butt ugly, though." She chuckled at her own joke.

"Hilarious, Robin."

"I am indeed, Krypto."

The traffic in the city was quiet. It was the deceiving calm right before the rush hour storm began at 4pm. Hart continued to eyeball him once they'd reached the police station car park and walked over to his black Audi. She passed him his car keys slowly, as if about to change her mind. He snatched them from her before she could. Wrestling a female coworker in the car park wouldn't be a good look for him.

"I'm going to call you in thirty minutes flat," she said before taking a step back to watch him as if he were a patient from Adrenna.

He nodded and jumped into his car. He threw an over the top wave her way as he rolled out of the station car park. She stuck her middle finger up. Being back in his own car gave him a sense of control that had been severely lacking throughout the day. In particular, the ability to control the heater.

Summer crossed his mind. Should he go back to the hospital? Would she even want him there? He couldn't very well sit next to her mum. What would he say to her? He knew her mum didn't know about their meetings to discuss finding Eddie, as she had no idea Summer was looking for him.

So he raced to his cottage instead, beating a further downfall of rain as he pulled up on his drive. He rushed inside and slammed the door behind him, not bothering to lock it, and kicked off his loafers at the bottom of the staircase.

The cottage was cold having sat in the low December temperatures empty and so with no heating on. He flicked on the central heating, then went to the kitchen to fill a pint glass with tap water. The water was bracing as it ran down his throat. He couldn't remember ever buying a pint glass in his life, and yet somehow he had half a shelf full of them in his cupboard.

The old floorboards creaked as he walked over to the sofa and took a seat where Hart perched earlier that day. Happy that he was sitting back where he belonged. He pulled out his laptop from underneath the ancient coffee table, which was yet another thing he didn't remember buying.

Hart said that the original doctor of Adrenna died 30 years ago, and his son died 20 years ago. Both were stabbed to death in the same room, and both were stabbed by a patient. Then there was the old man that nobody else wanted to admit to seeing. Who the hell was he, and how was he connected?

He blinked hard and held back a yawn. Christ, he'd already had a nap in the car park that morning, and in Hart's car on the first drive to Adrenna. The exhaustion was a killer. His tumour hadn't even caused tiredness prior to today. Maybe it was getting bigger.

Either way, sleep would have to wait. He needed to do something useful for Summer and if he wasn't able to get to the patient who'd actually hurt her, or visit her, research would have to do. He opened up Google and typed Adrenna hospital into the search bar. As he waited for the old laptop to do its job, he drummed his fingers on his knee.

Almost a million search results popped up. He scrolled through the results until one caught his eye. It was entitled *'The Dark History of Adrenna Hospital'*. Interesting. He checked the name of the website. *Haunted*

Asylums UK.

He groaned inwardly. What a crock of rubbish.

He fought the urge to close the laptop and opened up the article. A grey image of the hospital appeared in a separate tab. It was a bird's-eye view and looked vastly different compared to the hospital Swanson had visited that day. It was the same building. The same shape. The same material. Yet somehow it seemed more peaceful, and grass surrounded it, not gravel, while one long driveway stretched from the gates to the impressive front steps.

The haunting turrets at each corner of the square U still stuck out. Raising up from the ground like some sort of monster from the depths or as his Sunday school teacher would have said, something from hell.

He tried to figure out which part of the building he had physically been in during his visit. His finger traced the right-hand side of the building on the screen, the side that had the steel door where they'd entered. A shiver tickled his spine at the memory of the door slamming behind them. The stairs were adjacent and led straight to the first floor. He moved his finger up the screen, roughly to the middle floor of the first turret. He had seen no stairs from there, so how did they get to the very top floor, and what was up there?

He grabbed a small notepad from under the coffee table and removed the pen that he'd shoved into the spine. He made a note:

What's on the top floor?

He scrolled down to read the article and skimmed through the introduction. Adrenna was one of the first purpose-built lunatic asylums in the UK, so it was super old, as he suspected, but it was the history section that caught his eye.

'Dr Brian Stockport was a renowned psychiatrist known for experimental psychosocial treatment with limited use of drugs. He took over Adrenna Hospital during privatisation in the early 1980s. He was well respected in his field and wrote many articles citing successful experiments with using small amounts of diazepam alongside different social treatments.

The history of the Stockport family is a sad one. Two years before taking the hospital over, in 1981, the wife of Dr Stockport was murdered by a burglar who broke into their family home just a couple of weeks before Christmas. She was stabbed to death in their downstairs living room. In 1991, Dr Stockport himself was stabbed by a patient he was trying to help at the hospital, and died. Two weeks earlier, the same patient had murdered a female nurse for the same reason. Both times, the patient stated the devil had told him to do it.

But that isn't the strangest part. Stockport had a son, Jamie Stockport, who took over the hospital after his death. Ten years later, he was also stabbed to death in the same room by a different patient. This patient also said the devil had told him to do it.

Staff and patients often report strange goings on at the hospital. Strange shadows. The devil lurking around corners. Flashes of old Dr Stockport lurking on corners. Is there really a devil who haunts the walls of Adrenna? It seems like it to us.'

Swanson scoffed. Yes. Of course, the devil is happily hanging out in a random hospital in Derbyshire. How can people believe this rubbish? Though Dr Randall had a book on his shelf... Swanson racked his brain. What was it called? *The Devil in Adrenna? The Adrenna Devil?*

He closed his eyes and concentrated on the image there of Dr Randall's office. He remembered looking at the bookshelf as he walked in through the door. Some books about psychiatry and... The Devil of Adrenna! That was it. The kind of stupid story his mother would believe.

Shit. *Mum.*

Should he tell her about the tumour?

With no children or wife, she must be his next of kin. Wouldn't she get his cottage if he died? And his meagre savings?

The thought of calling her filled him with dread. Though her house was only a few streets away, it must have been three years since their last stilted conversation with his stepdad, Ronald, in the background. Listening to every word. Always watching her. She might not even have the same phone number. He had spotted her once since, when he was walking through town with Summer a few weeks ago. She appeared from nowhere on the other side of the cobbles. Their eyes had met, her mouth opened, but quick as a flash Ronald appeared and she turned away. Hurrying off in the other direction.

He wondered if it would be easier to visit and get it over with, rather than call. But as he imagined himself walking down the slabs of her driveway, knocking on the door, and Ronald answering the door... he knew he couldn't face it. She knew where he lived. If she was bothered about how he was she would have visited him before now.

She might even be glad if he was dead. She wouldn't need to feel guilty about not seeing him anymore. Maybe she'd be happier.

Ronald would certainly be glad.

He sat back on the sofa, momentarily putting off his research at the thought of his messed up family. At least if hell was real then his real father would be there to meet him. And if the devil really was at Adrenna, Swanson couldn't wait to ask him all about hell.

He brought up a separate search and googled the book, clicking order before he thought about it too much. One day delivery, nice. There was definitely something off about Adrenna Hospital, and Swanson was going to find out what.

Swanson

Swanson opened his heavy eyes, but the darkness was all-encompassing. He couldn't make out a thing. His body ached all over and he stretched his arms with a groan. It must be the middle of the night. Once again, he'd fallen asleep on the sofa.

A rancid, burning smell infiltrated his nostrils. It clogged his throat and made him gag, forcing him to sit up straight on the sofa. What the hell was that? Had he left something in the oven? Meat? A red light in the corner of the darkness caught his half-open eye. He squeezed his eyes and opened them again to focus his blurred vision. The light needed to be turned on. He needed to–

Nausea heaved up from his stomach.

The devil had come for him.

Red eyes were staring at him from a horned and grotesque head. No mouth or body was visible, but Swanson knew what it was.

He tried to stand up, but his body wouldn't move. He was frozen to the spot. Sentenced to sit there and die without a fight.

"You're here for me." He heard his own voice say the words, but his lips didn't move.

The devil didn't reply, but it began to bleed. Blood seeped from the red eyes, just a few tear drops at first. Within seconds the blood ran like a tap, and then a river.

And still Swanson couldn't move.

The blood surrounded him and filled the living room floor. It rose over his feet, then his knees, and he knew he was going to drown in the devil's blood. He closed his eyes and waited for death.

And the heaviness in the room disappeared.

Swanson opened one eye, and the devil had gone. Instead, Dr Randall stood there, surrounded by a pale light. He wore a maniacal grin and pointed a grotesquely long finger at Swanson.

"The devil is here," he said.

"What do you mean?" Swanson again heard his own voice speak, though his lips never moved.

"You already know," Dr Randall said, and disappeared.

As soon as he was gone, daylight filled the room. The heavy feeling and disorientation dissipated. He was free. He stood up and rubbed his face roughly, trying to shake off whatever the hell he had just experienced. His work shirt was soaked through with sweat, as were his hair and beard. His breath came in heavy pants. *What the fuck was that?*

A nightmare? He never even dreamed, never mind had nightmares so vivid. Can you have a nightmare whilst awake? He rubbed his face again. He should have read the side effects on those damn painkillers.

He looked down at his crumpled, damp mess of a suit. It wasn't unusual for him to fall asleep on the sofa, but he usually managed to at least strip down to his pants first. He stretched and twisted to get his aching body to move and get rid of the pain in his neck. But the memory of Summer made him freeze.

He had to know if she was OK. He rubbed his tired eyes hard and forced them back open to search the living room for his phone. He eventually found it on the floor next to his makeshift sofa bed. Luckily, he'd remembered to put it on charge before falling asleep in a crumpled heap. He had one new text message from Hart sent at 8:00am.

Summer is stable. Go back to sleep.

The clock on his phone informed him it was now 8:30 a.m. He stretched again and yawned loudly. His head was pounding, and his tongue felt like sandpaper. Had he drunk ten bottles of beer last night and forgotten?

He padded through the living room to the kitchen and grabbed a large glass of water, which he downed in one go. He filled it to the brim again and drank another glass full. Flashes of the nightmare kept playing on his mind. What the hell did it mean?

The devil and the blood were fairly obvious. It was clearly something to do with Summer, Adrenna and that damn book he'd ordered. In his mind, images of Summer being attacked had been sneaking in since he heard about what had happened to her. So the blood made sense.

But why on earth would the devil be coming for him?

That was weird as hell.

He needed to speak to Hart. She might have some ideas. After she'd mercilessly taken the piss out of him for letting Adrenna give him nightmares, anyway.

A hot shower washed away the sticky sweat and made him feel more awake. His brain was working clearly again, his thoughts alive. God knows he needed to feel alive after one of the worst weeks of his life.

He left the bathroom feeling more stable and grabbed the first work suit he saw. The accompanying shirt wasn't ironed, but it would do. He sent a message to Hart to ask her to meet him in the station car park.

He rarely ate breakfast, but his stomach growled. Had he eaten dinner? He couldn't remember. He made a slice of toast and chomped down half of it before jumping into his car.

It had clearly been raining a lot in the night; it soaked the ground through. The sky was still grey, but that was fine. It suited his mood.

It wasn't until he was halfway towards the office on the A52 that he realised what was bothering him. It was now December 2021. The wife died in December 1981. Someone had stabbed the doctor in 1991, and the son in 2001. Each murder was a decade apart, and now someone had stabbed Summer two decades since the last murder. A familiar adrenaline tingled his skin. He punched in Hart's name to the centre console to call her on the hands free system.

"Morning, Krypto," she said in a strangely bright voice.

"What's wrong?" Swanson asked, momentarily thrown by her cheeriness.

"Eh? Nothing. I was being nice. Can't I be nice?" she snapped in her usual, more comforting tone.

"Don't be weird because I have a tumour. It's... weird."

"OK, OK. You're a dick. Better?"

"Much better. Now listen, I was reading up on Adrenna's history and saw all the stuff you mentioned."

"Ooh, the devil stuff and the murders? It's creepy, eh?"

He saw her smug grin in his mind.

"Yeah, and obviously not real."

She tutted, but he continued.

"The doctor who took over the hospital, his wife was killed in 1981. Ten years later, a patient killed the doctor. Ten years after that, a patient stabbed his son. Twenty years later, someone stabs Summer."

"So there's a possibility that the murders are happening every 10 years for whatever reason." Hart cut him off.

"*Attempted* murder in this case," he said quickly, "and yeah. I mean it's strange and a long shot and probably a coincidence. But I think it's worth looking into at least. Though we're missing 2011."

"Hmm," there was a pause, 'where are you?'

"I'm five minutes away from the station, but I need to stay away from Murray," he said.

"OK, chat to you in the car park in five." A beeping noise filled the car as she hung up.

Swanson raced through the last few streets and reached the car park quicker than he thought. Hart was already there. She was easy to spot in her long red winter coat. Glamorous as ever, despite her sailor's mouth. He pulled up next to her and she jumped into the passenger seat. He drove off, not heading anywhere in particular but wanting to hide away from Murray.

Hart started talking straight away as she pulled off her black leather gloves. "OK. Are you ready for this? I agree with you. And not because you have a tumour. That's purely coincidental. What are you gonna name it, by the way?"

Swanson glanced at her. "Name what?"

"The tumour." She turned to face him.

Swanson was thrown. "Why on earth would I name the tumour?"

"Because... it's a thing." She waved her hands around as if it would prove her point. "That's what people do. Jeez."

Swanson threw her another look. She was on form today.

She pouted. "Google it and educate yourself rather than looking at me all weird."

"I'm not sure me googling brain tumours is the best idea right now." He pointed out.

She shrugged. "Good point well made."

He needed to change the subject. "So, we need to find out whether someone who thought they were acting on behalf of the devil stabbed Summer."

"OK. I'll call Dr Randall, I guess." Hart pulled her phone out of her handbag. She fiddled around with it and put it to her ear.

"Hi, it's Detective Inspector Hart, I visited yesterday... Good, thank you. Can you put me through to Dr Randall, please?"

She fell silent. Swanson waved a hand to get her attention, but she pushed it away in a huff and ignored him.

"Hello Dr Randall. I need to ask you about the hospital's history, please. I'm aware of what happened to the two Dr Stockport's 10 years apart, and needed to know if there were any other stabbings in the last 20 years that resulted in a death?"

She fell silent for a moment. Swanson glanced at her impatiently. She stuck her middle finger up at him. The supermarket loomed in front of him and he suddenly swerved into the car park. Hart grabbed on to the handle above her passenger side door and shot him an angry look.

"Right, so nothing to do with the doctors?" she said, "OK, thanks for your help."

She put the phone down and sighed as Swanson pulled into a free space at the back of the car park.

"So?" he asked.

"Nothing to report, really. No other deaths other than a suicide and that was 12 years ago, so doesn't fit with the timeline."

"Fair enough. I knew it was probably a dead horse. Too far-fetched that someone would murder people every ten years. I doubt anyone's even been there that long."

"There is Glenda." Hart turned to look at him with a big grin on her face.

"Glenda?"

"Yes! The old bag receptionist."

Swanson grinned. "Yeah, I imagine she's been there a while!"

"I wouldn't put murder past her. Maybe the doctors didn't sign in one day on her register. A woman's been reported missing, by the way. The day before Summer was hurt. She's a nurse at Derby Psychiatric Unit. She worked on the bank sometimes and covered the odd shift at Adrenna. Bit weird, isn't it?"

Swanson's phone vibrated, and he grabbed it from the centre console. He threw it down and immediately kick started the engine.

"Woah! What's wrong?" Hart asked.

"Forest texted about Summer. She's awake."

The Servant

I stared at the text on my phone. The advocate wasn't dead. She hadn't been given to the Devil. The corners of the room blurred into a darkness I couldn't see through. A guttural scream escaped my throat and I let it ring out in the silent room.

Rage coursed through my veins and gave me a new strength. I closed my eyes and time disappeared. But when I opened them a moment later, panting heavily, the room was a whirlwind of mess. The table was turned over, abandoned in the corner of the room. My paperwork from months of research covered the floor like a carpet. The bookshelf was overturned and my precious books were stuck underneath it.

Did I do that? Or did He?

A sharp pain in my hand made me look down. Blood seeped through the cut in my hand. The muscles in my legs and arms ached. And I knew it must have been me who destroyed the room. How could I do that without even realising it? I had to get a grip.

That lying advocate would pay for making me lose myself. How the hell did she survive when I slashed her right in the throat, as the Devil had asked? A clean but deadly wound with a sharp blade. Well, it should have been deadly. Clearly I'd messed up.

The Devil would not be happy with me. I'd finally found the perfect woman and yet she'd resisted. I had to make it up to Him pronto. She would pay for her insolence. But first, I needed that detective out of our way. Once he was on our side, the rest would be easy.

Swanson

Swanson raced out of the car park and spun a left turn, barely beating another car coming from the right which blared its horn. He glanced at the driver in his windscreen mirror and saw him waving his arms about, but ignored him and continued in the direction of the hospital.

"You know, she probably isn't ready to speak to us yet." Hart reminded him. She clung on to the handle above the car door, her knuckles turning white.

"I know. I only want to see if she's OK. She's an important witness. She won't be ready for a full statement."

"Uh, huh. Maybe now you'll finally ask her out." Hart gave him a look.

"Shush," he said, his brow crinkled.

It didn't take long to reach the hospital. Luckily, it wasn't far from the supermarket. And it didn't take that long to reach anywhere in the city centre, really. Swanson sped through Kingsway, his hands sweaty against the steering wheel, and pulled into the colossal car park of the hospital.

Hart pointed to the side of the grass verge. "Pull over here. Let me park it while you go talk to her. She won't want to see me," she said.

Swanson snorted. "No way. I've seen your parking skills, remember?"

"Do you want to get in there quickly or not?" she huffed.

"Look, there's a space right there." Swanson nodded to a small space on the right-hand side.

"Pfft. You won't get this in there," she said.

"No, *you* wouldn't get this in there," he stopped the car, "if you get out now, I'll pull it in."

Hart jumped out of the car and Swanson forced his brain to focus for one minute as he pulled expertly into the tight space, and squeezed himself out of the car.

"Impressive. I'm surprised you got your massive head out of the door," remarked Hart.

"Me too," he replied.

He marched off in the direction of the entrance whilst Hart hurried behind him. His focus had turned back to Summer. Her face and soft voice filled his head. He entered the hospital and was surprised to find he remembered the way to Summer's room, despite the haziness of his memory when he walked there yesterday.

Hart followed behind him, mostly in silence, much to his relief. Though he probably wouldn't have heard a word she said. His mind was whirring as he waded through the sea of patients, nurses, doctors and porters and everyone else who filled the hospital corridors.

He reached the ward and looked over at the chairs in the corridor. Summer's mother was not there, nor Aaron Walker or her brother. He pressed the bell outside the ward door and waited for a nurse to buzz him inside. Nothing happened.

He buzzed again, and within a few seconds a nurse stalked over to the door. Instead of buzzing them inside, she left the ward and closed the door behind her. She gave them a small smile.

"Hello, can I help?" Her voice was notably light and contrasted with her stern face.

It took Swanson by surprise, and he felt his mouth fall open in shock for a few too many seconds before he closed it again.

"Yes, please. We're here to see Summer Thomas. We heard she's woken up," Hart said when Swanson didn't answer.

"Oh, and are you a relative of Summers?"

Damn. Why hadn't he thought about what to say? Should he say he's a relative?

"I'm... er Detective Inspector Alex Swanson."

"She isn't ready for questions yet," she said.

"Oh no, sorry. I'm not here to ask questions. I want to know if she's OK. I'm also a friend, who happens to be a detective." Christ, he hoped he'd said the right thing.

The nurse considered him for a moment. Then her smile widened, giving her a much friendlier appearance.

"OK. She has a couple of visitors already, so let me tell her you're here, and I'll be right back. You can sit in the chairs there if you like." She pointed at the chairs in the corridor and disappeared back to the ward whilst Swanson stared at her back.

Frustration filled him. His need to see Summer was making him want to lash out. He clenched his fists and stared at the door, focusing on it and willing it to open. Hart stepped back and he glanced around at her. He'd almost forgotten she was there. She'd moved over to the side of the corridor that was lined with chairs.

"I'll wait here. No point in me going in too," she said. "Summer needs friendly faces and rest."

Swanson shrugged and turned back to the ward doors, which he was almost nose to nose with. Had he been that close a moment ago? He took a few steps back and saw the nurse heading towards the door. She was still smiling, at least.

"She's happy to see you. Her other visitors are leaving, so you can come in. You can have a minute or two, then she needs to rest," the nurse explained. He looked down at her name tag which said Sally. She had bruising around her wrist, he assumed from a patient.

He followed her into the ward. Aaron and Summer's mother were inside the door. Her mother didn't look up. If she did she probably wouldn't have recognised him, anyway. But Swanson nodded at Aaron, who had a big grin on his face. He nodded back. Her younger brother followed behind them. He set his mouth in a straight line, and he raised his eyebrow at Swanson as he passed.

Sally led him through the ward to a small private room at the rear. His eyes were drawn straight to the bed, and he smiled his first proper smile in

24 hours. There she was, lying on the bed with her eyes closed. Her skin was even paler than usual, almost grey, and her hair fell limply around her shoulders. A large bandage took up most of the left side of her neck, but she looked peaceful. Serene, even.

"Here's your detective!" Sally said in a loud voice.

Swanson turned to the nurse, ready to shush her. But Summers' eyes flew open, and he forgot about the nurse. Their eyes locked together, and she gave him a small smile.

"I'll leave you to it. Just a couple of minutes, though." Sally wagged one long finger at Swanson before leaving the room.

He stood awkwardly in the middle of the floor, not really knowing what to do now she was in front of him.

"Hey," he said. It was the only word which came to mind.

"Hi," her voice was quieter than usual, and croaked. She waved him closer.

He stepped over to the bed and looked down at her. She pointed behind him, and he turned to see a couple of those plastic chairs he loved so much. Without a word, he reached out to pull one closer; the legs clattering against the tiled floor.

"Oops, sorry," he said as he sat down, "how do you feel?"

She waved a hand at her throat. "Pretty sore, but I'm OK. I need to get home. So hopefully I won't be here long."

"Why the rush? What do you need?" he asked.

"Joshua," she said, her smile disappearing.

"Oh, where is he? Is he OK?"

"At his Dad's. He'll be OK, but he'll also be confused, bless him. He hates being without me. And I hate being without him." She cleared her throat and shifted back into her pillows.

"He'll be fine with his dad, and you need to rest."

The sadness in her eyes made him reach out to her hand and grip it tightly. He looked down, frozen. It was warmer than he expected. Her skin soft. He squeezed her hand gently and put his own back on his lap.

"Don't worry, I'm not here for a statement. But I wondered what you remembered so we can get a head start on investigating what happened?" He got back to a subject he was more comfortable with.

She looked away, her lips pursed. "Erm, it's a bit of a blur. One minute I was talking to Andy and the next someone came at me from the side, hit me in the neck, or at least that's what it felt like, then not much."

That same uncomfortable feeling that had been bugging him since he visited Adrenna Hospital returned.

"Wait, what? Someone came at you from the side?" he asked.

"Yes. Andy was sitting there, but he was pretty out of it. He might tell you more to be honest. But he doesn't talk much. His medication is quite strong."

"Andy is in confinement for attacking you." He instantly regretted saying the words out loud. She snapped her head around to look at him, but winced. She needed to rest, not be bogged down by who did what.

"What?" her face crumpled in confusion, "no. I remember. It definitely wasn't him."

"Are you 100% positive? Don't take this the wrong way, but you're on a lot of painkillers, I presume?"

She let out a soft laugh. "It's not the painkillers. I'm absolutely positive. In fact, it's the only thing I am sure of, because I was looking at him the whole time. He never usually talks at all, like I said. But yesterday he said something to me. He said something about a devil coming for me? But he did not move. I'm sure of it. I think he saw someone behind me, because I heard another voice and blacked out."

"They said something? What was it?"

"Something about the devil. That voice definitely came from behind or on the other side of me. Andy didn't move."

Swanson's nausea returned. Why was the damn devil a constant thing in this?

"Do you know about Adrenna's history?" he asked her.

She looked confused. "Er... no. It's old, I guess. But nothing specific. Why?"

"There's been some weird happenings there. An old Dr went mad, then got stabbed by a patient. His son was stabbed ten years later, in the same room, by a different patient. Both times a nurse was stabbed and killed a week before. And both patients said they were doing it on behalf of the devil."

"What? That's so strange. So you think this patient knew about that and tried to kill me?"

He shrugged. "I don't know what to think yet."

There was a noise as nurse Sally returned through the open door. "Time's up," she said. Her voice was strict again, though she wore a smile.

Swanson glanced at her, and buried the urge to tell her to piss off. He turned back to Summer.

"I'll come back tomorrow?" he said.

"Yeah, if I escape before, I'll let you know." She winked at him.

Swanson reached out to squeeze her hand again, and didn't move at first. But he felt Sally staring at him, and Summer's eyes closed. One short cough from Sally made him shift to his feet. He stalked out of the ward and back to Hart, who was still sitting alone outside.

"How is she?" Hart's face was serious for once.

"She seems OK. A bit sore and groggy from the painkillers," he said, looking back at the ward.

Hart nodded and stood up with a stretch. "Let's get out of here."

He turned back to face her. "She did say something strange, though. She's positive it wasn't Andy who stabbed her."

Hart scrunched up her face. "What? How can she be so sure?"

"She said she was staring at him the whole time. He didn't move."

"Well, I guess that means we're going back to that damn hospital to see doctor smiley," she replied.

He rubbed at his beard and let out a deep sigh. Adrenna was the last place he wanted to go. But seeing Summer made him even more determined to figure out who had hurt her.

"Fine, but I'm driving."

Swanson

Swanson drove them to Adrenna this time, though not as fast as Hart had done. The snaking country roads were wet from earlier rainfall and he wasn't risking his Audi on those twists. They didn't pass many cars on the way. Rush hour was over and most people were now at work or back at home after their school runs.

The high walls surrounding Adrenna loomed into view, and an urge to turn around and drive the other way overcame him. The sight of the prison-like walls made his headache worse and the pit of his stomach filled with dread. There was a god awful feeling about this place, even aside from the fact Summer was stabbed there.

"We should tell Dr Randall to come into the station now," he said, "I'm sick to death of this place."

"Same," Hart muttered, "I agree we should ask him. Get his statement on record properly, seeing as he appears to be mixed up on who hurt who."

Swanson pulled into the car park and chose a space close to the unused front entrance. He raised a hand to the back of his head to dull the ache that had come back with a vengeance. He saw Hart glance at him through the corner of his eye, but she said nothing and clicked her seatbelt. They exited the car and walked around the front corner of the building. He let Hart walk in front of him so he could get a proper look at Adrenna as it towered above him. He wanted to stare it in the eye, get a sense of what was actually causing the sickening feeling in his stomach every time he was here. But the feeling became instantly worse.

Someone was watching them through the top-floor window.

Swanson took a step back to get a better view of the face, but the person disappeared. The curtain fell back into place. Swanson peered at the other windows on the top floor.

"What do you reckon is on that top floor?" he called to Hart, who didn't seem to notice him stop and was now a fair way in front of him.

"I don't know. Storage?" she replied.

He took one last glance at the window, but there was still no face. He jogged over to Hart. "I didn't see any stairs to it anywhere, did you?"

She shook her head and stopped in front of the side entrance. She pressed the buzzer and stood back, waiting for the friendly receptionist to respond. Swanson caught up to her. There was no crackled voice this time though, and the door stayed firmly shut.

Hart buzzed again. They waited, shifting on their feet and kicking gravel. Nothing happened. She put her face up to the camera above the intercom.

"Helloo," she said, waving a hand around above her head as if that would somehow help.

Swanson took a few steps back to the grassy verge and looked again at the top floor.

"Someone was watching us," he told her.

"What?" Hart stepped back to join him on the verge and looked up. She scanned the windows but looked down again and peered at him. "You're seeing things again. Was it an old man with white eyes?"

"No, there was a face in that window. I don't really know what the person looked like. It was a face." He pointed up at the top floor.

"Yeah, a ghostly face with no features... OK. You need to check your meds."

She stepped forward again to the door and pressed the buzzer.

"Third time's a charm," she announced, but she reached into her bag and took out her phone. "I'm going to call Dr Randall. See if he'll come and answer the door."

She raised the phone to her ear as Swanson continued to stare up at the window. He knew he'd seen someone, but who would be on the top floor? Were patients up there or staff?

"No answer." Hart broke him out of his thoughts.

"What the hell is going on at this place?" Swanson gave up on the window and walked forward to stand next to Hart.

She shrugged, one hand on her hip. "Should we wait around, do you think?"

"Let's take a walk around and see if there are any other ways in."

They strolled down the side of the building and rounded a corner to the rear of Adrenna. The wind wasn't so bad here, though Hart still held her coat tightly around her and shivered. Swanson took his woolly hat out of his pocket and threw it at her. She caught it mid-air and pulled it over her head.

Their feet crunching against the gravel was the only noise that echoed out into the silent surroundings. They happened upon another door, barricaded up with wood. No buzzers.

"Where's the secure patient garden?" asked Hart, "you know, like the one in that other psychiatric hospital in the city centre? The one that Lucy disappeared from."

He shrugged and continued around the far corner and down the other side of Adrenna. There were no doors on this side. He kicked the gravel as they reached the car park once again.

"Come on, let's try the buzzer again," Hart said, "one last time before we give up."

"We could really do with finding Summer's brother, Eddie. He was a patient here.' Swanson said as they walked once more to the grey door.

"Yeah, good luck with that," Hart scoffed, "he's long gone."

Once again, no one answered their buzzer, and the pair walked back to the car. Heads down and each lost in their own thoughts.

Swanson snapped his head up suddenly.

"I've got it. We can speak to Aaron. He hasn't worked there for too long, but might be able to help." Adrenaline reignited his brain, and he mentally made a list of questions Aaron might help with.

"Not a bad idea for once," Hart said.

"Thanks, Robin. He might even be inside the hospital as we speak."

"Call him."

His face dropped. "I don't have his number."

"Text Summer and ask her for it. I'm freezing. Let's at least sit in the car."

"You're always bloody freezing," Swanson mumbled. He couldn't understand how anyone could live their life always being so damn cold.

They walked over to the car and climbed inside. Swanson turned on the engine and put the heater right up, against his better judgement. He texted Summer to ask for Aaron's number.

"I guess we may as well wait here, in case he is inside." Hart sighed as if it was a massive inconvenience.

"She might be sleeping, though. She might not text back for hours, and I'm not waiting here that long. Let's wait five minutes and see what happens. If not, we'll go get a late lunch."

Hart's phone buzzed, and she lifted it to her ear and barked a hello.

"Where? OK. We'll be there soon."

Swanson raised an eyebrow at her. He didn't want to go anywhere yet.

"Someone's found a body. They think it's that nurse. They found her at the site of the devil stone."

Summer

The tears threatened to fall, but Summer held them back. She didn't want to scare Joshua off from visiting her.

"I'll come and kiss you better soon, Mummy," Joshua said. His serious blue eyes tugged at her heart.

"I would love that, honey. Maybe tomorrow if you think you'll be OK visiting the hospital?"

He nodded fiercely. "I definitely will be OK. Will you be OK without me now?"

"Aw, honey. I miss you lots, but I'm going to sleep and rest until you get here. I'll be fine."

"And when I come and see you, you'll feel better!" he grinned.

"Absolutely! Have your dinner. I love you lots." She blew him a kiss.

"Love you more!" he shouted.

She laughed. He thought if he said it louder than her, it must be true. She repeatedly blew kisses until he hung up the phone, and plonked it back on the tray in front of her and sat back into the cushions. Her eyes were heavy and thick with sleep, thanks to the morphine. She rarely took so much as paracetamol unless desperate.

The worst part of being stuck in hospital was being away from Joshua. She was lost without her sidekick, and although he was putting a brave face on; she knew he'd struggle to sleep away from her for more than a couple of nights. Though having her own room and being able to sleep uninterrupted was definitely an unexpected bonus of being sliced in the neck.

She closed her eyes and shuffled her head to get more comfortable. Her neck wasn't as painful as she thought it would be with such a wound. A constant dull ache acted as a reminder, though. And having been a side sleeper all her life, getting comfortable on her back was no easy feat.

Despite being in a private room, the staff always left the door wide open and the noise of the ward seeped through. Machines beeped constantly. Conversations were never ending. Then there was the general hustle and bustle of busy nurses, health care assistants and doctors. Luckily, the morphine was strong enough that her mind drifted off even through the noise. Images of Joshua and her cuddling on the sofa played on her mind, with Toy Story or some dinosaur film playing in the background.

Sally's voice brought her back into the hospital room.

"Hey- Oh sorry, I didn't realise you were sleeping! How are you feeling?" She peered at Summer with her head cocked to one side, and gave her a big smile.

Sally was one of the happiest nurses Summer had ever met.

"Hi, Sally. I'm OK. Just tired," she replied, her eyes closing again as though she had no control.

"Oh, good. Are you feeling up to another visitor? Your brother's here."

"Oh sure, let him in." Summer's eyes flew open again, and her heart warmed at the thought of seeing Dylan. He always cheered her up.

"Not for long, though! You need rest," Sally instructed as she swanned back off through the door, returning a few moments later with her brother.

Summer shot up off the pillow and shouted out at the pain in her neck.

"Woah!" Sally put her hands up, "be careful, Summer."

But Summer couldn't speak through the lump in her throat that had appeared.

Standing behind Sally wasn't Dylan, it was Eddie. Summer stared at him. He stared back. His mouth opened, and then closed. He dwarfed the small nurse. Has he always been that tall? He was so clean for a homeless man. His coat and jeans looked brand new.

"Hi, Summer," he said, and looked down towards the floor.

Sally raised her eyebrows at Summer. "Are they happy tears, or does he need to leave?"

Summer shook her head and managed a smile. "No, they're happy tears," she croaked. She waved Eddie over to her bed. He stepped closer but didn't move far. She swallowed hard and lessened the lump in her throat.

"Eddie! Come here," she ordered with a laugh.

He took another couple of steps forward and she reached out and grabbed his hand to drag him in close enough to throw her arm around him awkwardly. He gently placed a hand on her back.

"I don't want to hurt you," he mumbled into her hair.

"I'm so sorry you had to leave, Eddie," she whispered. The lump returned and this time, she couldn't stop the tears from flowing.

Eddie stepped back from her awkward embrace.

"It's me who needs to say sorry," he replied in a quiet voice, looking at the floor again.

After watching for a moment with a small smile on her face, Sally left the room and closed the door behind her.

"Grab a seat. Sit down," Summer gestured towards the stacked pile of chairs.

"OK." Eddie carefully pulled off the top chair from the stack and laid it gently on the floor next to her bed.

"We've been looking for you since Astrid disappeared. Where did you go?" Summer asked. "Are you OK?"

She looked him up and down, taking in his clean cut stubble and freshly washed, short hair. Someone had been looking after him.

"Yes, I've been OK. Better than I've been in years if I'm honest sis. I was in a hostel but got a flat with a friend I met there. I would have told you, but I wasn't sure… and I heard about what happened to you on Facebook and knew I had to see you."

"On Facebook? I didn't realise you were on there?"

"Yeah. I log on sometimes to check up on some people. You included." He smiled at her, but it didn't reach his eyes. "A couple of people have written on your wall saying they were shocked about what happened. I think Dylan put something on. I thought you were dead at first."

His smile disappeared and his face paled. He reached out and took her hand.

"I'm so glad you're OK." He squeezed her hand gently.

"I'd be better if my big brother were around to protect me," she replied. "Maybe we could sort this mess out somehow?"

He took his hand away. "I thought the same thing. You know I didn't bring that gun into the house with Astrid, right? I was trying to get her to admit the truth. I only brought a knife in case she attacked me."

Summer nodded. "I know, Eddie."

"If I speak to the police, they might cart me off to Adrenna, but you and I could at least meet for coffee now and then?" His eyes were wide as he waited for an answer.

But Summer couldn't speak. *Eddie* was right in front of her after all this time. It was as though she were watching the conversation from above.

"Summer? We don't have to meet up if-"

"-No! We can absolutely meet up. I'd love that. And you can meet Joshua."

"Yes, I'd love to meet him.'" He grinned widely and his entire face lit up.

They sat in silence for a moment. It was much quieter with the door closed over, though dulled sounds of machinery and nurses could still be heard. Summer took in the way his hair fell in the same awkward way as Dylan's. And the wrinkles she hadn't noticed amongst the action of their last meeting when he'd saved Astrid. Right before she betrayed him to protect herself.

"If I'm allowed to be a protective big brother now, I need to ask you something important," he suddenly said, breaking her out of her thoughts.

"What is it?" She cocked her head but instantly regretted the movement as pain shot through her neck. Had she pulled a stitch?

"Please don't go back to Adrenna. If I'd have known you were working there, I would have warned you already. It's a hellhole, Summer. You shouldn't go anywhere near it."

Summer kept her face poker-straight. Patients told her many things about the hospitals they were in and it was rarely true. Patients sometimes thought they had been kidnapped, or under a government conspiracy. Summer had to help them call the police. Hospitals were often corrupt to a patient with paranoid schizophrenia and dangerous hallucinations in their head.

If Eddie was paranoid about Adrenna, was Dylan right, and he was still ill? If he was, he'd *have* to stop hiding and get medical help. She squeezed his hand and prepared herself for the worse.

"Why is it so bad?" she asked.

"It's the staff. They're messed up. I used to think it was me, my mental health, my visions. But now I'm doing better, I can distinguish between what was reality and what wasn't."

"I know. The receptionist is awful," she agreed. "But the nurses seem OK?"

He scoffed. "She's more than awful. Glenda Randall is a matriarch. She's the lead psychiatrist's grandma. She was married to the original Dr Stockport before he went mad and stabbed himself."

"Sorry I'm confused. Who stabbed themselves? Is Glenda the receptionist? I thought that was the manager's name."

Eddie nodded. "Some doctor called Stockport in the eighties or nineties, I forget, stabbed himself. Glenda was married to him."

"She was married to the doctor that died? I heard a patient stabbed him." This was giving her a headache.

Eddie shook his head. "He tried to kill a patient as a sacrifice for the devil. He failed, then stabbed himself. And so did his son ten years later. Rumour has it that Glenda killed Dr Stockport's first wife, too. They are doctors who accuse other people of being nuts. But they're the messed up ones, Summer. The rumour is that Adrenna is home to a possessive spirit who calls himself the devil and takes over the doctors. Although now there's only one left."

"There's only one what left?" she asked.

"One Doctor from the family. Doctor Randall. And he's just as nuts as his dad and grandad before him."

Swanson

Swanson and Hart arrived at the Hemlock Stone in Stapleford twenty minutes later. Summer had replied with Aaron's number, so Swanson sent him a text to ask if he was at work. The two-hundred-million-year-old sandstone tower stood almost thirty feet tall, the top half black and the bottom half red. Otherwise known as the devil's stone because of the myth that he had thrown it from the nearby town of Castleton when the ringing of church bells across the town annoyed him.

"The Stone Cross is in Stapleford," Swanson muttered as they sludged across a muddy field.

"What are you muttering about?" Hart threw him an unimpressed look.

"The oldest Christian monument in the midlands is over there." He pointed toward St Helen's Church, which lay on the other side of the small town.

"Full of useful information you, aren't you?" She pulled one stuck boot out of a particularly muddy piece of grass, staring down at it with distaste.

"Yep. More useful than ghost stories."

She jabbed him in the side and stumbled off the grass, onto the path that led towards the stone. Someone had already erected a large white tent and various forensic specialists donning white gear swanned around the area.

"Do you know anything about this nurse?" Swanson called after her as he reached the path. He traipsed his shoe along the path to get rid of the muddy chunks.

She slowed her pace and turned around to face him. "Er, not much more than what I said. I saw the press briefing. Didn't you see it?"

"I've been preoccupied." He pointed to his head.

"Well, her name was Sharon Vaughan. She was fairly young, about our age, maybe early thirties. And not married, because her boyfriend called her in as missing. No kids, I don't think. Her primary job was at Derby Psychiatric Hospital, but she took the odd shift at Adrenna as a bank nurse when they were short staffed. She disappeared early Wednesday morning after finishing a night shift."

"The day before Summer got stabbed," Swanson mused as they reached the crime scene boundary.

A uniformed officer checked their ID's and allowed them to pass through. Swanson spotted a familiar face a few feet away. Detective Inspector Ryan Thomas. An ex-colleague from Nottinghamshire Police and a useful person to have on your side. He raised a hand to Thomas in acknowledgement, who grinned and walked over to meet them.

"Hi, stranger. What's the great Alex Swanson doing back here in Nottingham?" He laughed, and nodded to Hart, who was around the same height as him. She gave him a small nod in return. "You haven't moved back over to the dark side, have you?"

"Not yet, mate." Swanson grinned. "But we do think you have one of our missing persons back there."

"Yeah, I heard someone from Derby would come over. Didn't hear your name mentioned though."

"It's not exactly our case, but we are working on something else which involves… well, a devil."

"Oh, I see. That's a pretty strong connection. Well, we can't get any closer at the minute."

"Can you tell us about the note?" Hart asked.

Thomas looked around to make sure nobody else could hear, then repeated in a low voice, "The dogs always bark, and the violets die a death, when the devil brings the dark, and when he gets inside my head."

Hart whistled. "Well, that's creepy as hell."

Thomas let out a short laugh. "You could say that."

"And the body?" Swanson asked.

"The body was left naked and in no particular position. Someone has dumped it as it lies. There's bruising and a big wound on the neck so it looks like a slit throat. There's also bruising to both wrists, as if they tied or cuffed her to something. Yet they'd piled the clothes neatly next to the body. Forensics are all over it at the minute."

"So, the body was just dumped? But they'd taken care to neatly fold the clothes?" Hart asked.

Thomas nodded. "That's what it looks like. I assume we'll be sending over the images and forensics to your teams soon."

Swanson nodded. "Thanks, Thomas."

"This reminds me a bit of that case we worked on years back, my first murder. Do you remember? A naked woman in a park. The suspect punched you in the face." Thomas snorted.

"Yes, busted my lip." Swanson grinned at the memory.

"Turned out not to be him. We never caught that guy. Might be worth looking into it."

Swanson stepped away as Thomas walked off and motioned for Hart to follow him.

"So, we have someone talking about the devil before stabbing Summer. A woman, a nurse who sometimes works at Adrenna, murdered outside of the hospital. Her body laid out similarly to a murder from years ago. A history of nurses being murdered, right before a doctor gets murdered. It looks like history is repeating itself alright."

"It must all be linked somehow. What happened to the previous body?" Hart furrowed her brow.

"Hard to remember now. It was about ten years ago. But she was naked in a park with her clothes folded neatly. She was a young student, not a nurse, but we definitely need to look into it. I think I'll talk to Summer again. She might remember more as she recovers."

"Ten years ago? Our missing 2011 murder? I think we need to talk to Dr Randall, too. He might know more about the history of the hospital and he might be in danger as the doctor. Don't some patients get leave that would enable them to leave the hospital alone?"

"Yes, sometimes. It's quite hard to get it approved, though."

"Not impossible that they could have attacked the nurse on leave."

"No, just unlikely. Still worth crossing off the list."

Swanson thought hard as they crossed the slimy field back to his car. Whoever had murdered Sharon Vaughan sounded like they were obsessed with the devil. Before all doctor murders, a nurse was stabbed. And now a nurse, followed by an advocate, had been stabbed again.

"So Summer being stabbed could be a coincidence, and nothing to do with this devil business. But it's unlikely because she heard someone say something about the devil right before she was stabbed. Or, scenario 2, they were not happy with only killing this nurse, and wanted another woman for some reason." Swanson thought aloud.

"Like what?" Hart asked.

"Maybe it was a mistake with the nurse. She wasn't right, so he stabbed Summer instead."

Hart treaded carefully through the sodden grass as they left the path, trying to miss the muddiest parts. "But Andy is locked away. He couldn't have killed the nurse."

"But Summer said it wasn't Andy who hurt her. We need to know what patients were on that ward, and if any are allowed unsupervised leave. Or if any have any kind of obsession or association with the devil."

Hart finally looked up at him as they reached the car park. "What if it wasn't a patient?"

"As in a member of staff? Don't tell me you're blaming Glenda." Swanson raised an eyebrow as he lifted the boot of his car. "Do not get in my car yet."

Hart snorted. "Wouldn't put it past her. And why am I not allowed in your car?"

"Here." He handed her two empty carrier bags.

"Erm. Thanks?" She said as she took them from him.

"They're for the floor. I don't want mud in the car."

She muttered something under her breath as she walked over to the passenger door, bags in hand.

"You're right, though," Swanson called over the top of the car as he pulled off his loafers and replaced them with the clean trainers in his boot. "We need the names of the staff on the ward and the patients. Whoever did this might have attempted two murders in as many days. We need to prevent a third."

He put his muddy shoes into a third empty carrier bag and threw them into the boot. No doubt he would forget they were there and be looking for them in the morning.

"Well, if this person knows Summer is alive, they might try to get to her," Hart called to him from the front seat.

Shit. She was right. Summer needed some sort of protection on the ward. The thought of her getting hurt again made him feel nauseous. His seat groaned as he jumped into the driver's side, when another thought hit him.

"Or, if they think Summer *is* dead, they might go after the doctor next if history is to be repeated," he said as he pulled his seatbelt across.

"So if it's the same pattern, a doctor's going to get stabbed soon. With the previous doctors, the nurses were stabbed two weeks prior."

"So if that is what's happening, we've hopefully got some time. But I think we need to at least warn Dr Randall that he could be in danger." Swanson reversed out of the park and pulled out onto Coventry Lane.

"I don't know if he is, but I find it strange that he didn't mention any of the history to us," Hart mused.

"Maybe he didn't know?" Swanson said, hazarding a guess, but it was a weak explanation. How could Dr Randall not know? He thought back to their visit to his office. He had been super friendly. His office was typical of a messy professor. He remembered seeing something there, though.

"The damn book!" he said aloud.

"You know what a book is?" Hart put her hand to her mouth and laughed.

"Dr Randall had a book. It was called The Devil of Adrenna or something like that. I ordered a copy yesterday. I conked out after and forgot all about it to be honest. Tell you what, I'll drop you off at the station so you can get your car and talk to Murray about protection for Summer. And I'll call you once I've gotten home if the book has arrived."

"Fine, but one way or another we are going to end up back at Adrenna, aren't we?"

Swanson didn't answer, though he knew she was right. That damn hospital would be the death of him. As long as it wasn't the death of Summer, he could live with that.

Swanson

Swanson carefully weaved the Audi through the labyrinth of inner city streets. Hart was trying to call Dr Randall for the second time after her first attempt went ignored. He glanced over at her and saw her expression set in a stubborn grimace.

"He's not going to answer now if he didn't answer five minutes-."

Hart suddenly jumped forward in her seat and waved a hand in his direction to shush him.

"Yes, hello Dr Randall. It's Detective Inspector Hart here. I'm sorry to bother you again, but we could do with asking you a few more questions. Can you come down to the station, please?"

Swanson heard the high-pitched voice of Randall, though he couldn't make out the words. He shuddered at the noise.

"Yes, that would be OK. Thank you, Dr Randall." Hart put the phone back into her bag.

"He said he will come down later today as long as nothing happens on the wards. He seemed quite happy to speak to us again."

"He's always happy, seemingly. Maybe I should sneak into the back without Murray seeing so I can chat to him with you."

"Yeah. You're great at sneaking. No one ever notices you when you walk into a room." She turned to him and smiled sweetly.

Swanson tutted. He couldn't deny she was right, though. "Fine. I'll go home. Call me as soon as he's gone," he replied as he pulled into the station car park.

He left the engine running as Hart jumped out. She turned to him before closing her door and gave him another one of her out of character looks.

"Listen, make sure you call me later. Or at least text, OK?"

"Jesus, Hart. Stop fussing. I appreciate it but I'm honestly fine." Swanson furrowed his brow and stared straight ahead out of the windscreen.

"Think if it was the other way round, how would you react? You'd want to know I was OK, right? So let me know. See you later." She waved, then slammed the car door. He watched her small frame stalk off to the entrance of the police station. She was right again, he supposed. It wouldn't be hard to send her a two second text later on.

He turned out of the station and headed toward his cottage. He circled Pentagon Island, intending to dive off onto the A52 towards home, yet something pulled him further on to take the exit back into the city. An urge to see Summer.

He considered what Thomas had said about the previous case in Grosvenor Park. They'd interviewed a weedy young student at the time, though his name escaped Swanson's tired brain. When Swanson pushed questions about his sex life, he'd gotten mad and punched Swanson in the face. His alibi had been watertight in the end, anyway. Swanson moved to Derbyshire, and they didn't find the killer.

He called Hart on the hands free and waited for her to answer. As usual, it didn't take her long.

"Hey, look can you look into that murder Thomas mentioned? It was at Grosvenor Park. I wanted to know the name of the suspects."

"OK. I'll look."

He hung up and found himself in Derby Hospital's car park a few minutes later, swearing once again at the tightness of the spaces. At least at Adrenna there was no one else around to park right next to you. Though there was pinging gravel to worry about instead.

He tried to forget about his car as he walked into the hospital and back to the lift to get to Summer's floor. His phone buzzed, and he tugged it out of his suit trouser pocket. He felt a little hole in the pocket and cursed. They were £45 from a well-known high street brand, and he'd expected them to last longer at that price. He looked at his phone and saw a missed call and a new text message. The hospital had left him a voicemail.

He stood outside Summer's ward and dialled voicemail to listen. His heart thumped in his chest as he waited for the message to begin.

'Hi, Alex. It's Dr Tiffin here. We don't have a date yet for your biopsy, but should have one by tomorrow. I need you to be ready to come in. I also wanted to remind you to take the medication I gave to you yesterday. It's difficult to admit that we're ill sometimes, but it's very important that you take it and don't allow yourself to suffer. I'll call again tomorrow to check in.'

Swanson let out a slow, controlled breath. No date yet. OK. He forced his mind to change to Summer, and buzzed the bell to be let into her ward. He saw the same nurse as before walking over to the door. What was her name? Sam? Sarah? She smiled and buzzed him in.

"Hello, Mr Swanson, wasn't it?" she said as he pushed open the door.

"Yes, hi..." he racked his brain, "Sally. How is Summer?"

"She's doing well. This way."

Sally led him through the busy ward to Summer's room and poked her head in to tell Summer he had arrived. He had a moment of panic. He really should have texted her first to let her know he was on his way. A wave of relief ran through him as he heard Summer tell her to let him in.

He stepped inside the room. To his surprise, Summer was sitting up on the bed. Her sallow skin made her look tired, but she looked much happier than on his last visit. He pulled out one chair and placed it next to her bed.

"How are you feeling?" he asked.

"I'm OK. It doesn't hurt as much as you'd think, actually," she said.

"Or you're super tough?" he smiled.

"Yeah, there's that too, obviously." She winked at him and laughed.

"Listen. There's been some developments." He stopped. How on earth was he going to word it without scaring her?

"OK. Go on?"

"Well, if you said it wasn't Andy who did this, we need to find out who it was. And that means we need to put an officer near you for a night or two to ensure whoever it was doesn't come back."

'So, do you think he might come after me again?' Her eyes widened.

He was silent for a moment, and caught sight of her pale hand in front of him. He reached out before he considered what he was doing and wrapped his hand around hers.

"I will not let that happen, Summer." He squeezed her hand. "Hart is with Murray right now asking for someone to sit with you. Or at least outside the ward."

Her eyes flickered downward to their entwined hands. She pushed her thumb out from under his hand and wrapped it around his palm.

"I have something to tell you." She didn't look up. "Eddie... left me a message. He said not to go back to Adrenna. It's dangerous. He said the receptionist is the wife of the old doctor who took it over in the 80s, and she killed his first wife. He also said that the doctor went mad and tried to kill a patient, and stabbed himself when he failed. And ten years later, his son did the same thing."

Swanson tensed and pulled his hand away from her, leaning back in his chair. "That's not what I read," he frowned, "and how did Eddie get a message to you?"

"He said some patients believe the devil himself lives there, and he's in the walls. Inescapable. If he chooses you then you have to do what he says." She shuddered. "I always hated going there."

"Maybe he's right. It isn't a safe place to work."

"You're the third person to say that in as many days." She turned away and shuffled back into the pillows.

"Well, you are in a hospital bed," he pointed out.

She laughed softly. "Yes, I can't argue with that, can I?"

"Did Eddie say anything else in this message that you're refusing to tell me how he delivered?" He wondered if Eddie had the balls to come and visit Summer in the hospital. Surely not?

"He said Glenda, the receptionist, is Dr Randall's gran. She was married to the original doctor, and Randall was his grandson, but changed his name somehow. Or just lies about his name. He wasn't really sure."

"Dr Brian Stockport? Dr Randall is his grandson? That nasty receptionist is his gran?"

Summer nodded, but winced and put her hand to her neck.

"You OK?" Swanson asked, though his brain was whirring. Little jigsaw pieces of information flew around his thoughts in a whirlwind.

"I'm fine." She put her hand down and rearranged her head on the pillows once more.

He gritted his teeth and forced his face to stay neutral to not alert Summer. He stood up and gave her hand one last squeeze before he walked away. "I'll let you get some rest. If you remember anything else, call me. No matter what time, OK?"

"Oh, I did remember something else actually," she called out as he was halfway towards the door.

He turned to face her.

She continued. "I meant to text you but I forgot. It's the morphine making me dozy. The devil brings the dark."

"Sorry, what?"

"The devil brings the dark. I think that's the last thing I heard. The muttering I mentioned about the devil? The devil brings the dark and gets inside my head."

Swanson didn't respond, didn't move.

"Are you OK?" Summer asked.

"Er, yes. Sorry. That's a weird thing to say, isn't it? Look, I need to go but I'll catch up with you soon. Let me know if you remember anything else, or need anything. An officer should sit outside the ward soon."

He walked off without waiting for a response. The familiar adrenaline of getting closer to the culprit was rushing over him. This was their proof that whoever was involved with the murder of Sharon Vaughan was also involved with stabbing Summer. Now, he had to find out who on that ward was obsessed with the devil. And if Dr Randall was the grandson of Brian Stockport, he must be intertwined with the story somehow. He might be the next one to die.

Swanson

Dusk fell as Swanson crawled through the tail end of the rush hour on the A52. The clock on his dashboard ticked past 6pm. Aaron hadn't texted back about whether he was in Adrenna, but it didn't matter now.

Randall had agreed to meet Hart in the station for a chat at 6:30pm. Swanson texted her a list of questions and told her about Summer's update. Now it was a waiting game. So he headed four miles east to the sleepy town of Ockbrook, where his cottage lay close to the top of the hill. It was half-hidden by the nave roof of the stunning Moravian Church building. Ockbrook was home to one of very few Moravian settlements in the UK, something Swanson tried not to think about since his last conversation with his very religious, and estranged, mother. She wasn't part of the settlement, but any church acted as a reminder.

He pulled into the driveway and stretched as he got out of the Audi. His eyes felt heavy already, such was the stress of the week so far. The air was still thick with the earthy smell of petrichor.

But the hair on the back of Swanson's neck raised despite the musty air, and he peered at the narrow street behind him, unable to shake a feeling that eyes were on him from somewhere.

There were no street lamps near his cottage on Bay Lane, and the tall church blocked out what little was left of the natural light. He watched for a moment, but nothing appeared.

He walked over to the front door, and there, on the doorstep, was a brown package. He picked it up, relieved it was heavy enough to be a book.

"The Devil of Adrenna," he muttered, "I'll be getting to know you soon."

He took one last look behind him before entering the cottage. The streets were still other than an overly fluffy cat sitting on the opposite side of the road. It stopped licking its front paw and peered at Swanson with untrusting eyes. He glared back for a moment, then disappeared inside the cottage, slamming the door behind him.

He kicked off his shoes as soon as he got inside, leaving them by the bottom of the open staircase in front of the doorway. The cottage was too small for a hallway. It was more of a 'hallsquare'. He walked through the wonky lounge to the kitchen, which was just as crooked, and tore the strip off the brown package from the doorstep. A small book fell out when he turned the package upside down.

The Devil of Adrenna was only an inch thick. He flicked it open and breathed in the new book smell. It had been a long time since he'd read a book thanks to work and general adult duties, but as a child that woody scent had been his favourite smell

He flicked through the pages and took in the detailed pictures of Adrenna in its heyday. The writing was fairly large, it wouldn't take too long for him to skim through. He'd pored through much bigger books in a couple of days as a teenager. He flicked through the introduction first, which went into the history of the development of the hospital.

From the late 1960s, the various asylums in the UK were closed down and emptied - of the living, at least.

Swanson rolled his eyes, but kept flicking through. He read more carefully as he got to the next chapter.

There are few buildings which remain and are used as modern day psychiatric hospitals, but Adrenna is one that lives to tell the tale. It doesn't take much to realise the rumours must be true. One step into the gardens of this beautiful building and you know that something is watching you.

The face in the window of the top floor at Adrenna came to Swanson. He shuddered, despite his belief that ghosts weren't real. He couldn't disagree that the feeling of being watched stayed with him. He looked up at the kitchen window. The plain green curtains were wide open, though all he saw in the window was his reflection. Anyone could stare right at him and he wouldn't have a clue. He walked over to the window and closed them tight, before double checking he'd locked the back door. Then he leant back on the kitchen counter and continued to read.

The book moved on to a quick overview of the victims of the Adrenna stabbings. At the last paragraph, he froze. He flicked his eyes back to the start of the line to re-read, but there it was in black and white.

This book will go into more detail about each victim, but one thing was the same for each one. The calling card of the devil himself. A poem, left by those who he has haunted:

'The dogs always bark,
And the violets die a death,
When the devil brings the dark,
And when he gets inside my head.'

Swanson

Swanson sent a quick text to Hart to remind her to call him about Dr Randall as soon as their interview was complete and crossed the cottage to the living room. He closed the curtains, which were the same plain green as the kitchen, and flicked on the TV for some background noise. Celebrity Catchphrase played out, though he only recognised one contestant, an ex-soap star. The laptop clanged off the side of the coffee table as he pulled it out from the underneath storage section, and he sunk into the end seat of his two-seater sofa, ignoring the creak it gave under his weight.

He tapped his leg as he waited for Google to load. The laptop always took a minute or two to get going. He watched the catchphrase contestants try to guess what the screen was showing. A stunt bike rider flew up and down a skate ramp, before taking off his helmet to reveal a winking devil. *'Daredevil'* shouted one contestant. Even watching random TV programs he couldn't get away from the devil.

He tore his eyes away and focused on his laptop. He typed in the words of the devil's poem and waited for the results to pop up. But a faint knocking sound made his head shoot up again.

Was that an actual knock at *his* door?

If there was one thing he didn't get, ever, it was unannounced visitors. He stared at the door. It didn't move. Had he expected it to?

It must be bloody charity door knockers. They would go away if he ignored it. There was no way he was dealing with salespeople right now. He looked back at the laptop and tried to focus on the random results that had popped up. Nothing seemed to match.

Knock. Knock. Knock.

Swanson threw the laptop to his side and stood up. He stared at the door for a moment angrily, building up to answer it and make the caller go away. He stalked over and yanked it open, ready to let loose at a cold seller who had ignored his signs.

A stocky woman in her fifties stood there, with the same fine hair and light eyes as him. Eyes that were peering nervously up at him. He sucked in a breath, and his body went rigid.

Was he dreaming again?

"Hi, Alex," she said, her voice soft.

"Mum?" His voice came out much higher than usual.

"Hi," she said again. She looked down at the ground and tucked a stray hair behind her ear. "I'm sorry for randomly turning up."

He said nothing at first. He had an urge to reach out and touch her, to make sure she was real. But he didn't want her to think he was losing the plot. Even though he might be, with old blind men following him around. She returned her gaze to him.

"Is something wrong? Are you OK?" Swanson racked his brain for any reason his mother would turn up unannounced at his doorstep after they'd barely spoken in forever. "Is Aunt Barb OK?"

She nodded and tucked a stray piece of flyaway hair behind her ear. "Yes, yes. Everyone is fine. But... are you OK?"

"Yes, of course." His face crumpled in confusion. "Why wouldn't I be?"

"I don't know. I felt a need to check." She fell silent.

It didn't happen often, but his mind went blank. He could interrogate all the 'no comment' givers all day long, yet here he was lost for words with his own mother. She said nothing either. He cursed himself. She peered up at him, and he cleared his throat. Her perfume seeped through. He hadn't smelt that in three years.

"Want to come in?" he asked, suddenly wanting to keep the smell. To hear her laugh. Maybe even to tell her about the tumour.

"Oh no, you don't need to invite me in." She waved a hand.

He hesitated, opened his mouth, then closed it again. He studied the woman in front of him. Since their last argument, he'd thought about her a lot. More wrinkles lined her face now. Her hands looked fragile as she clasped them together. If anything were to happen to her…

"No. It's OK. Come in, if you want to?" he said.

She peeked behind him shyly. "Do you live alone? I actually thought I saw you a few weeks ago… with a woman? I didn't want to intrude."

His cheeks flushed with warmth. "Yes, but I'm sure Aunt Barb keeps you updated on that front."

She laughed softly. He felt a lump in his throat. It had been too long since he'd heard her laugh.

"Actually Mum–"

"Well I–"

Their awkward laughter rang out into the empty street, and the lump in his throat disappeared. It felt good to laugh with her again.

"You go," Swanson said.

"I, well, I was about to head off. I wrote my address down though, in case you ever wanted to pop by." She handed him a piece of scrap paper.

He eyed her warily as he took the piece of paper with her address neatly written in black ink. Her handwriting had always been super neat. Not like his own, which was so bad he could barely read it back himself.

"I've left Ronald so, you know, it would be nice to see you. I know you'll need time to think about it, so I'm going to go, and give you that time." She hesitated, but turned around and stepped away from the front door.

Swanson stared at the piece of paper she had given him, unable to look back up at her. Halfway down the drive, she called out, "I love you." and continued on her way.

He didn't move from the open doorway as she walked away. He watched her leave his drive and disappear down the street. Part of him wanted to run after her, but she was right. He needed some more time. He needed to think about it and have a plan, so it wasn't too awkward. And he had to decide if he was going to tell her about the tumour. Once she'd disappeared out of view, he stepped back inside and closed the door softly behind him. He leant against it, worried he'd made the wrong decision. *Would she even want him to run after her?*

His phone buzzed from somewhere in the living room and broke his trail of thought. He looked up and saw it flashing on the sofa next to the laptop. He crossed the room in a trancelike state, his sense of urgency momentarily lost thanks to his mother's impromptu visit.

And he'd thought having a tumour would be his shock of the week. *Pfft.*

Though if he was going to be sick, having his mother around certainly wouldn't be a bad thing. After all, he might not be around much longer to make things up with her. And if he really was at risk of dying soon he wanted to make up with his mother. He should call Aunt Barb. She was great for talking things through.

Time seemed elongated as he walked to the sofa, as if an hour had passed when it had only been sixty seconds. He grabbed the phone. It was from Hart.

'Hey, no officer for Summer yet. Murray is looking into who to assign. Randall hasn't shown yet, going to call him now. Suspect from the Grosvenor Park body in 2011 was called Billy Logan.'

No officer for Summer and Randall was missing? Panic fluttered through Swanson like a swarm of butterflies. He grabbed his car keys and rammed his feet back into his trainers. As he left the house, he locked the door behind him and called Summer. He reached the Audi, and pressed the button to unlock the door.

The swishing sound of the car unlocking was the last thing he heard before everything went black.

The Servant

Getting Alex Swanson back to Adrenna wasn't as hard as I thought it would be. Not with the help of the Devil. I couldn't stop grinning. He would be a prize for the Devil and he'd be Summer's protector. I'd be honoured forever by His side. I studied him through the darkness. The light wasn't good down here, only one bulb worked and that was in the far corner. He slumped against the wall, his eyes still closed. I'd made sure I locked his cuffs tight. They were unbreakable, made for keeping severely disturbed people shackled up. He wouldn't be going anywhere.

Not until I knew what the advocate had told him about the attack. Then he would go to see the Devil. It didn't take long for him to stir and stretch. He groaned and the rattling of metal rang out, echoing through the cellar. I stepped back, suddenly unsure of how far the metal chains stretched. His eyes flicked open, but closed again.

"Hello." I tried to sound concerned, but couldn't prevent a hint of glee entering my voice.

His eyes flickered open again, and he tried to move an arm. The chain rattled and stopped short, making a loud clanging noise. His eyes suddenly opened wide and peered around his surroundings. And finally, he spotted me.

"Hello, Alex Swanson," I tried again. I could be patient. We had all night.

"Who is that?" his voice was dry and croaked.

"Dr Randall," I said. He needed some water. I picked up the bottle I'd left on the floor and opened it up, stepping forward. "Here."

I held the open bottle to his lips. He looked up at me and shook his head, his squinted eyes flashing with rage.

" Maybe later," I said, moving back towards the door and giving him some space to acclimatise to his surroundings. He looked all around the room and took heavy breaths, eventually his eyes settled back on me. The rage was gone, and his breathing slowed.

"Why am I tied up?" he asked.

"Well, because you're bigger than me, and I didn't think you'd listen to me otherwise. We need to talk. I have a fantastic proposition for you." I would have thought that was obvious.

"I agree we need to talk. That's why my colleague Rebecca Hart asked you to come and see us at the station. I won't hurt you."

He lied to me. I snorted and shook my head. "Of course you will. Why wouldn't you?"

"Why would I?" He feigned confusion, but I *knew* he realised what was going to happen. He must have some sort of idea, at least.

"Because I'm going to kill you," I said simply.

He didn't react at all to my words. He continued to stare at me, his neutral expression giving nothing away. It was impressive.

"What did you do to me?" he asked.

"Ah. Well, sometimes we have to help patients to sleep quickly if they need to settle down. I used an injection of Halmodol to pop you off to sleep so we could get you into the van."

"Well, I feel like shit," he groaned.

"Yes, it can do that to you. I apologise. But that won't matter for long. Water will help." I pointed to the bottle, which still lay full at my feet.

"Wait." His head snapped up. "You said '*we*'?"

I said nothing. Did I say *we* or was he trying to trick me?

"Did you mean the devil?" he asked.

"The Devil?" I asked slowly, unsure of what he already knew. How would he know about my connection to Him?

"Has the Devil spoken to you?" I asked. "Or was it her?"

"Who?"

"That stupid advocate who was supposed to die. Summer." I spat her name out, still furious with her. "Your friend, so I've heard." I watched his reaction. His face turned a shade of red, fists closed over. Yet his face was still neutral.

"It was you who hurt her, wasn't it?" he asked.

I chuckled. "No, of course not. It was Him. And only to give her a better life, Alex Swanson. Which is why I want to talk to you. "

"Who is *him*?"

"The Devil. He's been with my family for thirty years and now I'm honoured to be a part of our history."

"I know about the devil and your family."

I thought I'd misheard him at first, but I didn't. He knew. Had I been tricked? How could he possibly know?

"What do you think you know?" I asked.

"I heard about what happened. That your grandad and dad stabbed themselves. They thought the devil was after them."

I laughed. "Is that what you heard? That's not true. You've been reading too many things on the internet."

He shifted on the ground onto his knees. I took a step back, wary of getting too close even if he had chains on.

"Don't step back, I just have a leg ache. OK? What happened? Tell me the full story."

I eyed him with suspicion. I'd told no one the full truth before. It might be good to share the story. Surely He wouldn't mind because Swanson was going to meet him soon, anyway.

"You're going to kill me, anyway. You may as well tell me the truth."

"OK. I'll tell you the truth. But will you tell me what the advocate said about me? I need to know to protect us."

"Of course." he nodded as if it was the most simple conversation in the world.

I suppose I had no choice but to trust him. And even if he didn't hold up his end of the bargain, there were other ways to get the truth out of people, and the Devil knew all about them.

Swanson

Swanson fought through the thumping pain at the base of his neck. He struggled to pick out coherent thoughts through the fog in his brain. He gently leant forward to pull on the chains around his arms. They felt weak, old. And as he leant, he felt them weakening further. He just had to keep Randall talking.

"OK. I'll tell you," Dr Randall said, nodding his head as if pleased with his decision.

He looked eerie in the warm glow of one yellow bulb glowing somewhere behind him in the cellar. At least, Swanson assumed it was a cellar. Darkness hid Randall's left side, but his right was lit up with the glow. With his floppy hair, large glasses and white doctor's coat, he looked more like a mad scientist than a psychiatrist.

"Thank you." Swanson forced the words out in a calm and steady voice, though his tongue was like sandpaper. Bits of previous training sessions floated around in his mind. *Create a relationship. Get them talking. Humanise yourself.* He kept glancing at the bottle of water. It looked untampered with. He was tempted to risk it.

"When I was a boy, I thought the devil was talking to me in my dreams. I didn't like it. I didn't appreciate how special it was at the time. But my dad knew. He told me how special it was. It was him that made me listen to these dreams. Though Grandma tried to stop it."

Swanson swallowed. This guy was more messed up than he'd realised. Randall looked down at the floor as he spoke, and Swanson took a chance to peer past him. There was no way he had dragged him here alone.

Someone else must be close by.

"Glenda is your grandma, right? What did the devil tell you to do?"

Randall looked back up, and Swanson forced himself to focus on him.

"Small things at first. Steal something from the local shop. Trip someone over at school. It was all to test my loyalty to him, you see. That's what Dad said."

A shiver ran through Swanson. The air was thick with damp, but his shiver had nothing to do with being cold. "Did you ever disobey?" he asked.

"Yes. The day my dad was stabbed to death." Randall looked down again. His eyes were watering as he reminisced.

"So, someone else stabbed your dad? He didn't stab himself?"

"What? Of course he didn't stab himself," Dr Randall spat, his eyes flashing. Swanson said nothing. "The Devil took control of my grandma, and *she* stabbed him."

So Glenda was a murderer, after all. Hart would be pleased. It took him a moment to realise he was laughing out loud.

"Why are you laughing?" Dr Randall demanded. "Do you not believe me?"

Swanson swallowed hard and forced the laughter back. "I believe you completely," he said as sincerely as he could. "I think the drugs you gave me are making me act funny."

Dr Randall relaxed. "Oh. Yes, they will make you more calm. Do you feel OK? I know about the tumour."

"What tumour?" It was Swanson's turn to tense up. How on earth could Randall know about that? Only he and Hart knew. "Do you have access to my medical records?"

A noise at the end of the corridor made them both snap around. Swanson couldn't see a thing from where he was shackled to the wall.

Randall grinned. "He's here."

A shadow appeared in the light of the weak bulb, then disappeared quick as a flash.

"The dogs always bark, and the violets die a death, when the devil brings the dark, and when he gets inside my head." Randall lifted his arms into the air, eyes closed tight.

Swanson heard quick footsteps heading towards them. His heart raced and he pulled again at the shackles. Maybe his Sunday school teacher was right, and he really was going to see the devil.

The Servant

He was coming. I squeezed my eyes shut tight as I waited for the familiar icy breeze to wash over me. He would be happy with me today. And I couldn't wait to show Swanson how special he was.

"To be a messenger of the Devil is a wonderful honour to bestow." I told him.

"Why would the devil want me?" he asked. I sensed the fear in his voice.

"You're everything he needs! Vigilant, alert, serious. You need to protect her when he's busy." I felt the Devil getting closer. His presence was engulfing.

"Who am I supposed to protect? Dr Randall, please listen to me. I think we need to talk some more."

"Your advocate, of course. Summer." I smelt the Devil now. His stench was overpowering.

"How can I protect her if I'm dead? You're not making sense."

"She won't be alive for long. She is perfect for Him. Don't you see?"

"And why would she need a protector if she's with the devil? This doesn't make any sense to me?"

"You're the protector for when He isn't around. She is for Him, the Devil himself. Do you feel weak yet?"

"Why would I feel weak?" His voice was high pitched now.

I opened my eyes to take him in one last time. His face was ashen, and sweat dripped down his forehead. He looked behind me and his eyes widened.

I grinned. He was here. I turned to wait for Him. I took the knife out of my pocket and held it in the air.

Footsteps sounded in every direction of the cellar. Getting closer and closer, I closed my eyes to wait with the dagger held out in front of me.

An electric pain engulfed my entire body, and I cried out. My scream bounced off the cellar walls. And everything went black.

Swanson

Swanson had never been so glad to see Hart in all his life. She stood over Randall with her arm still raised in the air, taser in hand. He lay on the floor, unconscious. She dug her foot into the side of his stomach. He didn't move.

"Shit, I think he's banged his head." She looked over at Swanson. "Oh my god he's chained you up like a frigging animal."

He tried to form words but his tongue wouldn't work. She ran over to him and pulled at the cuffs.

"What the fuck has he done? We'll need to find the key."

"Water," Swanson gasped and pointed at the bottle of water.

Hart grabbed it and opened it up. She sniffed the bottle and held it out for him to drink from, the pain in his head too much to manage without a drink. At least if it was poisoned Hart could get him to a hospital. The cool water soothed his throat and the pain in his head lessened. He jerked his head back and Hart put the water back down on the floor.

"Maybe he has a key on him," she said, returning to Dr Randall's motionless body.

"I think I can break these. They feel weak." Swanson finally made his tongue work now it didn't feel so much like sandpaper. He leant forward and pulled with all his strength.

"You'll still have cuffs round your wrists, you donut, hang on a minute." She fished through Randall's pockets and triumphantly held up a key a moment later.

"Hurry please," Swanson urged, pointing his head toward the cuffs.

She ran over and after a few seconds of fighting with the old locks she released the cuffs one by one.

"Thanks," Swanson managed, though it wasn't enough to convey his relief. "I'll get you lots of chocolate cake."

"Never mind that. Do you need a doctor?" she asked.

"Well, yeah. To get rid of the tumour," he replied with a grin.

She tutted. "Can't you ever be serious? I haven't got my handcuffs for him. Have you got cuffs?"

He shook his head. He took a deep breath and put both hands flat on the floor, pushing himself up. The blood rushed from his head and he swayed as he waited for it to pass. He felt Hart by his side and almost laughed at the thought of her trying to catch him. It only took a moment for his vision to restore, and the dizziness to pass. He turned to her. Her concerned face stared up at him, and he put a hand on each shoulder.

"Thank you for saving me from that fucking psychopath."

She smiled. "Wow, you can be serious. You owe me BIG! Like I am going to go on about this for a long time. I don't go about getting myself kidnapped like a damn damsel in distress, so god knows how you will make it up to me. Also, I don't think you're allowed to use the word psychopath anymore."

He laughed. "I will find a way to make it up to you. Don't worry. And yes, Summer would slap me if she heard me use that word. How did you know I was here?"

"I didn't, not at first. Summer called me. She had my number saved because apparently you gave it to her?"

"Yes, for emergencies."

"Well, I would say I'm not sure what you think would happen to her, but after all the shit that has happened, I'll let it pass. She said you called her, but when she answered she heard some sort of thud and the line went dead."

"I forgot all about calling her, actually."

"I called, and you didn't answer, so I went to your cottage. Your phone was on the drive, and your car door was unlocked. Talk about alarm bells with you and your bloody car. Anyway, a lady came over–"

"A lady?"

"Yes. She, er, she said she was your mother." Hart looked at him as if waiting for a reaction. He didn't give her one. "She said she'd been round once, but came back again. And as she rounded the corner she saw two people driving erratically in a van which had windows that were painted black, and I remembered we saw a van like that in the Adrenna car park. Plus, you didn't answer your door yet your car was there. She waited around to see if you'd gone for a walk but you didn't show."

"Oh, I see." Swanson wasn't sure what else to say.

"And I worried it was something to do with Dr Randall cos I read your text and obviously he didn't show up for his interview, so I came to Adrenna and saw the van in the car park."

"Fair enough. Did you speak to Glenda?"

"She wasn't there, someone is headed to her home address. But someone had propped the side door open, and weird wheel marks were made on the grass verge. So I knew something was going on. Something had been brought into the hospital on wheels. Listen, you know how you owe me one?" she said with pursed lips.

"Yes?"

"And saving your life is the best thing I could ever do for you, right?"

"Spit it out, Hart."

"I messed up." She winced and looked away.

He shrugged. "OK... tell me what you did and we'll fix it. It can't be that bad."

"Er... I let it slip to your mum about the tumour."

He sucked in a breath and looked away. "Well. That is a mistake."

"I know, I'm sorry. It just came out. I was speaking to her, and I said something like 'the tumour could have made you faint again.' i.e. the thud that she heard."

He let out his breath in a slow, controlled sigh. At least the decision about whether he told his mother he was ill was out of his hands. "Not to worry. It was an accident. It doesn't matter."

"Yeah. And I saved your life, so we're even, right?"

"Right. No chocolate cake for you though after that." Swanson pushed his mother to the back of his mind. He'd worry about her later. "Come on, let's sort out the good doctor."

He turned to check on Randall and saw a space where the doctor had lain. He went rigid and stepped back against the wall. The low light flickered, and shadows danced. The room was silent. He pulled Hart back against the wall next to him and peered around the cellar.

"Dr Randall," called out Hart, "please don't run away. It's OK. We'll look after you and get someone to check out your head."

"And you can tell me more about the devil," Swanson added through gritted teeth.

Footsteps came from the other side of the cellar. Swanson jumped forward and saw the dark outline of Dr Randall.

He was right next to the only exit.

Swanson ran. Hart was hot on his heels as they raced towards Dr Randall.

"Don't make the situation—argh."

A clash rang out from behind and Swanson turned. Hart was on the floor. She groaned in pain. Swanson stopped running.

"Are you OK?" He bent down to check on her.

"I've twisted my ankle, I think. Go get him quick. That door locks. It doesn't open from the inside without a key."

"Shit." Swanson leapt up from the floor and ran towards the door.

But Randall was already there. He gave Swanson a serious look.

"I'll tell Summer you said hi, and you two will be together soon," he said.

And he slammed the door behind him.

It took Swanson a few seconds to reach the door. He yanked on it with all his might but it was no use. Even with his strength the heavy steel door was not moving. He reached into his pocket for his phone, but it was empty. Where was the last time he'd seen his phone?

He had no way of warning Summer that Dr Randall was on his way.

Summer

Summer lay back in her hospital bed having eaten a mushy meal of fish pie and mashed potato. She felt nauseous as the food sat heavy in her stomach, and resting her head back on the soft pillow felt good. The nice pillows were one benefit of staying in the hospital.

The stay hadn't been as bad as she'd feared. Other than missing Joshua, it was almost nice to have a break from the mundaneness of life. Though it was hard to sleep at night in the noisy hospital, despite still being in her own private side room, and her eyes were so heavy now from lack of sleep and morphine, she couldn't keep them open. She closed them and thought of Joshua. He wore his favourite dinosaur top in her reverie and laughed as he cuddled into her, his little body fitting perfectly with hers.

"Love you, Mummy," he said as he squeezed her far too tight.

"Love you more, baby," she replied.

A click of a door made them both glance up, and Summer opened her eyes. A tall man stood in front of her. He dressed like a doctor with the white coat and a badge around his neck, but not one she recognised.

"Hello there, Summer." A thick, dark stubble lined his smile. "I'm here to check up on you."

"Hi." Summer smiled back. "Sorry, I was so tired I couldn't help but close my eyes."

"Oh, that's OK. You need plenty of rest," the doctor said.

Summer smiled and waited for him to begin whatever it was he needed to do. Yet the doctor didn't move.

"Do you usually work on this ward?" she asked, breaking the awkward silence.

"No. I normally work with patients who have... more neurological disorders. I'm standing in due to short staffing."

"Oh, I see. I saw a doctor for a checkup before dinner, mind, about an hour ago. He said everything was OK? So you can move on to someone else if you're busy," Summer said, hoping he would go away. There was an uncomfortable vibe emanating from him, though she wasn't sure why.

"Did you? Well, that's great. Let me check if they have filled your notes out and I'll be on my way."

The doctor moved to the foot of the bed and pulled Summer's folder of notes from the holder that was attached there. Summer watched his face. His right eye twitched. She looked over at the closed door. The staff never closed the door unless she asked. The man looked up at her and their eyes met. A chill ran through her. Whoever this was, she wasn't safe. Her hand vibrated, and relief flooded her. She whipped out the phone from under the sheets and pressed the green answer button.

"Hi, baby," she smiled into the camera, "I'm here with the doctor, look." She pointed the camera at the doctor. She made sure the doctor realised he'd been seen in her room. Though it was by a child.

"Hi, doctor." Joshua waved into the camera.

The doctor's mouth was ajar, but he said nothing. He put up one hand in an awkward wave to Joshua.

Summer turned the camera back to her. "Get Daddy for a sec, hun," she said.

"Daaaaaaaad, come here." Joshua's voice rang out.

She braved a glance at the doctor. The way he stared at her made her want to run.

"Hey, you OK?" Joshua's dad, Richard, appeared on the camera.

"Hi, yes I'm doing OK, thanks. I wanted to say, can you call me back in five minutes? I'm here with the doctor, see?"

She pointed the camera at the doctor again and lingered on his face. He cleared his throat and looked down at her notes, pretending to be busy.

"Yes, sure. We'll call in five minutes. Speak soon." He gave a little wave and hung up.

Summer smiled sweetly at the doctor.

"So you're a mother?" he asked her slowly.

"Yes. Sorry about that. He gets really worried if I don't answer. We're very close! Don't know what he would have done if I hadn't made it."

The doctor put down her notes and stumbled backwards. "Oh, no problem. I can see your notes are fine, anyway. So I'll go now."

His hands were shaking, but he rushed off through the door before she said anything else. How strange. Was that her anxiety about being in hospital making it seem worse than it was? Or was he just a weird man? He left the door open, and Summer saw her favourite nurse standing outside.

"Sally?" she called out, her voice breaking because of her sore throat.

Sally made her way into the room, sighing and smiling as she usually did. You could tell with one look Sally was born to be a nurse. Summer had never seen her in a bad mood.

"Yes, my cherub?" she asked. Despite only being about ten years older than Summer, you'd think she was her grandma by the way she acted.

"A quick one. Who was that doctor who just left my room?" Summer asked.

"Oh, the tall one? Yes, what was he doing in here?" She glanced behind her as if to check he wasn't standing outside the door.

"He said he was filling in because you're short staffed. He was strange, to be honest," Summer said.

"Well, yes, considering I'm pretty positive he works in neurology." Sally chewed on her lip, deep in thought.

"What would he be doing here?"

"Who knows with these doctors, love? They help each other out sometimes, though. Usually they would come and speak to us first at reception so we can tell them about the patients."

"What was his name? He didn't even say."

"Oh, that was Dr Tiffin." Sally smiled. "I'm sure it was nothing to worry about."

The Servant

I sat outside Derby Royal Hospital and took deep breaths in a vain attempt to soothe my banging heart beat. My pocket vibrated. He was calling me. My hands shook as I reached into my jeans pocket and pulled out the phone.

He was going to kill me.

"Hello?" My voice sounded strange and far away, as though it didn't belong to me, and instead it belonged below somewhere, the way it echoed up from the ground.

"What do you mean, you've locked the police officers in the basement?" His angry voice was so loud I had to hold the phone away from my ear.

"I didn't mean to! It was the woman's fault. That stupid cow snuck up on me. I'll show her." I clenched my fist and felt the sharpness of nails digging in against my flesh.

"I don't know why I trusted you with Swanson. You couldn't even kill the advocate. You need to fix this."

"I can't kill them both. I need you."

"You don't need to kill them. Let them out and let them arrest you. Do not mention my name."

My mouth fell open in horror. He didn't understand. "I can't let them go! I told you, the Devil needs Swanson. You know this."

"It doesn't matter now. You bring only women to me, *untouched*. And I give them to the Devil. Your only other job is to get rid of the body."

"No. I saw Him. I told you."

There was a pause before He sighed loudly. "That was in your head,

James."

I scoffed. "How do you know which visions are in *my* head?"

"Because he talks to me properly. I'm not nuts like you are. Now go away and sort it out. Do not mention my name."

"No. They'll have no signal down there. They won't be able to call anyone. They'll get weak and–"

"And what, James? Die? What will the police do when two of their own are missing, and the last case they investigated was a stabbing at your hospital? The only reason I helped you get Swanson to your hospital was because he isn't someone I want looking into us. And if you did it by yourself you'd mess it up. And now you've messed it up, anyway. Yes, it would have been good to get Swanson out of the way. But I give the orders, not you, and now you've gotten caught."

My heart felt heavy as I realised the weight of his words. I had messed it up. If I got caught, I would no longer be of any use to Him. The only thing left to do would be to spread the word and tell everyone about my deeds. Recruitment might be my only survival.

"So the Devil will come for me?" It was more of a statement. I already knew it to be true.

"Yes, he will. You're in serious trouble."

"When will He come?"

"I don't know. But if you finish off the advocate, at least she can't talk anymore. Sally will let you in. Do it quickly. I tried but she's clever. She got me on camera. It's down to you now."

I hung up the phone. There was only one thing I could think to do. Kill everybody and run. That's the only way I might get away without going to prison and carry on doing what I was supposed to be doing for Him. The hospital loomed in front of me. It would easily intimidate most people. But not me. This was my domain. The advocate would be in there somewhere. Alone. Helpless. She started all this by not dying. Tonight, she will die first.

Swanson

Swanson continued to push all of his weight against the door, yet it barely budged. Adrenna was reminiscent of a time when such buildings were indestructible. One thing he knew for sure, he wasn't stepping foot in a fucking asylum ever again.

"It's not going to work. We need to be clever. I'm going to see if there are any signal spots at all. Sit tight. We'll get to Summer. Here's your phone, by the way. I saw it in your driveway." Hart limped over to him, wincing at her ankle.

Her words didn't have a reassuring effect, though he took his phone from her. He was grateful to be reunited with it, but there was no signal. Just a few missed calls and messages from Hart whilst it sat on his drive.

A scuttling noise echoed through the basement, and their heads whipped around to check out the sound. Short squeaks accompanied it and Hart looked at him in disgust with a shiver. She got her phone, turned the flashlight on and pointed it at the floor.

"Someone must know you're in here?" he said to Hart, "how did you find me?"

"I told you. The door was left propped open and Glenda was gone. I walked around the side of her office where Randall took us last time." She shuddered. "It was creepy. And I went to his office looking for him. Remember that door we saw there last time?"

"Yes." He motioned for her to continue.

"Well, that leads to some stairs, which lead to that door." She pointed at the steel door in front of them. "And a book held it open."

He studied the door and noted the cracks of light around the loose fitting top. He looked around for something that he could at least hit it with to make some noise and draw attention. If they were in Adrenna, there must be staff around in the wards at least. Maybe even Aaron. There wasn't much in the cellar. There were bars that ran from floor to ceiling, the remnants of old cells. He spotted a few more old shackles, though most were rusted or broken. He walked through the middle of the cellar, what he imagined must have been the corridor originally, and turned on the flashlight on his phone. The third 'cell' down had the most gaps in its bars, and broken metal tubes lay on the floor. Bingo. He grabbed a metal bar from the floor and ran towards the main basement door. Hart leant against the wall, with her bad foot in the air. She looked disdainfully at the metal bar.

"If it's sound proof no one's going to hear it, are they?" she asked.

"If there's light the sound will travel." He pointed at the crack in the door. "Stand back and cover your ears."

She raised an eyebrow at him, but took a few steps back and held both hands to her ears without arguing. Swanson held the metal bar high in the air behind him and brought it crashing down onto the steel door. The clashing noise echoed off every surface in the cellar and made Hart wince. He did it again, and again, until Hart couldn't take it anymore.

"Stop!" she yelled, "for one minute. It's too much."

"Just for a minute." Swanson's own ears were ringing. They might both be deaf by the time they got out. At least they'd be alive, though. As the ringing in his ears slowed, another sound caught Swanson's attention.

Slow footsteps. A flash of darkness against the crack of light in the door. Someone was standing outside the basement.

Instead of letting them out, the person was pacing. Swanson nudged Hart to get her attention, and once she looked up, he pointed to the moving light behind the doorway. Her eyes widened.

"Hello?" she yelled out.

The movement stopped, the unknown figure frozen.

"Can you let us out please?" Hart tried again.

The pair stood deathly still, but there was no response from the figure outside.

Hart looked at Swanson and shrugged. She stepped closer to him, gingerly putting her sore foot down on the ground.

"Maybe it's Dr Randall?" she whispered to him.

"I doubt it. I bet he's done a runner. Surely. Any sane person would," he whispered back.

"He's not sane though, is he?" she replied.

"Hello? It's the police here. Please open this door at once." Swanson tried with the unknown person.

"Detective Inspector Swanson?" Came a woman's voice. It sounded familiar. He racked his brain trying to figure out who it was. Hart stared at him with wide eyes.

"It's that receptionist," she whispered.

"His grandma? Stay quiet," he whispered to Hart. He raised his voice to speak to Glenda. "Hi, yes, is that Glenda? Can you open the door, please?"

Silence filled the air once more, and Swanson's heart deflated. She wasn't going to let them out.

Would she help Dr Randall?

"I can't." Came Glenda's beaten voice eventually. "I am sorry, Officer Swanson. But I have to protect my grandson."

"You can call me Alex. Why does leaving us in here protect him?" Swanson tried to make his voice sound friendly and neutral.

"You will take him away. But he isn't well," Glenda stated simply. "He needs someone to keep an eye on him."

"I agree. We can help look after him, you know."

"I'm not sure anyone can help him while he listens to his devil friend. He's just like his father, unfortunately. And I won't let my grandson end up in a place like Adrenna. The so-called care is appalling."

He bit his tongue at the irony of her calling the hospital run by her crazy grandson appalling.

"Tell me about his father?" Swanson asked. He got a nudge in the chest from Hart, but he put his finger to his lips for her to be patient. Glenda might let them go, if he could just convince her he cared.

"He was a troubled soul. It all stemmed from his dad, Dr Randall's grandfather. My husband met a tragic end in this very hospital after visions of seeing the devil. And the devil told him to do terrible things. He killed a woman here. A nurse. And he killed himself two weeks later. He couldn't live with the guilt. Our son, Dr Randall's dad, suffered after that. A few years later, he told me the devil had been passed to him. That he saw it, too. And he met the same fate. James was the one who broke the curse."

Swanson tried not to snort. He obviously hadn't broken the so-called curse at all. "He broke the curse? How?" he asked instead.

"Yes. He was fine all his life. A couple of years ago, he started going downhill. He made a new friend. Another doctor who tried to help him, but he kept getting worse."

"How so?"

"This Dr Tiffin gave him medicine to help, but it made him worse and now he only believes Dr Tiffin. He doesn't listen to me at all. I hope you don't think he's done anything to harm anyone. He wouldn't, you know."

Dr Tiffin? Swanson's head span. He tried to focus on what to say next. To focus on getting out and protecting Summer. He clenched his jaw.

"I don't know what he's done at the moment, Glenda. But you need to let us out so he doesn't have two dead police officers to worry about. And if you don't do it soon, another nurse might be killed and I won't be able to save him from that."

Again, there was silence. The shadow under the door didn't move. Swanson counted slowly to thirty. Still no response.

"Glenda?" he breathed.

He heard the jangling sound of keys, and the shadow moved. Hart looked at him with her hand in a prayer position and he tried not to laugh. He got Summer's number ready to dial as soon as he had signal. He needed to warn her, and he had to be quick.

Summer

Sally picked up Summer's medical notes from the caged box at the bottom of the bed. The same notes that were in the hands of Dr Tiffin moments before. She stood, tapping one foot off the floor as she flicked through the file.

"Hmm. He doesn't seem to have written anything," she mused.

"Can you make sure he doesn't come in again, please?" Summer asked.

"Well, I don't exactly have the authority to keep a doctor out. You look tired. Are you in pain?" Sally threw her a sympathetic look. She moved around to the side of Summer's bed and increased the morphine dose through her intravenous catheter in the back of her hand. The sleeve of her uniform lifted as she reached up, and Summer spotted yellow bruising around her wrist. "But I can promise to let you know if he returns."

Summer nodded. "Thank you. I know it's silly to be wary of a doctor. There was something weird about the way he looked at me."

Sally cocked her head to one side and sucked on her lip. After a moment, she said, "I'll tell him you're sleeping if he comes back. I won't let him in here unless I'm with him, OK?"

"Yes! Thank you, Sally. That would be great." Summer smiled gratefully.

Sally smiled back. "No problem, my duck. You go get some sleep now, OK?" She walked over to the door and turned to give Summer a wink before stepping out of the room, firmly closing the door behind her.

Summer smiled to herself and settled back into the soft pillows. Sally made her feel much safer. Her eyes were heavy with sleep as the increased morphine ran through her veins like a smooth blanket being pulled over her body. The room was far too quiet now the door was closed, and she found herself unable to relax even with the extra dosage. She flicked on the TV and an old episode of Time Team flashed up. Her heart leapt at the sight of her dad's favourite TV show. She'd always moaned when it came on as a child.

'Why can't we watch Sabrina, Daddy?'

But he'd say it was time for adult TV now and she'd cuddle up with him, anyway. He'd stroke her hair and she would take a nap, listening to the music and droning voices as she fell asleep. She wished he was here now, stroking her hair once more.

The familiar dull ache in her chest appeared, and she swallowed back a lump in her throat. She closed her eyes and focused on the familiar music and chatter of the Time Team crew, lost in memories, oblivious to her phone vibrating, or the creaking of her bedroom door as a quiet hand slowly pushed it open.

The Servant

I stalked through the hospital, not stopping to say hello to anyone. I kept my head down, sweat dripping from my forehead. Derby was a large hospital, and most staff didn't even give me a second glance. They assumed I was a doctor that belonged there. I took the stairs all the way, not wanting to be stuck in a lift with people who might spot the beads of sweat or the shake of my hands.

I knew where the High Dependency Unit was from my time as a junior doctor in the hospital years ago. It had changed little since, if at all. I pressed the buzzer and waited for the nurse to let me in. It didn't take long for a plump young nurse with thick black hair to arrive at the door.

"Oh, hello. Are you here to see any particular patient?" She smiled up at me, her accent rough. I spotted the top of a tattoo peeking through the top of her uniform on her chest.

"Hello, no, I'm here to fill in for someone. Can't remember his name." I smiled widely, certain she was going to see through my lie. To my relief, she waved me inside. Another nurse stalked over. She was older than the tattoo lady.

"I'll take it from here, thanks Bella," she said, and motioned for me to follow her to the reception desk.

"Right you are, Sally," Bella replied, and walked off in the other direction.

"I'm here for Summer?" I said to the nurse in a low voice.

"Yes, I know. Come here." She led me to a small private room off the left of the initial entrance to the ward.

"We recently moved her to this room because she's doing so well. She'll be out of this ward tomorrow," Sally said in a strange warning tone.

"Yes, alright. I know I messed up," I whispered back.

"Shh! Not here." She pushed open Summer's door and shoved me inside before anyone saw. She stepped in behind me.

"I increased her morphine dose. She'll be flat out so go do what you need to do and be quick," she demanded.

I stood open-mouthed for a moment. The last time I'd seen Sally Tiffin she'd been quiet and sweet. She was certainly taking a leaf out of her husband's book.

"Go on." She nodded at Summer and stepped out of the room. She swiftly closed the door tight behind her.

And it was Summer and me alone at last. Well, almost alone. The TV blasted out and interrupted my thoughts. I grabbed the remote from her bedside table and flicked it off. Silence.

Her head had almost disappeared into the pillow she'd sunk so far into it. Her skin was so pale it would soon match the white pillow. I watched her chest move up and down rhythmically for a moment. The rhythm calmed my own breathing, and I ran two fingers across the back of her hand. She did nothing. I wrapped my fingers around her hand and squeezed it tight. Still, nothing. Sally really had dosed her up.

So I continued to run my fingers up along her arm. The sparse little hairs rose at my touch, and goosebumps raised up as if she was excited to be touched by me. Maybe she knew what was going to happen to her. Maybe she already understood how lucky she was.

I traced one finger up her neck and across her cheek. Her skin was soft and smooth. And I knew what I was doing was the right thing. She would be a delight for the Devil.

I ran my finger back down her neck, to her chest, and caressed one breast. Still, she didn't move. I squeezed, watching her face for any signs of her waking. She didn't even flinch.

She was mine for the taking. I wrapped my fingers around the top of her hospital gown to pull it down.

But a growl stopped me in my tracks. It came out of nowhere and pierced my brain and I heard nothing else. I bent over, both hands flew up to my head to cover my ears.

   The Devil was here.

   And He wasn't happy.

Swanson

Swanson rang Summer again as he raced across the gravel car park to Hart's red car, but there was still no answer. God damn it. How could she be too busy to answer her phone in the hospital? Maybe he was already too late.

"Throw me your keys," he shouted at Hart.

"No way!" she yelled back, running behind him despite her weak ankle.

He stopped and turned around to face her. She also stood still and bent over, wincing at the pain in her ankle. "Now, Hart. I need to get to Summer before he does, and he had a pretty big head start. Come here."

She reluctantly pulled her keys out of her pocket and threw them at him as he walked towards her. He took hold of her arm and helped her to hurry to the car.

"I'll call the hospital," she said as he helped her into the passenger seat.

Swanson jumped into the driver's seat and raced out of the car park. Hart clung on to the handle above the door.

"Don't kill us both trying to get to her," she mumbled as she grabbed some spare cuffs out of the glove compartment.

Swanson ignored her as he flew down the country lane to get into the city. They'd make it in ten minutes if he was quick, and if nobody got in their way. Hart called the hospital and asked them to check on Summer and call her back asap, as well as calling for some backup in case Randall was indeed at the hospital.

Swanson made it to the hospital in eight minutes, abandoning Hart's car on the side of the entrance. The hospital hadn't yet called them back, and so the pair raced up to the high dependency unit, Swanson out in front and Hart still hobbling behind him. They ignored the stares and open mouths of sickly patients and staff in their blue uniforms. Swanson didn't stop for breath until he reached the buzzer for the ward. Hart was nowhere to be seen.

A few seconds passed by, and no one came to the door. He banged on the glass of the door instead. A nurse stalked over to the door. She put a finger to her lips and narrowed her eyes. He recognised her from before, nurse Sally. He flashed his ID against the glass of the door.

"You need to calm down please, Sir," she shouted through the door, her arms crossed.

He did not have time for some random nurse's tantrum.

"This is an emergency. Let me in now or you will be arrested," he yelled.

Her narrow eyes widened, and she took a step back. Her hand flew up to the release button on the wall, and the door buzzed open as Hart caught up with him. Swanson pushed open the door and Hart followed closely behind. He ran through the ward to the small private room at the other end, but as he pushed open the door, his heart fell through his stomach.

Her bed was empty.

He turned to see a different nurse standing behind him with wavy black hair, looking up at him with wide eyes.

"Where is Summer Thomas?" he demanded.

"Summer's been moved down there." She pointed to the other end of the ward. "On the right near the entrance."

Swanson moved before the nurse finished her sentence, but Hart was already halfway down the ward. Her ankle must have felt better because she darted to the other end and careened straight into nurse Sally and another doctor. Sally had her hand on the doctor's elbow and was dragging him towards the exit. She let go as soon as Hart ran into them, but he was certain of what he'd seen.

"Hart, that's Randall!" he yelled.

Randall cried out in fear and put his hands to his face as if he thought

Hart was going to hurt him. Hart jumped up and grabbed Randall's arm, pushing him up against the wall. He didn't fight with her, but he sobbed. His wails rang out through the ward as Hart pulled his wrists behind his back and cuffed him. She sat him down firmly in a chair near the reception desk, and he continued to sob quietly.

Swanson looked at Sally. "Show me where Summer is," he demanded.

Her eyes were wide and brimmed with tears, her whole body tremoured. She lifted one hand and pointed to a door right next to them.

"You come with me," Swanson said, grabbing her skinny arm and dragging her with him to the room. She didn't argue. He felt her shake under his touch, but until he found Summer, he didn't care.

But as they entered the ward, he threw Sally to one side and heaved. Summer was in bed, nestled between the thick sheet and pillow.

Her pure white sheet stained red with blood.

Swanson

Summer's skin was translucent against the shine of the bright hospital lights. Intense voices echoed around the room from the ward, but Swanson ignored it. He pushed Sally into a chair in the corner and dashed towards Summer.

"Don't move," he ordered as he turned to check on Summer, and put one hand against her neck to check her pulse. As he moved his hand across her face, he felt her warm breath tickle his fingers. The sick feeling in his stomach dared to lift.

"Summer?" He whipped off the blood stained duvet. Where was the blood coming from? She lay in pale pink pyjamas. They weren't stained or torn. He saw no blood anywhere on her body.

"It's not her blood," Sally said, sucking in a deep breath, "it's his. She's sedated with morphine. She's fine."

She put a hand to her mouth and sobbed quietly.

"It's 'his'? Who do you mean? Dr Randall?" Swanson asked.

Sally pointed under the hospital bed, and for the first time, Swanson looked down and noticed a small river of blood converging at the tip of the bed. He'd been too worried about Summer to notice much of anything else. He bent down and almost toppled back, unprepared for the sight that awaited him.

Dr Tiffin lay under the bed on his back. His skin was pale, and his face contorted into a scream. Swanson's nausea returned. That image would not disappear from his brain for a while. He took a breath, reached out and checked the doctor's pulse. But his skin was ice cold, his eyes wide open and unblinking.

"He's dead," Sally sobbed. "I already tried to save him."

"What the hell was he doing in here? Dr Tiffin doesn't work on this ward." He stood up and turned to face Sally.

"They knew each other for years, from med school apparently, though they've been best mates for a couple of years." She put her head down and sobbed hard.

"Listen, Sally. I don't know what you've gotten yourself involved with here, but you need to start talking. Tell me what happened. Is anyone else in danger?"

She shook her head and took a deep breath. "I'm Nick's wife."

"And Nick is Dr Tiffin, right?" Swanson asked.

"Yes, He tried to pretend to be the devil. He was trying to talk James out of killing Summer, but James got confused. I don't know what really happened. He pulled out a knife and stabbed Nick." she collapsed into tears again.

"You're going to need to come with us to the station, Sally,"

Swanson stepped back to the ward door to check on Hart. She stood above Randall, who was still sitting at reception with his cuffs on. He sat quietly and made no fuss. Hart was on the phone and looked up at Swanson to give him a thumbs up.

At that moment, a buzzer rang out and Swanson looked over at the door. Backup had arrived, and several uniformed officers stood outside the door.

***

Two officers took Randall and Sally away to the police station for questioning, whilst Swanson and Hart stayed behind to await forensics for Dr Tiffin.

"Have they moved Summer?" asked Hart as they sat outside the room where the body lay two hours later.

"Yes, she was a bit disorientated, to be honest. Not sure she had a clue what was happening."

"Christ. How much morphine did they give her? What a day." Hart exhaled slowly.

Swanson nodded, unable to add anything useful to her conclusion.

"We need to speak to all these nurses and patients," he looked over at her. "Question them all. See what they saw."

"Yeah, we do." Hart agreed.

He looked around the ward. Many patients lay in open beds, with no real clue as to the drama that unfolded around them. There were three open wards, with eight beds in each, plus six private side rooms. Doctors, nurses, health care assistants and other staff all milled around assisting patients.

"There's quite a lot of them," he sighed.

"Yes, there are." Hart nodded.

Neither one moved. They continued to allow the hustle and bustle to happen around them. Swanson's headache had returned with a vengeance, but he'd left his pills at home. He rested his head against the wall and tried to focus through the pain on what had happened tonight between Randall and Tiffin.

"Coffee first," Hart said eventually, "want anything?"

Swanson shook his head. "I'll wait here. There are a few things I need to get my head around before we ask questions."

She got up and walked away towards the kitchen that the nurses had allowed them access to, and Swanson considered what they knew so far. Randall killed Tiffin. They knew each other, and somehow Sally got involved. But if Sally was so upset with Randall for murdering her husband, why was she trying to help Randall get out of the ward? It still didn't make any sense. Somehow, he had to find the missing piece of the puzzle.

Swanson

Twenty-four hours later Swanson nestled into his favourite corner of the sofa. His thinking space. Usually, after catching a culprit he would feel lighter, elated even that he won the chase. Yet his mind was full of questions. None of it made any sense.

Why had Sally not screamed the place down when Randall killed Tiffin, her husband? And if she'd tried to revive him, how come she wasn't covered in blood?

The buzz of his phone ringing tickled his leg, pulling him out of his thoughts. He checked the caller ID before answering, Hart.

"I'm done with Glenda," she said, "she knows he has visions involving the devil but vehemently denies he's done anything to hurt anyone or that she killed Stockport's first wife. She didn't really want visitors in the hospital because of it, though."

"True protective grandma style?"

"Yep. So she was no help, really. But we've got Sally in soon, so that will be interesting."

"Mmm. I was thinking about why she would help Randall clean up the room and escape after murdering her husband." Swanson peered out of his window. Right at the spot Randall had knocked him out. He supposed it was Tiffin who helped him. He needed someone stronger than Sally. But why would Tiffin have wanted to hurt Swanson, unless he really did see the devil too?

"Yes, it is strange. I know Tiffin was giving Randall medicines to help him with his visions, but Glenda said he got worse, and so did his erratic behaviour."

"Well, yes. He did murder a nurse *and* a doctor, attempt to murder an advocate and a police officer. He's clearly not all there, but he is sane enough to make plans and hide what he was doing. Quite ingenious for someone whose mental health is so poor their thoughts must be all over the place." Swanson thought aloud. "Funny really, because my own symptoms were also worse after taking Dr Tiffin's prescription medicine."

Hell, the dizziness never even occurred until he'd started taking the tablets. And there was that damn old man he kept seeing. He actually felt better in the last 24 hours from not taking them.

Wait a minute. He really did feel better for not taking them.

"I'll call you back in a minute, Hart," he said, jumping up off the sofa.

He pulled out the pills the doctor had given him and read the side of the bottle. He hadn't bothered before with so much else on his mind, but kicked himself now. The label on the side read:

Tramadol.

Hmm.

That seemed normal enough. He'd definitely heard of Tramadol, though it wasn't something he'd taken before. He brought up Google to check it out and clicked on to the NHS website. The side effects listed were dizziness, nausea, headaches… the list went on.

His eyes flicked down to serious side effects. Extreme dizziness. Hallucinations. Seeing or hearing things that aren't there.

The man with white eyes? Was that what he was?

He checked the dosage of the pills. The label read as 50mg tablets. He pulled out one long, oval-shaped pill and peered at it. It looked like the image of a white tablet on the screen in front of him, but as he leaned in he realised the number on the pill said 400mg. A lot more than 50mg.

He checked the standard dosages on the NHS site. 50mg was the normal measure for pain that comes and goes. Which is what Swanson's pain did.

The 400mg tablets were slow release, and should be taken once a day only, starting off at 100mg a day until your body got used to it.

Well, Dr Tiffin never mentioned that. Why would he not mention that?

Swanson had been taking two at a time. Unless he wanted Swanson to be disoriented?

But *why* would he want Swanson to feel like that? He grabbed his phone to give Hart a call.

"Hello Mr yes I'm just going to randomly hang up," she grumbled.

"Sorry about that. Listen, Dr Tiffin gave me some medicine for pain relief. He said to take a couple of tablets whenever I needed it. It turns out it's 400mg of slow release Tramadol. He either made a very unlikely mistake or he's been spiking me."

"What? And I thought he was the good doctor?"

"So did I, but there you go. And a mistake this big by someone with his vast experience seems extremely unlikely, doesn't it?"

"Well, I was going to tell you before you hung up that I had a quick chat with Randall, and he's started to talk. He blamed Tiffin mostly. He said Tiffin was like some kind of great messenger and Randall had to do what he said. Tiffin told him to get a woman and bring her to him alive. I wasn't really believing him but if Tiffin has been spiking you, then yes, he's possibly our second bad guy."

"Did he say anything else?"

"Yes. He said he chose the nurse, and he brought her to Tiffin who murdered her. Randall picked up the body and dumped it. But Tiffin said the devil told him Randall touched the body first. She'd already been raped, so she was no good and Randall needed to get another one. Someone more... *pure*."

"Hence him trying to stab Summer?" Swanson asked.

"Yep, hence Summer. He thought if he did it on the ward, someone else would take the body away, she'd go to the devil, and he wouldn't be tempted to, er, play with her."

A shot of nausea put an end to Swanson's hungry stomach.

"Anyway, Tiffin told him that he needed a strong man to protect Summer in the afterworld when he was busy, and Tiffin told him all about you."

"Why would Tiffin want me dead, though? Unless he really was crazy, too." Swanson put his head in his hands and racked his brain.

"You definitely don't know him?"

"No. Never met him until the hospital. I mean, he looked vaguely familiar but he had one of those faces I think."

"OK. Well, we'll see what happens today. Now piss off and get some sleep. You still have a tumour, you know."

After she hung up, Swanson moved into the kitchen to fix a cheese and pickle sandwich to cure his rumbling stomach. He felt much better from not taking those damn tablets. He sat at his tiny dinner table, which had two chairs slotted underneath it in a perfect oval. His random Ikea purchase on the second day of living in the cottage. He tucked into his sandwich and reflected on his first meeting with Dr Tiffin. He had felt familiar now as he looked back, but he'd been too preoccupied with worry to think about it.

He picked up his second sandwich, but it fell back to the plate as the memory hit him. That was not the first time he'd met Tiffin.

And he realised why he'd told Randall to kill him.

The Servant

I sat alone in the interview room. The door was open, and an officer they called 'Forest' was standing right outside. My solicitor had gone to get a drink. I hadn't seen the Devil since yesterday. His presence was gone and Tiffin was dead. I wouldn't get my messages anymore. They only happened around Tiffin or after he'd given me a message. He gave me special pills too, so I could see the Devil myself. An ache tugged at my heart as I realised that without my pills, I wouldn't see a thing.

I didn't want to kill Tiffin, but the Devil insisted once Tiffin told me to leave Summer alone. He stood tall and powerful behind Tiffin and told me what to do. Being so trusting of my service to him, Tiffin hadn't flinched as I drove the knife into his heart. Sally told me I did the right thing. She was correct, of course. I hadn't had a choice. I had to do as I was told. But the police wouldn't see it that way. I knew.

Especially Swanson.

I looked up as footsteps echoed through the corridor. It was Hart. I knew by the way her heels hit the floor. But this time there was someone with her. Her face was cool as she walked in, but I could tell she wasn't happy about something. Behind her came DI Swanson. I'd grown quite fond of him. I saw why the Devil wanted him.

He didn't look too happy either, but I hadn't seen him smile once. I'm not sure he smiled all that often.

"Dr Randall, you remember my colleague, Detective Inspector Swanson?" DI Hart asked as she pulled the chair across from me over the tiles with a loud scrape. I shuddered at the noise.

I nodded and turned my attention to Swanson instead. He took the other chair adjacent to me and nodded a hello. My solicitor, Bobby Jones, followed them into the room and sat down next to me, the chair creaking under his considerable weight. The smell of Bobby's cheap cologne filled the room and stuck in my nostrils. I cleared my throat to keep away the nausea it gave me. He looked more like a pub landlord than a solicitor.

I waited for Hart to formally start recording and introduce the interview and smiled patiently at them both, but focused on Swanson as he talked.

"Dr Randall, can you tell me how you knew Dr Tiffin please?" he asked, his pen and notepad ready in front of him. He seemed far more interested in what I had to say than DI Hart.

I leant forward. "Of course. I really do want to help, Sir. I've known him for years. We went to medical school together in Nottingham."

"And how did you become friends?" he asked.

I sat back and sighed. I was going to have to go into more detail here than I originally thought to get him to understand what he could have been a part of. There was still a chance the Devil would come back to me if I proved myself worthy. If I convinced Swanson to give himself up.

"Well, we shared most of the same classes, and for the first year we shared a dorm. Our bedrooms were on the same floor. We both kept away from most other students. I was a bit shy, and the other students were so stupid. Always getting drunk and being loud and acting like animals really. They didn't take anything seriously. Tiffin was the same as me. He liked to keep himself to himself. He was always out doing something or other, but always alone. In the second year, we moved into a flat together and shared the bills. We became quite good friends and opened up to each other. It turned out our families were... special."

"Your grandma said you only became friends a couple of years ago," Swanson said.

I stifled a laugh. I could never have told Grandma about Tiffin back then. "No. You know what grandmas are like. She never met him whilst I was at university. She never visited the flat. Tiffin and I lost touch after we graduated, and he got back in touch a couple of years ago via social media."

"You don't strike me as the type to be active on social media," DI Hart piped up.

"I'm not, but I am on work related media for my career." I didn't bother looking at her, and kept my gaze on DI Swanson instead.

"And why did he get back in touch?" he asked.

"He needed help with something. We met up for a coffee. The thing is, I helped him with something once before in university." I hesitated. It felt strange to say these words after keeping it a secret for so long.

"You don't have to answer," Bobby piped up. I glanced at him with disdain and wished he would go away.

"We'd really appreciate anything you can tell us, Dr Randall," Swanson said, "you said you wanted to help us?"

"OK. Yes, yes, I do want to help *you*, Detective Inspector Swanson." I pointed at him to ensure he understood my meaning. He nodded for me to continue. "When we had our own flat, a year into living together, he had an accident with a young girl. Well, she would have been our age roughly at the time. She was about 19, we were 20ish. He'd taken her out and they'd come back to ours for… you know… things." I waved a hand.

"Sex?" DI Hart suggested.

Trust her to have no shame.

I nodded and swallowed. "Yes. That. She had *asked* him to choke her, and so he did. She kept asking for it and suddenly she wasn't breathing. He was in a complete mess over it. He could barely breathe. His life ruined because of one stupid girl."

"You don't need to say anything more, Dr Randall," Bobby grunted, his face looking sweaty and pale.

"What about her life?" DI Hart asked, her disdain obvious.

I closed my eyes and took a deep breath, washing away the irritation she brought about in me. I looked at her for the first time since the interview began.

"The whole thing was her fault. She *asked* him, remember?" I explained again.

"Do you really believe that?" she asked, her eyes narrowing.

"Of course I do," I scoffed, "there were no secrets between Dr Tiffin and I."

The clear memory of the perfectly formed, naked girl spread out on Tiffin's bed suddenly hit me like a brick. I closed my eyes and cleared my throat, trying to think of something else to focus on to push away the memory of the first girl I'd ever seen naked.

"Are you OK, Dr Randall?" Swanson's voice broke through my thoughts.

I opened my eyes again and focused on his face. The memory faded into a wisp of an image. I kept focused on his beard and nodded.

"OK. So what happened after he told you he'd murdered a young girl?" Swanson looked at me. He scribbled notes on his pad as he spoke.

"When the girl accidentally killed herself, you mean? Well, like I said, he was in a mess. Couldn't breathe properly. I calmed him down, and told him I would sort it out." I took a deep breath and closed my eyes. Talking about this was harder than I thought it would be. I wanted to be back there before everything went wrong. Me and her alone. She lay there quietly, eyes closed, while I explored her. She was beautiful. I opened my eyes. They were staring at me, patiently hanging on to every word.

"I went into the room, and dressed her as best I could and wrapped her up nicely in bin bags. Rigor mortis was settling in at that point, but I knew we only had a couple of hours before it set in properly. Luckily it was 2am and our flat was in a very quiet part of town. There were no cameras. Tiffin had checked that before we moved in. He didn't like being watched. He helped me put her in the back seat and I drove to a park nearby so police could find her easily."

"That was nice of you," DI Swanson said.

I nodded, glad he understood.

"I wanted her family to find her, but when I got there I realised they needed to know what she'd done, too. They needed to realise it was *her* fault that she was dead. I made it clear by cutting off the bin bag and clothes and burning them a few days later."

DI Hart cleared her throat. She didn't understand like DI Swanson did.

"Weren't you worried about being caught?" she asked.

"No. Tiffin said the Devil would protect us, and he did. Although that wasn't his name back then." I wondered if he would understand the Devil was real now. I couldn't understand much from his face. DI Swanson must be amazing at poker.

"Sorry? That wasn't the devil's name?" DI Swanson asked.

"What? No. It wasn't Tiffin's name. His name was Billy." I saw Swanson's eyes widen, though his set jaw gave nothing away. "Why?"

"What was his surname?" he asked.

"It was Logan. Billy Logan."

He cleared his throat, and I noticed the subtle clench of his jaw.

"And you left the girl in which park?" Hart asked.

"Grosvenor Park."

"And when did this happen again?" Swanson asked.

"Well, I think that's all I want to say right now." I sighed. They didn't seem to understand like I'd hoped so far.

"OK. So can I ask, before university, did you live at Adrenna? I'm confused about your family background. It's quite a tragic story," DI Swanson asked.

"Yes. I realise you don't know about the Devil. You haven't had the pleasure of being chosen by Him. But all the men in my family have had that. It isn't tragic at all." I shrugged.

"Let's start with your grandad's first wife. She died in 1981. What happened?" he asked.

"My Grandad took her for the Devil. He did panic and make up some story about a burglar, but he did a very noble thing in giving up his love for Him. She was the first in our family to go. But after giving her up, he couldn't bring himself to kill anyone else, and the Devil sentenced him to live for ten years without her before trying again. Though he met and married Glenda within a year. Ten years later, Grandad killed a nurse the devil chose for him, and he tried to kill a male patient to protect the nurse, but he failed with the patient, and couldn't take his failure. He killed himself."

"Quite the story," muttered DI Hart, "and your dad?"

"Yes. It's incredible, really. It quite troubled my dad as a boy. He got into a lot of issues at school and ended up being home schooled. He lived on the top floor of Adrenna. And Grandad would tell him all about the Devil. He passed his gift to my dad when he died, but the Devil made him wait ten years to make sure he was worthy. He killed a nurse chosen by the Devil, and instead of killing a male patient, he got greedy. The nurse was the one he wanted to be with. He wanted to be the one to protect her, so he killed himself."

"And where is your mum in all of this?" DI Swanson asked.

"I have no idea." I looked away and shifted in the chair. "Can I have a glass of water, actually?"

The whereabouts of my mother was one thing I was not prepared to share, even with DI Swanson. I looked around for her nervously. She liked to appear when I was in trouble. But I would take what happened to her to my grave, no matter what she did to make me tell.

Swanson

Two days later Swanson and Hart sat outside Adrenna for the last time. Swanson had driven and the pair still sat in his Audi in the bleak car park. Neither were in a particular hurry to return to Adrenna. The temperature was still cool despite the sky brightening and the clouds giving way to strong beams of sunlight, which bounced off the foreboding turrets and made the usual eerie atmosphere of Adrenna appear a bit lighter.

"It doesn't seem as…" Swanson paused, struggling to find the right word as he unbuckled his seat belt.

"Scary?" Hart suggested.

"Just not as atmospheric or something." He pushed open the car door and climbed out, the sun surprisingly warm on his face. Hart climbed out too and met him at the bonnet of his car. The pair crossed their arms and looked up at Adrenna as other officers arrived around them.

"Well, we do know most of her secrets now," Hart said, "maybe it's the mystery that's gone."

Swanson nodded slowly. "Yeah, I think that's it. Come on. Let's get this over with and find out any last secrets."

They stalked down to the side door of Adrenna and two separate groups of six officers followed behind them. Adrenna was a big place, and the warrant Swanson held was for private areas of the hospital which were not occupied by patients. He shuddered at the thought of the dark basement where Randall had shackled him. He would not be the one searching down there, that's for sure. Anyway, whatever was hiding on the top floor was probably more interesting.

Glenda was not on the reception desk today, and instead a junior nurse had taken on the role of receptionist temporarily. She let Swanson and the other officers straight in as soon as she saw them on the camera, and greeted them in the corridor with a cheery smile as he explained the warrant, and that they needed access to non-patient areas of the hospital.

"I've been expecting you. Aaron is going to show you where you need to go," she beamed.

"Oh, OK. That would be great." Swanson tried not to show his shock at how easy it had been to get access. The team walked through into the reception area where Aaron was waiting. He nodded at Swanson and gave a perfunctory, brief smile.

"I hear you're going to give us a tour of the non-patient occupied parts of the hospital?" Swanson asked him.

"Yes, though I haven't seen all of them myself, so we'll be exploring together a little." He shrugged and gave Swanson an apologetic glance. "We'll start in the offices though, if that's OK."

Aaron led them through to the back of the reception where Dr Randall had taken them a few days prior.

"I'll need his office first, Aaron," Swanson said, "take this first team to the door that's in there. The basement."

"I didn't realise there was a basement," Aaron replied with a frown.

"Yes, in Randal's office, through the door within," Swanson motioned for the first team of 6 officers to follow Aaron and stood to one side to let them through. "Make sure you keep the door open with something heavy."

Aaron reappeared a couple of minutes later, looking paler than he had done.

"Are you OK?" Swanson asked.

"Er, yes. Yes. Fine."

"Bit of a sight down there, isn't it?"

Aaron nodded and swallowed before raising his head to look Swanson in the eye. "Where do you need to go next?"

"The third floor. What's up there, by the way?"

Aaron shrugged. "I've never been up there. I haven't actually worked here that long. After all of this, it is time to move on again. I don't seem to have much luck with these places. But I opened that door by accident once when I was trying to find Dr Randall." He motioned to the door across from Randall's office. "And Dr Randall suddenly turned up behind me. He was weirdly annoyed that I'd opened the door."

Aaron opened up the door and jerked his head for Swanson to look. It was a small, square space, the only purpose of which seemed to be to hide the stairs going up to the third floor.

Aaron went first, huffing by the time he got halfway. Swanson's chest felt tight, but he took slow, deep breaths and refused to appear out of breath to anyone. Particularly Hart, who had watched him like a hawk since learning about the tumour.

At the top, Aaron took out his set of his keys and attempted to unlock the door. The key didn't work, so he tried the next one. And the next one. Before eventually turning to look at Swanson with pink cheeks.

"Sorry, I don't know what to do if it's none of these keys. They're the only keys I have. These are the same keys all nurses get."

"It's OK. We can break it down if we have to," Swanson said, looking warily at how thick the door appeared, and at the small space of the stairway. "But let's see if we can find a key first."

"If you were Randall, where would you hide the key?" Hart looked up at Swanson.

He thought for a moment, focusing on a cobweb in the corner of the landing ceiling. A fly was trapped in the intricate spool weaved by the tiny spider. Though to the fly, the spider was a monster.

A devil.

"His office," Swanson said. He turned to Aaron and the other officers. "Wait here."

He pushed past them all, but Hart followed close behind him. They went back down the stairs and into Randall's office. There were two officers already inside, who looked up from their rifling in surprise.

"Have you found any keys?" Swanson asked.

They looked around at each other and shook their heads. Swanson scanned the room. Where would that psycho hide keys? He went over to the desk and rummaged around the paperwork. Nothing.

He opened up the drawers and dug through the contents. But there was nothing other than paperwork and pens. Hart surveyed the shelves of books and boxes of paperwork, but she turned to him and shook her head.

He examined the room once more. It had to be in here somewhere. They were so close to finally accessing that damn third floor. Then his gaze landed on the bookshelf.

The Devil of Adrenna.

Bingo.

Swanson

Swanson's heart raced as he ran to the bookshelf and yanked *The Devil of Adrenna* off the shelf. He ripped it open and relief hit him. A rusted, bent key was sellotaped to the first page of the book. He peeled back the tape and released the key. It was heavy. Certainly a remnant of the asylum period. He held it up to Hart, and her face broke into a grin.

"Come on, let's find out all about that top floor," she said.

The pair raced back up the stairs to the top floor and pushed past the officers and Aaron, who had been standing in awkward silence judging from the relieved smile Aaron gave Swanson.

Swanson pushed the key into the lock and jiggled it to make it fit. Despite being bent out of shape, it turned, and the lock clicked open. He turned the handle with a shove and pushed open the bulky door. It was four inches thick, and creaked loudly as it opened. The nine of them stood still. No-one said a word.

The door opened up to a long corridor with a white-tiled floor and one large window halfway down on the left-hand side. The first part of the corridor was gloomy, but the sun shone through the window and gave it an eerie light. Specks of dust floated in the sunlight. Two doors across from the window caught Swanson's attention but he stood rooted to the spot, lost in the feelings of wretchedness that escaped from the corridor.

Something was in that room, and he wasn't sure he wanted to know what it was.

And that was before the stench hit them. It snuck out as if trying to catch them unaware. Swanson held his arm up to his nose to block the foulness. Not that it was much use.

"Well, go on inside." Hart's voice brought Swanson out of his reverie and he turned to glare at her before stepping forward into the sorrow. Slow footsteps followed him. No one was in a rush to be first.

"Er... I'm going to stay here." He heard Aaron's voice pipe up. "You know, to keep out of your way."

Swanson would have laughed, but he didn't blame him. A part of him wished he could stay outside, too. He'd had enough of creepy asylums. But he kept moving one foot in front of the other until he reached the window. He swiped away the dust in the air, which made no difference as the tiny particles continued to surround him as if trying to shoo him away.

He surveyed the car park below. This was the window he'd seen someone staring at them from. The deep burgundy curtain hung to one side now, but it had been closed. The face had disappeared behind it. Someone had been here since, and opened up the curtains fully.

"Holy hell, Swanson. Come look at this," Hart's yell cut through the thick atmosphere.

He turned and saw her standing a few feet behind him. She'd opened one door and was standing in the doorway staring into it. He walked over, and the scene took his breath away.

A winged statue of a creature he'd had never seen before stood in the middle of the room. Horns stuck out from the forehead and black staining mottled the grotesque face. It was positioned on top of a sort of unit with doors.

"I'm not going near that thing," Hart said with a look of disgust, "I'll wait here, go on boys."

She smirked as Swanson rolled his eyes and motioned for the other officers to follow him in.

"You can wait outside on your own," he said as he walked past her.

Her smirk dropped and she turned to look behind her. Swanson stepped over to the statue and ran a gloved finger across the face. It felt like stone under the rubber of the glove. He examined the dark, mottled parts, and a shiver ran through him as he realised it looked like old blood.

He moved his attention to the dark wooden cupboard underneath and opened up the door. It contained a few strange rocks and smaller statues, and a large, heavy book. He opened up the book and spotted an inscription written on the first page.

'The dogs always bark,
And the violets die a death,
When the Devil brings the dark,
And when he gets inside my head.
To the men lucky enough to be chosen to serve, may Satan be with you.'

His stomach felt cold. He flicked through the pages. It was all handwritten nonsense. He passed it to an officer to put it in a bag as evidence. Underneath the book was a pile of handwritten notes. More nonsense, probably. He picked them up. Not notes, letters. Letters to the devil. Each one was signed off by Billy Logan.

Swanson felt sick as he read through the letters. Letters written by his own doctor. Each one with detailed instructions on which women to kidnap.

Their names, addresses, jobs.

How to restrain them.

Where to take them so Tiffin could do the killing, apparently for the devil.

Randall really was only the servant. Tiffin was the real devil.

Swanson put them down and stepped out of the room. He needed to breathe. Hart still stood there, looking warily down the corridor.

"What? What did you find?"

He rubbed his face hard, as if trying to wipe away the memory of reading the letters. "Letters with detailed instructions on women to kidnap for Tiffin, or Billy, whatever the hell his name is."

Her face paled. "So there's more kidnapped women?"

"Dead women, probably. Not all of their addresses are Derby based."

"OK. And that smell?"

Swanson nodded down the hallway.

"Let's keep looking."

The pair kept their arms against their noses as they continued down the dim hallway. One more door lay at the end and from the vileness of the stink, they both knew there was only one thing it could be. They were still tentative as they made their way towards the door, and Swanson grimaced as he pushed it open.

The pair fell backwards as the stench hit them full pelt, gagging as they leant against the wall. Swanson's eyes streamed, but he turned to force himself to double check what he was calling in.

A room full of bone fragments and naked bodies. His eyes desperately searched for anyone that might be alive. But there were no signs of life. There were at least eight bodies in the room.

Here lay the women who were not good enough for the devil, Billy Logan.

Swanson

Swanson sat in his makeshift office, hiding from Murray. It was supposed to be his peaceful hideaway, but yet again Hart perched on the end of his desk.

"What a messed up family," she said slowly, staring off into space.

"Mmm," Swanson agreed, "you can see why Randall was drawn to Tiffin, and vice versa. It's a match made in heaven."

Her head snapped around. "Randall killed him!"

"Well, yes. Apart from that. That went wrong for him, didn't it? But that's what you get if you give someone as mentally disturbed as Randall drugs to enhance his visions. I mean, he might have been a doctor, but he wasn't the brightest spark, was he?"

She shuddered. "I know we shouldn't say it, but good riddance."

"Well, I wonder about Tiffin's family, though. What made him so messed up?"

"You've been spending too much time with Summer and her patients," Hart grinned, "how is she, anyway?"

"She's doing good. Should be out of hospital in a few days."

"And looking for a new job, I expect."

"Would you get a new job if a suspect stabbed you?"

"No, but I'm usually well surrounded by good guys. She's mostly surrounded by dangerous guys, and she has no backup. Hey, she should come work with us. Not long till she's a qualified forensic psychologist, right?"

Swanson raised an eyebrow. "True. Maybe she should."

"Well, just a thought. I'm going for food. Want anything?"

He shook his head and Hart walked off, finally leaving him with some peace to gather his thoughts. The dead bodies were being examined, and a few had matched up with missing women already. It appeared that Billy Logan had changed his name to Nick Tiffin not long after he'd punched Swanson in the face all those years ago. He'd finished medical school and became a doctor. A damn good one, apparently.

Until his urge reappeared, and he once again wanted Randall's help. Drugging Randall with small doses of LSD and telling him it would enable him to see the devil as he did. Not that Randall believed Swanson, yet. But maybe in time he would realise that Tiffin used him. One body had been a woman in her late forties to fifties named Brenda Randall. Swanson assumed that this was Randall's missing mother, murdered by her own son. And then there was Sally Tiffin, who was covered in bruises and scars from her husband, and had been glad to see him dead.

Hart's idea also played on his mind. Summer would make a great addition to the team as a profiler or something similar. She'd be safer and might enjoy it more. A smile spread across his lips as he thought about the pair of them working together, a plan already forming in his mind.

Summer

Summer couldn't remember the last time she'd been so excited. It had been two weeks to the day since Randall attacked her, and the hospital was finally allowing her home. Although she was under strict instructions to rest, a plethora of daily medication and no driving under any circumstances.

None of that mattered, though. She was finally to be reunited with Joshua.

He was waiting at home for her in their flat with her mum. Apparently, he was 'helping' to clean, which Summer had smiled at the thought of.

"You all good to get out of here?" Swanson asked her.

She patted the bag slung around her shoulder.

"Think so!"

"After you." He pointed at the exit.

"Don't think I won't be coming back here with you for your hospital appointment," she warned him.

"Yes, yes. I know," he muttered.

"I can't believe you left it to Hart to tell me."

"She's bloody telling everyone."

"Someone has to look after you and you're too stubborn to ask."

The pair walked out and into the busy corridor, dodging hospital beds and porters and busy nurses.

"Are you excited to be going home?" Swanson asked.

"Are you kidding! I feel like a kid at Christmas. I could even do a dance right here!"

He laughed. "Go on!"

She gave him a playful glance. "Maybe later."

Swanson stopped and turned to her. "What are you doing for dinner?"

"Oh," she paused and looked deep in thought, "I don't know. I haven't thought that far ahead."

"Well, it has to be a special one. Why don't you let me take you out if you're feeling up for it?"

"Oh, that would be lovely, but it's not that easy with Joshua."

"Bring him along. He knows we're friends. I'm sure he wouldn't think anything of it."

"Is it a dinner for friends?" She peered at him.

He cleared his throat, looking more nervous than usual. "Well, tonight, yes. But next weekend, maybe not?"

She nodded, but couldn't help her face breaking into a grin. "That sounds great."

"Excellent. So it's a date, finally."

She laughed and pushed his arm. He grabbed her arm and pulled her to him. She looked up at him, their eyes locked together.

"I sort of have a job offer for you," he said, "well, a career change."

Summer looked away and took a breath to calm her beating heart. Jesus. Why on earth would he kiss her when she looked so awful? Greasy, matted hospital hair and pale as snow were not a good look. Although he asked her for dinner.

"Summer?" Swanson said with a laugh.

"Oh sorry, I was miles away. Yes? A job offer?"

"Yes. Come work with us once you're qualified. You can do profiling or intelligence. You'll be surrounded by good guys, always someone to help. It'll be safer."

She opened her mouth to laugh and refuse, but hesitated. It wasn't such a bad idea. Joshua had nearly lost his mum.

"I'll think about it," she replied as they walked off down the corridor together.

"You can let me know on our date next week," he said with a grin. She hadn't seen him grin like that before, ever. She had a feeling there was still a lot about Swanson she had left to learn.

And she was going to find out about it all.

Also by Ashley Beegan

The Holiday Home

The beautiful, old cottage in the Peak District was the perfect place for Simone to take a much-needed break following a horrific attack. Surrounded by nature and peace, she can finally relax.

Until she realises she isn't alone.

Her partner and therapist, Chris, insists there's nobody else there. She just needs to rest. But Simone finds out that this particular cottage has some dark secrets.

Secrets that people will kill to protect.

Printed in Great Britain
by Amazon